THE GOODBYE BODY

The Claire Malloy Mysteries by Joan Hess

Strangled Prose

Murder at the Murder at the Mimosa Inn

Dear Miss Demeanor

Roll Over and Play Dead

A Diet to Die For

A Really Cute Corpse

Death by the Light of the Moon

Poisoned Pins

Closely Akin to Murder

Busy Bodies

Tickled to Death

A Holly, Jolly Murder

A Conventional Corpse

Out on a Limb

The Goodbye Body

THE GOODBYE BODY

JOAN HESS

 ST. MARTIN'S MINOTAUR ✻ NEW YORK

www.minotaurbooks.com

ISBN 0-312-31304-7
EAN 978-0312-31304-3

First Edition: April 2005

10 9 8 7 6 5 4 3 2 1

For Alexandra Ripley

A gracious Southern lady and a warm and loving friend,
whose stories will always keep me smiling

Acknowledgments

I would like to thank the following people for providing me with useful information, intentionally or otherwise:

Robin Burcell, the regional U.S. Marshals office, Parnell Hall, Sara Koenig, Terry Jones, and James Gandolfini.

THE GOODBYE BODY

Chapter One

Rats!" I said, gripping the receiver so fiercely that it almost squealed. "I am speaking of rats, and don't think I don't know one when I see it, Mr. Kalker! This creature was the size of a large squirrel, but without the endearing bushy tail. What's more, Mr. Kalker, it was in my kitchen! What are you going to do about it?"

"Well, Ms. Malloy, I reckon you got a problem."

"Oh no, *you* have a problem. Not only did I see this wretched rat in the kitchen this morning, I've seen others in the garage during the last month, cavorting in the banana peels and pizza crusts provided by the downstairs tenants after they toss their plastic bags down the steps. The bags do not bounce—they split open! Every day is Mardi Gras for the rats! I've never had more than an occasional cockroach, but now hordes of them are coming in through the vents. I have mice in the cabinets, ants along the baseboards, fleas in the rugs, and flies everywhere. The downstairs tenants are slovenly, to put it politely, as well as noisy, inconsiderate, and surly."

Mr. Kalker sighed. "I'll have a word with them, Ms. Malloy, but it's damned hard to find renters in the summer. It ain't like rocket scientists are lining up to rent an apartment in an old duplex. And I still got to make the mortgage payment to the bank every month."

I paused to glance up as the door of the Book Depot opened and one of my favorite customers came inside. I wagged a finger at her, then flung myself back into the fray. "You leave me no choice, Mr. Kalker. As soon as we've concluded this pointless conversation, I'm going to call the county health department and report the duplex as a hazard. After that, I'm going to call the fire department and do the same, since the downstairs tenants have piled newspapers, boxes, magazines, and greasy rags all over the garage. Oh, and the sanitation department, which can issue violations with hefty fines. As a finale, I'll call the Farberville Police Department and offer an anonymous tip that there are drug deals taking place down there every night. It will take you months and months to do battle with the paperwork before you can collect a penny's worth of rent. Then, Mr. Kalker, which one of us will have a problem?"

"Why don't you just move out, Ms. Malloy? I just bought a nice little house on the south side of town. It needs some fixing up, but—"

"I will not move out! I've lived here for years. I can walk to my bookstore, and my daughter can walk to the high school. I like the view of the campus. At my own expense, I've painted and wallpapered, and last year I had every intention of refinishing the hardwood floors. The downstairs tenants have lived here only long enough to turn this place into a slum. Don't you care about the value of your property?"

"Hold on," he said, then covered the receiver and demanded that someone bring him a bottle of aspirin and a quart of whiskey. "All right, Ms. Malloy, I get your point. What do you want me to do?"

I tried not to sound unbearably smug. "Send over an exterminator right now to find that filthy rat and dispose of it, humanely or otherwise. Give the downstairs tenants twenty-four hours to move out. Once they're gone, the entire structure needs to be fumigated, from the garage to the attic. You'll need someone with a truck to haul away all their debris. Oh, and while we're at it, I'd like tile countertops in the kitchen and a new sink in the bathroom. That ought to do it, Mr. Kalker."

"Tile countertops?" he said, choking.

"I cannot live with countertops on which rats have prowled. You're lucky I haven't demanded new cabinets."

2

"And the bathroom sink?"

"Cockroaches and spiders come out of the drain. My daughter may require extended counseling."

Mr. Kalker was silent for a long moment. "Okay, Ms. Malloy, but you'll have to move out in a day or two and stay gone for a couple of weeks. I can't just snap my fingers and make an exterminator appear."

"Two weeks, then," I said in the gruff voice of a sheriff giving the boys in black hats until sundown to get out of town. I replaced the receiver and stood up to see where my sole customer was browsing. Dolly Goforth had appeared in Farberville about six months ago, and had since won my heart by buying armloads of books every time she came into the Book Depot. She was in her fifties, but handling it with great grace—as in meticulous skin and makeup, stylish silver hair, and a trim build. Her idea of casual street wear consisted of linen slacks and silk blouses, but not all of us are of the fashion school that dictates jeans and T-shirts on a daily basis.

Her head popped up from the cookbook section. "What on earth was that about, if I may be so bold to ask?"

I sank back on the stool behind the cash register. "I saw a rat in the kitchen this morning. The only reason Caron didn't have hysterics is because she's been staying with Inez. She compares the apartment to a bad address in Calcutta. Both of us have flea bites on our ankles, which is peculiar since we don't have any animals."

"Except rats," Dolly murmured.

"Is there a vaccination for the bubonic plague, or at least a cure?" I went on to relate the entirety of the conversation with dear Mr. Kalker, adding a few choice adjectives concerning the downstairs tenants. "I don't even know how many there are. They look identical, which is to say they have stringy dark hair, sallow skin, filthy clothes, and their communication skills go no further than porcine grunts. There's at least one mangy dog that barks half the night. Not that it keeps me awake, though. I'm much too busy listening to the scritching in the vents and the rustling in the cabinets. I can hear the pitter-patter of ants marching in a tight column, keeping cadence with their antennae."

Dolly brought over a stack of cookbooks, including the pricy coffee-table-sized ones with color photographs of esoteric ingredients. "It sounds as though you won the skirmish, if not the war. Why don't you come to my house after you've closed for the day? We can have a drink by the pool. I've been thinking that we ought to organize a book club. Several of the women who do fund-raising for the various charities said they might be interested, and of course we can go after the college faculty."

"I don't know if I have the energy to take on a project like that," I admitted. "Summer is not my busiest season, so I've decided to keep the store open until six every day, even on the weekends, in hopes of luring in some innocent pedestrians. Even though Caron's not in school, she finds ways to keep herself entirely too busy to help out." I smiled ruefully. "And I haven't had much sleep lately. As a kid, I watched too many movies about mutant insects rampaging across the countryside. Now I can almost hear them plotting in the living room, their tiny exoskeletons crackling with satanic glee."

"You definitely need a drink. Bring Caron and Inez, if they'd like to swim."

I agreed, and after she'd left, sat down on the stool and tried to savor my victory. The only glitch was that I didn't really have anyplace to stay for the next two weeks. My closest friend, Luanne Bradshaw, had turned over her vintage clothing shop and her apartment above it to a couple of grad students for the summer and was now trekking in South America or some such place. Peter Rosen, with whom I romantically tangled quite often, would be delighted to accommodate me, but I wasn't sure it would be wise. If and when I decided to marry him—and it seemed likely—I wanted to do so from a position of independence. Sally Fromberger would gladly take me in, but she'd probably discovered a way to brew coffee from tofu—and I was way too old to sleep on a futon with half a dozen cats.

Then again, the only motels I could afford might well be infested with quite a few more of the one hundred thousand species of insects than I'd been encountering. The downstairs tenants, having been evicted (at my behest), could be in an adjoining room. Not only would I be treated to their atonal, bombastic music, incessant profanities, and barking dog, but I'd also be able to overhear XXX porn movies all night.

I was still brooding when Caron and Inez came into the store. "How was the mall?" I asked idly. "Did you buy anything?"

Caron, who has my curly red hair and freckles but not my mild manner, said, "No, I'm saving up to hire a hitman. Do you think I can find one in the classified ads?"

Inez Thornton settled her thick glasses on her nose and regarded me somberly. "Rhonda Maguire was there, with Emily, Ashley, Carrie, and Aly trailing after her like suicidal lemmings. They all just stared at us. I felt as if I were half naked."

"I am not going to survive the summer," said Caron. "There is simply No Way. Why don't you have some distant cousin in Paris or Rome who needs a nanny for a few months? I can change diapers and that kind of crap. Or London, so I can show up at the end of the summer with a pretentious British accent and invite everybody over for tea and cucumber sandwiches."

"I might be able to get you a job on a potato farm in Idaho," I said without sympathy. "Better yet, you can put in some hours here and save enough money to buy a Jaguar convertible and a pair of designer sunglasses."

Caron shot me a withering look. "But then I'd be seventy-five years old, wouldn't I? My eyesight would have deteriorated so much that I couldn't get a driver's license. Maybe I could park it out front and sit there, waving like the Duchess of Farberville."

Inez had wisely sidled behind the rack of paperback fiction. "Have you been able to catch all the mice, Ms. Malloy?" she asked.

"Not exactly," I said. It did not seem prudent to elaborate. "Would the two of you like to go with me to Dolly Goforth's house later today to swim?"

"Who's that?" Caron said suspiciously.

"A very pleasant woman who has invited you to swim in her pool. Take it or leave it."

"Where does she live?"

"Good grief," I said. I took an index card out of the file box, where I keep tabs on my more loyal customers. "She lives on the hillside west of the football stadium. She reads bestsellers in hardcover and a smattering of genre fiction in paperback. She's partial to international cuisine, needlepoint, unauthorized biographies, and travel guides. More important, she has a pool. If you two aren't back here at six, I'll assume you've got better things to do, like flipping through the classified ads. Don't forget about the Yellow Pages. You might have better luck if you put on false eyelashes and miniskirt and hang around outside the Dew Drop Inn. I'm afraid I don't know what the going rate is these days for a simple hit. There may be a discount in the summer."

"I've got eleven dollars and change," Inez called helpfully. "I may be able to talk my father into an advance on my allowance."

Caron rolled her eyes, which she always did with impressive eloquence. "Come on, Inez. We can go to the library and use the Internet to search for ads for nannies and scullery maids. At least we won't be stuck here all summer, watching Rhonda suck the brains out of our former friends."

I spent the rest of the afternoon peddling books when the opportunity arose, dusting the artful display of beach books in the window that opened out to the covered brick portico of my dusty, musty bookstore in what used to be a bustling train depot, and wondering what I could do with myself while the Pied Piper worked his magic.

By six o'clock, I'd concluded that my only option was a pallet in my office. There was a tiny bathroom with a sink, which was adequate for superficial hygiene. I could put my microwave on the desk and keep my fingers crossed that it didn't blow every fuse in a six-block area.

Dolly's house was surrounded by a white brick wall made less formidable by thickets of ivy and honeysuckle. I pulled into the circular driveway and parked behind a sleek red Mercedes. The two-story house was also constructed of white brick, and probably dated to the late nineteenth century. I wouldn't have been surprised to learn it had served as the residence of the president of the college at one time, or at least a pompous state politician.

Dolly opened the front door as I came up the steps. "Let's head straight for the patio. You look exhausted. Scotch?"

"Absolutely." I followed her along a hallway that passed by a formal living room and a dining room with a table adequate to seat the U.S. Supreme Court and its clerks. All the windows had treatments, of course, and the knickknacks had not come from flea markets. Mings and things, I supposed.

She settled me down on a padded chair and returned shortly with an ice bucket, glasses, and a lovely bottle of a brand I'd tasted only in my more self-indulgent fancies. I gave her a moment to produce a peer of the realm in full regalia and a discreet string quartet, then took an appreciative sip.

"I could get used to this," I said as I gazed at the well-tended garden, weathered gazebo, and pristine pool. "Caron's convinced she was born to it, and all that stands between her and a personal maid is my pitiful inadequacies in the world of marketing."

"Bibi and I were very lucky. Forty years ago he devised a modification for certain machinery that provided significantly less maintenance and therefore great savings for its owners. He turned what once had been a small shop into a factory with three hundred employees." She turned her head and wiped away a tear. "When he died, almost every one of them came to the memorial service. He was generous to a fault, providing health care, added retirement benefits, day care centers, scholarships, picnics, and holiday bonuses. They called him 'Mr. Bibi,' and their children called him 'Uncle Bibi.' He knew all of them by name."

"When did he die?"

Dolly moistened her lips. "Only a year ago. This week would have been our twenty-fifth wedding anniversary. He'd been promising me a South American cruise. We both loved ballroom dancing, especially the tango. We even entered competitions, although just for the fun of it. He was looking into buying a yacht when he had the heart attack."

7

"I'm so sorry," I said lamely, which is about the only way such a cliché can be said.

"Things happen." Dolly refilled our glasses, then went into the house and brought out a platter of antipasto. "I hope you like this sort of thing. Bibi and I used to indulge ourselves on special occasions. Luckily, we found a way to make every day qualify as one." She nibbled an olive, then looked at me. "You're a widow, aren't you? One of the women who volunteers at the arts center gift shop mentioned that your husband was a professor at the college."

"Yes, but I wasn't his preferred partner when it came to the tango. He was killed in a car accident some years ago." I opted not to describe the flurry of chicken feathers that had covered the highway like light snow when he'd had an unfortunate encounter on a slippery slope. "Caron and I are doing well, though. She'll graduate in two years, and I'm praying her grades will be good enough to get her a scholarship to a college in Manitoba or a design institute in Helsinki."

"Bibi and I never had children. He had a stepdaughter from his first marriage, and several nieces and nephews who spent summers with us at the lake house. Most of them came to the memorial service. We haven't been in touch since then, but that's understandable. They always seemed more fond of Bibi's money than of his second wife. He was very generous to them in his will."

The topic was making me uncomfortable, so I stood up and went to the edge of the pool. "Do you swim often?"

"Laps in the morning, for the most part. I was hoping Caron and Inez might come with you."

"They're trying to hire a hitman," I said, speculating on how much it might cost to keep the water as clear as the Caribbean but devoid of all the creepy denizens. I've never understood the allure of beaches, with all the unhealthy lumps of seaweed, crabs, bits of debris, and scuttly little bugs. And entirely too much sand.

"A hitman?" she echoed, alarmed.

I sat back down. "The delusions of postadolescent minds are beyond adult comprehension. Anyway, I doubt they'll have much luck, and by now they're probably off debating shades of toenail polish or the wisdom of dyeing their hair purple. Or shaving their heads, for that matter."

Dolly smiled as she refilled my glass. "Better than tattoos, I suppose. Claire, I had an interesting idea while I was driving home this afternoon. I've been thinking for quite some time that I'd like to visit my sister in Dallas for a few weeks. She's an invalid, and her health is, well, unpredictable. If I can persuade you to stay here while I'm gone, then I won't have to worry about the house and yard. All you'll have to do is collect the mail, make sure the pool maintenance guy shows up once a week, and water the houseplants. Caron can have her friends over to swim and barbecue by the pool. I have a big-screen TV and hundreds of videotapes. Whenever Bibi saw a movie that he liked, he bought it. The freezer in the garage is packed with hamburger meat and steaks."

"I couldn't possibly take advantage of—"

"You're not, dear. This will solve your problem as well as mine. I haven't seen my family since the funeral. I'd love the opportunity to see my sister, shop with her eldest daughter, and perhaps indulge myself at a spa for a weekend. You can water houseplants, can't you?" She held up her hand before I could speak. "Yes, I know you're going to say I'm just doing this to help you, but it's not true. Now, I've already made airline reservations to fly to Dallas tomorrow afternoon. If Caron can take me to the airport, she can use my car while I'm gone. If you slip away from the bookstore at noon, I'll give you the keys and show you how the security system works. The cleaning service comes once a week, as does the yardman."

"But, Dolly," I protested, although I could almost hear Caron screeching at me from behind a perfectly pruned shrub, "you truly don't have to do this for my sake."

"Please don't throw me in that briar patch?"

I shrugged. "Something like that."

"You would not believe this place!" Caron said as she and Inez came out onto the patio the following evening. "The kitchen has so many appliances that it's frightening. It's like one of those cooking shows

9

where the chef has more obscure utensils than a surgeon. There's probably something in there to peel peas."

"Why would anyone peel peas?" asked Inez, whose inquiring mind tended toward pragmatism.

Caron ignored her and sat down beside me. "We're going to take that blue bedroom at the end of the hall, if that's okay. The bathroom has skylights and a Jacuzzi, along with what I presume is a bidet. Inez turned the spigot and about drowned."

I noticed Inez's hair was a bit limper than usual. "Use it at your own risk. Did you get Dolly to the airport with time to spare?"

"Yeah, I guess. She insisted that we drop her off at the curb. I offered to park and help her with her luggage, but she just laughed and told me she'd be fine. Her car is just incredible! It's got an electronic control for the sunroof, leather seats, eight speakers for the radio and CD player, and a dashboard that tells you pretty much everything except what's on TV. It's also got this computer that shows you where you are and when to turn. I could practically live in that car."

"Until you ran out of gas," I said.

"Dolly—she insisted we call her that—gave me her gas station credit card."

"Well, then," I said, "there's no need for you to unpack. Instead of the 'Man Without a Country,' you can be the 'Teenager Without a Stationary Abode.'"

Caron gave me a condescending look. "Sometimes you edge perilously close to being amusing, Mother. Inez and I thought we'd swim for a while. What's for dinner?"

"We found a package of steaks in the freezer," said Inez.

"Let's settle for pizza tonight. I spent last night and most of the afternoon packing away our worldly possessions to protect them from toxic fumes. I assume you've brought everything you'll need for two weeks."

"Yeah," muttered Caron, "unless Louis Wilderberry has an epiphany and invites me out to a really fancy French restaurant. In that case, I can wear one of Dolly's outfits. She has some really cool clothes."

I gave her an icy maternal stare. "You are not to go poking through her personal things. Stay out of her closets, jewelry, and bathroom cabinets. She has been kind enough to allow us to—"

"I know, I know. I was kidding, okay? Louis Wilderberry will never stop nuzzling Rhonda's neck long enough to notice I'm on the same planet. Dolly did tell us to help ourselves to anything in the house, though. She even said we could have big parties."

"Over my dead body," I said. "I don't even want you to invite a few people over without checking with me first. Unless Dolly adopts you, this is not your house. We're going to leave it exactly as we found it. Understand?"

"She said to help ourselves to the food and sodas," said Inez.

"Which we shall do, but with moderation." I poured a scant inch of scotch in my glass, hoping they wouldn't notice the label (or realize its significance, anyway). "Why don't you take out enough hamburger meat for a barbecue tomorrow night? You can invite a couple of friends and I'll invite Peter."

Caron's eyes narrowed. "So he can arrest us if we track mud into the living room?"

"Exactly."

The next morning I drove by my duplex on the way to the bookstore. The downstairs tenants had piled boxes and duffel bags on the porch. No vans with plastic insects on the roof were parked in the vicinity, but perhaps Mr. Kalker was worried that any attempt to fumigate would be fatal to said tenants, who may well have been aberrant variations of bedbugs and silverfish.

Caron and Inez had been asleep when I left, which was not worrisome since they had watched movies most of the night. I'd fallen asleep to spates of machine-gun fire, squealing tires, and an occasional shriek. Bibi had not been a Disney fan.

Peter Rosen, man of my dreams (and occasional nightmares), wandered into the bookstore late in the morning. He looked as though he belonged in an ad in an upscale men's magazine, replete with tennis racket in hand and a sweater flung over his broad shoulder. However, he was but a lieutenant in the Farberville Police Department, and his warm brown eyes were twinkling at me rather than at a bottle of imported vodka.

"What's happening at your place?" he asked.

I told him about my various infestations and successful resolution with Mr. Kalker. "Instead of living on the street and standing in soup lines," I added, "Caron and I have taken residence in a house west of the stadium. Would you like to inspect the property and have hamburgers by the pool with us this evening?"

"Do you know how to use a grill?"

"Of course I do. Dolly showed me how to turn it on and off. I'm not promising the burgers will be Cordon Bleu, and I'll be serving ketchup instead of Dijon mustard. Shall we say around seven?"

Peter grinned. "A gourmet meal, a moonlit patio, the lapping of water, and the distant call of whip-poor-wills. Any chance the girls might be enticed to go out to a movie while we engage in a bit of skinny-dipping and other unseemly activities?"

"No farther than the den, I'm afraid. There's an enormous television set and more videos than the average rental store, as well as unlimited sodas and frozen desserts. By the end of two weeks, they won't just be couch potatoes—they'll be the size of Idaho."

We chatted for a while, even ducking into my office for a bit of activity, albeit pubescent, that would have earned him a reprimand from his superiors had he been spotted while on duty. Eventually his beeper beeped, and he left to find out what felony was in the process of being perpetrated. I returned to the unenviable chore of matching invoice lists to stock. Without the somewhat reliable influx of Farber College students clutching reading lists (or seeking condensed versions of said contents), customers appeared only sporadically, and often to buy only a thick paperback to take on vacation. My science fiction hippie came by, as he did on a daily basis, to goggle at the covers of the more preposterous paperbacks and assess his chances of shoplifting. I frisked him before he left, but he seemed to enjoy it. I'd ban him from the bookstore if it weren't for his puckish demeanor framed by a frizzy beard and shoulder-length hair. I could easily imagine him living under one of the quaint wooden bridges in the nearby park. Billy goats, take care.

I sat down on the stool behind the counter and picked up a pencil. In my naïveté, I'd assumed that owning a bookstore meant surrounding myself with more books than I could ever read. As it was, I found myself immersed in invoices, bills, IRS paperwork, and hard, uncaring numbers that were the anthesis of lovely, lyrical words.

My thoughts were far from lyrical when the phone rang.

"Mother," Caron began abruptly, "you have to come here right now! I mean it. The police are on the way. Inez is about to throw up, and I'm feeling kind of queasy myself."

I dropped the pencil. "What's going on? The police? Has someone been hurt?"

"I really don't have time for dumb questions. I can already hear sirens. Just get up here, okay?"

She slammed down the receiver. I replaced mine more gently and tried to make sense of the call. Police, rather than paramedics or firefighters. That was good. Caron and Inez were still breathing, if unsteadily. That, too, was good. Caron had promised to ask my permission before inviting anyone to Dolly's house to swim, so presumably they'd been the only ones there. A burglar would not have ventured into a home in the middle of the afternoon, especially when it was obviously occupied.

I stopped myself from further speculation, locked the front door of the store, and drove as quickly as I dared through the campus and labyrinth of shady streets on the hillside. A police car was parked in the driveway, its blue lights still flashing. I hurried into the house, where I found Caron pacing in the living room and Inez hiccuping in a corner. The two uniformed officers, both of whom resembled junior high basketball players, glowered at me as I halted.

"You know anything about this, ma'am?" asked one of them.

"Nothing whatsoever," I said. I caught Caron's arm. "Are you okay? Did someone attempt to . . . hurt you or Inez?"

Caron pulled herself free. "He was already dead, for pity's sake."

The second officer smirked. "But not real dead, since he upped and left before we got here."

"Like in some stupid zombie movie?" countered Caron, who does not tolerate any smirks aimed in her direction. "He was dead. I saw him, and so did Inez, and we can assure you that he was 'real dead.' "

"That's right," Inez said between hiccups. "At my uncle's funeral, there was an open casket and—"

"Would somebody please tell me what's going on?" I said without my customary mild modulation. "Who is this dead man?"

"He wasn't dead, ma'am," said one of the officers.

Caron spun around. "He most certainly was!"

"Then where is he?"

"How should I know?" she said, then resumed pacing. "All I know is that Inez and I saw him, and He Was Dead! Why don't you stop scratching your pimples and go find him?"

"So you think he's a zombie? Maybe you and your girlfriend have been drinking beer all afternoon out by that fancy pool? Smoking a little weed, too?"

I pointed at the officers. "You two go wait out front while I talk to the girls, understand?" Once they were gone, I made Caron sit down, then said, "Tell me exactly what happened."

She took a few deep breaths. "Inez and I got up about noon, and—"

"It was actually almost one," said Inez as she joined us. "I was supposed to call my mother at noon because she and my father were scheduled for a three o'clock flight to Toronto, where they get on a train to British Columbia. My mother likes to leave in plenty of time to get to the airport in case they have a flat tire or something."

"Continue," I said to Caron.

"Well, we heated up some pizza and ate it while we watched some totally bizarre cooking show. Then we changed into bathing suits and went out to the patio. I took the cordless phone and called Carrie and Ashley to see if they wanted to come over for hamburgers, but neither of them was home. I suppose they were at Rhonda's house, kissing up to the cheerleaders."

"Or shopping at the mall," Inez added wistfully. "My mother won't let me buy any school clothes until the sales start in September."

"And then . . . ?" I said, poking Caron.

"Inez and I decided to look around the yard. We found some rafts and a beach ball in the little shed with the pump and chemicals and stuff. Then we went behind the gazebo, and that's when we saw the dead guy stretched out on the ground." She held up her hand before I could interrupt, which I was intending to do. "He was kinda short and bald, with pudgy cheeks, wire-rimmed glasses, and a crooked nose. His eyes were wide open and he had a bullet hole in the middle of his forehead. Trust me, Mother, he wasn't taking a nap."

"How close did you get?" I asked.

She gave me a level look. "Close enough to see he was dead. We ran back to house, locked the doors, dialed 911, then called you. When the cops showed up, I told them where the guy was. They came back in about two minutes and said they hadn't found anybody or anything. Then again, I doubt they could find the pool without a map."

"And that's when you arrived," said Inez.

She'd stopped hiccuping, but she was shivering and both of them looked distressingly pale. "Go upstairs and take hot showers," I said. "I'll talk to the police officers and have them do a more careful search of the yard."

"You don't think we're making this up, do you?" Caron asked me in a voice reminiscent of elementary-school days.

I tried not to think of the times she'd come home and regaled me with tales of lions lurking behind bushes, kidnappers posing as crossing guards, and cafeteria ladies recruited from Siberian prison camps. "I believe you saw something very peculiar," I said carefully. I gave them each a hug and sent them upstairs, then went out to talk to the police officers.

Although it was an excellent plan, it did not come to fruition in that the officers and their vehicle were gone. Harrumphing under my breath, I went back through the house and onto the patio. It all seemed quite idyllic. I located the shed and glanced inside, where I saw the pool equipment and anticipated accouterments. The gazebo was octagonal, made of redwood siding and roofed with cedar shakes. I continued behind it, where the ground was covered with pine needles and speckled with shadows. Wildflowers tolerant of shade grew in abundance. I studied the ground for any signs of blood or indentations, but saw nothing more suspicious than pinecones and twigs.

Midway along the back wall was an arched opening with a wrought-iron gate. The gate creaked painfully as I opened it. Beyond the wall was an unpaved alley, somewhat overgrown but obviously still in use. A shortcut for those residents farther up the hill, I surmised without much mental exertion. However, it did mean that someone could have come into the yard through the gate and, if not too terribly dead, left in the same fashion. A dearly departed, so to speak. Caron had sworn his eyes were wide open, but he could have been experiencing a severe panic attack or some sort of seizure. The bullet hole in his forehead could have been nothing more than a smudge of dirt. He'd been strolling down the alley, felt faint, and for some reason came in through the gate to recuperate for a moment. Caron hadn't admitted that she and Inez screeched, but it was probable. Justifiably alarmed, the man had picked himself up, dusted off his trousers, and slipped away. I was sure the police offices had already written up a report saying as much.

Or, on the other hand, something very odd had occurred.

Chapter Two

Well, he has to live in the neighborhood," I said to Peter as we sat on the patio that evening, idly watching swallows swoop and dive for unwary insects.

"And why is that?"

"It's hard to imagine that this man would drive over here, park in the alley, and come into the yard for a little snooze in the middle of the afternoon. He had to have been on foot. Otherwise, why not just pick a shady spot in the park, which, among other things, is public property?"

Peter pulled another beer out of the cooler. "We definitely need a backyard like this. I can just see you curled up on cushions in the gazebo, reading Proust as you waft away the mosquitoes with your fan. I'll insist on a hairy, unintelligible pool boy, though. I wouldn't want you to find yourself gazing at some young hunk's rippling, bronzed muscles as he skims—"

"Did you check the missing-persons report before you left the office?"

"Yes, dear," he said with a sigh. "You'll be pleased to know that all the citizens of Farberville are accounted for except a junior high school girl who skipped her piano lesson and may have run off with her ne'er-do-well boyfriend. No one has reported the inexplicable absence of an elderly man with wire-rimmed glasses and a crooked nose." He popped open the beer and leaned back. "Isn't it more likely that he was a drunk who wandered by and thought the pine needles looked inviting? Assuming the sliding glass doors to the house were closed, he would have had no reason to think anybody was at home."

"Caron was convinced he was dead," I said. "She and Inez were both seriously upset."

"If he got up and left, he wasn't dead. Maybe he does this every afternoon, and Dolly just forgot to mention it to you."

I ate a slice of salami while I thought this over. The plate of antipasto I'd prepared lacked Dolly's artistic flair, but I'd been touched by her romantic vision. I wondered if Peter and I would feel that way about each other after twenty-five years of marriage. Or one, for that matter. In the past, he'd been more than irritated when I'd taken it upon myself to assist in various murder investigations, and even more so when I'd arrived at the correct solution. He'd gone so far as to use the word *meddlesome* on occasion. And had my car impounded not once, but twice.

"Dolly wouldn't forget to mention it, but I suppose you're right," I conceded gracefully. "Do you want to swim while I see to the hamburgers?" I caught his leer and added, "The girls went for a drive, but they'll be back any minute."

"Later, then," he murmured as he stood up and went over to examine the gleaming gas grill. "Who ever said only boys want toys? You could roast a cow in this thing."

I picked up the antipasto platter. "Perhaps we will, one burger at a time."

Caron and Inez were not convivial companions while we ate dinner on the patio, responding in monosyllables to questions. Peter's attempt at a joke about the missing body was met with frigid stares. After we'd all taken the plates and bowls to the kitchen, he said goodnight and left for a warmer environment. I wished I could do the same, but instead told the girls I'd finish cleaning up and sent them to the den.

After I'd tucked away the leftovers and put the silverware and dishes in the restaurant-sized dishwasher, I decided to go upstairs and read in relative tranquillity. The machine-gun fire was blasting away as I reached the staircase, but the sound that caught my attention was the doorbell.

Wondering if Peter had left his beeper by the pool, I opened the front door. Two girls were standing on the porch, shifting impatiently. One had short blond hair, pouty lips emphasized by cerise lipstick, and the physical endowments of a *Playboy* cover girl (or perhaps a centerfold; such things were beyond my realm of expertise). The second girl presented a more mature demeanor, with dark hair that fell below her shoulders and a shrewd, appraising expression.

"Is Dolly here?" asked the blonde.

I must have looked blank, because the dark-haired girl said, "Dolly Goforth? This is her house, isn't it?"

"Yes, it's her house," I said, "but she isn't here. I'm Claire Malloy." The blonde stared at me. "And . . . ?"

I felt as though I was being challenged to explain before they took the matter to the authorities, who would pull out the rubber hoses and force a confession. "She's out of town. I'm house-sitting." They continued to stare, so I said, "It's like babysitting, only in this case the baby has three and a half bathrooms and a Jacuzzi."

The girls stepped back and had a whispered conversation that was interspersed with suspicious glances in my direction. It was obvious they were both distressed, and the blonde went so far as to wipe away a tear before she looked at me and said, "This is really awful. How long will she be gone?"

"About two weeks," I said, not especially impressed. Sixteen years with Caron has given me a high threshold for melodramatics. "She went to visit relatives in Dallas."

"I'm Madison Hayes, and this is my cousin, Sara Louise Santini. Dolly invited us to come see her whenever we could, so we just tossed our stuff in the car and decided to surprise her. We've been driving for two days. It was okay until Sara Louise's car broke down about twenty miles from Farberville. We had the car towed, then took a cab here."

Sara Louise frowned. "My car did not break down, Madison. You snapped off the key in the ignition switch. It seems there is no Maserati dealership in this town. The guy at the garage said it'll take him a few days to get a replacement." She growled under her breath, then looked at me. "Can you recommend a cheap hotel?"

"Not sleazy, though," said Madison. "Last night we stayed at a horrible place where some pervert kept scratching on our door all night. I was too terrified to close my eyes. Sara Louise locked herself in the bathroom."

I noticed two bulging backpacks at the edge of the driveway. "Why don't you bring your things inside and we'll try to clear this up? Dolly left a number where she can be reached in Dallas."

"That's really kind of you," said Madison, then recoiled so abruptly that she and Sara Louise nearly tumbled off the porch as a sputter of gunfire ripped through the house. "Who's here? What the hell is going on?"

"My daughter and her friend are watching old movies." I herded them inside and led them to the kitchen. With the door closed, the violence emanating from the den was muted, if not entirely inaudible. "It seems Bibi was fond of gangster movies, where the hills may have been alive with the sound of music but the cast most assuredly was not by the time the credits rolled. Would you like a sandwich or something to drink?"

Sara Louise sank onto a stool. "I'd love almost anything, Ms. Malloy. We shared a sandwich while we waited for the tow truck, but that was all we've had to eat today. Do you have white wine?"

I took an opened bottle from a shelf in the refrigerator, along with whatever I could find for sandwiches, and set it all on the island in the center of the room. "Please help yourselves while I find the phone number Dolly left." I went back to the hall, where I could hear Big Al warning Stinky that he'd be swimming with the sharks if he didn't cough up the goods. I retrieved the pad of paper and the cordless phone, and retreated to the kitchen. Madison and Sara Louise had located wineglasses (it might have taken me weeks) and were assembling thick sandwiches. Neither acknowledged my presence as I sat down and dialed the number.

A haughty mechanical voice informed me that the number was no longer in service and that I ought to dial more carefully in the future. I did so, and listened to the same message, which this time seemed to drip with contempt at my ineptitude. "That's odd," I said as I put down the receiver. "Dolly must have written down the number incorrectly. Do you know her sister's name?"

Madison shook her head. "Sorry, but we don't really know much of anything about her before she married Uncle Bibi. I think she was from the Midwest. One of those states that begins with a vowel."

"So you were among the nieces and nephews who spent summers at the lake with them," I said. "That must have been a pleasant vacation."

Sara Louise poured me a glass of wine and slid it across the tile surface. "Yeah, we always had a great time. Uncle Bibi used to insist that we watch those very same movies with him. He wouldn't believe me when I told him that they gave me nightmares. Maybe that's why I ended up studying international banking. Numbers are very quiet."

"Where did you go to school?" I asked.

"Yale, and then the London School of Economics. London's a marvelous city, isn't it?"

Not wishing to expose my lack of savoir faire, I looked at Madison. "And you?"

"Drakestone, a liberal arts college in the wilds of Connecticut," she said. "After my parents heard about Sara Louise's escapades, they wanted to keep me closer to home. I did do a year in Europe after I graduated, but I was chaperoned every step of the way. Most of it was really boring, like being forced to watch other people's slides from their summer vacation, with their grubby children sneering on the steps of old cathedrals and their fat wives teetering on malnourished donkeys. The only way I survived was to slip away for torrid trysts with unwashed peasants and Australians in tight shorts. Aunt Gabby would have choked on her dentures if she'd known."

"I guess we'd better figure out what to do," I said. "I wish Dolly had told me that you were coming. I'm reluctant to invite you to stay here, since it's not my house."

21

Sara Louise managed a sickly smile. "We understand, Ms. Malloy. If you'll call a cab for us, we'll find someplace to stay until my car's repaired."

"As long as it doesn't have any perverts," added Madison, again looking teary. "I'm so exhausted that I could sleep on a bench."

"Get over it," Sara Louise said as she finished her wine and stood up. "If it has deadbolts on the door and a decent shower, we'll be fine. I told you we should have called first, but you swore Dolly would be delighted to see us. I'll call home tomorrow and ask my father to send some money."

"He and your mother are in Hong Kong," Madison said sulkily. "My father doesn't even know that we took off on a crazy whim, and I'm not about to tell him. The last time I pulled something like this, I was threatened with a convent school."

"You were fifteen and you skipped off to Bimini with the golf pro's son."

"Wasn't that while you were in rehab?"

I let them bicker while I tried to come to a decision. They were Bibi's nieces, if not Dolly's, and she had invited them to visit her. She'd impulsively gone to see her sister as a favor to me because of my predicament. It seemed harsh to force them to suffer the consequences.

"How about this?" I said, cutting off a discussion of the golf pro's son's virtues in matters of sexual prowess. "You can stay here until your car is ready. There are two unoccupied bedrooms upstairs and more than enough food and beverages to keep all of us content for a decade. You can lie out by the pool or watch movies with Caron and Inez. If Dolly happens to call, you can explain the situation to her."

Madison put her hand on her chest. "Are you sure? We really don't want to be a bother, but I just don't know what else we can do. I promise we'll stay out of the way, Ms. Malloy. You won't even know we're here."

"How could she not know we're here?" Sara Louise said tartly. "She just now told us we can stay. Do you think she has short-term memory problems?"

I wished I did. "Why don't you take your backpacks upstairs and get settled in? I'm afraid you'll have to share a bathroom. The girls are in the master bedroom at one end of the hall, and I'm at the other end. I'll have to leave early in the morning, but you can sleep in and introduce yourselves when you come downstairs. Ignore the machine-gun fire as best you can."

"I could sleep through a terrorist attack in Timbuktu," said Madison. She and Sara Louise repeated their gratitude, then went upstairs, murmuring to each other.

I had no idea what Caron and Inez would make of the situation. They might be intrigued by the glamour of Europe and its trappings of sophistication, or they might feel as if their two weeks at Farberville's version of a stately home would lose its enchantment with the intrusion of those who'd stayed in the real thing. I considered warning them before I went to bed, but instead tidied up the kitchen (for the second time, I might add), turned off the light, switched on the alarm system, and retreated to bed with a book.

Late the following morning I found out exactly what Caron and Inez had made of the situation, and it wasn't pretty.

"They are Utterly Intolerable," Caron announced as she sat down on the stool behind the counter at the Book Depot. "They're like . . . like older versions of Rhonda Maguire, but with perfect teeth and pretentious accents. What's more, they treated us like housemaids. I kept waiting for the blond one to ask me to do her dirty laundry. You have to make them go away, Mother, preferably to someplace in Africa where cannibalism is practiced on a daily basis!"

"What do you think, Inez?" I asked.

"Well, I suppose they thought they were being nice, but they left a mess in the kitchen, and when they got back—"

"Back from where?"

"Back from wherever they went," Caron said, regaining the spotlight. "They were gone when we got up. They waltzed in while we were having breakfast and said they'd borrowed Dolly's car to go to some garage. They told us who they were, then went upstairs and changed into bikinis. When they came back down, Madison sweetly asked if we'd bring them Diet Cokes—in glasses with lots of ice, please—out by the pool. Sara Louise slapped her perfect forehead and said they'd forgotten towels, and if I'd be a dear and find some for them, she'd be ever so grateful."

Inez attempted to insert herself into the conversation. "We were so dumbfounded that we did all that, then Madison said she needed to give herself a pedicure, but she'd left her case upstairs and—"

"And asked me," Caron said, then paused for maximum dramatic effect, "if I'd mind moving the umbrella back a little bit so the sun wouldn't be in their eyes. Can you imagine? I kept waiting to be told that they'd like salmon mousse and asparagus for lunch, and strawberry sorbet for dessert. Did you put mints on their pillows last night when you turned down their beds, Mother?"

"Oh, dear," I murmured, trying my best not to look amused by their tale of horrific abuse. "Did it occur to you to say no?"

"I don't think they would have noticed," Inez murmured.

Caron slid off the stool so she could better express her frustration by stomping around the store. "What are you going to do about them, Mother? They practically stole Dolly's car. They left dishes and coffee cups all over the kitchen, and they didn't bother to wipe breadcrumbs off the counter or put anything away. They said they might want to take naps this afternoon, so we had to keep the volume down if we watched movies. By now they've probably moved our stuff out of the master bedroom so they can have the Jacuzzi to themselves."

"As well as the bidet," I said.

"Dolly didn't say anything about them coming," growled Caron as she disappeared behind a rack of travel books. "All she mentioned were the pool boy, gardener, and cleaning service. I don't think Madison and Sara Louise qualify as any of those. I don't see how you can allow Total Strangers to move in like this. You told me I couldn't even have a party, for pity's sake!"

"I tried to call Dolly last night," I said, "but she must have left the wrong number. I'm hoping she'll call tonight to see how we're doing, but she's likely to say that the two girls are welcome to stay until their car is repaired. I really couldn't send them away in an unfamiliar town to find a motel, could I?" I immediately sensed that my rhetorical question was about to be taken literally, and quickly added, "It's only for a day or two, and then they'll leave. You have the car now, I presume. Why don't you find some back roads and pretend you're James Bond being pursued by evil men with heavy accents and plans to conquer the world?"

"I'm a little too old for make-believe," Caron said from some corner of the store.

Inez sniffed. "You like the Harry Potter books, don't you?"

Caron's head popped up from behind the mystery fiction. "But I don't straddle a broomstick and wait to whoosh into the sky. I suppose we can buy some sandwiches and drive out to the lake. This is so pathetic, Mother. For the first time in my life, I'm staying in a really cool house with a pool, a Jacuzzi, and a humongous TV screen, but can I enjoy it? Noooo, because you decided to let these two snooty girls stay there so they can Make Me Miserable. It's like some kind of insidious torture. I feel as if I'm on one of those ghastly reality shows where they have to eat maggots to win a million dollars."

"We could stay at my house," said Inez, "but I don't have a key. My father's afraid I'll lose it and someone will sneak into the house to steal all of his research on the weaknesses of the Dewey Decimal System. He's been working on it for nearly ten years."

"Your father is too weird," said a voice from the self-help section.

I opened the cash register and took out a few dollars. "Here's enough to buy sandwiches and sodas. Go to the lake, or even the park. You can each take a paperback. When I get to the house, I'll lay out the rules to Madison and Sara Louise, and also find out when their car is supposed to be ready."

Caron appeared long enough to accept my paltry offering, then trudged out the door with Inez in tow as though they were headed to a funeral home to make prearrangements for their untimely demise. I would have felt more sympathy had Caron not been scheming a few days earlier to find a job as a scullery maid or a nanny. I gave myself a figurative pat on the back for not saying as much, then returned to the tedium of the invoices. The Dewey Decimal System sounded almost invigorating in comparison.

Dolly's car was not parked in front of the house when I pulled into the driveway shortly after six o'clock. I could hear music from the backyard, which led me to cleverly deduce that Madison and Sara Louise were out by the pool. I went upstairs to change into tattered shorts, then peeked into the master suite to make sure Caron and Inez had not been dispossessed of the Jacuzzi and the bidet. Evidence to the contrary was scattered on the floor, the dresser, and the unmade bed.

Being of high moral standards, I did not look into the bedrooms occupied by the unexpected guests, although I will admit to temptation. They presented a somewhat contradictory demeanor. Obviously they were from wealthy families and had impressive educational credentials, yet they were broke and traveling with backpacks instead of steamer trunks. It was hard to imagine Madison and her aunt taking third-class trains around Europe and staying in hostels. Living in London requires more pounds than pence.

But mine was not to reason why, so I went downstairs and poured myself a drink. I debated cleaning up the kitchen, but decided that the two princesses could do so, even if it required them to plunge their exquisitely manicured nails into hot water. With a tiny twinge of optimism, I returned to the hall and picked up the pad in hopes Dolly might have called. Nothing had been noted. The message light on the answering machine was blinking, however. I crossed my fingers, then pushed the button (which was a bit harder than one might expect). All of the messages were from women wanting to either spread gossip from committee meetings or finalize arrangements for upcoming events. Although disappointing, this did not preclude the possibility that Dolly might call during the evening.

I opened a drawer and took out an address book. I had no idea what the sister's name was, but it took me only a few seconds to flip through the pages and note that all of the entries were for Farberville locals, including those charitable souls who'd called during the day.

There was most likely another address book for family and old friends, but it was not in the drawer or among the oddments of mail that I'd tossed in a wicker basket under the table.

I picked up my drink and was preparing myself to have a few stern words with Madison and Sara Louise when the doorbell rang. Pleased by the diversion, I opened the front door.

On the porch stood a dark-haired man of perhaps thirty or so. He was as tall as I and dressed in a khaki jumpsuit. His thick black hair was slicked back as if he were in the cast of a seventies musical. He appeared to be harmless, so I merely raised my eyebrows and said, "Yes?"

"I'm Nick from Manny's PerfectPools. Are you Ms. Dolly Goforth? If so, I must say you are looking attractive this evening."

"Ms. Goforth is not available right now. May I help you?"

"Manny had to take off for a couple of weeks on account of a family emergency. I just started working for him, so I thought I'd go around and introduce myself to all his customers and get the lay of things. I'm supposed to clean this pool tomorrow. I wouldn't want Ms. Goforth to get upset if she should see a stranger in the backyard. Manny warned me that she does not care for strangers on her property."

"Very thoughtful of you," I said. "Ms. Goforth is out of town. I won't be here tomorrow, but there are some girls who might be. I'll let them know you're coming."

"Do you mind showing me the pool and the pump?" He looked at the glass in my hand. "Unless you're busy, of course. I can probably stumble around and find everything on my own. Swimming pools are pretty damn hard to hide. Then again, Manny was telling me about this crazy client he had a couple of years ago that insisted he come once a week to clean her pool, even though she didn't have one. They'd sit on her back porch and drink gin, then she'd insist on paying his regular fee. He felt bad about it, but it was her idea. And he is fond of gin."

I gestured for him to follow me through the house. "You said your name is Nick?"

"Yeah. Manny and my old man were in business together a long time ago. When Manny couldn't stand the rat race any longer, he retired and moved down here. Nice little town you got. Are you and Ms. Goforth old friends?"

I opened the sliding door and went out to the patio, where Madison and Sara Louise were indeed sprawled in lounge chairs. The table between them was cluttered with glasses, plastic bottles of suntan lotion, and the paraphernalia necessary for perfection as defined by fashion magazines. Beside me, Nick began to cough uncontrollably, as if he'd swallowed a fly.

Both of them glanced up at us. "Holy shit!" said Sara Louise, pulling up a towel to cover that which her scanty bikini top did little to hide, as well as her chin and mouth. She peered at us over the edge of the towel. "Sorry, Ms. Malloy. I didn't know we had a visitor."

Madison had rolled over to scrabble through her purse. When she reappeared, she was wearing oversized sunglasses that made her resemble a grasshopper. She sucked on her lower lip until she could say, "Neither did I. I guess we lost all track of time. I am so sorry about the mess in the kitchen, Ms. Malloy. We really did intend to clean it up before you came back."

"You still have time to do it," I said. "This is Nick from Perfect-Pools. He's going to clean the pool tomorrow and wants to see where the pump and the chemicals are kept. Don't let us stop you from cleaning up the kitchen."

Nick nodded at them. "I hope you will forgive me, young ladies. When Ms. Malloy said girls, I was expecting pigtails and braces. I won't be a nuisance tomorrow. It shouldn't take me more than a couple of hours."

"No problem," said Sara Louise as she lowered the towel a few inches. "We can stay in the house and watch movies or something."

"The smell of chlorine gives me a headache," Madison added.

I chose not to offer sympathy for their impending inconvenience. "The storage shed's next to the gazebo," I said to Nick. "I assume everything you need is there."

Nick showed no inclination to locate the shed, but was instead staring at Madison and Sara Louise. "Manny didn't mention anything about you two. Are you visiting?"

"Only temporarily," I answered for them. "They had some car trouble yesterday. Did the owner of the garage give you any idea today when he expects the part?"

Sara Louise shook her head. "He's still trying to locate it. Once he does, he says he'll have it overnighted. I'm sorry we're in the way, Ms. Malloy."

"I'll bet your daughter and her friend were complaining about us," said Madison, giving me a complacent smile. "I think they were planning on having a little party this afternoon. They rummaged through the liquor cabinet while we were gone, and I saw some beers in a cooler. You can't really blame them. God knows I did the same thing when I was their age. I'm sure they'll settle down when they get older."

I gave Nick a nudge in the direction of the shed and, when he reluctantly headed that way, said to Madison, "How do you know they rummaged through the liquor cabinet?"

"Sara Louise and I are planning to cook dinner tonight. It was going to be a surprise, but I guess it won't be now. We're fixing a really lavish Thai food spread, and I was looking for rice wine. This morning I was totally flabbergasted when we stumbled across a little Asian shop that carries lemongrass, spring roll wrappers, hoisin sauce, cellophane noodles, peanut oil, shrimp, water chestnuts, and just about everything we'll need. You do like Thai, don't you? It's so healthy and organic, you know, low in calories and no cholesterol."

I was more in the mood for red meat that I could gnaw off the bone with my fangs. "That's very nice of you. I'm sure we'll all enjoy it."

"We'd better get started," said Sara Louise as she stood up, dropping the towel beside the chair. "We need to chop, slice, dice, and marinate. When will your daughter and her little friend be back?"

"I don't know," I said, "but while we're on the subject—"

"Oh, you shouldn't worry about them, Ms. Malloy," said Madison. "As I said, they'll grow out of this petulance sooner or later. And they certainly can't have a pool party tomorrow if that man's going to be here. Sara Louise and I will make sure that nothing goes on upstairs in the bedrooms. We'll patrol the hall and wear whistles if we need to."

"You won't need whistles," I said darkly.

"Never underestimate teenagers."

She and Sara Louise went into the house. I sat by the table and forced myself to calm down. Surely they would be gone within a day or two, and I would no longer be regaled with Psych 101 wisdom in matters of child rearing. Caron, Inez, and I could celebrate with ribs and baked potatoes slathered with calories and cholesterol. If Peter wasn't involved in some high-profile case (and I hadn't seen anything in the local newspaper to suggest he was), then he might be willing to join us. I'd even rummage through the liquor cabinet for an imported bottle of red wine.

Nick interrupted my pleasant musings. "I found everything. You said Ms. Goforth is out of town. You know when she will be back? Manny always presents a bill and waits for a check. He has had problems in the past when he mailed them. It seems rich people aren't any more eager than the rest of us to pay bills on time."

"You'll have to settle up with her. I doubt you'll have any problems."

"I can always come after you," he said with a grin. "Your name's Malloy, right?"

"Yes, and I own a bookstore that doesn't show enough profit for you to clean my kitchen sink."

"A bookstore, eh?" he said. "Out at the mall?"

"On Thurber Street, next to the railroad tracks. Come by and browse when you have time. Customers are always welcome."

"If I should come by about the time you're closing, could I persuade you to have a drink with me?" He held up his hand. "Please don't think I'm being pushy, Ms. Malloy. It's just that the only person I've met in Farberville is Manny's bookkeeper. She's seventy-seven years old and refuses to wear a hearing aid. I tried a couple of bars, but everybody there was in college. I'm getting so old that I've never even heard of the bands they talk about, and their music is crap."

I had a feeling that under the jumpsuit was the buff pool guy Peter had mentioned as a potential nemesis. However, I doubted Nick would show up at the Book Depot in a skimpy pair of shorts and a bare chest. "Maybe in a few days," I said.

"Okay, then," he said, sounding disappointed but not inclined to do himself bodily harm anytime soon. "I will leave the bill on the table in the hall if that's okay. I'll just let myself out so's not to disturb you anymore."

I nodded, then watched him as he went into the house, glanced back at me, and assiduously closed the sliding glass door. Muscles were definitely rippling under the khaki, like a tawny lion stealthily moving in on an oblivious gazelle. I warned myself not to entertain heretical ideas and leaned back in the chair. Peter was far from flabby and could ripple with the best of them. I imagined him swimming laps in the pool, effortlessly, his shoulder blades cutting through the water, his adorable rump surfacing every now and then. . . .

Several minutes later I was roused from my reverie by the sound of a car door slamming and an engine starting. If the girls had once again fled rather than clean up the kitchen, I thought crossly, they very well might end up sleeping with the squirrels. It might not prove to be comfortable, but at least it would be preferable to sleeping with the sharks.

"Ms. Malloy," called Madison from the doorway, "do you know where Dolly keeps her wok?"

Caron and Inez were surly during dinner, but roused themselves to offer halfhearted expressions of appreciation whenever I kicked them under the table. I'd expected Madison and Sara Louise to chatter, but they were subdued. I dug into the lemongrass and other exotica with some degree of enthusiasm, but I couldn't help feeling as though we were at the mess hall in a prison, with steely matrons watching us.

Madison set down her fork. "I just love Thai. One of my very favorite places at home is this tiny little restaurant run by an immigrant and his family. It's so quaint and authentic."

"Then you've been to Thailand?" I asked politely.

"Heavens, no." She wrinkled her nose. "It's one of those Third World places with lepers and cripples on every corner. I know it would just break my heart to see little children begging on the street. And the lack of hygiene would revolt me."

Caron pushed away her plate and crossed her arms. "So how do you know this tiny restaurant is authentic?"

"Please," said Sara Louise, "let's just drop it. Madison and I thought we might borrow Dolly's car, if it's not a problem, and catch a movie or something. We may stop at a bar before we come back, so don't wait up for us."

I felt the lemongrass beginning to intertwine with my intestines. "What about the kitchen?"

"We'll clean up and put everything away when we get back," she said.

Madison smiled at me. "We certainly don't expect you to lift a finger, Ms. Malloy. This meal is our special treat. It's just that we'd like to see more of this little town before we leave because it's so . . . typical, if you know what I mean. True Americana. I'm sure the pollsters love this place when they want to know what the average citizen thinks—or doesn't think—about vital issues."

I looked at Caron, who was rolling her eyes in a most unattractive fashion. "Are you and Inez planning to go out tonight? I suppose you can take my car."

"No, Mother. We thought we'd watch movies. If we get hungry, we can make peanut butter and jelly sandwiches."

"Or nachos with Velveeta cheese," said Inez. "Maybe we can have tuna fish and noodles tomorrow for dinner. We can eat on trays and watch reruns of *Green Acres*."

My lips quivered. "Then we're settled. Madison, I do expect you and Sara Louise to clean up the kitchen before you go to bed. I'm not sure when the cleaning service comes, but I doubt that's in their job description."

Sara Louise sounded offended as she said, "I can assure you we'll take care of it. Please don't even bother to take your dirty dishes to the kitchen. It will be spotless in the morning."

"And I'll be engaged to Prince Rainier," muttered Caron as they went into the hall, took the car keys from the table, and called good-night as they left. "I swear, Mother, if you don't get rid of them soon, I'll move back home and take my chances with the cockroaches and the fleas."

"And the rats."

"Rats?" Her lower lip shot out as she recoiled with revulsion. "We have rats?"

"I've only seen one in the apartment," I said, "and Mr. Kalker promised to send over an exterminator. I myself prefer to stay here until the exterminator has had plenty of time to set out poison and spray the entire building. If you want to go home, it's up to you."

"Did you really see a rat?" whispered Inez. "How big was it?"

"Does it matter? Are you two sure you don't want to see what your friends are doing? You can invite them over to swim or just sit out by the pool if you'd like."

Caron sighed. "Have you already forgotten that we don't have any friends, Mother? I don't know how I'll survive until I graduate and can go away to a college where everyone isn't a pathetic syco-phant. Maybe Dolly will let us spend our weekends here watching old movies and eating stale popcorn."

"And knitting," said Inez in an equally morose voice. "My mother says it can be very soothing. She made a sweater for my father, but the sleeves weren't the same length."

"This problem with your friends is temporary," I said. "Once they get tired of Rhonda, or she of them, they'll be back."

Caron slumped back in the chair. "You don't understand, Mother. We're going to be juniors when school starts in August. You know how the politicians have to fight during the primaries so they can win the nomination? This is our primary season. We have to get our dele-gates in a row this summer."

I had to think about this. "And there are elections in the fall?"

"No," said Inez, blinking at me, "but once we have a solid political base, we'll be ready for the elections for senior class officers in the spring."

"And we have to line them up this summer, so they can begin campaigning," said Caron. "Aly's on the varsity basketball team, so she can work on the athletes. Emily's a shoo-in for the National Honor Society, which will give us the geek faction. Carrie is in the choir and the drama department. I may use her as a coach."

"Then they're just puppets in your Machiavellian scheme to seize power in your senior year?" I asked, appalled.

"You think Rhonda Maguire really likes them? She probably can't keep their names straight." Caron stood up. "Come on, Inez, I can hardly wait for the St. Valentine's Day massacre. I just wish I could insert a few more characters."

She and Inez went into the den. I looked at the dishes on the table, then decided to trust Madison and Sara Louise to follow through on their promise to clean up when they returned. I had well-founded doubts, but I was not in the mood to wash the wok. Unlike Caron, I harbored no desire to be a scullery maid. Or a nanny, for that matter. I'd received an honorable discharge from that position and would, when the time came, be relieved of all maternal obligations and allowed to retire with great fanfare. In my dreams, anyway.

I poured the last of the tepid tea in my cup and went out to the patio. Lights sparkled on the water. The neighbors—professors and retirees, for the most part—were ensconced in their homes, reading erudite tomes, groaning over freshman essays, or watching baseball and sputtering maledictions at the umpires. Whatever their vices, they were engaging in them peacefully. A pine-scented breeze rustled the leaves. I was imagining Peter next to me, our fingers entwined, our thoughts decidedly amorous, when the phone rang. I dashed inside, but was not quickly enough to beat Caron.

She glared at me, then said, "Hello?" After a moment, her shoulders slumped and she thrust the phone at me. "It's for you."

"Claire? It's Dolly. I'm just checking in to let you know I made it to Dallas and am having a lovely time. My sister's doing a bit better,

34

I think. She's not able to leave the house, so I picked up some Tex-Mex and a bottle of tequila. My niece makes a very tasty margarita. I really must get her recipe before I come home."

"Oh, yes," I said, almost giddy with relief. "I tried to call you last night, but apparently the number's not in working order."

"She's been having a problem with the telephone company. I tried all afternoon to get things straightened out, but each time I actually spoke to a real person, we were disconnected. You'd think *they'd* know how to make their own system work, wouldn't you?"

"There's something I need to discuss with you," I said. I explained about Madison and Sara Louise, then nervously waited for her reaction.

After what felt like an interminable pause, she said, "I don't have a problem with them staying there, Claire, unless they're bothering you. Did they happen to mention how they got my address?"

"No, they didn't say anything, and it never occurred to me to ask. Is there some reason why they wouldn't know it?"

"I'm just a little surprised, that's all. As I told you, I haven't been in touch with Bibi's family since the funeral."

I waited for a moment in case she wished to elaborate, which she did not, then continued. "We had an odd experience yesterday afternoon. Caron and Inez swore they saw a dead body under the pine trees behind the gazebo."

"A dead body in my yard? Are you sure?"

"I'm not, but they are."

"Are you making this up, Claire? If this is meant to be a joke, it's in very bad taste. I . . . I don't know what to think."

"I wish it were a joke," I said. "The girls ran into the house and called the emergency number, but by the time the police arrived, the body had disappeared. The police were convinced that he was more likely drunk or ill, and left under his own power."

Dolly exhaled slowly. "So it was a man. Did the girls get a good look at him?"

"They said they did." I repeated their description, then asked, "Does this sound like one of your neighbors?"

"I haven't really met anyone. I tend to keep to myself when I'm home, and the wall prevents me from seeing anyone who uses the alley as a shortcut. I do hear voices out there every now and then. Are the police investigating further?"

"There's not much they can do. No one has filed a missing-person's report, and as I said, the body was gone when the police arrived."

"And they believe he simply got up and left? Why would he have come into my yard in the first place?"

"It doesn't make a lot of sense," I acknowledged, "and Caron and Inez had been watching Bibi's gangster movies half the night. Their imaginations may have gotten the better of them."

"I heard that!" Caron squawked from the den.

Dolly chuckled. "Perhaps we'd better drop the subject. It sounds as though you have matters well under control, Claire. I'll call you once I get the mess with the telephone company resolved. Go have a glass of brandy and don't worry about a thing." On that cheerful note, she hung up.

I decided to take her advice. Ignoring the disastrous mess in the kitchen, I poured myself an inch of brandy in a bona fide snifter, wished the girls goodnight, and went upstairs. Dolly was not distraught, and therefore I had no reason to be so, either. I opened a window, puttered around until I was ready for bed, then crawled under the covers with a cozy tale of murder most foul in the quaint village of Quirky-by-the-Sea.

The vicar had just presented himself in the drawing room when Caron and Inez stumbled into the room like knock-kneed foals.

"The body!" Caron shrieked, clutching Inez's arm in a bloodless grip. "It's back!"

Chapter Three

"What do you mean?" I said as I scrambled out of bed, allowing the vicar to flop facedown on the carpet. "Where? Behind the gazebo? What were you doing out there?"

Caron sank onto the edge of the bed and began to snuffle. I stared at Inez, who said, "By the pool. We saw him through the sliding glass door. He's most likely still there."

"By the pool," I repeated weakly. I went to the window and looked down. There was most definitely someone in one of the lounge chairs, although the umbrella blocked my view of all but trouser cuffs and shoes. I stared for most of a minute, expecting a sudden disruption to the surreal placidity of the scene, but not so much as a moth fluttered by. "Are you sure it's the same . . . person?"

Inez nodded. "Oh, yes. Chubby face, wire-rimmed glasses, bald head, all that. It was too dark to tell if his eyes were open. He didn't look like he was breathing, though."

"As if you could tell," muttered Caron. "Maybe you should have gone outside and asked him if he needed CPR."

"I guess I'd better go have a look," I said without enthusiasm.

Caron scrambled to her feet. "You can't go down there, Mother! What if this is some kind of trick to lure you outside so they can get you? Then I'll be a foster child and be packed off to live at a pig farm. I'll have to go to a one-room schoolhouse. I won't be able to get into a college, so I'll just stay at the farm, drive a pickup truck, and grow old and stinky. When I die, they'll plow me under a field for fertilizer. Maybe they'll put up a crude wooden marker that reads, 'Here lies Caron Malloy under forty acres of organically grown alfalfa.' "

I caught her shoulder before she could throw herself on me with further capricious descriptions of her fate. Holding her at arm's length, I said, "I promise I won't go out to the patio. As soon as I've taken a better look at this . . . person, I'll come right back up here and we can decide what to do."

"You really should be careful, Ms. Malloy," said Inez. "Caron could be right, you know." She hesitated. "About someone luring you outside. I'm not sure about the pig farm and the alfalfa."

"Of course I'm right!" Caron snapped, then gave me the piteous look she had perfected after years of practice in the bathroom mirror. "Promise you won't go outside, Mother."

"I won't even open the sliding door. Now just wait here." I went out to the hall and started down the stairs, hoping I would be able to keep my promise. I would have to ascertain if the man was dead, as Caron and Inez fervently believed, or if he was merely enjoying the evening ambience (and oblivious to the transgression of trespassing). The latter theory certainly made more sense, in that corpses, unlike buffalo, seldom roam.

I'd reached the bottom step when I heard frantic pounding on the front door, along with shrieks of distress. I froze in mid-step, as much out of confusion as of panic.

"What's going on?" howled Caron from the top of the staircase. "Should I call 911?"

My grip tightened on the banister. "Not yet. There's someone at the front door."

"Don't open it," Inez quavered.

The pounding increased in urgency, as did the shrieking. I finally realized the voice belonged to Madison, rather than a B-grade movie heroine resisting the advances of a hand-sewn suitor. I went to the door and swung it open. "What's wrong?"

She barged into the entry hall. Seconds later, Sara Louise followed her, locked the door, then leaned against it and groaned. Madison was struggling to find a breath, having spent her reserves rousing the entire neighborhood, and perhaps the west side of town. Both were disheveled and ashen.

"Well?" I said.

Sara Louise recovered first. "We started feeling guilty about the mess in the kitchen, so we decided to skip the movie and come back here."

"Besides," added Madison, having finally found a few wisps of oxygen, "we'd already seen everything playing. Like over a year ago, if you can believe it. Do they send movies here by mule train?"

It was not a topic worthy of debate at the moment. "So you came back. Did you discover you didn't have a house key and could think of no other way to attract our attention? There is a doorbell, after all."

Sara Louise glared at me. "When we got out of the car, a man came charging at us from the bushes. He grabbed Madison's arm, so I whacked him with my purse. Then he swung around and knocked me down. I grabbed his leg, but he kicked me until I let go. Madison screamed and ran onto the porch. The man took off. I went to the end of the driveway and tried to see which way he went, but I couldn't tell. You know the rest."

"It was horrid," Madison said as she examined her arm. "I'm going to have the most hideous bruises tomorrow."

"Do you have any idea who he was?" I asked, shaken if not stirred.

She shook her head. "It was awfully dark and it happened so fast. I guess it was just a redneck bastard who followed us here to mug us—or worse. I don't want to think what might have happened if I'd been alone."

I glanced at Sara Louise, who shrugged and said, "I agree with Madison that someone must have followed us, or maybe it was just a kid looking for something to steal. It certainly wasn't anyone we know. It's not as though we were beaten or raped."

"Mother!" said Caron. "Should I call 911?"

"Let's not get hysterical," said Sara Louise. She winced as she straightened up and pushed back her hair. "There's absolutely no way I can identify the creep—and neither can Madison."

"Yeah, just forget about it, Ms. Malloy," Madison said in a sulky voice.

I was beginning to feel as though the house belonged to Vincent Price rather than Dolly Goforth. "I'll decide what to do in a minute. There's another problem that requires my attention."

Sara Louise arched her carefully plucked eyebrows. "Another problem? Is this typical when you house-sit?"

"Stay here, or go upstairs and whimper with Caron and lnez." I went across the living room, switched on the outside lights, and stared through the glass at the lounge chairs on the patio. None of them was occupied. No shoes, no cuffs. No dark blobs floating in the pool. In essence, no body. The bottles of lotion were upright on the table, and the towels were still discarded on the concrete. The whole area looked exactly as it had when I'd been out there earlier.

Caron and Inez had ventured downstairs and were waiting with Madison and Sara Louise, if not precisely consoling them. I went to the phone, took a breath, then dialed 911. When a voice responded, I said, "I need to report an attempted assault in the front yard. It took place less than five minutes ago, and the assailant might still be out there." I then dutifully answered a barrage of questions as best I could, acknowledging that I was not the homeowner, spelling my name, and so forth.

"You the lieutenant's girlfriend?" the dispatcher asked.

"That's hardly the issue. Are you going to send a patrol car, or should I call Lieutenant Rosen at home? We both know how fond he is of being disturbed when he's off duty."

"A patrol car's already on the way. Are you sure you don't need an ambulance?"

"Very sure." I hung up.

"What about the dead man?" said Caron. "You didn't even mention that pesky little detail."

"Not there. Were you or Inez keeping an eye on him from the window?"

"Believe it or not, we were more concerned about you, especially after they"—she tilted her head at Madison and Sara Louise—"started screeching. We assumed one of them had broken a nail or something equally earth-shattering."

Madison smiled sweetly at her. "I do hope you grow out of this stage at sometime in the not-too-distant future. Precociousness is appealing only in toddlers and prodigies."

"What dead man?" demanded Sara Louise. "In the backyard? Why would there be a dead man in the backyard? That's ridiculous!" She went to the sliding door and peered out. "There's nobody there. What are these two talking about?"

"You'll hear all about it when the officers arrive," I said. "Why don't you take this opportunity to clear the dining room table so we won't look like squatters?"

"I don't think either of us can be trusted to carry china right now. We'd better have some wine to steady our nerves. Do you know if Dolly keeps any aspirin in the kitchen or guest bathroom?"

"Oh, dear," said Madison, "I need to lie down before I faint. Caron, would you be a sweetie and fetch me a damp washcloth?"

"Only if you promise to use it for a gag, you oleaginous bitch!"

"I may be a bitch, but I can assure you I'm not . . . whatever you said I was. How can I be? I don't even know what it means!"

"Oily," Inez said helpfully.

Sara Louise pointed a finger at her. "Like your complexion?"

I was almost sorry the conversation was not allowed to escalate, but the arrival of the police officers stopped all of them in mid-sentence. They questioned Madison and Sara Louise, who were unable to add anything to what they'd told me earlier, except that the man was of average build and dressed in dark clothes and that Sara Louise had heard a car engine start up somewhere away from the house. One of the officers called the station to request a thorough search of the neighborhood, although he implied it would be fruitless to expect even the most clueless perp to wait around.

The other turned to me. "Anything to add, ma'am?"

Caron and Inez cut me off and began to gabble about the dead

41

man who kept popping up. Madison and Sara Louise contributed sniffs of incredulity and comments concerning the effects of violent movies on hormonally contaminated imaginations.

"Didn't I see a similar report from yesterday?" the officer asked, unsuccessfully attempting to hide his derision.

I was considering how to respond when Peter came into the living room. He silenced Caron and Inez with a look, then took the officers aside and had them explain the situation. Madison and Sara Louise were openly assessing him, from his slightly hawkish profile to his Italian shoes, and apparently finding the entire package of interest. Once the officers had finished, Peter sent them out to search the backyard and came over to me.

"Did you see the body this time?" he asked.

"I couldn't see anything more than the man's cuffs and shoes because of the umbrella. He was indubitably there, although I can't attest to his well-being or lack thereof. But there was a five-minute gap when he could have left."

"Or been carried off," said Caron. "I know what I saw."

"Were the outside lights on?" he asked her.

"No, but I saw him and he was dead."

Inez offered a timid "There was light from inside, though. It glinted off his glasses and bald head."

Caron nodded. "It was the same man we saw yesterday. Do you want us to take a lie detector test or something?"

"I don't think you're lying," said Peter, "but you do see my problem, don't you? Dead bodies don't just appear and disappear like this."

"We saw him," she said stubbornly, "and so did Mother. She doesn't even have hormones anymore."

Madison positioned herself next to Peter and gazed up at him. "Well, I think it's some kind of prank. Whenever there are reports of poltergeist, the investigators always trace it back to the children in the household. The pitiful little things are begging for attention. What's more, children can be very rigid about changes in their immediate environment and routine. They lack the flexibility that comes with maturity."

I could sense that she was in danger of something far worse than a poltergeist attack. "Madison," I said, "you and Sara Louise are still looking pale. Why don't you go upstairs and try to relax? I'm sure the pitiful little things won't mind if you use the Jacuzzi."

"Come along, Madison," said Sara Louise. "A long, hot soak sounds divine. I feel as though I were run over by a truck. If I don't feel better in the morning, I'll have to see a doctor about the possibility of broken ribs."

"Oh, all right. Lieutenant, if you have any more questions about our assault, I'll be happy to come by the station tomorrow morning and do absolutely everything I can to help. We can do it over lunch, if it's better for you. There must be one restaurant in this town that doesn't specialize in barbecue or catfish."

"If you think of something you haven't already told us, just call and leave a message at the police station."

Sara Louise gestured to Madison, who gave Peter a little wave as they started upstairs. I had a feeling Madison would remember at least one minor detail that would necessitate a phone call, if not a visit around noon.

"What about us?" Caron demanded. "What if we want to go to bed and those two are snickering and making rude remarks in the bathroom? Maybe we ought to make a quick run to the grocery store so we can put catfish fillets in their lingerie drawers."

"And barbecued beans in their designer shoes," said Inez, always a willing accessory to a misdemeanor.

I cut them off before they added further embellishments to the menu. "Go watch movies in the den. I'll make sure the doors are locked and the alarm is on before I go upstairs."

Caron glanced at Peter. "By yourself?"

"Yes," I said firmly, "by myself. Now scoot before I suggest you clean off the table and wash the wok. Someone's going to have to do it, and if we wait for Madison and Sara Louise to recover from their ordeal, the lemongrass will require mowing."

Once they'd gone, I leaned against Peter and said, "This is so bizarre. I feel like the housemother of a satanic sorority."

He led me into the living room and we settled down on a sofa. "I won't argue with you about that. Do you have any ideas whatsoever?" When I shook my head, he continued, "For starters, who the hell are those two who're upstairs bubbling away their bruises—and why are they staying here?"

I explained what I could. "I have no reason to doubt their story, and I think it's just a coincidence that they arrived the day after Dolly left. Maybe it's not, but they haven't shown any inclination to make off with the jewelry or the VCR. Then again, they could be waiting for an opportunity when we're out of the house to have a moving van pull into the driveway."

"Do you believe their story about being assaulted?"

I nodded. "They were truly upset when they came inside. Madison's arm was red, and Sara Louise's backside was dotted with grass. There were smudges of dirt on her shirt where she was kicked. What am I going to do if she really does have broken ribs? Is there any hope they'll keep her in the hospital? Not that it would get rid of the insufferable Madison. I can't envision her sitting at her cousin's bedside, peeling grapes and reading *Vogue* magazine to her."

"Don't even think about tossing a hair dryer into the Jacuzzi," Peter said. "That only works in fiction. Could they have anything to do with this body that won't stay put for five minutes?"

"I don't see how they could. They were waiting for a tow truck when it first appeared. And even if they were in some way involved, where would they have stashed the body for more than twenty-four hours? I didn't search their rooms, but I would have noticed if they were carrying a rolled-up carpet when they left this evening."

"Nothing escapes Miss Marple's keen eye."

"Cool it, Sherlock," I said as I punched him in the rib cage, albeit gently enough to cause no damage. "I'm not on the case. There's no way this can have anything to do with me, or with Caron and Inez. If all of this has to do with someone, it's Dolly."

"What do you know about her?" he asked idly, as though attempting to gain the confidence of a recalcitrant witness. He'd probably been given a fingerprint kit on his sixth birthday and dressed up like a Pinkerton agent for Halloween.

"Not much. Her husband died a year ago. I gathered that he was exceedingly wealthy, but generous in his will with bequests to family. Dolly didn't seem to think there was any animosity when the estate was settled. She obviously inherited a substantial amount, and moved here from the Chicago area. Oh, and she and Bibi loved to tango. I wish I had the phone number in Dallas, darn it."

"You said she called earlier. Didn't you ask her for it?"

"I would have, but she just said she'd call back when she got the problem with the telephone company resolved. Before I could say anything else, she hung up. Can you trace the call?"

"I can, but it'll take as long as a week. This is hardly a high-priority situation. A simple assault isn't going to do it, and we can't make a case for murder until we have evidence."

"You told Caron you didn't think she was lying."

"And I don't," he said. "I believe she's telling the truth as she sees it, but she's almost a legend at the PD. Remember when she and Inez were arrested for trespassing in people's yards while dressed in gorilla suits?"

"They weren't technically arrested," I said loftily. "They were picked up by an overly zealous animal control officer. The theft of the frozen frogs destined for dissection in the biology lab was never reported to the police. Inez did kidnap a baby recently, but for what she perceived to be a valid reason. In any case, that's history."

He flinched at the gunfire from the den. "And now they're training to be interns for the Mafia?"

I rested my head against his shoulder. "What should I do, Peter? Dolly was kind enough to invite me to stay here, but it's been a nightmare since we moved in. I've got to consider Caron's and Inez's safety, as well as my own."

"You can all stay with me."

"If ever there was an invitation issued in haste," I said. "You have two bedrooms. Although Caron knows precisely what's going on between you and me, she pointedly refuses to acknowledge that we do anything more than exchange chaste kisses. Do you really want to sleep on your sofa for ten days?"

"I can pay for hotel rooms," he murmured, nuzzling my neck. "As long as they don't have adjoining doors, you and I can—"

"And what about Madison and Sara Louise? I can't allow them to stay here by themselves. Even if they're not murdered in their beds, the house would look as if it had been used as a clubhouse for spoiled preppy princesses. The cleaning service would refuse to set foot inside. Even the pool guy might quit when he saw wine corks bobbing in the pool and martini glasses on the diving board. Dolly entrusted me with her house."

Peter was not overwhelmed with compassion. "Throw them out. You never agreed to host them."

"So they can sleep under a bridge until the car's repaired? They're Bibi's nieces, for pity's sake. I feel as though I should take them up cups of tea."

"I can't arrange for twenty-four-hour surveillance in the back-yard. The best I can do is have a patrol car drive through the alley every few hours. That's not likely to produce results, since this body is not on a regular schedule. If it appears tomorrow, have Caron or Inez stay with it while the other calls 911."

"Now there's a splendid idea," I said coldly. "Either the man is not dead, and is therefore capable of doing physical harm, or he's dead and someone is waiting nearby to whisk him away. I doubt said person is a benevolent employee of the sanitation department."

The conversation drifted toward topics of a more intimate nature, although both of us were aware that Caron and Inez were in the next room. I finally told Peter I needed to resuscitate the vicar and sent him away, then conscientiously made sure the exterior doors were locked before I set the alarm. Caron refused to respond when I went into the den to say goodnight, and Inez's smile was several degrees weaker than usual. I wasn't sure if they thought I should sit by the pool all night with a shotgun in my lap or call the FBI and demand a forensics team to search the yard for DNA traces.

I opted for bed.

No one was about when I rose the next morning. Rather than set foot in the kitchen, I stopped by a drive-through window to pick up a cup of coffee and a politically incorrect muffin, and retreated to the Book Depot. The solitude, if not financially advantageous, was agreeable. A few students trudged toward the campus, laden with backpacks to hold not only their textbooks and notebooks but also all the vital electronic apparatus deemed necessary for survival of the fittest. Caron and I had engaged in numerous arguments about cell phones. I had not been swayed by her assertion that I was a pathetic example of a throwback to the twentieth century (a *Librasaurus extincta,* so to speak).

Sally Fromberger, the ever so enthusiastic chairperson of the Thurber Street Improvement District, stopped by with a stack of flyers for the upcoming Summer Solstice Fair. I declined to supervise a mock battle performed by the Society for Creative Anachronism knights in aluminum foil armor, consented to tape a flyer in the window, and hedged when she invited me to a planning session. A meeting by any other name is still a meeting.

An elderly woman dropped by and nattered to me about her cats as she thumbed through quilting books. A teenaged boy dressed in black leather came in, asked if I carried interactive computer games, and stomped out when I suggested he might interact more wisely with classic literature. A sorority girl shed a tear when I told her I did not carry any condensed versions of world history with, like, you know, pictures and maps and that kind of stuff. The head of the philosophy department came in to buy several westerns, and gravely declined my offer to wrap them in plain brown paper.

I was finishing the crossword puzzle when a pair of more promising customers came into the bookstore. The man had short gray hair, an uncompromisingly square jaw, and the tan of a dedicated amateur golfer. His plaid Bermuda shorts were not a good fashion choice, since they emphasized his bony knees and hairy calves. His companion, perhaps twenty years his junior, was dressed in a short skirt, sleeveless blouse, and a visor restraining cropped auburn hair. Her brown eyes were wide-set, and her shoulders broad. She looked as though she would be a fierce competitor on a golf course, a tennis court, a conference table, or even a Scrabble board.

"Looking for anything in particular?" I asked.

"We're here on vacation," he said, "staying at a condo by the country club. You have much in the way of military histories and biographies?"

I headed for the appropriate section against the back wall. "Just a few. I hate to say it, but you might have better luck at one of the bookstores in the mall."

"Oh, I'll find something. Lucy's taste runs toward frivolous choices like mysteries. If you ask me, they're a waste of one's time, as well as one's intellect. Don't know why she bothers to read at all. She might as well watch decorating shows on TV."

"Goodness, Daniel," she said, "I don't recall hearing anyone ask you. Why don't you go bury your nose in Napoleon's armpit while I have a look around?"

I showed her the rack of paperback mysteries. "I don't carry much in the way of bestsellers. I prefer traditional mysteries, so that's what I order. Do you have any favorite authors?"

She mentioned a few names that happened to be among my own favorites, so we had an amiable time searching for titles that she might have overlooked.

"You're the owner?" she asked as we headed back to the cash register with a dozen paperbacks. "I'm Lucy Hood."

"Claire Malloy. Are you enjoying your vacation?"

"It's nice to get Daniel away from the office, even if he does spend all day playing golf. I ran out of books to read two days after we arrived. I was invited to play bridge at the clubhouse, but I declined. Local gossip doesn't intrigue me, and bad bridge irritates the hell out of me."

I began to ring up the sales, feeling increasingly kindlier toward her with each ka-ching of the cash register. "Why did you choose to come here?"

"We were told it's a wonderful retirement area, so we decided to investigate. We're going to tour a few gated communities adjoining golf courses later in the week. The weather's purportedly mild, and—"

"Low property taxes," Daniel asserted as he approached with a couple of books. "What's more, the area's booming, so we can rely on a profitable resale price if we decide to move elsewhere. The cost of housing in Southern California is exorbitant, and even if we were interested in southern Arizona or Florida, we'd have to invest too much of our—"

"Get out your wallet," said Lucy. "I'm sure Claire's not interested in the details of your IRA and pension plan. I know I'm not." She looked at me. "So what's the truth about the weather? We're from Virginia and not at all accustomed to annual blizzards and relentless summer heat waves."

"'Purportedly mild' is a good description." I took Daniel's credit card and began to fill in numbers on the receipt. "Occasional snow, but it doesn't linger. August is usually pretty hot." I glanced up as the bell above the door jangled and my science fiction hippie slithered in. "Spring and fall are lovely, though, and you don't have to worry about hurricanes, earthquakes, or tornadoes."

Daniel peered at the license displayed on the wall behind me, as dictated by the local powers that be. "Claire Malloy, eh? How long have you lived in Farberville? Did you attend the college?"

I handed him his card and a pen to sign the receipt. "I've lived here quite a few years, and I went to college elsewhere. Would you like a bag for the books?"

"Yes, please," said Lucy, "and do forgive Daniel. He's as snoopy as a little old lady who hides behind the curtains and spies on her neighbors."

"Like that witch in the condo next to ours?" He laughed in a rather unconvincing way. "I think she's hoping we're going to skinny-dip in the hot tub. Why don't you invite her over for coffee some morning, Lucy? She probably has some juicy stories about illicit liaisons behind the fourth green."

"Let's go, Daniel. I enjoyed talking with you, Claire. I'll come by later in the week to replenish my book pile."

I wished them a pleasant stay, and after they'd left, went to see what nefarious tricks were being perpetrated behind the science fiction rack. The hippie was squatting to peruse the lower rows, his jacket pockets bulging suspiciously.

"Find anything?" I asked.

Startled, he stood up. "No, just browsing. Who were those two that just left?"

"A couple of tourists. Unlike some, they paid for their books."

"Spooky."

I frowned at him. "Because they paid for their books?"

"No, them. Real spooky, if you know what I mean."

"I have no idea what you mean," I said, hoping he wasn't in the throes of a hallucinogenic flashback from substances he'd ingested in the seventies. "They seemed very nice."

He began to edge toward the door. "I'm talking real spooky. Don't get all worried if I don't come around here for a few weeks. I think I'd better go to an ashram to get my head straight. Nothing like meditation to realign your karma."

I had a feeling he might benefit more from medication. "I'll try to be brave. Send me a postcard if you have a chance."

He backed through the door and headed up the street. I sighed as I noticed a few gaps on the rack, then went into the tiny office to collect a stack of catalogs. His absence might be the closest I'd come to a vacation, I thought as I sat down on the stool behind the counter. Lucy and Daniel had seemed to be the epitome of a normal, upper-class couple, bickering in a genteel way while they searched for a gated community where they would be sheltered from even a glimpse of the untouchable caste.

At noon, I put the CLOSED sign on the door and drove to Dolly's house. There were no signs of activity in the front yard, and no blare of music from the back, which suggested that all concerned parties were still in bed. I was not inclined to rouse them and suggest we have lunch by the pool. I didn't know of an antacid that could combat the level of acrimony and antagonism that would surface between bites of tuna salad and sips of iced tea.

I went inside and stopped to gape at the dining room table. Not only had the dishes been removed, but the center of the table sported a modest arrangement of fresh flowers. I numbly continued to the kitchen. Every countertop was immaculate and the sink was empty. Pots, pans, and the wok had been put away. The dishwasher was humming softly. A ceramic bowl filled with glistening red apples was centered on the island. The kitchen looked as if it had been prepped for the arrival of a television crew and a professional chef eager to share his secrets with bored housewives.

I was trying to remember which day the cleaning service was scheduled when Madison came into the room.

"I felt really bad about the mess we left last night," she said.

"You did all this?"

"It didn't take all that long. There's something I need to tell you. Would you like a glass of wine first?"

I shook my head. "Tell me what?"

Madison went around me and took a bottle from the refrigerator. "I really must find a wine shop and stock up. Dolly's taste is so provincial. Have you ever tried the New Zealand sauvignon blancs?"

"You needed to tell me about Dolly's taste in wine?"

She filled a glass and sat down on a stool. "Sara Louise had a really miserable night. She couldn't sleep at all, and aspirin didn't help. This morning I took her to the emergency room. They did some X-rays and found two badly cracked ribs, so they taped her up and gave her a prescription for pain pills. She's upstairs now, zoned out. She's supposed to go back for more X-rays in three days. The doctor's worried that the cracks may splinter and put her at risk for a punctured lung."

"But she's okay for now?"

"As long as she stays in bed and doesn't try to go any farther than the bathroom."

Despite my better judgment, I poured myself a glass of wine. Three days. If the assailant had been in the kitchen, I would have stuffed him in the dishwasher along with the china and silverware. And adjusted the temperature for scalding water.

51

Madison misinterpreted my stunned expression. "Please don't worry about her. The doctor said she ought to be fine as long as she follows orders. I know this is a major inconvenience for you, Ms. Malloy, but I don't know what else we can do. I can't cram Sara Louise in the backseat and drive fifteen hundred miles on my own."

"No, of course not." Unable to come up with anything else to say, I took a drink of wine.

"I'll stay out of your way, I promise. Sara Louise can't even come downstairs. I thought I'd take her some soup later, if she feels up to it." She refilled her own glass and looked at me. "I really would like to explain all this to Dolly. Are you sure there's no way to get in touch with her? She didn't mention her sister's name, for instance?"

"I wish she had," I said truthfully. "I checked the address book, but it has only local names and numbers."

"I'm sure she has a cell phone. Maybe we can find a bill and get the number off of it. Do you think it would be all right if we looked through her papers?"

I didn't, but this was an extraordinary occasion in which the end would certainly justify the means. "There's a desk in the den. I suppose we might see if she keeps a folder with that sort of thing."

Madison brightened. "Uncle Bibi was very meticulous about records and canceled checks. I used to tease him about keeping our school photos in alphabetical order, as well as chronological. He had a separate bank account for birthday and graduation checks. Whenever I blew my allowance and needed a loan, he'd have me sign some sort of legal form that specified when I had to repay him—and charged me interest. Can you believe it?"

We went into the den. The desk was along the wall opposite the impressive (and somewhat oppressive) entertainment system. I noted the rows of boxed videocassettes in a bookshelf large enough to accommodate the collected works of pretty much all the authors worthy of being collected. It was unfortunate that Bibi had preferred Scarface and Bugsy over Shakespeare.

With Madison hovering behind me, I sat down at the desk and

began to open drawers. I found a thick manila folder and removed it. "Utility bills, all local," I said, flipping through the contents. "A contract with Manny's PerfectPools, another with the security-system company. A receipt for work done on her car. A warranty for a food processor. I don't see a contract with a cell phone company."

"What about telephone bills?" asked Madison, literally breathing down my neck.

I retrieved several of them. "No long-distance calls."

"Everybody makes long-distance calls, so that proves she has a cell phone. The credit card receipts have to be somewhere. Keep looking."

I tried to recall when I'd last made a long-distance call that hadn't involved a publisher and a 1-800 number. Clearly, I needed to reach out and touch someone more often. When I felt Madison's fingernails dig into my shoulders, I said, "Back off and I'll keep looking. Otherwise, the folder goes in the drawer and we wait for Dolly to call us."

The fingernails receded. "Sorry, Ms. Malloy," she said in a voice meant to convey penitence. Petulance overshadowed it. "It's just that we're like a couple of private detectives hot on the trail. Uncle Bibi used to read that kind of book all the time." She stopped for a moment. "I still can't believe he's really dead. Nobody knew he had this terrible heart condition, except Dolly and his doctor. When my father called to tell me, he was so choked up that he could barely talk. The family had a wake after the funeral, but it was like a scene from a movie or stage play. My godfather made a toast that left us all in tears."

"I'm sure he would have been pleased," I said for lack of anything more insightful to say. I returned my attention to the papers. "Here are five months' worth of bank statements. All the checks are local, however, and the cell phone bill isn't paid by bank draft."

"What about credit card bills?"

I found those at the bottom of the stack. "Purchases at local shops and stores, including mine. A couple of orders from candy and fruit catalogs. A donation to the NPR station. Other than those, nothing."

Madison plucked them out of my hand. "It's like she has no life outside the city limits. That's ridiculous. Surely she stayed in contact with a few old friends. There has to be another folder!"

I opened the bottom drawer and stared not at an innocuous manila folder, but at a large, shiny handgun.

Chapter Four

Is it loaded?" I asked, mesmerized by the gun.

"What's more useless than an unloaded gun?" Madison picked it up as if it were no more lethal than a box of cookies. "It's a little bit dusty, so I don't think it's been handled lately. It must have belonged to Uncle Bibi. He kept one in his bedside drawer, and another at his office. I wouldn't be surprised if he kept one in his glove compartment, too."

"Would you please stop playing with that? Just put it back where we found it."

She gave me a wounded look as she replaced it. "It's just a little Beretta, Ms. Malloy. Everybody should have one for self-defense. I mean, what are you going to do if somebody comes in your store and demands all the money in the cash register?"

"I'd hand it over, apologize, and offer to write a check. I don't understand why Dolly feels the need to keep a loaded gun in her house. This is Farberville, not some city teeming with armed robbers. Besides, she has the whole house wired so that no one can break in without causing a major hullabaloo."

"If I were you, I wouldn't worry about it. Dolly just feels safer with a gun, that's all. Did you find any personal correspondence?"

I looked through the remaining drawers. "No, nothing. She hasn't lived here long enough to acquire much clutter. I guess I'd better go back to the bookstore. Please let Caron and Inez know that the pool guy is coming. I don't want them to get hysterical if they see a strange man in the backyard."

"They are excitable, aren't they?" she said, sounding as though we were both PTA mothers leaving a workshop on parenting skills.

I stopped. "There's something I have to say to you, Madison, and it goes for Sara Louise as well. Caron and Inez are sixteen years old, not eight. Stop speaking of them as if they're incapable of adult conversation. Furthermore, neither is in your employment. Don't expect them to clean up after you or run little errands. If you want room service, check into a hotel. Do you understand?"

"I'm very sorry, and I'm sure Sara Louise is, too. We'll make every effort to be nicer to them in the future."

I didn't buy a word of it, but I nodded and said, "Then perhaps we can all get along until Sara Louise recovers. Have you heard anything from the garage?"

"I wish I had," she said, still acting as if my rebuke had pierced her heart. "Sara Louise and I went to the emergency room right after you left, and then we had to find a pharmacy to get the prescription filled. By the time we got back here, she could barely walk. It's a miracle I got her upstairs and into bed. After that, I cleaned up the kitchen and went to check on her. I'm feeling so lost, Ms. Malloy. Sara Louise has always been smarter and braver than I could ever be. The way she attacked that man last night was just unbelievable. She didn't even hesitate. Now she's like a baby, all curled up in bed." Her eyes filled with tears. "I don't know what I'll do if she has to have surgery and . . ."

I patted her on the arm, careful to avoid the bruises. "She'll be fine, Madison. Why don't you fix yourself something to eat and go watch something tame on TV?"

"I wouldn't want Caron and Inez to feel as though I'm violating their sanctuary. I'll just read in my room, where I can hear Sara Louise if she wakes up."

I stopped in the hall and picked up the day's mail, which included a small package. It was addressed to Dolly, naturally. The return address was more intriguing.

"What is it?" asked Madison, who looked as though she could barely restrain herself from ripping it out of my hands and chewing off the wrapping paper with her teeth.

"My Spanish isn't all that good, but it appears to be from a music shop in Buenos Aires. CDs, from the size of it. Dolly told me that she and Bibi were big fans of the tango."

"Yeah, they even used to compete. The photos are hysterical, if you enjoy pathos. Dolly wore this low-cut dark blue gown with swirls of sequins, and Uncle Bibi wore a matching tuxedo. I think the best they ever did was second place in what amounted to a local talent show, but they were thrilled. I guess when you get to be that old, you take your excitement wherever you can find it."

"I guess so." I flipped through the rest of the mail, then put it all in the basket on the floor. "Why don't you take some steaks out of the freezer for dinner? On the way back, I'll stop by the store and pick up potatoes and salad greens."

"Shall I take one out for Lieutenant Rosen?"

"Why would you think I'd invite him?"

She gave me a facetious frown. "I just happened to be looking out the front window when he left. Investigators don't usually hang around for an hour, questioning suspects." She gulped, then added, "Not that you're a suspect, Ms. Malloy. I have to admit I don't understand about this body Caron and Inez claim to have seen, but I can't picture you having anything to do with it. Or them, either. It's got to be some kind of really peculiar practical joke. Dolly could probably explain it if we could just figure out how to get in touch with her. How can anyone survive with one credit card and no cell phone? This is so incredibly frustrating. It's . . . it's like the Middle Ages! No, worse than that. The Dark Ages!"

"Indeed," I said. "Take out four steaks, or five if Sara Louise is feeling better. If Lieutenant Rosen wishes to join us, I'll call and let you know so you can take out one for him. Don't count on it, though."

She headed toward the kitchen door. I went upstairs, peeked in on Sara Louise, who was asleep, and continued down the hall to the master bedroom. Caron was sitting cross-legged on the bed, staring out the window at the backyard. The shower was running in the bathroom, leading me to cleverly deduce Inez's whereabouts.

"What do you want?" growled my loving daughter.

"For starters, I wish you'd stop sulking. I left my tights and cape at the apartment, so I cannot transform myself into a superhero and resolve this mess in the name of truth, justice, and the American way. Peter believes you, and so do I, but there's nothing any of us can do until there's concrete evidence."

"Like a dead body."

"Exactly." I sat down on the bed and squeezed her knee. "I'm sorry to have to tell you that we're stuck with our uninvited house-guests for three more days. Madison took Sara Louise to the emergency room this morning. She's been ordered to stay in bed and go back for more X-rays at the end of the week. I can't boot them out of the house at this point." I squeezed her knee harder to cut off her response, which would not have been sympathetic. "I had a conversation with Madison about their rudeness toward you and Inez. She promised to do better, but you're going to have to stand up for yourselves. You might consider doing the same to Rhonda Maguire. When she's snide, give her a dose of it right back instead of running away and whining about it. Tell Carrie and Emily and those girls what you think of their behavior."

"Sure," she said, "as long as I don't mind being ignored until I graduate. Inez and I will have our own table in the cafeteria, and not even the dorky freshmen will want to sit with us. Maybe we'll skip lunch altogether and shelve books in the library for Miss Guillotine."

"Miss Guillotine?"

"There's a story that forty years ago, she chopped a kid's finger off when he brought in a stack of overdue books and wouldn't pay the fine." She flopped back on the pillow and closed her eyes. "Do you really believe us?"

"Of course I do, dear." Surely mothers were allowed a certain leeway in matters of maternal mendacity. Hadn't I assured Caron she looked fine when, at the age of four, she'd cut off all her curls and announced she was going to be a bulldozer driver when she graduated from kindergarten? Dr. Spock would have awarded me a silver star for stoicism in the face of disaster. I stood up. "The pool guy's coming this afternoon. Madison's taking steaks out of the freezer for dinner. Perhaps you might want to invite your friends over afterwards to swim."

"Only if Rhonda promises to wear concrete boots."

I hesitated in the doorway. "I need to ask a favor of you, dear. Would you please have a look in here for an old address book or a Christmas card list or something like that? It's important that I get in touch with Dolly."

She lifted her head to gaze balefully at me. "I seem to remember being ordered not to snoop. I was Totally Humiliated that you thought for one second that Inez and I would ever do something like that. After all, the Constitution guarantees the right to privacy, as well as protection from unlawful search and—"

"Just do it, okay?" I went downstairs, grabbed my purse, called to an unseen Madison that I was leaving, and was reaching for the knob when the doorbell rang. I fleetingly entertained the image of a man with a bald head and wire-rimmed glasses, his face unnaturally white, his eyes glassy. I will admit I opened the door with some degree of caution.

Nick, dressed in the same khaki jumpsuit, stood on the porch. The man looming behind him was well over six feet tall, with long, unkempt dark hair and bushy eyebrows. He looked capable of wrestling a grizzly bear. His identical jumpsuit fit so tightly that I expected the snaps to pop off.

"Ah, Ms. Malloy," Nick said, "I thought you'd be at your bookstore. This is Sebastian, my temporary assistant. I do not think I told you about him when I was here yesterday."

"How do you do," I said.

Sebastian grinned, exposing neglected teeth, and mumbled, "Pleased to meet you."

"Sebastian helps Manny out every now and then," Nick went on. "He changed his plans so he could work this week."

I felt as if I were expected to invite them in for a glass of tea and a chat about the weather. "Well, then," I said, "I'm sure you two want to get started on the pool. I need to get back to the store. If you run into any problems, don't bother to call me because I won't have any solutions."

I went around them and out to my car. After picking up a salad at a fast-food place, I returned to the Book Depot, flipped over the CLOSED sign, and tried to immerse myself in the tiresome but ultimately profitable task of ordering books on the fall reading lists supplied by members of the high school and college faculties. *Beowulf* was no longer fashionable, but Shakespeare was holding his own. Students would be subjected to the Greeks, a smattering of German philosophers, verbose British essayists, and nineteenth-century American novelists. As always, a predominance of dead white males, with only a token female writer or two. No one had included *Zen and the Art of Pool Maintenance* on his or her list.

Toward the middle of the afternoon, Peter wandered in with lattes and cookies. I invited him for dinner, but he declined with a lame excuse about a baseball game of particular fascination. He was no more convincing than Madison had been when she expressed regret for her patronizing remarks about Caron and Inez.

"Any bodies lately?" he asked.

"No," I said as I nibbled on the cookie, "which is the good news. The bad news is that the houseguests can't leave for three more days." I told him about the emergency room and the diagnosis. "Now I'm truly stuck with them. Have you had any luck finding the assailant?"

"Several of the officers canvassed the neighbors, but nobody saw or heard anything. The girls are attractive, and they were cruising in a very expensive car. The obvious explanation is that someone followed them to the house. A drunk, possibly, or drug addict, planning to snatch their purses. We don't have much to go on, especially without a description."

"Sara Louise said she heard a car start up."

"It was nine o'clock. Someone in the neighborhood developed

a craving for ice cream, or a dinner guest went home after a glass of brandy."

I tossed the cookie wrapper in the trash can. "And this body?"

"We talked about that last night," he said, sounding a wee bit exasperated. "I checked again this morning, but no one has been reported missing. There's no physical evidence that someone was deposited on the pine needles behind the gazebo or in the lounge chair. There's no way to follow up on the matter."

"You could have Caron and Inez work with a police sketch artist," I said.

He thought about it for a moment. "I suppose so, although I can't see how it can do any good."

"If he hasn't been reported missing, he must live alone. A friend or landlord might recognize him from the sketch and call you."

"Or he could be from out of town, or an indigent with no local ties, or a respectable citizen pulling a prank and currently going about his normal routine. The sketches aren't as accurate as, say, mug shots or photos from the morgue."

I wasn't pleased to have my idea dismissed. "So go twiddle your thumbs until the rest of us are found floating facedown in the pool. Do the autopsies in a timely fashion; the chlorine and other chemicals might accelerate decomposition."

Peter smiled. "I'll keep that in mind. Any chance you can sneak away for the seventh-inning stretch?"

"Even if I knew what that was—and I don't—I should be at the house, if only to protect Madison from Caron and Inez. She has no idea how creative they can be when their honor has been impugned. And I keep hoping Dolly will call."

He wandered away, and I resumed filling out order forms within the limits of my budget and whatever credit I could wheedle out of the publishers. I sold a few books and shooed out some junior high girls who were reading aloud steamy passages from romance novels. The telephone remained silent, which meant no crises were taking place at Dolly's house that were deemed worthy of my intervention. This did not mean that I wouldn't arrive there to find fire trucks, ambulances, police cars, a SWAT team, and perhaps a vehicle from the UN with a multinational force to restore order.

I was putting the catalogs in my office when I heard the telephone ring. I made sure I was seated before I picked up the receiver.

"Ms. Malloy," began Mr. Kalker, my less than revered landlord, "I reckon I got some bad news for you."

"You rented the downstairs apartment to a family of rats—or should that be a pack of rats?"

"No, it's just that all the insulation has been infested, so it's got to be replaced. I got carpenters going over there tomorrow to start tearing down the Sheetrock. They know to be real careful with your stuff, but it might get dusty. After that, they—"

"How long will this take, Mr. Kalker?"

"I'm in real estate, not remodeling."

I took a bottle of aspirin from a desk drawer and tried to open it with one hand. "So now we're talking about the full two weeks?"

"Along those lines, yeah. Do you have any idea what this is costing me? I might as well level the site and put in an apartment building. I ain't sure about the zoning, but I figure I can squeeze in maybe six, eight units."

I put down the receiver, opened the bottle and shook out three tablets, then picked up the receiver. "The duplex is on the Historic Register. You can't make any changes to the exterior, much less raze it. Penalties range from a hefty fine to imprisonment, or both. If you don't believe me, go look it up at the courthouse."

"You sure about that?"

"Absolutely," I said, having no idea what I was talking about. "Call me when you're ready for me to look at paint chips. I've always thought sage green might be nice in the living room. Goodbye, Mr. Kalker."

I went back to the front room and was preparing to lock up when Lucy Hood and an unfamiliar man came across the portico.

"Oh, dear," she said as she came inside, "are you closed?"

"I'm in no rush, but I can't believe you've read all the books you bought this morning."

"Only one of them. I wanted to show Gary your store. He's staying in one of the condos, and invited me to lunch at the clubhouse. He's looking for bird books."

"Gary Billings," he said.

He was definitely Hollywood material, with tousled blond hair, intense blue eyes, and broad shoulders. Despite the fact that he was wearing a sports jacket and crisp trousers, I could see him in the role of a debonair tennis pro resisting (or acquiescing to) the advances of shapely matrons laden with sterling-silver baubles.

"You're a bird fancier?" I asked.

"Nothing of the sort. I'm looking for bird recipe books," he said gravely. "Roast robin, fried dove, sparrow à la king."

Lucy shook his arm. "You are such a liar. This is Claire Malloy, the owner of the store. She was about to close, so let's not delay her with your feeble attempts at humor." She looked at her watch. "I didn't realize how late it is! Daniel and I promised to meet another couple for drinks in half an hour, so I need to run. Claire, will you please find something for Gary and then kick him out? Gary, do try not to be insufferable." Twitching like Alice's White Rabbit, she darted out the door.

"Goodness," he murmured. "I sense that Lucy has ulterior motives, although I want to assure you that I do not. I'm looking for the Audubon guide for birds west of the Mississippi."

I agreed with his assessment of Lucy's motives, but said nothing and led him to a nearby rack. "I don't have a wide selection, but I do have the Audubon and a few other field guides."

He selected a couple of books. "Shall I assume you're single?"

"Why would you assume anything about me?"

"Lucy is one of those women who cannot bear the idea of single people drifting about like free spirits. She would have made a fine dowager in a Jane Austen novel. When I told her I was divorced, I saw a distinct glint in her eye. We continued to chat, but I could tell she was distracted. Now I know why."

"Perhaps she overestimates herself," I said as I rang up his purchases. "I said nothing earlier about my marital status."

63

"You're not wearing a wedding ring. Divorced, or still waiting for a prince?"

The conversation was taking a disturbingly personal bent. "I'm a bookseller, which is the only variable of any consequence. Cash or credit card?"

Gary gave me an impertinent smile. "Hey, don't blame me. I would have been perfectly content to sit on the deck and identify birds as best I could. Lucy insisted that I accompany her here. The store's charming, by the way."

"Thank you."

"So, are you single?"

I bit back what might have been interpreted as a caustic reply. "Your total comes to thirty-two dollars and seventeen cents. Would you like a bag?"

"I'd prefer a drink. Might you be able to join me at the establishment across the street?"

"I think not. If you'll excuse me, I need to lock up and be on my way. Happy birdwatching, Mr. Billings."

His smile faded. "Hey, I'm sorry if I've offended you. The last time I asked a woman for a date was when I was in college, and familiarity was the rule. I've only been divorced for a couple of months—make that sixty-seven days—and I'm clearly stumbling into a brave new world."

If he hadn't been drop-dead gorgeous, tanned, poised, and somewhat witty, I might have believed him. As it was, I doubted he'd been a bashful husband who could barely conduct a conversation over martinis at a chic restaurant. "You did not offend me," I said. "It's just that I have a complicated situation that requires both my attention and my presence. Drop by again if you'd like to browse."

"Lucy will be disappointed."

"I'm sure Lucy has only the best intentions, but not all of us are characters in novels who can be manipulated at an author's whim. I really do need to go now."

He followed me to the door. "I've always thought I'd make a great Gatsby."

"Then you'll have to look elsewhere for Daisy. Goodbye, Mr. Billings."

"Daisy? I could have sworn her name was Dolly."

I caught my breath, then managed to say, "No, her name was Daisy Buchanan. Next time you're by, I'll sell you a copy so you can refresh your memory."

He obligingly stepped out onto the portico so that I could lock the door, which I did with an unsteady hand. His mistake could have been entirely innocent, I told myself as I switched off the lights and left through the office door. The names were similar, and he'd probably last read the novel in college. I'd obliquely brought up the subject by claiming I was not a fictional character. Gary Billings and his type no doubt fancied themselves to be ruthless tycoons. And I was hypersensitive, albeit justifiably so. Sometimes a coincidence is just a coincidence.

The campus was closed down for the day, with only a few students ambling along the tree-lined sidewalks. It looked so safe and serene that I had to hold in a whimper as I speculated on what might be awaiting me at Dolly's house, but sitting on a bench was not on my agenda. I parked behind the Mercedes and went inside. There was no sound of carnage from the den, which was an agreeable respite. I stopped in the hall to listen to messages on the answering machine. As usual, they were all from women and concerning luncheons, committee meetings, and fund-raisers for causes that were undoubtedly worthy of fashion shows at the country club and champagne receptions at the arts center.

I went into the kitchen, which remained pristine, and poured myself a glass of scotch. When I came back out, I heard Caron's and Inez's voices from the patio and continued in that direction. They were sprawled in lounge chairs, with glasses of soda within reach and magazines spread across their laps.

"Everything okay?" I asked as I sat down by the table.

"As far as I know," Caron said. "We stayed in the den until the pool guys left. After that, we came out here."

Inez sat up and looked at me. "My mother called to see how everything was going. I didn't think she would want to hear about the dead body and the attack in the front yard, so I didn't say anything."

"That was for the best," I acknowledged with a weak smile, feeling as though I'd been tacitly accused of masterminding some devious scheme. "Where's Madison?"

Caron shrugged. "How should we know? She wasn't around when we came downstairs, and we haven't seen her all afternoon. I looked in on Sara Louise, who's still asleep."

"Could Madison have been in the bedroom across the hall?" I asked. "She implied earlier that she was planning to stay there to be near Sara Louise."

"No, the door was open and I didn't see her. The bathroom door was open, too."

I took a sip of scotch. "That's odd. What about the rest of the house?"

"About the only place she might be is in the garage or the attic," said Inez. "If there is an attic."

Caron snorted. "And what would she be doing in the attic? Having a tea party with dolls and teddy bears? After four hours, that might get a little old."

"Dolly's car is out front," I said, "so perhaps she went for a walk."

"Right," said Caron. "After all, the park's only two or three miles. She's probably sitting under a tree, writing sonnets. 'How do I love me? Let me count the ways . . .' The list could take hours."

I tried again. "Maybe the mechanic called to say the car was ready, and offered to pick her up. She might still be on the telephone with her father, explaining the situation and persuading him to pay the bill."

"So call the garage." Caron turned the page of the magazine. "Who wears this crap, anyway? The principal would have a stroke if I showed up in purple leather pants, stiletto heels, and a transparent bustier. If I wore it on Thurber Street, I'd be dragged into an alley."

Inez leaned over to look. "I don't think anybody actually wears that sort of thing in public. Well, maybe in Paris or Rome."

"Or Alpha Centauri," added Caron. "Can you believe somebody would pay nearly two hundred dollars for a pair of sunglasses? I feel faint. Inez, would you be so kind as to fetch me a damp washcloth?"

"Oh, yes, Miss Caron. When I get back, would you like me to massage your feet?"

"I would be ever so grateful if you'd just sprinkle them with champagne. My toenails are absolutely parched. A Mont Blanc, I should think, or a Moulin Rouge . . ."

I ignored them. I could call the garage, but neither Madison nor Sara Louise had ever mentioned its name. Farberville might lack an opera house and a museum of modern art, but it boasted innumerable garages and auto repair shops. And, to be candid, her absence was not intolerable. Caron and Inez had reverted to a more mellow level of cattiness. The pool could have been featured in a landscaping magazine for those with exorbitant incomes. The only noises from the neighborhood consisted of car doors and modulated voices; no one seemed to feel the need to mow a lawn or blow away an errant leaf.

However, I was puzzled by Madison's behavior. She'd professed great concern about Sara Louise at noon—but shortly thereafter, had cast off her Florence Nightingale trappings and disappeared, not into the night but into the midday sun. I told the girls I would return shortly with some crackers and cheese, then went inside. Madison had not left a note on the pad next to the phone. I did a quick tour of the living room, dining room, and den. The only evidence of any occupation was in the den, where there were soda cans and an empty pretzel bag on a coffee table. Fingerprinting and DNA testing were not required to identify the culprits.

I went upstairs and into Sara Louise's bedroom. She appeared not to have moved since I'd been there earlier. I was not surprised, since the prescription bottle from a pharmacy contained pills strong enough to knock out the most valiant cavalry troops on the Crimean battlefields. Sara Louise's color was adequate and she was breathing evenly.

The bedroom directly across the hall was untidy, but no more so than the master suite. Madison had been able to cram quite a bit into her backpack, I thought as I picked up clothes and tossed them on the

67

bed. She clearly preferred silk to cotton, and the sunglasses atop the dresser were replicas of the ones in Caron's magazine. I stopped as I saw her purse on a chair by the window. I advanced cautiously, as though it might be a booby trap left by fashion terrorists. Echoes of stern warnings blared over loudspeakers in airports flashed through my mind.

I finally opened it. Rather than sticks of dynamite, it contained a thick wallet, a makeup kit, scraps of paper, pens, a checkbook, a key ring, a brush, a small address book, wadded tissues, and other necessities.

I could think of no reason why she wouldn't have taken it with her, unless she'd anticipated being gone for only a few minutes. It would have been firmly affixed to her backpack had she attempted to climb Mount Everest, or strapped to her life jacket had she chosen to go white-water rafting on the Colorado River. A dearth of lipstick would pose a greater threat than mere frostbite.

Perplexed, I did a quick search of the guest bathroom, master suite, and my bedroom. If there was an attic, I saw no telltale trap-door in the ceiling. Madison was not the type to risk climbing a rickety ladder in order to brush away cobwebs and amuse herself by snooping through whatever Dolly might have stored there.

There was likely to be a more mundane explanation, I told myself as I went downstairs. The doctor at the emergency room could have been as handsome as the most recent customer at the Book Depot, and called to invite Madison for a leisurely lunch. A grad student might have met her while she was at the mailbox and suggested watching racy videos at his house. She'd felt the need for a spontaneous trip to the mall to alleviate her stress and called a taxi. She'd gone for a walk, turned her ankle, and was now being treated by a bearded professor with a fondness for whiny blondes in tiny shorts. But she wouldn't have left her purse behind in any of those scenarios.

There wasn't much point in worrying about it, I concluded. Remembering my offer to appear poolside with cheese and crackers, I went into the kitchen and opened the refrigerator door. The shelves were crowded with containers of leftover Thai delicacies, cold cuts, cans of soda and beer, a curling piece of pizza, jars of pickles and relishes, and so forth. I found packages of cheese in a lower drawer. I took out what I preferred, along with a jar of olives and a salami, arranged a platter, and was about to go outside when I realized I hadn't seen any steaks. When I'd last seen Madison, she'd been on her way to the freezer in the garage, but apparently had lost her way or allowed herself to be distracted by the heady redolence of detergent in the laundry room by the door.

I put down the platter and headed for the garage. I wasn't sure how many steaks we'd need, since Sara Louise was unavailable for comment. Madison would surely drag herself back in time for dinner, though, which meant we needed at least four. I'd forgotten to stop by the grocery store, but Caron and Inez would not mind an excuse to drive Dolly's car.

In painful contrast to the garage at my apartment, this one was fastidious. Hoses were neatly coiled around hooks on the wall, and the few gardening tools were aligned on a metal shelf. No stacks of newspapers or boxes of books cluttered the floor, which looked as though it was scrubbed on a weekly basis. And, of course, no rodents scurried out of sight or eyed me with disdain.

The freezer was large. I had no idea of cubic feet or whatever measure was used to gauge capacity, but this one had lots of them. I raised the door, then stopped as a blast of arctic air engulfed me. My eyes bulged in a most unattractive fashion.

For the first time, I had a decent view of the body Caron and Inez claimed to have seen. And this time, he wasn't going anywhere.

Chapter Five

I dropped the freezer lid and backed into the pantry, fighting the primal instinct to dash through the kitchen and out the front door, squawking in a most unseemly manner. My knees were wobbling so badly that I had to grab the edge of the counter to steady myself. I stared at the freezer as if I were expecting to see the lid slowly rise of its own accord—or propelled by an icy, misshapen hand. I grabbed the door, slammed it closed, and locked it. Only then was I able to exhale the gulp of air that had crystallized inside my lungs.

I'd seen dead bodies before, in that my modest attempts to assist the police had at times led to sticky situations of a somewhat gothic disposition. But none of them had been so ghastly as the man in the freezer, his skin gray, his eyes flat, his face reflecting only minimal surprise, his arms curled around his bent legs. He was loosely wrapped in some sort of transparent plastic. And, as Caron and Inez had claimed earlier, he had a small wound ringed with blackish blood in the middle of his forehead.

Still unsure of my gelatinous knees, I risked letting go of the counter and made it into the kitchen, where I sank down onto a stool. From the patio I could hear the girls cheerfully prattling about ads in the fashion magazines. Could the person or persons who'd done this be in the house? I'd looked around for Madison, but I hadn't opened closets or peered under furniture. With its gazebo, shed, pine trees, and bounteous azaleas and rhododendrons, the backyard could have provided cover for a platoon of malefactors. I began to shiver, either from shock or the sudden realization that we might all be in danger. I tried to yell Caron's name, but all I could produce was a strangled croak.

I finally forced myself up and went to the sliding door that led to the patio. "Girls," I said evenly, "come inside now."

"Yeah, okay," Caron said without looking up. "We'll be there in a few minutes."

"Come inside now," I repeated.

Inez turned her head. "Goodness, Ms. Malloy, is something wrong? You look like you're about to throw up."

Caron snickered. "She probably found Madison in the butler's pantry panting with the butler."

"We have a butler?" said Inez, glancing over her shoulder as if Jeeves might be bearing down on them with a plate of sticky buns.

I bit down on my lower lip for a moment, then said, "Both of you, now. Inside."

They put down the magazines and came across the patio. "You do look pretty awful, Mother," said Caron with the faintest flicker of concern. "Has something happened?"

I nodded. "I've found your missing body. Go upstairs to Sara Louise's room, lock the door, and stay there until I come get you."

Inez's eyes widened. "He's in the house?"

"All you have to do is wait five minutes," said Caron, "and then he'll vanish. I know how this works, Mother. Trust me."

I was not amused. "I'm going to call 911, and then Peter. If I don't hear you lock the bedroom door before I pick up the receiver, I will drag you upstairs by your hair and fling you inside. Understand?"

"Don't get all huffy." Caron went past me, with Inez trailing after her. "So where's the body this time—watching a movie in the den?"

I reached for the cordless. "Think of the money you'll save on shampoo and conditioner." After they'd trotted up the stairs, I punched in the numbers, waited until I heard a voice, and then said, "I've just found a body in the freezer. Please send someone immediately. I'm afraid the perpetrator might still be in the house or yard."

71

"On Dogwood Lane." The dispatcher groaned. "Third time this week, right?"

"Send someone immediately!"

"Look, Ms. Malloy, I realize you're the lieutenant's girlfriend, but this is getting old. The officers on duty have more important things to do than come chasing up there whenever one of you claims to have found a body that turns out not to be there after all. Why don't you have yourself a stiff drink, then call me back if the body hasn't taken a hike?"

"Then you're not going to send a patrol car?" I said, grinding out each word.

"If I send a patrol car every time some nutcase hears Nazis in the attic or sees little green men in the backyard, I wouldn't have anyone available—"

I hung up, then dialed the more mundane number of the police department and asked to speak to Peter. I was informed that he was gone for the day. I called his house, but no one answered. He could have stopped to pick up a pizza or Chinese—or taken Madison on a scenic drive to a country inn for an intimate dinner, despite the fact he was old enough to be her father (presuming she'd been conceived on his prom night).

I'd about decided to take the dispatcher's advice and have a stiff drink when a bedroom door opened and Caron called, "What on earth is going on, Mother? If we're all going to be murdered, I'd like to change into something more flattering."

"No one will notice if you're wheeled out in a body bag," I replied.

"I'm talking about the crime scene photos, with the victim awkwardly sprawled on the carpet. Did you call 911?"

"Yes, I did. Now get back inside the room and stay there."

"While you do what?"

I was very nearly hysterical, and the conversation was not helping. Her question was a good one, though. What did I think I was going to do? Sit on the top of the freezer to prevent someone from retrieving the body? Go outside and scream until one of the neighbors called the police? Search the house while clutching a corkscrew to defend myself? Make spaghetti for dinner, since steaks were off the menu unless I rolled aside the body to fetch a package of sirloin strips?

What I needed to do was go back to the garage, open the freezer, and make sure that I hadn't mistaken the body for a side of beef—which I knew perfectly well I hadn't. On the other hand, I really didn't want to so much as unlock the door to the garage.

I was in the hallway, dithering, when the front door opened and Peter came in. "I hear you found the body again," he said in a conversational tone, as though commenting on the traffic. "The dispatcher started worrying and paged me. I assured him I'd look into it."

"How kind of you," I said in an altogether different tone. "I do hope this isn't interrupting your baseball game."

"It doesn't start for another half hour." He went into the kitchen. "I assume the freezer is back here somewhere. Would you care to show me?"

"It's in the garage." I wanted to stay where I was, but reluctantly led the way. My hand began to shake as I unlocked the door to the garage, but I managed to do so. "Right there."

Peter lifted the freezer lid, then stepped back and let out a low whistle. "Any idea who he is?"

"According to what Caron and Inez said earlier, it's the same man. It would be too much of a coincidence if it weren't."

He lowered the lid. "I suppose it would be a stretch." He continued across the garage to a door that led to the side yard. "It's not locked. Anyone could have come in this way."

"Anyone lugging a dead body," I said. "Are you planning to do something more useful than counting the rakes?"

He put his arm around me and took me into the kitchen. "Wait here while I make a call." After barking orders at the dispatcher (who deserved a great deal more than that, I thought acerbically), he returned. "Where are Caron, Inez, and those two girls?"

"Madison has been gone all afternoon. The others are in a bedroom upstairs, waiting for me." I blinked as my eyes began to burn.

"I wasn't sure there might not be someone hiding in the house. I'm still not, for that matter. Maybe you should—"

He put his hands on my shoulders. "It's okay, Claire. Officers should be here in a minute. I'll have them do a thorough search of both the house and the yard. After that, I'll have to deal with the crime boys and the medical examiner. It's too bad you couldn't have waited until the game was over."

"This is hardly my fault. I've never been consulted about the scheduling of baseball games. If that were the case, they'd all start at midnight." I moved away from him and leaned against the refrigerator, my arms crossed. "Up until now, it could have been some sort of twisted practical joke. Maybe he was a friend of Dolly's and was acting out scenes from a movie or a mystery novel they'd enjoyed together. Or he could have been an enemy, trying to frighten her. He wouldn't have known she went out of town or that we're house-sitting. Once she decided to go to Dallas, she made a reservation and left the next day. Dolly did not dillydally."

He saw the glass I'd left on the counter. "Is this yours?" When I nodded, he put it in my hand and made sure I had a grip on it. "I hear cars out front. Please join the girls for a few minutes. As soon as the house has been searched, you can all come downstairs and wait in the den. I don't think you'll be having steaks tonight, but you can come in the kitchen long enough to find snacks to hold you. At some point, I'll have to get statements from everybody, but it shouldn't take long." He paused and gave me an appraising look. "Unless there's something you're not telling me."

"Something I'm not telling you? I've told you every last blasted detail of what I know, which isn't much." My voice began to rise. "Are you insinuating that I'm withholding information? I cannot believe this, Lieutenant Rosen. Here I am, being terrorized, and you have the nerve to even think such a thing!"

"If you recall, there have been investigations in which you went to extremes to do exactly that."

"I never lied to you," I said.

"I didn't say you did, but you certainly withheld evidence."

74

"I never withheld anything that you couldn't have discovered on your own—if you hadn't been so pigheaded. Some of us see the forest, while others of us insist on blundering into trees. Now, if you'll excuse me, I'll go upstairs."

I swept out of the kitchen, seething. By the time I was halfway upstairs, I realized I'd overreacted in a post-traumatic bout of suppressed hysteria. A fine diagnosis, worthy of a veritable babble of psychologists, but nevertheless requiring an apology. However, I could hear voices in the hallway, and I knew I would encounter unsuppressed hysteria in Sara Louise's bedroom if I didn't explain what was happening.

Inez unlocked the door and dragged me inside. "What's going on? Is there a murderer in the house? All I could find to use as a weapon is a nail file." She held it up like a diminutive carving knife. "I don't know if I could actually poke somebody. I guess I could."

Sara Louise was sitting up in bed, looking pale and bewildered. "There's a body downstairs—and a murderer? This really doesn't make any sense, Ms. Malloy. I feel like I'm in a hazy dream. Did somebody get shot? The same guy as last night? Where's the body?"

"In the freezer in the garage."

"That is way creepy," said Inez as she set aside her weapon of less than mass destruction. "Is he frozen?"

"Frozen stiff."

Inez gave me a wary look. "Are you sure you're okay, Ms. Malloy?"

Caron turned away from the window. "The cops took their sweet time getting here, didn't they?"

"Calls from this house lack credibility, I'm afraid," I said. "Peter saw it this time, so we won't be subjected to ridicule again." I told them how I'd come to find the body in the freezer, then glanced at Sara Louise. "Do you know where Madison is? I can't believe she'd wander away without her purse."

She pushed her hair out of her face. "I was asleep all afternoon. Do you think something's happened to her?"

"I don't know what to think. She was fine when I saw her at noon. You know her better than we do, Sara Louise. Has she met any men in Farberville whom she found attractive? You did say something about the golf pro's son, after all. Does she pull that kind of stunt often?"

Caron waggled her eyebrows. "The golf pro's son? What did she do with him? Hold up caddy shacks?"

Sara Louise blinked at her, then said to me, "To be frank, Madison's gotten herself into trouble on several occasions. We haven't met any especially attractive men, but I was in the emergency room or being wheeled off for X-rays most of the morning. I suppose she could have encountered someone and made a date. She tends to be . . . spontaneous."

"That's not what it's called at the high school," murmured Inez.

A police officer knocked on the door and identified himself. "The lieutenant wants you all downstairs for questioning."

"Can you make it?" I asked Sara Louise.

"I may need a little help. The pain's not as bad as it was last night, but I'm still sore. What are you going to do about Madison?"

"It's not even seven o'clock," I said. "We need to tell Lieutenant Rosen about it. I don't see what he can do, though."

"She probably saw the perps putting the body in the freezer," said Caron. "They grabbed her and took her to a meat locker. By now she looks like that Neanderthal some scientist found frozen in an iceberg at the North Pole." She held up her hands, fingers contorted, and screwed up her face in a mockery of a silent scream.

"Is she for real?" said Sara Louise.

"Let's go downstairs," I said, giving Caron a sharp look. "All we need to do is tell the lieutenant everything we know. Sara Louise, put your arm around me. We'll take it one stair at a time."

Eventually we arrived in the hallway. The door from the kitchen to the garage was open, and I could hear Peter issuing orders in a manly fashion. Sergeant Jorgeson, his minion, was waiting for us in the den.

"Should I get her some water?" he asked as I deposited Sara Louise on the sofa and put a comforter over her legs.

"I'd prefer a glass of white wine," she said with a grimace.

Caron and Inez sat down on an ottoman, attempting to appear

blasé but no doubt thrilled to be key players. And, I noticed, rather self-satisfied, as if savoring the calls they would make later to Emily and Aly and the rest of the traitorous lemmings. Rhonda Maguire might have the unflagging devotion of her coterie (as well as that of Louis Wilderberry), but my two politicians had their very own dead body. Surely that would merit several points in the polls.

"I'll get it," I said to Jorgeson. I went to the kitchen, poured the wine, and gathered up an armload of sodas, chips, and sandwich fare. Sara Louise accepted the glass with a grateful smile. The girls made sandwiches and retreated to the ottoman. I would have preferred a more potent potable, but settled for a soda.

Peter kept us waiting over an hour. From the den, it was hard to hear what was happening in the garage, but I had a feeling Jorgeson's assignment was to keep us (or more specifically, me) away from the scene. At some point the garage door proper was opened, perhaps to expedite the removal of the body. Vehicles came and went. Several plainclothed investigators paused in the doorway to stare curiously at us. I began to feel as though we were in a department store window for the entertainment of passing shoppers.

At last Peter came in and sat down. "Do you want to stay here to-night?" he asked me. "I can assure you that whoever's responsible for the homicide is not in the house or hiding in the yard, but you may feel uncomfortable. I can arrange for the department to put you up in a motel for a few days."

I considered his offer. "No, we'll be okay here. We'll keep the doors locked and the alarm set at night. Do you all agree?"

I expected Sara Louise to demand a suite with a minibar, so I was surprised when she said, "Ms. Malloy is right. I think we should stay here. What are you going to do about my cousin?"

"The blonde?" said Peter.

"Madison has been missing all afternoon, and now it's almost eight-thirty. Shouldn't you be trying to find her?"

He looked at me. "You said she was gone. That's not quite the same as 'missing.' "

77

I decided it was not the time for a discourse on semantic technicalities. "I came here at noon and asked her to take steaks out of the freezer. She agreed to do so. I went upstairs to have a word with Caron, then came back down and was about to leave when the pool guys showed up at the front door. Maybe you should talk to them."

Caron leaned forward and said, "When we came down about ten minutes later, we didn't see her. The pool guys were doing whatever it is they do."

"They probably knocked her out," Inez added, "and stuffed her in the shed. She may still be there, tied up and gagged."

Sara Louise attempted to throw back the comforter and sit up. "We've got to go look," she said frantically. "The stench of all those chemicals could—"

"She's not there," Peter said. "We did a very thorough search that included the shed as well as every inch of the yard. I would like to have a word with the pool guys, though."

"Manny's PerfectPools," I said. "There should be a bill on the table in the hall."

Jorgeson cleared his throat. "I'll call 'em, Lieutenant. Could be they saw something."

While we waited, Peter made himself a sandwich and opened a can of soda. Sara Louise sank back down and began to fidget with the hem of the comforter. I could see that she was in pain, but I didn't want to encourage her to take more medication until we had an inkling where Madison might be. Questioning the unconscious is rarely productive.

Jorgeson came to the doorway and said, "No one there, and not even an answering machine. Guess we'd better go by early in the morning. You need to talk to the ME before he takes away the body?"

Peter frowned for a moment, then shook his head. "Tell him I'll call later when he has something for us." He finished his sandwich, meticulously wiped his chin with a napkin, and put down the soda can. "To save you the trouble of asking, we don't know who the man was. He carried no identification of any kind. There's an indication that he normally wore a watch and a ring, but they're missing. We'll send his fingerprints to the FBI database in case he has a criminal record. Cause of death is most likely to be the result of the gunshot to his forehead. No weapon has been found."

"Of course not," said Caron. "He was shot at least two days ago. Inez and I would have noticed if someone killed him fifty feet from where we were sitting."

"I'm sure you would have," Peter murmured. "Now tell us about this missing girl. Does she know anyone in Farberville?"

Sara Louise shrugged. "Not really. The only thing I can think of is that the garage called to say the car was fixed and offered to pick her up. I can't imagine where she'd go after that, though."

"There's a phone in the bedroom," said Caron. "Nobody called except some woman wanting to know if Dolly had talked to a florist about a luncheon next week. I said I really didn't know, which was true, but the woman acted like she didn't believe me and—"

Peter held up his hand. "Well, I believe you. Jorgeson, get a description of the missing girl and have the patrol boys keep an eye out for her. I don't see what else we can do for now. The neighbors have all been asked if they saw anything suspicious or even out of the ordinary this afternoon, but no one did. We'll check with the garage to make sure she didn't call them; if they have a towing service, they'll have an emergency number."

"If I can remember it," Sara Louise said as she rubbed her face. "I called AAA and they sent the tow truck. Once we got to the garage, we were both so exhausted and hungry that I just gave the guy the telephone number here and told him to call as soon as he had an idea when the car would be repaired." She began to shiver. "Maybe AAA can help. I've got my card upstairs."

I gestured at Inez and Caron. "Help her back to bed and bring down the card."

The girls did not look pleased to be excluded, however briefly, from the potentially more promising discussion, but they dutifully waited until Sara Louise stood up and then each took an arm and steered her toward the stairs. Jorgeson pulled out a notebook, and

Peter and I described Madison as best we could. I maintained a stoic expression when Peter added a few comments about her figure, although I did notice that Jorgeson glanced in my direction.

Once Peter and I had the den to ourselves, I said, "So now are you going to make an effort to find Dolly? It's not what I would call low-priority anymore, unless finding dead bodies in freezers in Farberville is more common than I realize. Perhaps it's so pedestrian that the newspapers don't even bother to run the stories."

"You are not attractive when you froth," he said wearily. "Yes, we are tracing the call she made the other night. If it came from her sister's house, we'll have the name and number in the morning. We're also getting the record from the telephone company of all the calls she made from here in the last month. I suspect that she's going to have to cut short her trip."

I felt a slight flutter in my stomach as I envisioned a row of sleeping bags in the bookstore. "It's hard to imagine Dolly caught up in something like this. She seems so kind and generous. Since she moved here, she's hooked up with a dozen charitable causes, including the Book Depot. Before she left, she wanted to help me organize a couple of book clubs."

"You sound as though you think she's guilty of something."

"I don't think she is," I said, "and neither will you when you meet her. Maybe it has to do with her husband's business."

"What was it?"

I tried to recall what Dolly had said while we nibbled antipasto by the pool. "A factory near Chicago that made some sort of terribly utilitarian widget. Rags to riches, so to speak. I don't think she has anything to do with it these days, though. I happened to look through her papers, and—"

"You happened to look through her papers?" Peter gave me a faint smile. "Did they happen to fall out of a cabinet?"

"Madison and I were looking for her telephone bills," I said coolly. "We thought we might find the sister's number. No luck there; she hasn't made any long-distance calls since she arrived, and we couldn't find any evidence that she has a cell phone. Furthermore, there weren't any letters or documents involving business concerns. Even if she were an inactive partner or a member of the board, she would have received copies of the minutes, dividend statements, tax information, that kind of thing. I think she just settled everything and walked away from it."

"And subsequently made enemies here?"

"I don't know," I admitted. "Maybe there's a vicious underworld split between those devoted to adult literacy and those who believe the only hope for civilization is free ballet classes for underprivileged children. Maybe it's escalated because of dwindling support from the government. You may have to install metal detectors at wine-tasting fund-raisers at the arts center and send bomb-sniffing dogs into soup kitchens."

Peter yawned. "We'll keep that in mind. We're done here for the time being. Someone will come by tomorrow to take everybody's fingerprints so we can eliminate them. I'd like Caron and Inez to come to the PD and give detailed statements."

"Are you going to take us out to lunch afterwards?" asked Caron as she came into the den. "Anything but barbecue and catfish. Why, I don't know what I'd do if I was confronted by a nasty little ol' hush-puppy."

Inez came over to Peter. "Here's Sara Louise's AAA card. I think it's platinum."

"All I can promise are stale doughnuts," he said. "In the meantime, don't make any comments to the media. I'm serious—not one word until we locate the man's next of kin."

"The media?" Caron said with studied indifference. "They'll want to interview us, put us on the news?"

Inez ineffectually pushed her hair out of her eyes. "The only time I've ever had my picture in the paper was when the math club won a regional competition. I was in the back row, and all you could really see was the glare on my glasses. My father said it was a good likeness."

I realized that anything I said would be just as ineffectual as Inez's gesture, but I tried anyway. "You heard what Peter said, and you'd better keep it in mind. Tomorrow, with the exception of the police department, you are to stay inside the house or in the backyard. Do not so much as answer the phone."

"What if Dolly calls?" asked my intrepid daughter. "I thought you wanted to talk to her. I suppose she might leave a message, but that won't do much good, will it?"

"We'll have to take that risk," said Peter. "And I don't want you to drive yourselves to the department. At eleven o'clock, a patrol car will pick you up at the back gate and deliver you there when we're finished."

Caron's lower lip shot out. "And what about Mother? I don't see why she gets to take all the credit. Inez and I are the ones who kept seeing the body. She didn't really believe us, any more than you did. Sure, you both said you did, but you were just patronizing us like we were little kids having bad dreams. Now that you have proof, you don't have any choice but to take us seriously for a change. But we're not allowed to defend ourselves, are we? Why don't you just send a helicopter and have us airlifted to a convent on some mountain? Or put us in the witness protection program and make us go live in Toledo or Tacoma?"

Peter did not smile. "Don't tempt me. I apologize for not taking you more seriously. However, we are obliged to limit media exposure until we can notify the victim's relatives."

"And protect you and Inez until the killer is in custody," I added. "If you start embellishing your story, you're liable to imply that you know more than you really do. Whatever's going on has been carefully calculated thus far."

"Are you implying that I'm too stupid to have figured that out?" she said in an icy voice. She turned around. "Come on, Inez, let's go drown ourselves in the Jacuzzi. That way, at least we'll get our obituaries in the local paper!"

"Goodness," I said as they left the room. "She seems to be regressing. Not all that long ago, I thought she was finally through all this adolescent rampaging and was showing some signs of maturity and compassion. I'd like to throttle Rhonda Maguire."

"Who?" asked Peter, understandably baffled.

"Never mind. Why don't you pack up your fingerprint kit and magnifying glass and go away? Tomorrow Madison will show up with some lame excuse, Dolly will appear and explain everything, the victim's ne'er-do-well nephew will step forward and confess to everything, and Mr. Kalker will carry away the last few cockroach corpses."

He glanced at the doorway, then pulled me up and wrapped his arms around me as if I might crumple. "An excellent scenario, particularly if we add a romantic dinner to top it off. Let's make sure all the other doors are locked, then you can escort me to the front door, where I will give you a very unprofessional kiss before I leave. You can then turn on the alarm, fix yourself a cup of tea, and go to bed."

I demurely acquiesced. Peter allowed me to wait in the kitchen while he locked the door from the pantry to the garage. I was pondering the possibility of adopting a vegetarian lifestyle as we went to the front door. We engaged in what was indeed a very unprofessional kiss, but reluctantly disengaged after a few minutes.

Peter's arm was draped over my shoulder as he opened the door. Camera flashbulbs exploded in our faces. Microphones were thrust in front of us from what seemed like dozens of directions. Television cameras began to whir like a swarm of demented locusts. Reporters screeched questions. Headlights came on to further illuminate the scene as if we'd stepped onto the stage of a Broadway show.

"Lieutenant Rosen, is it true—"

"Over here, Ms. Malloy!"

"Have you identified the body?"

"Was the body in a freezer?"

"What did you first think, Ms. Malloy, when—"

"Is this the first time a body has—"

"Could we have a word with you, Ms. Malloy, about how you—"

"Lieutenant, do you have any suspects?"

Despite the increasingly frenzied jumble of questions and demands, the only noise I could truly hear was a howl of outrage from a Jacuzzi on the second floor.

Chapter Six

I did not sleep well, but my expectations had been low and I hadn't looked forward to strangling myself in the sheets if the nightmares became too vivid. Which they might have. I took an unusually long shower and assiduously avoided looking at my reflection as I brushed my teeth. Poor little man, I thought as I went downstairs, started a pot of coffee, and stuck a couple of slices of bread in the toaster. Not only had he been murdered, but he'd also been carted around like a mannequin. The crimes I'd encountered in the past had been motivated by passion and anger. This one was cold-blooded, to put it mildly.

The toast popped up and the coffeepot stopped gurgling. I conscientiously switched off the alarm system and opened the front door, poised to slam it if any reporters had camped overnight or arrived under cover of the dawn's early light. The lawn was a muddy mess, but the coast appeared to be clear. I darted out to the driveway, grabbed the newspaper, and retreated without being captured on film for all of Farberville to scrutinize.

Peter and I had agreed that I should stay away from the Book Depot until the media coyotes had moved along to their next hyperbolic crisis. Even a few days of no income would come back to haunt me at the end of the month. I was still paying utilities for my apartment, but I figured I could argue my case with Mr. Kalker, pointing out that the dwelling was uninhabitable due solely to his neglect. It was worth a try. And, of course, Caron and I would save a bundle when I renounced our carnivorous ways. It would be an interesting conversation.

I poured a cup of coffee, fetched butter and jam from the refrigerator, and settled down on a stool for a peaceful breakfast. And promptly choked on a mouthful of coffee as I stared at my photograph on the front page, with a headline that proclaimed LOCAL BOOKSTORE OWNER FINDS CADAVER IN FREEZER. The photograph was far from flattering. My eyes were rounded, as was my mouth, as if I'd been stung by a hornet. Peter was scowling with the fury of a Samurai warrior. His hair, which had been ruffled during our charming interlude in the hallway, stuck up in tufts. We could have been celebrities sneaking out of a sleazy motel room at some unholy hour in the morning, unaware that the paparazzi had gathered like maggots on a dead animal.

I moved on to the article. The reporter had done his best to imply there was something scandalous afoot, but was obliged by what ethical standards he'd picked up in Journalism 102 to acknowledge that it was ten o'clock in the evening and we were both, sadly enough, fully clothed and superficially sober. Details about our names, careers, and current addresses had been provided, along with a rehash of Peter's homicide cases and my occasional contributions to some of them. With almost no information released about the crime itself, column inches, like dental cavities, had to be filled. Jorgeson had declined to comment, as had the medical examiner and the uniformed officers who'd struggled to constrain the media to the driveway and yard. I suspected there would be quite a few comments being made in the sanctity of the PD—and primarily of a derisive nature. Farberville's chief of police had undoubtedly choked on more than a mouthful of coffee.

The story continued onto a second page. An ambitious underling in the newsroom had ferreted out a photograph of Dolly at a formal affair, surrounded by local luminaries. She was identified as the owner of the house "in which this vicious murder" had taken place. The only personal tidbits they'd uncovered were quotes lauding her charitable activities. They'd found nothing about her background prior to moving to Farberville, but it was early in the day. Without a chainsaw murder, a school bus crash, or the arrest of a college athlete, they certainly would pursue it. Farberville provides them with few sensational stories in the summer months, which often leaves them with nothing more newsworthy than a boating accident or a fender bender in a discount-store parking lot.

I was rereading the article when the doorbell rang. I was hardly in the mood to have a camera stuck in my face. I did want to talk to Peter, however, to find out if he'd identified the body. It was possible Madison had finally decided to drag herself back, wagging her shapely tail behind her. Dolly might have taken a cab from the airport. The victim might have slipped out of the morgue and come looking for his watch. Or cows might be flying in formation across the sky, mooing happily as they migrated north to the cornfields of Nebraska. Nothing would have surprised me.

I went to the door and opened it a few inches. There was definitely someone there, but he or she was hidden behind a vast flower arrangement that had missed no hues in the spectrum, or species in a botanical garden.

"Claire Malloy?" mumbled a male voice. "Delivery."

"Come in," I said. I wasn't completely convinced this was not a pernicious ploy perpetrated by a reporter, and I was more than ready to snatch a snapdragon from the arrangement and retaliate.

A septuagenarian with dark, deeply creased skin, a dusting of gray hair, and a well-trimmed beard and mustache peered at me from behind a spray of lilies. "Can I put this down, lady? It must weigh a ton, and my back ain't what it used to be. I shined shoes at the student union for forty years, always bent over with my polish and rags. It wasn't nearly as bad as this job. My kids keep telling me to quit and stay home, but I ain't about to spend my years watching those damn fool talk shows. Afore too long, I'd be talking to my dog. Let me tell you, he's one stupid dog. I tell him to fetch, he just lies there farting and twitching his legs. When he starts answering me, that's when I'll quit."

I took the flowers, which were indeed very heavy, and set them on the dining room table. "Would you like a cup of coffee before you leave?"

"That'd be real nice. You are Claire Malloy, aren't you? I'm supposed to have you sign for this on account of how expensive it is."

I took the proffered pad and scribbled my name. "Cream, sugar?"

He followed me into the kitchen and sat down. "Black's fine. In all my years at the student union, I never forgot a face. You look familiar, but I can't rightly place you." He glanced down at my sandals and sniffed. "Don't reckon I polished the likes of those. Maybe you were a student. A lot of the self-proclaimed liberals used to stop by the stand and say good morning. Made 'em feel good, I suppose, letting us underprivileged minority folks know they cared."

I set a cup in front of him, then said, "I didn't go to school here. My husband taught English, but I never had a reason to go to the student union."

He was still studying me. "I guess you'd know if you did. You look familiar, though, and I'm going to worry about it all night."

I folded the newspaper to the front page and slid it across the island. "Because of this?"

"Oh, that. I glanced at it before I went to work. Is this really you? If you don't mind me saying so, you look like you stuck a fork in an outlet. Did you really find a dead man in the freezer?" He cackled. "He'd have to be dead, wouldn't he? Freezers are mighty cold."

"Yes, they are," I said, nodding.

"The cops think you did it? Is that why this Lieutenant Rosen was questioning you so late? Looks like you and him had quite a tussle."

"We did not have a tussle, and I am not a suspect." Abruptly, I wondered if I was. Surely not. Peter had heard the whole sordid chain of events. His superiors, on the other hand, were less impressed by my indisputable investigative prowess, and quite possibly would enjoy nothing more than to see me implicated. I'd spend my last nickel on lawyers, lose the store, and be forced to move somewhere where the redolence of notoriety would not cling to me like stale cigarette smoke. Mr. Kalker would immediately rent out my apartment to drug dealers and pornographers who could pay exorbitant rent. Caron and I would not sleep comfortably in my hatchback. Both of us might end up shoveling manure at the pig farm.

"Hey, lady," the delivery man said, patting my hand, "don't go getting all upset. I was just making a joke. It says right here that this isn't even your house. Where's the woman who lives here? Shouldn't she be the one to explain about the body in the freezer?"

"She asked me to house-sit so she could visit her sister." I took a swallow of coffee. "The police are trying to track her down."

He stared at me. "Visit her sister? Is that all she said? If I was going to visit my sister, all I'd have to do is go to the cemetery. Maybe she's pulling a fast one on you, honey, trying to make you look guilty on account of something she did. Didn't she leave a phone number in case you need to get hold of her? What do you know about her, anyway?"

It was oddly comforting to talk to someone who was interested, but at the same time disinterested. He probably wouldn't have cared if I'd broken down and confessed to the evil deed. Then again, he might have deemed me unworthy of the flowers and hauled them off to the cemetery. "I thought I knew her pretty well," I said, "but now I'm not sure. I happened to look through her papers—"

"On account of how they fell in your lap?"

He and Peter would make a fine team, I thought irritably. I should have run him off, but the house was peaceful and he was an astute listener. And, for the most part, nonjudgmental. "Your name is . . . ?"

"Call me Cal. So you snooped through her papers? Find anything?"

"Not really." Sighing, I refilled his cup and mine, then sat down across from him. "There wasn't one thing that related to her life before she moved to Farberville several months ago. It's as if she was swooped up in a tornado and deposited here with nothing more than a very respectable bank balance." I tried to remember what I'd noticed on her bank statements. "And a very respectable deposit every month, for that matter."

"Where's the money come from?" he asked, leaning forward.

"I don't know. I think it's transferred, most likely from a trust. Her husband was rich."

He looked around the kitchen. "No question about that. You sure you don't know how to get in touch with her so she can explain about the body? She doesn't sound like much of a friend if she just waltzed off and left you to deal with the police. I'll bet she hasn't even bothered to call you since she left. Some friend she is!"

Now I felt the need to defend Dolly, even though his assessment had a degree of validity. "If she had any idea about this mess, I'm sure she would fly home immediately. All she did was go to visit her sister in Dallas."

"You know for certain she went to Dallas?"

"Of course she did," I said. "My daughter took her to the airport."

"And watched her get on the plane?"

"No, but I'm sure the police will confirm it. And she did call from Dallas the next night."

Cal nodded slowly, like a bobble-headed judge with a flask in his hip pocket. "Then she must be in Dallas, because she called and told you that she was in Dallas. You interested in investing in a mighty fine parcel of swampland out by the sewage plant? Even my dog knows enough to stick up his nose when he smells something rancid. You sure she even has a sister? She ever mention a name?"

It occurred to me that I'd not seen a single photograph in the house, not even of her beloved Bibi. No casual snapshots from a vacation, or more formal shots of the two of them attired to tango. "I don't know if she has a sister," I admitted grumpily, "but if she wanted to spend a couple of weeks relaxing at a resort or having discreet cosmetic surgery, all she had to do was say so. Why would she bother to lie about it?"

"Why was there a body in her freezer?"

"If I knew, I'd tell you, the police, and the media. If you'll excuse me, I have some things to do. Thanks so much for delivering the flowers."

He trailed me to the front door, then paused. "Anytime you want to talk to ol' Cal, just give me a call." He put a slip of paper in my hand. "Here's my home number. I don't get out much at night on account of my eyesight not being what it used to be. If a dog answers, hang up and try later."

I thanked him again. He drove away in a muddy white minivan with a large, stylized rose painted on its side. I returned to the dining room, moved Madison's offering to a sideboard, and then hunted for a card among the roses, lilies, carnations, daisies, birds-of-paradise, gladioli, dahlias, snapdragons, and sprigs of greenery. After an unpleasant encounter with a thorn, I gave up. Whoever had shelled out big bucks for the flowers would have to identify himself if he wanted credit. They might be from Peter, I thought as I stood at the sliding glass door and watched birds hopping about in the grass in search of the elusive early worm. I considered calling him, then decided to wait until later in the day, when he might have information about the identity of the body or even Dolly's whereabouts. In Dallas, I told myself firmly. Visiting her sister. Having a problem with the telephone company, as we all did on occasion.

I was rinsing the coffee cups in the kitchen sink when the doorbell rang. If flowers were to be delivered at this rate, the house would soon resemble a funeral chapel—or a little shop of horrors. Inez would have an asthma attack. Caron would achieve a personal best in sarcasm. Sara Louise would be politely appalled at the gaucheness.

Again, I opened the front door cautiously. Rather than a deliveryman burdened with nature's finery, Nick, the temporary proprietor of Manny's PerfectPools, stood on the porch. Sebastian towered behind him, shuffling his feet.

"Ms. Malloy," began Nick, clutching my hand, "I feel like I should talk to you about all this mess. Do you mind if we come in?"

"Please do." I forced a small smile. "Coffee?"

We went into the kitchen. I took cups from a cabinet, poured coffee, and then stood at the end of the island, waiting for an explanation. It clearly wasn't going to be forthcoming from Sebastian, who was hunched over his cup, his eyes downcast, his lower lip wet with saliva. Nick poured milk into his coffee, stirred it carefully, and finally looked at me with such anguish that I wanted to squeeze his shoulder and mumble vague yet reassuring sentiments. Unless, of course, he was about to confess to something that would force me to threaten him with a damp sponge and a dish towel.

"The police were at the shop when we got there this morning," he said. "I'd seen the newspaper, so I figured that's what they wanted to ask about. Which they did, at length. Sebastian and I could not help them. After we got here, we went out to the pool. I tested the water and adjusted the chemicals. Sebastian cleaned the traps and the filters. We vacuumed, skimmed, and then put everything back in the shed. It took us maybe two hours. If there was trouble inside the house, we didn't see or hear any of it. When we got finished, we went around the side of the house and headed for the next job a couple of blocks from here."

"Did the police ask you about the blond girl who was on the patio when you stopped by to introduce yourself?" I said.

Nick shrugged. "Yeah, but there wasn't much to tell them. A little while after we got here, no more than ten or fifteen minutes, she came out of the house and left through the gate in the back wall. We didn't see her after that."

At least Madison had left of her own accord, I thought. "What was she wearing?"

"Jeez, I wasn't paying much attention. That's not to say I did not notice she was a fine-looking broad, what with her tanned legs and big"—his ears turned the shade of one of the carnations on the dining room table—"sunglasses. Real pricy sunglasses like the movie stars wear. White shorts and a skimpy halter. Sandals. No purse or canvas bag."

If he'd been paying any more attention, he could have reported the number of freckles on her arms. I looked at Sebastian, who had not so much as twitched since he sat down. "Anything to add to that?" I asked him sweetly.

Nick intervened. "He's kinda shy, Ms. Malloy. Anyway, that's all we could tell the police. It'd be a damn shame if something bad happened to a pretty girl like her. I just didn't want you to think we had anything to do with it. Before he left, Manny gave me a long lecture about minding my own business and staying focused on the job. He's real proud of his reputation. He says the most important thing these days is customer satisfaction and referrals, and you won't get those if you bring a portable radio and start goofing off. He fired his own nephew when he found out the boy was smoking weed in the van between jobs."

"He was real pissed," Sebastian said hoarsely. He seemed startled by the sound of his own voice, and quickly resumed staring at the coffee cup.

"I'm sure you did a professional job, Nick," I said, "and you, too, Sebastian. The pool looks lovely." I paused to replay the scene he'd described. "Did Madison say anything to you?"

"No, she acted like she did not even notice us. That kind never does. When I was in school, I used to deliver pizzas. You wouldn't believe how many girls would come to the door wearing nothing but a T-shirt or underwear. Why bother to make yourself decent for the pizza guy? After all, he's nobody."

I was not in the mood to discuss social and economic inequalities. I could have given him Cal's telephone number so that they could hash it out together, but instead moved toward the hallway. "It was thoughtful of you to come by, Nick. The police must have been satisfied with your story, so you shouldn't have to waste any more time. I'm sure you have a busy schedule for the day, and I don't want to keep you from all those dirty pools."

"Tell you what," he said as he nudged Sebastian into motion, "when we come next week, I will give you a discount, say, twenty percent off."

"You don't need to do that."

"I realize that, Ms. Malloy, but I don't want to lose your business on account of you thinking Sebastian and me might be killers and kidnappers. I know twenty percent is not much, but I'll have to answer to Manny when he gets back."

"And Miss Groggin," said Sebastian.

Nick shoved him out to the porch. "Miss Groggin is the

bookkeeper. She's worked for Manny for twenty years, and acts like it's her own business. She could stand a helluva lot more sugar in her lemonade, if you know what I mean."

I wished them a pleasant day and closed the door. Two of my three visitors had been remarkably garrulous, the third perilously close to mute. I could only hope that when Caron and Inez appeared for breakfast, both would be sullen. My photograph on the front page would not help the situation.

I'd returned to my coffee and the newspaper, and was preparing to tackle the crossword puzzle when the doorbell rang. Muttering an expletive, I once again opened the front door. Three unsmiling women of indeterminate age stood on the porch, armed with mops, buckets, cleaning supplies, and brooms. They were dressed in identical industrial-style aprons, hairnets, and thick-soled canvas shoes.

"Squeaky Clean," said the spokeswoman as they marched inside. She gave me a piercing look. "Is Mrs. Goforth here?"

"No," I said, not bothering to explain. "She told me to expect you."

"We are seven minutes late, but it could not be helped. I shall see that it does not happen in the future. If you do not mind, we'll get started. We do the downstairs first, then the second floor. We do not vacuum or clean bathrooms unless the floors are clear. Personal items must be stowed away. We will replace towels and linens only if the dirty ones are left in the hall outside the appropriate doors. Do you have any questions?"

Any questions I might have had were of a frivolous nature and would not be well received. I shook my head, then hurried upstairs to warn the girls. Sara Louise was emerging from the bathroom, clad in a robe and with her hair hidden under a terry-cloth turban.

"Did you hear something about Madison?" she asked.

"Not yet." I followed her into her bedroom and told her about the imminent invasion of the fearsome Squeaky Clean trio. "If you want them to clean in here, I'll help you strip the bed and pick up your things. You'll have to stay out of their way. Do you feel up to sitting by the pool?"

93

"You're being awfully kind," she said. "You didn't have to invite us in and let us stay here, you know. Most people wouldn't have bothered to do anything more than call a cab. Now we've caused all this trouble and you have every right to tell us to leave. If Madison and I hadn't both maxed out all our cards, it wouldn't be such a problem."

"How are you planning to pay the garage?"

She pulled off the towel and began to dry her hair. "I'll think of something when the time comes. It's not like we're paupers or anything. When my father gets back, he's going to set me up as a vice president in his firm. I've already made arrangements to have my office redecorated." She dropped the towel on the floor and put on a pair of shorts and a blouse. "But in answer to your question, I would like to go downstairs. This room is very tasteful, but it's hardly spacious and I'm feeling a bit claustrophobic. I need to eat something, if only toast and tea. The pain's not nearly as bad as it was yesterday, so perhaps I can get by without any more of the medication." She began to walk unsteadily toward the top of the stairs. "Madison's room is likely to be an absolute catastrophe," she added over her shoulder as she disappeared.

I stuffed her clothes into her backpack and tossed it in a closet, stripped the bed, and piled the sheets in the hall. I did the same in Madison's room, then went to the bathroom and swept all the cosmetics into a drawer. The two had used enough towels to mop up after a major hurricane. After dumping a second armload in the hall, I went to the master suite and knocked on the door.

I waited for a moment, then went inside. Neither lump on the bed acknowledged me. "The cleaning service is here," I announced as I began to gather up their clothes. "You need to get up and vacate the room if you want clean sheets and towels. And don't forget that Peter's sending a patrol car to pick you up at eleven."

"For a press conference on the courthouse steps?" said a very unfriendly voice from under the covers. "Did Diane Sawyer call yet?"

I dumped their clothes on a chair. "I am not responsible for what happened last night. Somehow or other, the media got wind of the story and showed up outside the front door. As much as you would like to see your faces on the front page"—I stopped and warned myself to choose my words carefully, since the newspaper was still on the island in the kitchen—"I hope you understand why it's important that you downplay your involvement. Even if you claim not to know anything, someone may decide that you might recall some significant detail and tell the police."

"We already told you everything," said Inez. "We're not going to make up stuff."

Caron sat up. "What kind of cleaning service makes you clean up before they clean up? Isn't that like going to a restaurant and being told to cook your own food? I mean, what's the point?"

"You're welcome to discuss it with them. In the meantime, I suggest you shower and get dressed. Stash all your makeup and hair paraphernalia in a drawer, and leave the sheets and towels outside your bedroom door when you come downstairs. You don't want to embarrass yourselves in front of Diane, do you?"

"You are so Not Funny," Caron muttered.

I had to agree with her. I breezed through my own bedroom and bathroom, which were pristine in comparison, then went to see if Sara Louise had been able to coax a cup of tea from Squeaky Clean. She was standing in the doorway to the dining room.

"Nice flowers, if you like overstatements," she said. "Are they from that police lieutenant?"

"Possibly. Why don't you go sit by the pool while I fix you something to eat? Would you like something more substantial than toast?"

"Toast is fine, and if it's not too much trouble, maybe some fresh fruit. I'm especially fond of melon if it's ripe. And coffee with cream rather than tea. Tea can be so vapid. When I lived in London, I was invited by the son of an earl to have tea at a fancy hotel. We opted for gin and tonics, and I ended up spending weekends at his country house. He was adorable and filthy rich, but too dim to notice that his parents despised me. I thought my mother would die when I told her I'd declined to become Lady Sara Louise Pompousass."

"Tragic." I heard vacuum cleaners approaching. "Go outside and sit down. I'll be there in a few minutes."

As I went into the kitchen, I made a mental note to pick up a can of fruit cocktail if and when I left the house. A generic brand if I could find it. I started a fresh pot of coffee, then dutifully cut up a melon, made toast, and arranged a rather artful tray. I did not, however, fold a napkin into a swan or raid the flower arrangement for a rose to poke in a bud vase. The newspaper went into the trash.

Once the coffee was ready, I filled a cup and took the tray out to the patio, where Sara Louise was reclining on a lounge chair. She assured me that I was too kind, then dismissed me with a vague smile and resumed leafing through a magazine. Reminding myself that she'd teethed on hapless nannies, I stalked inside and was considering where to hide from the omnipresence of Squeaky Clean when the phone rang.

I answered it with a guarded "Hello?"

"This is Sonata Wells from the *Waverly Gazette*. I'd like to speak to—"

"No comment," I said, then hung up.

The phone rang again. This time I snatched up the receiver, repeated my previous response, and hung up. I glowered at the offending instrument, daring it to try once more, then picked up the accumulated mail in case I'd failed to notice an out-of-state return address from someplace like Texas.

The phone rang yet again. At that moment, I would have preferred to toss it in the pool or put it down the garbage disposal, but instead picked up the receiver. "How many times do I have to tell you that I am not—"

"Claire," Peter interrupted, "don't hang up. I need to talk to you."

"Okay," I said, feeling a bit foolish.

"When the patrol car comes to pick up Caron and Inez, please come with them. I have some questions to ask you about Dolly."

"Have you located her? Does she know anything about the body in the freezer?"

"I'd rather discuss it in my office."

"Whatever you say." I paused, then added, "I'm not comfortable leaving Sara Louise here by herself, and she's not well enough to come with the rest of us. I don't suppose you've found Madison?"

"We're doing what we can, but it's not at the top of the list right now. I'm going to send up the crime scene team to do some further investigating. Sara Louise will have plenty of company for a couple of hours. If we're not finished by then, one of the officers will stay with her. It won't be hard to find a volunteer."

"A couple of hours? I can tell you everything I know about Dolly in ten minutes or less."

"I'll see you at eleven."

I was annoyed at his officiousness, but not appalled at the idea of getting out of the house for a while. My only refuge until Squeaky Clean left was the patio. When Caron and Inez joined Sara Louise, the ambience would be less than amicable. And once Peter finished with us, I would ply my indubitable charm and convince the officer who was escorting us to make a quick stop for carry-out carbs.

I was still standing in the hallway, debating whether to urge the girls to hurry up or allow them to take their chances with Squeaky Clean when the phone rang. I picked it up with some reluctance.

"Ms. Malloy!" whispered a voice. "Thank gawd you're there!"

"Madison? Where are you? Are you okay?"

"I can't tell you where I am. I need to talk to you, but I'm afraid your line's tapped."

I took a breath, then said, "Why can't you tell me where you are? We've all been worried sick about you."

"I just can't." Her voice grew more urgent. "Dolly's in terrible danger, and so are you. I can't say any more until you're on a safe line. Go to your bookstore. I'll try my best to call you there in fifteen minutes."

"I don't think it's wise for me to go the bookstore, Madison. The media might be waiting, and I've had quite enough coverage already."

"Promise me that you'll go. It's really, really important!"

97

"Okay," I said without enthusiasm. "I should be there in fifteen minutes, but if you don't call within five minutes, I'm coming back here."

"I'm so sorry about all this, Ms. Malloy. I wish I could explain." Instead of doing so, she hung up.

Frowning, I replaced the receiver. The phone line tapped. Madison held prisoner by party or parties unknown. Fifteen minutes. It was likely that Dolly was "in terrible danger," although I had no theories why. But I had no part in it. I was only a befuddled spectator. Fifteen minutes—and counting. What would happen to Madison after that?

I grabbed my purse and opened the front door. The only recent arrivals in the driveway were a van with the Squeaky Clean logo (a coat of arms created from a mop, a broom, and a ferocious mouse in an apron), and a patrol car. The garage door was criscrossed with yellow tape; all it needed was a bow to resemble a birthday present. A second police car drove up and discharged two plain-clothed detectives, who stared at me before disappearing around the far corner of the garage. I walked quickly to my car, dug the key from the bottom of my purse, and drove away before one of Peter's growing army of minions could challenge me.

The Book Depot looked forlorn, but my customers were not the sort to gather under the portico and pound on the door to demand their inalienable right to purchase paperbacks. I parked in back and let myself in through the door that opened into the office. Out of habit, I started toward the front room, then froze in the doorway. Everything that had been on the counter or on the shelves beneath it was now strewn on the floor. The racks of fiction had been pushed over, scattering the books like debris in the aftermath of a squall. I spun around and looked more closely at my desk. Drawers had been emptied onto the floor. A stack of folders had been dumped in the metal trash can.

I went behind the desk and picked up the telephone. After

ascertaining that it was functioning, I set it on the desk. My immediate instinct was to call Peter, but I did not want to preclude Madison from calling in the next five minutes. And although the police might arrive with sirens shrieking, they were not likely to find any evidence that might lead to the vandal. If indeed this was the work of a vandal, I thought numbly. As far as I could tell, there was no actual damage to the building or its contents, just a hellacious mess that would take a couple of hours to undo. It was possible that some misguided soul had been looking for cash, and then pushed over the racks out of frustration. I'd resisted the impulse on occasion.

The phone rang. I picked up the receiver, but before I could say anything, Madison said, "Ms. Malloy, I was so scared you wouldn't be there." She wasn't whispering, but her voice was low and tainted with the same urgency. "I can only talk for a minute."

"Where are you, Madison?"

"I can't tell you. Listen, you've got to find Dolly and persuade her to come back to Farberville. She's the only one who can clear this up. Are you positive she didn't say anything about where she was going to be? Has she called again?"

"No, she hasn't called," I said impatiently, "and I don't understand why you can't tell me where you are. If you're being held hostage, say so. The police are trained to deal with the situation."

"This isn't about me, Ms. Malloy—it's about Dolly. You're her best friend. Surely she must have said something about other family members or a place she's always wanted to visit. Did she buy any travel guides lately?"

"The only thing she mentioned was a twenty-fifth wedding anniversary cruise with Bibi. We both know that's not going to happen."

"Has anything else come in the mail? A message on the answering machine, maybe?"

"Nothing. You've got to tell me what's going on, Madison. You're clearly the one who's in danger right now."

The only response was a dial tone. I may have looked less than winsome as I replaced the receiver and returned to the doorway, my

99

hands on my hips, to glower at the books and papers on the floor. I was muttering a long and colorful stream of Anglo-Saxon expletives unsuitable for a lady when something smashed against the back of my head with enough fury to send me sprawling facedown on the splintery floor. My exact thoughts at that moment are regrettably lost to posterity.

Chapter Seven

A hand on my shoulder startled me enough to pull myself out of what felt like an eddy of strobe lights. I tried to move, but an unexpected eruption of pain inside my head paralyzed me. I kept my eyes squeezed tight as I tried to remember where I was and why I seemed to be glued to the floor. Neither explanation was forthcoming.

"Are you okay?" asked a wary male voice.

"Get away from me!"

"Whatever you say." The hand was removed, and the voice grew a bit more distant. "You going to stay there?"

I concentrated on sorting out the various physical symptoms, all quite unpleasant: head pulsating, elbows hot, face warm and sticky with what I suspected was blood. It would have been overly optimistic to assume the blood was anyone else's but my own. "Yes," I growled, "I'm going to stay here."

"Forever?"

"Am I in game-show hell? Is the next question worth a million dollars?"

"Maybe you should sit up."

I opened one eye and watched muddy workshoes approach. "Don't come any closer or I'll . . . do something."

"Why don't you let me help you up first? It might be easier to do something that way."

"Stay where you are." I opened both eyes, then winced as another bolt of pain careened inside my head. I waited until it subsided, then managed to struggle to a sitting position, albeit an ungraceful one. Only then did I look up at what I'd assumed was my assailant. My science fiction hippie gaped back at me. "You did this?" I asked incredulously.

"Trashed the store and hit you on the head? Not me, lady. I believe in nonviolent confrontations, with maybe a little laser swordplay. I just stopped by to get a few more books before I take off to the Buddhist commune over in Lloyd County. I looked through the window and saw you lying on the floor. The back door was open." He squatted next to me. "You want I should call for an ambulance or something?"

"No, I'm okay. Just help me up." He obliged and clung to my arm until I was seated on the stool. I touched my face, then sighed as I looked at the bloody smears on my fingertips. "Will you please get me a wet paper towel from the bathroom?"

"You ought to call the cops."

"I will as soon as I've cleaned myself up," I said. "I have no desire to spend the rest of the day sitting in a chair at the emergency room, waiting for some adolescent resident to determine that I was hit on the head and then try to keep me overnight for observation. If I have a concussion, I'll topple off the stool in a few minutes. While we wait, I'd appreciate that paper towel. I feel like a Jackson Pollock canvas."

"Yeah, okay," he mumbled as he went into the office, "but—" There was a pause, and then what sounded like a scuffle. "Who're you, buddy? Get your hands off me! I'm a third-level apprentice warrior of the Realm of Zaderith!"

"And I'm friggin' Genghis Khan!" snarled a second male voice.

"Who is it?" I called. I was too bruised and battered to be alarmed, protected as I was by a third-level apprentice warrior of whichever fantasy realm my hippie had adopted. And I doubted the situation could get worse.

"Claire," said Gary Billings as he came into the front room, "are you okay? What the hell happened? My god, you're bleeding. Did that maniac do this to you?"

I eyed him with suspicion. "What are you doing here? Didn't you see the CLOSED sign in the window?"

He put his arm around me and gazed down like the slightly constipated male models who grace the covers of romance novels. "Let me take you to the hospital."

"Don't even try." I shrugged off his arm and accepted a dripping paper towel from my hippie. The bump on the back of my head, approximately the size of a Quarter Pounder with cheese, had quit bleeding. I wiped my face and neck, then tossed the noticeably pink towel on the floor. "So what are you doing here?" I asked Gary, who was still hovering and looking more likely to faint than I.

"I saw the mess through the window. The door was locked, so I came around to where you'd parked your car. He"—he gestured at the hippie—"was prowling around the office. Should I restrain him until the police get here?"

"No." I told the hippie that if he picked up the racks and replaced the books, he could select a couple of paperbacks to take with him on his quest for recalibrated karma. After a brief negotiation, we settled on six and he went to work.

Gary seemed to find the exchange odd, and was watching me for symptoms of incipient delirium (or whatever romance heroines resort to in moments of distress). "You did call the police, didn't you? This is clearly breaking and entering, vandalism, theft, and bodily assault. He may be destroying evidence."

"I'm sure he is," I said as I looked around for the telephone, which had been swept off the counter along with all the files, catalogs, folders, pencils, complimentary bookmarks, and so forth. I finally spotted it and asked Gary to hand it to me. "I'm now going to call the police, if only to satisfy the two of you."

The hippie came to the counter and leaned forward until I could feel his breath on me. "Too spooky for me," he whispered. "I'm out of here."

Before I could respond, he went out the front door, hopped on a bicycle, and wobbled away. No crowd of pedestrians had gathered under the portico to stare and mutter among themselves. I suspected only my bloodied corpse in the window might attract any attention.

I called the police station and asked to speak to Peter. I was, of course, put on hold and regaled with tips to prevent bicycle theft. I was unable to think with my customary lucidity, and idled away the time watching Gary wring his hands. I'd had limited interactions with men who were entirely too attractive for their own good. Peter was the exception, but he had just enough deviations from perfect symmetry to redeem himself. My deceased husband, Carlton, had been compelled to rely on his position in academia to woo his distaff students. Thinking of him brought to mind the poor little man in the freezer rather than soap opera celebrities.

Peter finally came on the line. I shushed Gary, who was in the middle of asking me for the twelfth time if he could do something for me, and told Peter what happened. He didn't bother to ask why I hadn't called 911, but instead told me to wait for him. I agreed, adding that if I saw so much as a flashing light on an ambulance, I would be out the back door and down the railroad tracks before he'd unbuckled his seat belt. He hung up, as he is inclined to do when he's less than pleased with the conversation.

"The police will be here shortly," I said to Gary, "so you don't need to stay any longer."

"I'm not leaving you here by yourself," he said, looking sharply at the front door. "Are you quite sure that—that peculiar man isn't responsible? He sounded almost delusional."

"He's very delusional, but he wouldn't hurt me or trash the store. Once he pointed his finger and threatened to cryotransmogrify me. We were both disappointed when nothing much happened."

"Then who did this?"

"I don't know. Did you?"

He shrank back. "Why would I do something like this? I just came by to apologize if I offended you yesterday afternoon. Lucy can be

104

rather forceful, as you must have noticed, and I . . . well, I don't know. I'm sorry."

"Apology noted," I said. "Now run along unless you want to explain all this to the Farberville CID."

"Are you sure you're okay?"

I was getting tired of the sensitive-male thing. "Yes, Gary, I can survive for another forty-five seconds without your masculine presence. Feel free to drop by in a couple of days if you need another bird book. I'll have to reduce the price on all the damaged stock."

He dithered for a moment, then left only seconds before Peter and his minions stormed the bookstore like a Mongol horde (sans Genghis). Much ado followed, but none of it was all that interesting.

An hour later, I was seated in Peter's office. I'd declined coffee and tea, but had accepted a cup of water, a couple of generic aspirin tablets, and primitive first aid for my knees and elbows. I was feeling steadier, although I would not have aced the SATs (or passed the vision test for a driver's license). Caron and Inez were in the front room, no doubt squawking about the lack of media coverage. An officer had been dispatched to babysit Sara Louise. Squeaky Clean was by now buffing the banisters or whatever they did, but they surely would be gone by noon.

Peter did not seem to appreciate why I'd felt the need to go to the Book Depot to take the second call. I once again pointed out that there'd been no time to sit down and contemplate the most judicious course of action. He rephrased his questions and I rephrased my responses until both of us were reduced to mute glowers.

After several minutes of silence, he sighed and said, "Do you know anything about Dolly that you've failed to tell me?"

"Why does everyone think I'm harboring some dark secret? I've told you every last blasted detail, including her preferences in books, her kitchen utensils, her window treatments, her wardrobe. She is a very nice, personable, intelligent woman. If she has neuroses, she's

105

kept them hidden from me. Call the president of the hospital auxiliary, the chairwoman of the arts festival, the director of the battered women's shelter. She asked me to house-sit and went to Dallas. That's all I know."

"Well, she may have gone to Dallas, but she didn't call you from there," Peter said. "We traced the call. It came from a cell phone in Atlanta."

"Atlanta?" I gurgled. "She told me Dallas."

"That's what we have at this point. What's even more interesting is that she didn't take any flight from the airport. None of the airlines had her on the passenger list."

I sat up to stare at him. "But Caron took her to the airport."

"And then she disappeared, as far as we can tell. One desk agent noticed her when she came in, but no one else seems to have seen a middle-aged blond woman wearing a black pantsuit, a red silk scarf, and oversized sunglasses. The car rental companies have no record of anyone who might remotely resemble her. It's not a large airport."

"But it's not a black hole," I said. "Did you check with the shuttle service?"

Peter gave me a tight smile. "Yes, Claire, even we thought of that. Dolly Goforth found a way to disappear in the Farberville airport and resurface in Atlanta a day later. It sounds like an Alfred Hitchcock plot, doesn't it?"

"Or H. G. Wells, I suppose." I took a sip of water and tried to think, although gremlins were still gleefully clogging inside my head. "Did she have a reservation to Dallas?"

"No, and we checked all the airlines. Several unaccompanied women flew that afternoon, but all of them had proper identification." He leaned back in his chair and gazed at me, as if waiting for an explanation.

The Farberville airport does not compete with LAX or O'Hare in terms of daily flights and passenger nose count. One airline caters to a hub in Memphis, and the other two to a hub in Dallas. Atlanta was a long walk from Farberville.

"You said she called from a cell phone," I said at last.

"Which is also interesting. The cell phone belongs to Petrolli Mordella. Does that sound familiar?"

"Only if it's on the menu at an Italian restaurant." I noted his failure to smile, and added, "No, I've never heard the name. Who is he?"

"He's the man who was in the freezer, but he wasn't nearly as innocent as a leg of lamb. The federal database politely ignored the shriveled state of his prints and popped up with an album of mug shots. Over the last fifty years, Mordella was arrested for extortion, possession of stolen property, transporting same across state lines, bribery, and intimidation of witnesses during a trial. None of the charges ever led to a conviction. Fifteen years ago he was found guilty of tax evasion and spent two years in a minimum-security federal prison. After that, he never had so much as an unpaid parking ticket."

"He was a hoodlum?" I said, stunned. "But he looked so ordinary, like somebody you'd chat with while standing in line at a bank. A retired history teacher or insurance agent. An avid stamp collector. Then again, I suppose people like that don't end up with bullet holes in the forehead. What else do you know about him?"

"We have his last known address, a house number in the Flatbush area of Brooklyn, but that's about all so far. The department there is sending officers to verify the address and try to locate his next of kin. I expect to hear something in a couple of hours."

I needed an entire bottle of aspirin to assimilate this, but none was in reach, which was for the best. "So Dolly's in Atlanta, using a cell phone owned by a criminal from New York City, telling me she's in Dallas with her sister. In the meantime, the Mordella's in the morgue at the hospital and—" I stopped, unable to continue the sentence.

Peter did not share my reticence. "The Brooklyn detectives asked for a current photo to show around the neighborhood. As soon as I finished talking to them, I sent one of my men to the hospital to take some facial shots that would be less distorted than the ones we took last night. It seems there's a problem."

I stared at him over the rim of my paper cup. "Please don't tell me the body disappeared."

"No one admits any responsibility for it. The exterior doors are locked at night, but that's the only security measure taken. There aren't any cameras in the hallways. The cleaning staff and orderlies with reason to be in the basement all claim to have seen nothing out of the ordinary, which one assumes would include the body being removed by person or persons unknown. The hospital administrator is reportedly apoplectic."

"The door to the morgue's not locked at night?" I said. "Anyone in the building can trot downstairs and borrow a body instead of going to the trouble of digging one up in the cemetery? Burke and Hare would have sneered at our present-day practitioners."

"It's no longer a viable occupation. Any valuables on the body are sealed in a manila envelope and kept in a safe. Medical schools aren't that desperate for specimens for dissection, and are required to keep records for the ones they acquire from legitimate sources."

"This is ridiculous. Maybe Mordella wasn't really dead. According to your very own officers, he has a history of rousing himself when he doesn't care for the accommodations. I have no idea why he chose the freezer, but he was clearly more at home there than in a drawer in the morgue. Maybe he's sitting in the gazebo as we speak."

"The medical examiner pronounced him dead at the scene." Peter went over to a table and refilled his coffee mug. "The scene being Dolly Goforth's house on Dogwood Lane, of course."

I glared at his back. "So now you're trying to put the blame on her."

"The medical examiner was planning to do the autopsy this morning to determine how long Mordella's been dead. He might not have been able to tell us much of anything if the body's been in and out of the freezer several times. You don't want to hear the details, but apparently it's a question of ice crystals and tissue decomposition."

"The day before Dolly left, she told me to help ourselves to the contents of the freezer. She couldn't have thought the body was there at that point." I stopped and thought about it. "Unless she wanted us to find it—but, no, I just can't believe that. Why would she have called on Wednesday? To see if we'd found it? That doesn't make any sense, since sooner or later we would have opened the lid to the freezer.

If she had anything to do with it, she wouldn't have asked me to house-sit. She would have told her committee members that she was taking a trip to some foreign destination, packed her bags, locked the house, and left. No one would have started asking questions for months."

Peter sat down at his desk. "I agree that her behavior was irrational. However, we know she couldn't have moved the body on Wednesday because she was in Atlanta when she called. It's seven hundred miles from here."

"Did she make any other calls?"

"Not on the cell phone. We obtained the record of calls from her home phone for the last several weeks. All of them were local, mostly to places like the arts center, the country club, a health club. One to a catalog company that specializes in gourmet cheeses and sausages. The only one that stood out was made early Sunday afternoon, when she called a local motel. We're checking it out now. If Mordella was a guest there, we can determine when he arrived in Farberville. And as for Dolly Goforth, we've got some serious questions about her. I'm beginning to doubt she actually exists."

I set down the cup before I spilled its contents in my lap, hoping that I wasn't experiencing symptoms of a concussion, which conceivably might include auditory hallucinations. "You've been in her house, for pity's sake. You saw her car. Your men have probably pawed through her lingerie by now. Half the caterers in town are on a first-name basis with her. She spends several hundred dollars a month on books."

Peter gave me a mug of coffee and waited until I'd taken a shuddery sip. "She may have a corporeal presence, but not much else. She leased the house and furnishings for six months and paid with a cashier's check. The agent, now panicked, is trying to run down the references. The car was leased as well, with cash from a dealer in Oklahoma. The Social Security number she used for a credit card and a bank account is valid as far as the government is concerned, but she apparently has never paid any income taxes or had money withheld from a payroll check. She doesn't have a credit rating, a passport, or a criminal record."

I took another swallow of bitter coffee. "What about Bibi? He owned a large business."

"Not in Illinois," Peter said with a grimace. "On a brighter note, he didn't die there unless he did so without the standard paperwork. No obits in any of the major newspapers, no death certificate on file, no notification sent to the government agencies, including Social Security, Medicare, and the armed forces."

"Dolly told me about his funeral. It wasn't held behind a barn. Bibi was obviously a nickname. Did you—"

"Only two people with that same last name died in Illinois in the last five years. One was an elderly widow living in a nursing home in De Kalb, the other a siding salesman in Peoria. Neither left an estate in excess of a few thousand dollars. Local authorities are hunting down the families, but it doesn't seem likely to lead anywhere. We have inquiries out to all the other states, but it'll take time to hear back."

I put aside the coffee before it did further damage to my stomach. "What about Sara Louise? Surely she can explain."

His forehead furrowed, which in other circumstances I usually found endearing. "Sara Louise took a pain pill and is asleep in the den. Had you bothered to notify us before you went to the Book Depot, we might have been able to trace the call Madison made to you. We're working on the call she made to the house."

"I didn't have time," I protested with more indignation than I felt. "She told me the line was tapped, so you should have known, anyway."

"We do not have a tap on the line. Even in this climate of disdain for civil liberties, we have to get a court order, and there was no evidence that any crimes were being plotted. Criminals tend to use cell phones or computers for such activities. You need to stop reading cozy mysteries and watch more cop shows on television."

"If you say so," I said as I stood up. "Are we finished for now?

I'd like to go back to the bookstore and assess the damage. I guess I'd better have the locks changed as well, and install some designer deadbolts."

Peter cut me off before I reached the door. "I don't want you at the store by yourself, and we don't have anyone available to stay there with you. An officer will take you to fetch your car, and then follow you back to Dolly's house. Caron and Inez should be there shortly. If Sara Louise rouses herself, give her very strong coffee and call me." He took advantage of his height to loom over me. "Don't go any-where and don't take it upon yourself to question the girl."

I was not impressed with his attempt to intimidate me, but smiled demurely and said, "We'll be out by the pool playing Scrabble if you need us."

Caron flung herself on me as I came out of Peter's office. After I'd assured her that I was all right, she released me and gave me a beady look. "Jorgeson told us you were attacked in the bookstore. I Do Not Like This, Mother. I think we should break into Inez's house and stay there. I personally will fight off any rabid librarians that creep into Mr. Thornton's study to steal his precious notes on the decimal system."

Inez looked up from a grimy plastic chair. "I don't think my mother would like that. She always wants the house to be perfect for guests. Before her sister from Boston came to visit, she painted the kitchen cabinets and waxed the garage floor. She even made me buy new under-wear, just in case."

"In case of what?" asked Caron, momentarily distracted.

I tapped her on the shoulder. "I'm leaving now. I'll tell you every-thing when you get finished and an officer brings you back to Dolly's. We can have a picnic on the patio."

Caron spun back around. "What if there are snipers on rooftops? I'm not setting foot out of the house, not even if somebody starts lob-bing in tear gas canisters!"

"Then you'd better ask Peter if the department will loan us gas masks."

An officer appeared, and I followed him out to a patrol car. Despite his visible discomfort, I insisted on sitting in the front seat. I recognized him from one of the previous 911 visits, but in that he wasn't smirking, I couldn't remember which one. I realized it would not be in my best interest to remind him of it.

"Quite a mess," I said lightly as he pulled away from the curb, "what with the body disappearing from the morgue. Security at the hospital must not be very effective."

"They're understaffed, same as everybody else. I got a friend that works there, and he says there's no way to secure all the ground-floor entrances. Nurses and orderlies go out for a smoke, then leave the door propped open. Delivery guys do it, too. The employees are supposed to wear ID badges, but they forget them half the time. Visitors come day and night. After ten o'clock, they have to use the main entrance. Nobody keeps track of them, though."

"Guess I'd better leave my diamonds at home if I go in for surgery."

"Yeah," he said. "My sister-in-law had her purse stolen from her room while she was off getting some kind of test."

We were approaching the Book Depot, which meant I had only a minute or two left to see what more I could weasel out of him. "Were you assigned to check out the victim's motel room?"

"Naw, but I heard they didn't find much. No wallet or personal papers, just a small suitcase, some clothes, bathroom stuff, a couple of paperbacks, and a bunch of racing forms all scribbled up. Hope the guy's horses won."

"The Wormwood Motel, wasn't it?"

He sucked on his lip for a moment. "I thought it was the Fritz out on the highway." He drove into the parking lot and stopped. "The lieutenant says that you're not supposed to go inside, and that I have to follow you home. Any problem with that?"

"I would never dream of ignoring the lieutenant's orders," I said as I got out of the car. "And I solemnly swear to drive well under the speed limit so you won't be compromised."

And so I did, even observing the fifteen-mile-per-hour limit through the campus, which meant the students attending summer school sailed past me. After I parked in front of Dolly's house, I waved to the officer, who backed out of the driveway and went racing down the hill. The Squeaky Clean van was gone. Dolly's Mercedes was parked near a magnolia tree; I toyed with the idea of searching it, but decided the police had already done so, no doubt fastidiously ascertaining that there was no body in the trunk.

I went into the house, where I found Sara Louise snoring in the den and a young female officer sitting on a stool in the kitchen, drinking iced tea and reading one of the fashion magazines. She was startled when I entered the room, but stopped short of pulling out her weapon. "Corporal Margaret McTeer, ma'am," she said.

I introduced myself, then poked around in the refrigerator for some cheese and salami. "Hungry?" I asked as I put everything on the island.

"No, thank you," she murmured. "I hope you don't mind that I fixed myself something to drink. There's not much going on."

I began to slice the cheese. "Anybody call?"

"Half a dozen reporters, and some friends of the woman who lives here. A lawn service guy, wanting to know if he should still show up. A dentist's office about rescheduling an appointment for next week. I kept a list on a pad by the phone."

"Is this what you envisioned when you signed up for the police academy?"

"I've had more challenging assignments, like directing traffic at high school football games. If you're okay with it, I'm going to call the department and have somebody pick me up. Maybe I'll get lucky and be assigned to patrol the mall for shoplifters. Most of the stores are having sales on swimwear." She held up the magazine and showed me a photograph of bony models in improbable poses and little else. "I'm thinking about something like this."

"Charming," I said. I wondered if I would feel vulnerable after the officer left. Although she was petite and could easily go undercover at the high school, she did have a gun. It occurred to me that I did, too—unless the investigators had taken it. I had no idea how to operate it, but I most certainly could pretend otherwise in a crisis.

Furthermore, it was not a dark and stormy night, and I was hardly destined to watch candles flicker in a mansion with creaky stairs and moans emanating from the attic. "We'll be fine," I added. "My daughter and her friend will be back shortly, and we'll restrict ourselves to the house and the backyard."

"If you're sure," she said. "I don't want Lieutenant Rosen hollering at me. I heard one of the 911 dispatchers called in sick this morning."

"I'll assume responsibility. Go ahead and call for a ride."

I turned my attention to making a sandwich. A few minutes later, she came into the kitchen to tell me she would wait outside. I nodded, and after I'd heard the front door close, poured a glass of iced tea and went into the dining room. Had Dolly been there, she would have effortlessly produced a mushroom quiche or a pizza with sun-dried tomatoes, prosciuto, and feta cheese. Salami and cheese, even with imported brown mustard, did not compare well.

I managed a few bites, then pushed aside the plate. I wished I could take a hot bath and a long nap, but I felt as though I needed to remain vigilant in case the body appeared on the front porch or on a rubber raft in the pool. I went into the den and looked down at Sara Louise, willing her to open her eyes and offer some explanations about Dolly and her beloved uncle Bibi. Who they were, for instance, and where they'd lived. Precisely where Bibi was resting in peace for all eternity. Why Dolly had lied to me, which she obviously had and in curious detail.

Sara Louise failed to so much as flutter her eyelashes. Irritated, I tossed the comforter across her bare feet. This elicited a faint snuffle. Short of poking her, there was nothing I could do until she roused herself. I went over to the desk and opened the drawer in which Madison and I had discovered the ominous gun—or little Beretta, depending on one's perspective. It did not seem likely that she'd familiarized herself with the nomenclature at Drakestone College.

In any case, the gun was gone. I closed the drawer and moved to the other side of the room to examine Bibi's extensive video collection.

Although I'd had the impression that all of them were black-and-white movies featuring mobsters, G-men, and machine guns, I found a selection of musicals from the forties and fifties and a few tearjerkers of an even older vintage. Caron and Inez had preferred to watch antiheroes bleed out in rain-slicked alleys, but I decided that were I forced to remain in the house too long, I would override them and settle in with the comforter to sniffle as fragile heroines succumbed to vaguely defined fatal illnesses, much to the chagrin of the steely-eyed men who'd secretly loved them throughout various tragic upheavals.

On a bottom shelf were exercise videos that did not tempt me, and a few that offered instruction in the basic tango steps, as well as more advanced moves. The covers of the boxes depicted women in long gowns and men in tuxedos, reminding me of Madison's patronizing remarks about Dolly and Bibi's passion. At least ballroom dancing was healthy and did not threaten the environment, I thought, although one woman was bent back so far that her vertebrae must have been crackling in protest.

I was about to replace them when I saw a video that had been cached behind the others. It did not have a protective box, but only a strip of masking tape and a handwritten notation that read: "Lookout Lodge, Catskills, 1991." I glanced back at Sara Louise, who was still asleep, then inserted the video in the VCR, located the remote control, and pushed buttons at random until eventually the VCR whirred to life and the screen began to flicker. Although I wouldn't have been stricken if the sound awoke Sara Louise, I muted the volume.

The video was clearly an amateur production, and an amateurish one at that. The camera wobbled and jerked, as if its operator were standing on a small dinghy in a rough sea, but eventually he found steadier footing and panned the room. The setting was a large banquet room, the players dressed elegantly, lights glittering off a rather scary mirrored ball above their heads. Gowns and tuxedos, as I'd anticipated. Round tables adorned with candles, flowers, and champagne glasses. Music must have begun to play, because most of the participants rose and began to glide past the camera. Silk and satin seemed to be compulsory. Some of the couples wore coordinating ensembles that were embellished with sequins and rhinestones. No one was smiling, suggesting this was serious business.

I waited patiently until I spotted Dolly, who was wearing an aquamarine gown. A fan of peacock feathers swayed in her hair. I assumed her partner was Bibi, the mysterious manufacturing mogul. He was significantly older than she, by as much as twenty or even thirty years. He appeared to be shorter, although it was hard to judge because of her towering hair. His hair, in contrast, had dwindled to a white ring around a shiny dome. A large, irregular nose and bushy white eyebrows dominated his face. If I'd encountered him on the street, I would have pegged him as a politician or a member of the European peerage. Both he and Dolly had expressions of dogged concentration, as though mentally replaying one of the instructional videos.

Eventually, everyone returned to the tables and the competition began. I was hardly qualified to judge the couples as they slunk, spun, whirled, and twirled across the dance floor, but I was impressed for the most part. Each move had been rehearsed and polished, if not always executed perfectly. I suspected that room service employees had been kept busy later that night with requests for footbaths, heating pads, and ice packs. The tango was not a dance for cowards.

After half a dozen performances, Dolly and Bibi had their moment in the spotlight. They looked pretty good to me, but I was biased. They were more cautious than some of the younger participants, but neither appeared to falter and Dolly did not limp off the dance floor, as her predecessor had done. The camera followed them as they returned to their table, then fizzled out.

I removed the video and replaced it at the back of the shelf. Dolly had brought no old photographs with her to Farberville, but she hadn't been able to resist the video. It was not dusty, suggesting she'd watched it on occasion. Imagining her on the sofa late at night, a glass of champagne nearby, watching Bibi and herself under the sparkling lights, brought a tightness to my throat. I am by no means a slave to sentimentality, but candor obliges me to admit I was blinking back tears as I stood up.

I was tidying up the kitchen when Caron and Inez came inside through the sliding glass door. Both of them looked as grim as tango dancers, although I doubted there'd been much twirling at the police department.

"How did it go?" I asked.

"Just dandy," Caron muttered as she sat down on a stool. "Peter asked us the same dumb questions over and over again, trying to trick us into confessing. It's not like we knew the man, much less conversed with him. Peter almost choked when I suggested that Rhonda Maguire might be behind it. If anyone deserves to be locked away in a clammy cell . . ."

Inez pulled off her glasses and rubbed her eyes. "I don't think he was really expecting us to confess, Ms. Malloy. Most of his questions had to do with hearing a voice or a car engine, or remembering something we'd forgotten to mention."

Caron snorted. "He didn't get too excited when you told him you saw a scissor-headed flyswatter on a power line."

"It was a scissor-tailed flycatcher," she said haughtily. "They're uncommon in populated areas. You certainly didn't contribute much except for some lamebrained theory about Rhonda Maguire climbing the wall out of jealousy. Why on earth would she even own a black ski mask?"

I dropped a loaf of bread between them. "Would you like some lunch?"

"Wow, another sandwich." Caron shoved the bread to the edge of the island, where it teetered briefly and then tumbled out of sight. "Are we under house arrest? Are they going to put manacles on our ankles?"

"Only if we attempt to break out," I said. "Peter's worried about us."

"Which is why we have to stay in a house where a body was found twenty feet from where we're sitting and those two sniveling morons claim to have been attacked in the front yard. It makes less sense than the Pythagorean theorem."

I looked at her. "I hear there's a cafeteria in the juvenile detention center. It probably includes a salad bar. I can't promise a big-screen TV and a Jacuzzi, though. If you'd feel safer there, I'm sure it can be arranged."

"I'll make a salad," Inez said, edging out of the line of fire. "Does everybody like olives?"

I gave Caron a moment to stop huffing, then said, "Did Peter tell you about the body?"

"I told him they should have stuffed it in a safe-deposit box at the bank. He did not appreciate my remark." She retrieved the loaf of bread and began to nibble on a slice. "What's the big deal with it, anyway? I mean, once the guy was dead, it's not like he was going to start blabbing state secrets. He looked way too ordinary to be a spy."

"Maybe he was disguised," Inez said as she took an armload of salad ingredients from the refrigerator. She dumped everything on a cutting board and found a cleaver. "Anyway, spies are supposed to look ordinary. That way nobody suspects them."

"Suspects them of what?" demanded Caron.

Inez whacked at an innocent head of lettuce. "Of creeping into the headquarters to photograph documents and maps. Everybody thinks they're just low-level bookkeepers or nameless secretaries. James Bond gets in trouble because he's so tall and handsome. Real spies don't get to be in movies because they never get caught."

"Gee, I hope the archvillains aren't bugging the room."

"Continue this discussion later," I said. "Caron, see if you can find a salad bowl. Shall we eat here or in the dining room?"

Caron remained where she was. "What's the deal with those aw-ful flowers in there? They're so gaudy that I assumed they were plas-tic. Did Peter send them? I would have thought he had better taste than that."

"I forgot to ask him," I admitted. "Did he say anything to you about Dolly?"

"Just that they're trying to find her."

Inez began to wreak havoc on a tomato. "Well, he did ask us if we'd snooped through her closets and drawers."

118

"About fifty times," added Caron. "Had we inadvertently found a packet of correspondence, or pulled any boxes off the top shelf, or forgotten to mention finding the crown jewels under the bathroom sink? I was quite offended. Inez, that tomato looks like it was run over by a truck. I mean, do you have something personal against it? Were you force-fed ketchup as a baby?"

"I happen to be chopping it," Inez said. "If all you're going to do is sit there and criticize me, you can open a can of tuna fish for lunch."

Caron rolled her eyes. "There are no cans of tuna fish in this kitchen. Anchovies, maybe, or smoked oysters in virgin olive oil. You are so utterly provincial. If you were someplace like Paris, you'd probably be looking for a McDonald's."

I was in dire need of a bus ticket to someplace like Billings, where I could sit on the porch of a log cabin at sunset and watch coyotes stalk prairie dogs. "I am going to sit out by the pool and read. The two of you may remain here, eat in the dining room, or go soak your heads in the Jacuzzi. You are not to come outside under any circumstances. Got it?"

I refilled my glass with ice and tea, and left the kitchen. Once outside, I did a quick tour of the yard on the off chance I might find the body in placid repose on a bed of aromatic pine needles. The gate was ajar. I made a note to ask Peter to bring a padlock when he came by later. It might not provide much of a deterrent, but nothing short of guard dogs and concertina wire would.

And why, I asked myself as I returned to the patio, would anyone find the need to keep making off with the body? As Inez had said, the corpse was no longer able to tell tales. Since there were no suspects, there could be no DNA samples or particles of fiber to be matched. Carting around a body was risky business. Stealing it from the hospital bordered on lunacy. Mordella had already been fingerprinted and officially identified. Photographs had been taken before and after the body was removed from the freezer. The cause of death was evident.

Dolly must have known him. She'd called his motel room, and

then called me three days later on his cell phone. His arrival precipitated her departure in some way. As hard as I tried, I could not see her as a killer. The last time I'd seen her, she'd been as warm and gracious as always. She'd invited us to enjoy the contents of the freezer, which she hardly would have done if she'd left her victim among the pork cutlets. I myself had removed a package of hamburger meat the day after she'd left.

I avoided the lounge chair where I'd seen Mordella's feet, sat down by the table, and let my gaze wander while I tried to construct a timetable that went as far back as Lookout Lodge. Peter and I could never tango, I thought with a sigh. The male led, and the female meekly followed (unless she was willing to risk a broken toe). It was his erotic fantasy, not hers.

Caron opened the sliding glass door. "Mother?"

"Do I look like Carmen Miranda? I thought I told you to leave me alone for a while."

"You have a call."

"Take a message," I said coolly.

"It's Dolly. She says it's urgent."

120

Chapter Eight

I brushed past Caron and snatched up the receiver from the table in the hallway. "Dolly?" I gasped.

"Well, yes," she said. "I saw something in the newspaper about what happened last night, and I want to be sure you and the girls are okay. What a horrible thing, so insane, discovering a body like that! You must have been hysterical."

Caron and Inez inched closer to me, their noses twitching. I shooed them toward the dining room, then went into the kitchen. "We're okay, Dolly. How about you?"

"I'm fine, of course," she said, surprised. "Why wouldn't I be?"

"And your sister and niece? Are they fine as well?"

"You sound very peculiar, Claire. I hope you haven't been drinking so early in the day. That's not to say I wouldn't understand if you have been. The shock of finding a body in the freezer must have been a nightmare. I can't begin to imagine what it must have been like for you. Now that I think about it, perhaps I'll have a martini for lunch."

"It was not pleasant," I said. "But you must tell me about your sister's condition. Has she improved since you arrived?"

"I suppose so."

"Has your niece made any more margaritas?"

"I really don't understand why you keep asking about them.

I called out of concern for you and the girls. Have the police identified the body?"

"A man from New York City named Petrolli Mordella. An old friend of yours?"

After a long pause, she said, "I don't recall the name. Is he the one Caron and Inez saw behind the gazebo a few days ago?"

"So it seems. The police don't know when he arrived in Farberville, but they do have the name of the motel where he was staying. Of course, you already had that information, didn't you? Otherwise, you couldn't have called him before you left for Dallas. How's the weather down there?"

"Very chilly," she said. "Why would you think I called this man? I don't even know who he is." When I did not reply, she added, "I did receive a rather odd message on the answering machine to call an unfamiliar number. It turned out to be a motel. I assumed it was an error and forgot all about it until now. I most certainly did not speak to anyone staying there."

"That doesn't explain why you have Mr. Mordella's cell phone."

Dolly's laugh echoed like that of a used-car salesman. "No, I don't guess it does. Perhaps I can explain when I get back from Dallas."

"Or Atlanta."

"Oh, dear, this is complicated, isn't it? After I got to Dallas, I realized that I'd needed to call an old friend in Atlanta. She'd called me the previous week to tell me that her husband of twenty-three years walked out on her. When I spoke to her, I was worried that she might go berserk and shoot him, his twenty-five-year-old secretary, or herself. I felt as though I needed to be there to talk her out of whatever she might do. I didn't want to mention it, because she's a bestselling author. If the tabloids were to hear about this, they'd destroy her reputation."

I wondered if she could be quite so nimble in the witness box. "That doesn't explain why you have the murder victim's cell phone."

"That must be a mistake. I used my friend's cell phone, but I simply cannot tell anyone her name. Friendships are very important to me, Claire, including yours. I would never knowingly put you in harm's way."

"Then why don't you tell me what's going on? Let's start with your real name, as well as Bibi's. Don't waste your energy coming up with more fanciful stories and coincidences. The police have already checked all that out."

The receiver began to crackle and buzz. "We're losing our connection," Dolly said loudly. "Cell phones are so unreliable. Can you hear me?"

"I hear you," I said, also forced to raise my voice as the staticky buzzing increased. "Give me a number so I can call you back."

Her voice faded. "I'll have to call you, I'm afraid. Has anything come in the mail for me?"

"Nothing important," I shouted. "Do you promise you'll call me?"

"Yes, I—" The line went dead.

"Damnation," I muttered as I continued to sit on the stool, scowling at the receiver. I was such a Luddite that no one even bothered to call me from a cell phone, so I had no idea if this was typical, or very convenient for Dolly. Was there a notation in the instruction guide for tactfully terminating conversations?

Caron opened the kitchen door. "What did Dolly say? Does she know who the dead guy is?"

"Did she shoot him and put him in the freezer?" Inez asked over Caron's shoulder. "If she did, I'm not sure I want to sleep in her bed."

I shrugged. "She's not hiding under it, if that's what worries you. Her earlier call was made from Atlanta, and she implied that she's still there. This doesn't mean she's not in New Orleans or Miami or Kalamazoo. I guess I'd better call Peter and tell him about this."

Caron grabbed Inez's arm. "You know what we ought to do? We should write a book about this. We'll call it something really provocative like *Ice Cold Corpse*."

"How about *Freezer Burn*?" suggested Inez.

"Not bad," said my daughter the seasoned crime writer, stopping short of posing for the jacket photo. "There's some paper in the desk in the den. The first thing we have to do is write down exactly how horrified we were each time the body appeared. After that, we can—"

"You can't use the den," I said. "Sara Louise is asleep on the sofa."

They stared at me. "No, she's not," Caron said. "She left half an hour ago. She came in the kitchen and said she was going upstairs, but a couple of minutes later we heard the front door close and the car start up. You were out on the patio and said you didn't want to be disturbed."

It seemed that, for once, my daughter had not only listened to me but also chosen to take me literally. "Did she say anything else?"

"I told you what she said, Mother. Why does everybody act like I'm holding back some earth-shattering revelation? She did not say that she was going to the morgue to collect another body, or that she'd remembered who shot that man and was going to make a citizen's arrest. I'm sure I would have noticed."

Inez blinked at me. "All she said was that she was going upstairs, Ms. Malloy. When we heard the front door close, we looked out the living room window and saw her drive off in Dolly's car."

"It's not like we were assigned to follow her around with a cold compress and a pot of tea," added Caron. "Besides, who cares? I wouldn't mind a bit if she decided to drive all the way back to wherever she lives. We can give her a couple of hours of grace, then report the car stolen. I'd like to see her try to explain that to some potbellied sheriff in Missouri."

I waved my hand at them. "Then go into the den, or out by the pool, or better yet, upstairs to the Jacuzzi. I read somewhere that all truly great authors think best when immersed in hot water. I need to call Peter."

"Is he going to be mad?" Inez asked timidly.

"I'm quite sure he will be. Now go off and write your bestseller. Dolly knows someone who can help you find an agent when the time comes."

Caron opened her mouth to respond, but closed it when she saw my expression. "Yeah, come on, Inez. We can write a hundred pages before dinner, which no doubt will be sandwiches. Pretty soon we'll be reduced to trapping songbirds and scooping frogs out of the pool."

I waited until they'd gone into the den, then dialed the number of the police station. While I was left on hold and treated to a recorded voice offering tips on protecting my home from burglars, I carried the receiver with me into the guest bathroom and found a bottle of aspirin in a cabinet. Although I was tempted to wash it down with scotch, I went into the kitchen and poured a glass of water. I was seated on a stool when Peter finally came on the line.

I warned him not to interrupt, then related the conversation with Dolly as best I could. "There's no point asking me to repeat it over and over again," I continued. "When the connection went bad, she promised to call me back. Please note that I'm not holding my breath."

"So noted," he said drily. "I suppose I'd better send a technician up there to rig the phone so we can tape any future calls. You took quite a hit this morning. How are you feeling?"

"Rotten. If I keep taking aspirin at this rate, I won't have a headache—but I'll start feeling as if I'm in a casino filled with slot machines. Caron's being her obnoxious self, and Inez seemed disconcertingly intent when she chopped a head of lettuce into shreds. Oh, and Sara Louise left a while ago."

All sympathy disappeared from his voice. "She what? Where did she go?"

"If I knew, Sherlock, you'd be the first to hear. I was out by the pool. She told Caron and Inez that she was going upstairs, presumably to lie down on her bed, and then drove away. Either the pain pill wore off, or she was faking it. I should have poked her after all."

"She took Dolly's car, right?" He told me to wait, then barked orders to have the patrol officers start searching for it. Once everybody had scurried off to comply, he said, "This is by far the screwiest case I've ever encountered. Please don't succumb to any flashes of insight and go storming off to confront the murderer in a cave or an empty warehouse—or the bookstore, for that matter. Jorgeson arranged for deadbolts, since there were no signs that someone broke in. He'll keep the key until this is resolved." He took a deep breath. "I don't want anything else to happen to you, Claire. You know how much I love you. I just wish I could trust you that much."

"I'm not going anywhere," I said solemnly, "and I promise to tell you the truth, the whole truth, and nothing but the truth."

"When have you ever told me the whole truth?"

"When it suited me," I said, smiling for the first time that day. "I have a lead on Dolly's identity, by the way. I found a video of her and Bibi competing in a tango tournament—or whatever it's called—in 1991 at a hotel called Lookout Lodge in the Catskills. Maybe they keep fastidious records."

"I'll put that on the list, right after bagging all the pine needles for evidence. As soon as I can get away for the day, I'll come over and let you know what we have thus far. Shall I bring something for dinner?"

"Anything but sandwiches."

I replaced the receiver on the base and went to the doorway of the den. Caron was draped across the sofa, reciting a litany of aggrandized emotions that had bathed her in perspiration, turned her blood to ice water, and left her paralyzed with fear as she stared at the corpse. Inez was perched on the ottoman, a notebook balanced on her knees, scribbling madly. I suspected Jane Austen and Louisa May Alcott had gone about it differently.

I decided to take a quick shower before the technician arrived to fiddle with the phone. My earlier sprawl on the floor of the bookstore had left a residue of dust on my T-shirt and shorts. Blood from the scrapes on my elbows and knees had discolored the Band-Aids. A long-sleeved shirt and jeans would cover the worst of it. The hair on the back of my head was matted, as to be expected, but less than alluring.

I was putting on clean clothes when Caron shouted, "There's some man at the front door, Mother!"

"Let him in and show him where the phone is," I called back. "I'll be down in five minutes."

I presumed the man had a badge rather than a bullet hole in the middle of his forehead, so I gave myself a few additional minutes to dry my hair with a towel. I still looked pale, I thought as I scrutinized myself in the mirror, and a faint discoloration on my cheekbone might evolve into a black eye worthy of an inept boxer. Various aches and pains had retreated for the time being. I gave my curls a final fluff, then went downstairs.

No police officer, uniformed or otherwise, was bent over the phone. Puzzled, I started for the den, then saw Gary Billings in the dining room.

"I came by to see how you're doing," he said. "I hope you don't mind. You're looking much better than you did this morning."

"It's very kind of you to be concerned," I said coolly. "Would you like something to drink?"

"Is it too early for a glass of wine?"

I suggested he go out to the patio, then went into the kitchen. The idea of a glass of wine appealed, but I dutifully fixed myself a glass of iced tea. I left the sliding door open so that I could hear the doorbell and save Caron from losing her train of thought in midsentence. Authors in a creative frenzy should never be interrupted by anything less significant than a tidal wave or an earthquake measuring at least eight on the Richter scale. Even the arrival of the Prize Patrol was iffy.

"No wine for you?" asked Gary, crinkling his eyes just enough to make them sparkle. "It seems to me you deserve one after all you've been through these last two days."

I sat down across the table from him. "I appreciate your efforts at a heroic rescue this morning, even though it wasn't necessary. I'm used to my science fiction hippie, but I can understand why he looked guilty to you. Usually he is guilty when he comes inside the store, but only of shoplifting. I consider it a charitable gesture. I wish it were deductible as well."

"I felt like an idiot."

"Some days there's no need for a knight in shining armor." I look a sip of tea, aware that he was doing his best to overwhelm me with his masculine charm. I had yet to decide if he actually had any. "The police have taken care of everything, including deadbolts. I should be able to straighten up the mess and open in a few days."

"Do they think it has any connection to that body you found in the freezer last night?" He gave me a lopsided grin meant to communicate both sympathy and amusement, as if we were sharing a private joke. His eyelid twitched but stopped short of a wink. "It was hard to miss the story on the front page of the newspaper."

"It must have been a hot topic over brunch at the country club."

Gary laughed. "It was, but then some duffer made a hole-in-one. From all the hoopla in the bar, you would have thought Elijah himself came down in a fiery chariot to buy a few rounds."

"It's nice to know somebody's having a good day."

"Have the police identified the body?"

"Yes. You'll be able to hear all about it on the local news tonight. It would take something along the lines of an alien invasion to supplant it as the lead story—and then only if the little green men sexually assaulted the mayor's wife."

"Who do the police say it is?"

I sat back and looked at him. "Why do you care? Did you bring a traveling companion in your golf bag who's gone missing?"

"It's interesting, that's all. How often do I meet a woman who subsequently finds a dead body in the freezer? I did know a couple who found a body floating in their pool one morning, but they'd had a wild party that lasted until dawn. It was deemed an 'unfortunate accident.' Gossip suggested otherwise, but the husband was a high-powered politician and his lovely young bride was notoriously friendly."

"I'm neither of those," I said, fighting back a yawn.

"What about the woman who lives here? Dolly Goforth, isn't it? I gathered from the article in the newspaper this morning that she's out of town. Have the police contacted her?"

"You know, Gary, if I wanted to be questioned about this, all I'd have to do is call KFAR. They'd love to send out a van with a camera crew and a perky little female reporter named Tiffany or Chantilly. They'd probably run over a grandmother and a couple of cats in their haste to get here. We could videotape the interview and watch it over and over and over again. My daughter and her friend, also known as Woodward and Bernstein, would cut a deal with a tabloid. I'd sell a few more books until the thrill-seekers had their fill and moved on to goggle at the next freak celebrity."

He leaned across the table and caught my hand. "I'm really sorry, Claire. I can see you're still upset about this. I just figured you might want to talk about it."

I have to confess that his touch unnerved me. There are people in this world who believe that hugs and kisses are integral to an introduction. I am not one of them. My blood pressure skyrockets when I'm handed a paper gown at my doctor's office. As far as I'm concerned, the slightest physical contact should be by invitation only. I disengaged my hand and picked up my glass. "I don't even want to think about it, but that hasn't been an option. All I know about the victim is that he lived in Brooklyn and was staying in a local motel. He looked like a retired teacher or an accountant. Of course, he may have been a world-renowned lion tamer, but I don't keep up with that profession. Dolly Goforth claims to be unfamiliar with his name and has no explanation why he was found in her house."

"So you've talked to her today?" When I reluctantly nodded, he went on. "If she didn't know him, then why was he left in her house? Why not his motel room or out in the woods? Don't the police have any theories?"

My patience was depleted. "I really don't know. It was thoughtful of you to stop by. If you don't mind, I'd like to take a nap." In case he did mind, I stood up and started for the door. "The Book Depot should be open in a few days. If you need another field guide, please drop by."

"Now I really feel like an idiot," he said as he followed me inside. "Is there any chance you might be able to sneak out for dinner tonight? I promise we won't discuss anything more sensational than the nesting habitat of the ruffled grouse."

"No, but thank you for asking." I continued to the front door and pointedly opened it. "Perhaps I'll see you later in the week."

"You realize that you've doomed me to a barbecue at Daniel and Lucy's condo, where the duffer will pull me aside and relate every last detail of his triumph."

I managed a faint smile. "I'm sure it will be fraught with drama. I'm expecting a technician from the police department, so you'll have to excuse me."

"To check the alarm system?"

"To examine each pine needle for DNA residue. He's bringing tweezers and a microscope."

"You're kidding, right?"

"Yes, Gary, I'm kidding. I have no idea what he's going to do, but you probably don't want to be here when he arrives. It might look suspicious."

Once he'd finally uprooted his feet from the porch and left, I went back to the patio, gathered up the glasses, and took them to the kitchen. Squeaky Clean would have been discouraged to discover how temporal their efforts had been. Caron and Inez had attempted to clean up, but bits of tomato clung to the edge of the chopping board, and an olive that had rolled under a stool was warily watching me. I started to bend down, then thought better of it and left the olive where it was.

I was eating an olive (from the jar, not the floor) when the technician arrived. He wore a fusty brown suit and a bow tie, and looked to be in his fifties, proving that geekiness was not solely the prerogative of the young. Although he was laden with a large black box and a tool kit, he insisted on showing me his identity card and badge before he came inside. "Not safe to let strangers in your house these days," he said. "My wife won't open the door more than a crack for the pizza man until she smells pepperoni. And in a case like this, you probably ought to call the station and confirm my identity. I've been a cop for more than twenty years, and I don't remember anybody finding a corpse in the freezer. It almost makes you think there might be a cannibal hanging around the area. You recall that Dahmer fellow—Jeffrey Dahmer? He kept body parts in his refrigerator."

"I'm sure Lieutenant Rosen will inform me if there's a starving serial killer in the neighborhood. Let me show you the telephone."

He seemed quite happy to examine the base and point out various screws and plates that would expose its interior. "You won't be able to make or receive any calls until I'm finished, ma'am. It should take about half an hour. Is that a problem?"

It would be if Dolly attempted to call, but the probability of that lay between highly unlikely and none whatsoever. "I think I'll go upstairs and rest. My daughter and her friend are in the den. Send one of them to fetch me if you need anything."

He nodded, already engrossed in disassembling the base. I contemplated mentioning his presence to Caron and Inez, then decided they were best left to entertain themselves in a fairly innocuous fashion. After I reached my bedroom, I realized I'd consumed entirely too much caffeine to lie down, much less close my eyes. Neurons, although misdirected, were firing away like guns in a video arcade. Even reading would be too tame.

I paced for a few minutes, then left the bedroom and went down the hall, loftily telling myself that I was merely inspecting the premises to make sure Squeaky Clean had done a thorough job. There were no piles of sheets and towels beside the doors of the other rooms. Sara Louise's room was pristine. The bedspread had nary a wrinkle, and the pillows had been fluffed to perfection. The backpack was in the closet where I'd tossed it. I didn't see a purse, but I couldn't be sure it had been there earlier. In a drawer beside the bed I found the prescription bottle with a cautionary label about imbibing alcohol, driving, and operating heavy machinery. I was surprised to see that it came from a pharmacy in Connecticut instead of a local one. The book in the drawer involved international banking regulations. It was dog-eared; scribbles and punctuation marks in the margins suggested it served as the source of her daily inspirational reading. Perhaps it had been given to her by evangelical Whartonians.

Madison's room had also passed muster. The bed was neatly made, and patterns in the carpet indicated that it had been vacuumed despite a shoe I'd overlooked in a corner. I sat down on the bed and tried to think where she might be. She'd left the house the previous day, seemingly without coercion. She wouldn't have left behind her purse if she'd planned to be gone for more than a few minutes. Her calls had suggested that she was unable to extricate herself from her present whereabouts. They were becoming repetitive with their enigmatic references to the danger that Dolly was in. As far as I knew, the only danger Dolly was in might be an overdose of peach daiquiris and pecan waffles. If she was in Atlanta, that is. If the police could do no better than to situate her somewhere in a city of nearly half a million people, it seemed unlikely that civilians could do any better. They had yet to find Madison in Farberville, with its population of twenty thousand.

I took Madison's purse off the dresser and dumped the contents on the bed. I set aside the scraps of paper for the moment and opened her wallet. Although the girls had led me to believe they were broke when they appeared on the doorstep, she had more than three hundred dollars, as well as enough gold and platinum credit cards to play gin rummy. Her driver's license indicated that she was twenty-three years old and lived in Sands Point, New York. She had declined to donate her organs, which were probably also gold and platinum. In case of emergencies, authorities were directed to contact Richard D. Hayes at Velocchio & Associates, Purveyors of Fine International Antiques and Antiquities, at an address on Madison Avenue in Manhattan. It seemed she'd been named after the address of her father's business rather than a dead president. It was fortuitous that the antiques store had not been located on Mott Street or Broadway. I scribbled the telephone number on a gum wrapper and tucked it in my pocket. Scattered among the credit cards were a few cropped snapshots of handsome young men, all with the arrogant posture of heirs to vast family trusts. One was astride a polo pony, another at the helm of a sailboat. None of them was wearing a hard hat.

The scraps of paper were for the most part credit card receipts from stores and boutiques in Manhattan. One was for a purse that had cost seven hundred dollars and change. I retrieved Madison's purse and studied it. I could see little difference between it and one that could be purchased at a local discount chain for less than twenty dollars. Then again, no one has ever accused me of harboring lust for the finer things in life, particularly those with bloated price tags.

I continued down the hall to the master bedroom. The bedding was so rumpled that I might have assumed, had I not had evidence to the contrary, that Caron and Inez were still asleep. Damp towels were heaped in the bathroom. Squeaky Clean clearly adhered to its standards. Although the detectives had searched the room, I opened the closet door on the chance a diary or journal might tumble off the top shelf. Unless Dolly had stored her winter wardrobe in a closet I'd yet to notice, she'd taken much of it with her. A red wool pantsuit that I'd admired was gone, along with the lined raincoat she'd worn through Farberville's drearier months. Other outfits of a similar nature were missing, as indicated by bare clothes hangers. It was an odd choice for Dallas—or wherever she'd temporarily taken refuge.

And that's exactly what she'd done, I told myself as I closed the closet door. She'd known Mordella, had spoken to him when he arrived at the motel, and at some point ended up in possession of his cell phone. He'd ended up dead, either before she left Farberville or shortly thereafter.

I briefly considered straightening up the room, then concluded that Caron and Inez had failed to strip their bed and were therefore doomed to sleep in it. There were plenty of towels in linen closets, and should the supply be deleted, the two could bite the bullet and run a few loads in the washing machine. Or take them to the creek at the park and pound them with stones while they chatted with my science fiction hippie about the prevalence of trolls.

I heard Caron call my name. I carefully closed the bedroom door behind me so I couldn't be accused of anything as gauche as snooping, then went downstairs. Caron pointed at the technician as she headed back to the den to further elaborate on the terror that would leave indelible scars on her fragile postpubescent psyche and require intensive analysis, if not incarceration in a mental hospital.

"Everything's all set," the technician said. "Let me show you how it works. If someone calls and you want to tape the conversation, push this button. You'll hear a little beep, but the party on the other end won't hear anything. A green light will come on and blink while the machine's recording. After you hang up, push this other button. There'll be a red light to remind you that there's something on the tape. To listen to it, push this. To erase it, hold this down until the red light goes out."

I nodded as if all this was as clear as bottled water from a European spa. "Would you be able to tell if the line's tapped?"

He began replacing tools and bits of wire in his kit. "I did a scan, and it's not. Why do you think it might be?"

"Somebody mentioned the possibility," I said.

"It's almost impossible for local authorities to get a court order. As for the feds, nobody knows what they can do these days. They could put surveillance cameras in your bathroom if they wanted to. Hack into your computer and read your personal e-mail. Dig through your trash bags. Bust into your house in the middle of the night and haul you off without reading you your rights or allowing you access to a lawyer. They can keep you locked up for months, claiming they have evidence of suspicious behavior."

"They wouldn't go after a modestly unsuccessful bookseller in a little Midwestern city."

He closed his kit. "You carry any copies of the Koran? Any foreign students from Middle Eastern countries ever come in the store? Ones with funny names like Ali or Rasheed?"

"One of the professors at the college teaches comparative religion," I admitted. "I stock some of the books on her reading list."

"Then don't be surprised if federal agents show up and demand to see your sales receipts."

"They'll be out of luck. I dispose of them every night."

The technician picked up the case and the tool kit, and headed for the front door. "By shredding them, or just tossing them in the trash? Let me know if you have any problems with the equipment."

Paranoia is not an agreeable sensation. I looked down at the black box, pondering what else it might be able to do. Secretly record any conversation within a fifty-foot radius? Analyze voices for abnormal levels of stress? Send alerts to the authorities if anyone used words remotely related to potential criminal behavior? Activate surveillance cameras that had been surreptitiously installed while we were asleep? Surely not in the bathrooms, but in the kitchen, hall, den, and patio? Had federal agents vandalized the Book Depot to cover up whatever perfidious acts they deemed vital to national security?

I stopped myself before I started speculating that the robins I'd watched in the backyard were avian agents. It was near enough the cocktail hour to justify a splash of scotch. I was annoyed to find my hand trembling as I took the bottle from the liquor cabinet. Earlier, I'd been uneasy—and with reason. However, I hadn't felt that Caron, Inez, and I were in any danger, since we were not withholding information or dark secrets. I hoped that Dolly was innocent, but I wouldn't have been stricken with anguish if evidence ultimately proved otherwise.

A guttural cry from the den distracted me from my disjointed thoughts. Most parents would have been alarmed, or certainly should have been. Listening to the ice cubes cheerfully clinking in my glass, I ambled to the doorway. Caron had the notebook. Inez was clutching her own neck and staggering backwards, her face distorted as if she'd taken a swig of vinegar. Her utterances were not indecorous, but they were highly creative.

When she finally collapsed on the floor, I said, "Have we arrived at a climactic moment?"

Caron looked up from the notebook. "Do You Mind, Mother? Inez is in the middle of a dynamite scene where—"

"Don't use that word!" I snapped.

Inez recovered from her self-induced death throes and blinked at me. "What word, Ms. Malloy?"

"The d-word."

Caron wrinkled her nose. "Dynamite? What's wrong with that?"

I glanced over my shoulder at the black box on the hall table. "Just don't, okay? I'm sure the scene was fantastic, extraordinary, and breathtaking."

"It's not an obscene word, Ms. Malloy," said Inez. "It was invented by Alfred Nobel in the middle of the nineteenth century, after he found a way to stabilize"—she gulped—"the n-word by combining it with the s-word."

Caron gave me a baleful look. "Some of us should be more concerned about the p-word, as in *peculiar*."

"Perhaps so," I said, sighing. "I'm going out to the patio to make a call. If Sara Louise wanders in, please be so kind as to inform me."

"You going to call Peter?" asked Caron.

"No," I said, wishing it were as simple as that.

But it wasn't.

Chapter Nine

I scooped up the receiver and went out to the patio. I was working up my courage to make the call when Caron opened the sliding door.

"It's not Sara Louise," she said in one of her better long-suffering, why-me whines that surely surpassed Job's rudimentary efforts. "It's these other people. Should I let them in?"

"Media?"

"Not unless they're in disguise. Some old guy and a younger woman. I could frisk them to see if they're wired with tiny microphones in their navels, but I'm not going to do a body cavity search." She paused. "Although navels might be considered cavities, in the precise definition of the term."

"I'll handle it," I said. "You might make better progress upstairs, where your creative flow won't be disrupted. Make your bed while you're at it."

She stomped back toward the den. I went to the front door, where I found Daniel and Lucy Hood. Before I could open my mouth, Lucy said, "I hope you won't think we're presumptuous in coming without calling first. I did try to call a while ago, but got one of those insufferable recorded voices telling me the line was out of order."

"Which stirred her up all the more," inserted Daniel. "I told her this was a bad idea, but she insisted. If we're bothering you, please say so and we'll leave."

Lucy nudged him aside. "Yes, I know we just met yesterday, and you can hardly consider us friends. But when I read that article in the newspaper this morning, I was so worried that I couldn't stop thinking about you. What a horrible thing, and then to have that ghastly photograph on the front page! The media have no respect for privacy, and what's more, they're all idiots. I'm sure they stuck microphones in your face and demanded to know how it felt when you opened the freezer. That's almost as tasteless as cornering some woman whose children perished in a fire."

I stepped back before she could hug me. "It's kind of you to stop by."

"And then Gary told us what happened this morning. If I were you, I would have checked into the hospital and made them let me stay for a week. Shouldn't you be in bed?"

Daniel held out a paper plate covered with foil. "Brownies are Lucy's version of chicken soup."

"Chocolate has been clinically proven to trigger endomorphins," she said as she came inside. "I like to think of it as a jogger's high, but without the shin splints and sweat."

"Thank you," I said. I accepted the plate, along with the inevitable. "Would you like a glass of wine or a cocktail?"

"If you're sure we're not disturbing you," Daniel said stiffly. I could imagine him rolling over in bed to pat Lucy's bottom and express the same sentiment.

Lucy squeezed my shoulder. "If you'll forgive me for saying so, you're looking a bit haggard. Point me to the bar and I'll fix the drinks. Bourbon and water, Daniel?"

"Yes, dear. Please don't panic, Claire. We're having a little party this evening, so we can't stay for more than a few minutes."

He and I retreated to the patio. "Nice place," he commented. "Very peaceful, and with the wall and gate, secure as well."

"I used to think so, too." I sat down at the table and picked up my glass. "Have you had any luck looking at properties?"

"We've seen a few promising ones."

Lucy came out with a glass in each hand. "And once we're settled, I'm going to write a twenty-first-century version of *The Stepford Wives*. I'll title it *The Stepford Golf Widows*. After that, I may update *Lady Chatterley's Lover*, but with a greenskeeper rather than a gardener. May I count on you to host my premier signing?"

I remembered the last signing I'd hosted, which also became the author's last in a different sense. She, like her prose, had been strangled. However, I smiled and said, "Of course. Then you've decided to retire in the area?"

"We're considering it." She sat down and gave me a searching look. "I have to admire you for remaining so composed. Are the police providing adequate protection? Will someone be patrolling the grounds at night?"

Daniel grunted. "Damned rude, if you ask me. First that woman who lives here goes off, leaving you to find the body in the freezer. Then some maniac makes an unholy mess of your bookstore and attacks you. The two events have to be connected. You have any idea who's behind it?"

"So you can give him a good thrashing?" murmured Lucy. "Daniel has some very old-fashioned ideas. His staff cowers when he swaggers in every morning, fuming about the difficulty in finding a parking place. The men avoid him, while the women fuss over him as if he were a befuddled great-uncle."

"Some of 'em find me sexy," he said, wiggling his eyebrows. "Like that Sean Connery fellow. And so do you, my dear, even if you won't admit it." He turned to me. "So what do the police have to say about all this? That man in the photo, Lieutenant Rosen, for instance. He have any theories?"

"None that he's shared with me."

"What about this Dolly Goforth? Have they found her?"

"Daniel, stop it," said Lucy. "The last thing Claire wants to talk about is all this. Claire, why don't you come over for a barbecue this evening? The conversation on the deck is likely to focus on state-of-the-art putters, and in the kitchen on recipes and drooling grandbabies.

Now that I think about it, it doesn't sound all that intriguing, but at least you can get away for a few hours. We'd love to have you, and your daughter as well."

"Did Gary put you up to this?" I asked.

Daniel adroitly cut her off. "Of course he did, but with Lucy's complicity. Both of them ought to take a few lessons from the pro and get out on the course. They could expend their excess energy fishing balls out of the pond or trying to get away from the geese. You hit a ball into their territory, you stay on the tee and take a second shot. The last damn fool who insisted on retrieving his ball ended up in the emergency room." He stood up. "Come along, Lucy. I need to pick up a bag of charcoal, and once you're in the store, you'll think of two dozen things you need."

She finished her wine. "Yes, dear, and I promise not to say a word when we drive all over town looking for some esoteric brand of charcoal." She paused in front of me. "This must be a terrible strain for you. How much longer will you have to stay here before Ms. Goforth returns to answer some questions? It's too much of a coincidence to believe she's in no way responsible."

"I couldn't say," I said vaguely. I led them to the front door, wished them luck in their search for the consummate briquette, and watched them drive away. I waited for a moment, hoping to see Dolly's Mercedes coming up the hill, then returned to the patio. The telephone call needed to be made, and I was the designated dialer.

I took out the gum wrapper on which I'd written the number, and reluctantly pushed the appropriate buttons. To my dismay, someone answered.

"Velocchio and Associates," said a female with a British accent. "How may I direct your call?"

"I'd like to speak to Richard Hayes," I said, wondering if she nibbled on crumpets between calls.

"May I ask who's calling?"

"Claire Malloy."

"And in reference to . . . ?"

"His daughter, Madison."

My response produced a long moment of silence. I was on the verge of asking her if I should arrange for paramedics to utilize the Heimlich maneuver to dislodge a crumpet crumb when she said, "Mr. Hayes is in a meeting with Mr. Velocchio. Would you care to leave a number so he can call you back?"

"Heavens no, I wouldn't dream of infringing on his time. I'll try again in a few days."

"Please allow me to put you on hold while I see if he's out of his meeting. I'm sure he'll be eager to speak with you. He's very fond of Madison, as we all are."

At least I was treated to Mozart instead of tips about pruning bushes under windows. I propped my feet on a second chair and tried to envision Madison's stroll across the patio and out the gate. Nick had not described her as upset or particularly grim. She'd ignored him and Sebastian, but that was unsurprising since they were mere peons. It seemed likely that she'd either made a call or had prearranged a time to meet someone in the alley for a brief conversation. At which time she'd either changed her mind and left, or had been forced to do so. If the latter were true, she had not screamed or cried out for help.

Mozart stopped in mid-crescendo. "Mrs. Malloy? This is Richard Hayes. You wish to speak to me about Madison?"

He spoke briskly and with irritation, as though I'd stumbled into the midst of a top-secret meeting of global powers. I was tempted to reply in the same tone, but instead said, "Yes, I do. It's complicated, but the bottom line is that she's disappeared."

"I am very much aware of that, Mrs. Malloy. When I returned from a business trip to Spain, the household staff informed me that they hadn't seen her for several days. She'd mentioned inviting some of her college friends to stay at our place on the Vineyard, but the caretaker went by and no one's been there." He paused for a moment. "Do you have knowledge of her whereabouts?"

"No, and that's the problem," I said. "She and her cousin Sara Louise—"

"Dammit, I knew she'd be involved in this! Madison's moderately intelligent, but Sara Louise is manipulative and too clever for her own good. She'll do well in the corporate world, where the most important attributes are greed and ambition."

"That may be, Mr. Hayes. In any case, Madison and Sara Louise showed up here on Tuesday—"

"Showed up where?"

"Farberville, in Arkansas. They—"

"Never heard of it, and I can't believe they have, either. Are you claiming they simply showed up in some backwoods podunk?"

"I am not claiming anything," I said through clenched teeth. "I'm telling you what happened. If you think this is a crank call, feel free to hang up and peddle Chippendale chairs and Grecian urns to blue-haired matrons."

"My apologies, Mrs. Malloy," he said smoothly. "I'm concerned about Madison. Do you have a daughter?"

"I do, and I know exactly where she is and what she's doing." I did not add that she'd yet to run off with a golf pro's son. "Shall I continue?"

"Please do."

He sounded grumpy, but I excused him on the grounds that the need to apologize had no doubt given him indigestion. Miss Treacle would suffer in the near future. "Madison and Sara Louise said they'd come on a whim to visit Dolly, since she'd given them an open invitation."

"Dolly? Who's that?"

"Dolly Goforth, the widow of Bibi Goforth, who presumably was a relative of yours. The girls referred to him as Uncle Bibi."

"Oh, Bibi, sure. He was an old family friend, not related. So they came to visit Dolly. That's very interesting. Just how do you fit into this, Mrs. Malloy?"

"Dolly asked me to house-sit while she went to see her sister. If the girls had come two days earlier, they would have caught her."

"Indeed they would have. I gather you're allowing them to stay there until Dolly returns, but now Madison has disappeared. When did this happen?"

"Yesterday. She's called twice, but refused to tell me where she is. I'm afraid she may be in some sort of trouble."

Now he was speaking slowly, as if calculating the weight of each word. "Have you notified the police, Mrs. Malloy?"

"Yes, but they don't seem to have any ideas where to find her. Despite your previous assumption, Farberville has more than a trailer park and a café."

"I'm sure it does," he murmured. "What does Sara Louise have to say about this?"

We would have been on the phone well past midnight (EDT) if I'd told him the entire story. I settled for a vague reply. "She said she was unaware that Madison had met anyone who—"

"A man, you mean."

"Well, yes, that's what she said. She also admitted that Madison has done this sort of thing before." I began to feel as if I were teetering atop a very slippery slope—with boulders at the bottom. "There's not really anything you can do right now, Mr. Hayes. I just thought you ought to be aware of the situation. There is something I want to ask you about Dolly and Bibi."

"And that would be . . . ?"

"Dolly told me that she and Bibi had lived near Chicago, and that he'd owned a factory before his death a year ago. The police can't find any records or documentation that they lived anywhere in Illinois. Did I misunderstand Dolly?"

"Give me a minute to decide how best to explain this." Apparently he'd given himself more than a minute. After an interminable silence, he finally said, "Dolly intentionally misled you, I'm sorry to say. She's been under a psychiatrist's care for years for bipolar episodes. Bibi was an accountant, not an industry mogul. They lived in a modest house. He did his best to curb her extravagant spending, but he wasn't always successful. When he died, she came into an appreciable sum from his life insurance policy. As for—please wait just a moment, Mrs. Malloy." He covered the mouthpiece of the receiver and spoke to someone who must have entered his office. After a few muffled sentences were exchanged, he said to me, "Something has come up that requires my immediate attention. I'm going to transfer you to the receptionist so you can give her your address and telephone number. Thank you for calling, Mrs. Malloy. I would appreciate it if you keep me informed of any new developments."

Mozart took over. I drummed my fingers on the table until the receptionist came on the line. After I'd given her the information, I turned off the phone and leaned back, attempting to sort out what he'd told me—and what he hadn't. He certainly hadn't been upset over Madison's disappearance. He hadn't demanded details or threatened to call the police or the FBI. Then again, he hadn't denied that she'd done this sort of thing before. He was annoyed, but not alarmed.

I wasn't sure what to make of his explanation concerning Dolly and Bibi. Dolly had lied to me and allowed me to make erroneous assumptions. Then again, evasive and psychotic were not interchangeable. Bibi Goforth had not died in Illinois, but she could have kept her maiden name when they were married. Bibi was a nickname; his last name could have been anything. Bernard Mordella came to mind. Ergo, Petrolli had been Bibi's brother, and therefore Dolly's brother-in-law. The one whose name she didn't recognize. Oh, *that* brother-in-law.

But she had recognized the name, despite her disavowal. She'd tried to explain away the call to the Fritz Motel, but she'd been unable to come up with anything remotely convincing to explain her possession of the cell phone. And so she'd created interference to end the conversation. Peter would have traced the origin of the call by now, as well as received more information from the Brooklyn police. And learned that I'd called a number in New York City, then failed to tape it. Which meant he'd be in a full-blown swivet when he arrived in a couple of hours.

I definitely needed an excuse that would soothe the savage beast. Technological ignorance would not cut it. I'd spent entirely too much time adamantly maintaining that I didn't have a concussion to offer it as an explanation. And if I did, Peter would insist on hustling me to the emergency room, where I would be exposed to every airborne virus known to the AMA. Sick people, I thought testily, should be quarantined at first sniffle.

The telephone rang. I froze, gaping at it as if it had reared back and bared its fangs. I allowed it to ring a second time before I answered it with a wary "Hello?"

"Hey, Mrs. Malloy, this is Aly. Is Caron there?"

"Yes, she is," I said weakly.

"Are you okay? You sound funny."

"I'm fine, Aly. It'll take me a minute to find Caron and Inez." I carried the receiver to the door of the den, where great leaps of literary lionizing had given way to pretzels and sodas. "It's for you," I said. "Aly."

Caron shrugged. "Tell her I'm busy."

I dropped the receiver in her lap. "Tell her yourself."

"The only reason she's calling," Inez said in case I was too dim to grasp the political significance of the call, "is because she saw your picture in the newspaper this morning. That's why she knew to call this number."

"You saw the picture?" I said.

Inez nodded. "At the police station."

"What do you want?" Caron said into the receiver. After a pause, she said, "Yeah, I suppose so, but only if you bring a pizza. And you'll have to leave when Lieutenant Rosen arrives to interview me again. Inez and I are the key witnesses, you know. We spent half the day at the police department being questioned by detectives and looking at mug shots. Luckily, we were able to assist them in identifying the victim. You won't read any of that in the newspaper, though. Our lives are in danger until they catch the murderer."

"Tell her we're in the witness protection program," whispered Inez.

I retreated to my bedroom to lie down and read. Eventually the vicar engaged my attention, and I dozed off during his explanation of why he'd forgotten to tape the conversation he'd had with Lady Pompousass concerning the pain pills he'd inadvertently given to her beloved mutt, Mott.

145

An hour later I was awakened by the sound of squeals, giggles, and the sort of music that I had not yet learned to appreciate. I went to the window and looked down at the patio, where Caron and Inez were holding court. Aly, Emily, Carrie, and Ashley seemed properly impressed by the recitation that had no doubt escalated to a climactic crisis that involved gunfire from rooftops and a dozen thugs coming over the wall. I hoped Caron and Inez would not decide to print brochures and lead walking tours of the crime scene. Caron had shown promise of developing into an entrepreneur at the age of eight, when a child down the block had opened a lemonade stand one summer. Caron had opened her own the following day, but her lemonade was garnished with maraschino cherries and paper umbrellas—and at half the price. Net profits had been minimal, but the competition had been vanquished.

The doorbell warbled. When no one on the patio so much as twitched, I went downstairs and opened the door. The van from the television station was parked by the front walk, and a camera was aimed at the perky reporter as she backed off the porch and pointed dramatically at the garage door. "As you can see," she gushed to her unseen audience, "the investigation is continuing on Dogwood Lane, where the victim was found crammed in the freezer only yesterday." She gestured at me. "Mrs. Claire Malloy, owner of a bookstore here in Farberville, told reporters that she'd gone to the freezer to take out steaks for dinner. Mrs. Malloy, have the police identified the victim yet?"

"You'll have to ask them," I said.

"Can you tell us exactly what you thought when you saw the victim? Were you surprised?"

I stared at her. "Of course I was surprised."

"Did you realize immediately that he was dead?"

"I didn't check his vitals, if that's what you mean. That's all I have to say. This is private property. Please leave immediately."

The reporter pouted for a brief second, then turned back to the camera. "This is Silkie Solomon for KFAR, on the scene of the brutal murder that took place yesterday, only a few blocks away from the football stadium. We'll have an update at ten, when we hope to have more details for you. Now, back to Edward in the studio with a report on the bass fishing tournament this weekend." She handed her microphone to an underling and took a compact out of her pocket to examine her face. "Damn," she muttered, "I look like that friggin' reindeer in the song. Pack it up, guys. I need to pee."

I closed the door, berating myself for answering her insipid questions but deeply grateful Caron or Inez had not heard the doorbell. I dithered for a moment, then found the receiver in the den and called Peter's number at the PD.

Jorgeson answered. "Lieutenant Rosen's office."

I identified myself and told him about the KFAR episode. "Is there any hope you can send someone here to thwart the media? Every time I glance at a window, I expect to see an inquisitive face or a camera. It's only a matter of time before they discover the gate's not padlocked. I feel like we're in a goldfish bowl. Or maybe I'm going stir-crazy, Jorgeson."

"You've only been there since noon, Ms. Malloy."

"I'm aware of that," I said, "but I'm about to start chewing my toenails. If you can send an officer to keep an eye on the girls and their friends, I can at least go to the grocery store. We're running low on olives and gorgonzola. Thirty minutes, Jorgeson, that's all I'm asking."

"The lieutenant won't like it."

I crossed my fingers. "So go ask him. I'll wait."

"Can't do it. He and the chief are in a meeting at city hall. The county prosecutor's pissed because he can't hold a press conference. The mayor's been getting hysterical calls from women who're afraid to open their freezers. The hospital administrator is accusing us of not providing adequate security outside the morgue. And by the way, Ms. Malloy, don't expect a Christmas card from the chief this year."

"Then it's up to you, Jorgeson," I said meekly.

"You can't get in the Book Depot, you know."

I struggled not to sound exasperated. "The grocery store is my sole destination. A glimpse of sanity, the chance to mingle with those whose worst crimes consist of buying premium ice cream instead of sugar-free sherbet. I may even discuss the weather while I wait in line to check out. Thirty minutes, that's all."

Jorgeson considered this for a minute. "Okay, Ms. Malloy, it's not like you're under arrest. I'll have a uniformed officer pick up a padlock for the gate, and then stay there in case the media show up. What you choose to do is your business. All I can say is that this meeting may go on all afternoon—or it may be over in fifteen minutes."

"Thank you," I said. "One of these days, I'll buy you a goldfish bowl and a couple of fish."

"Don't go doing that, Ms. Malloy. My wife has so many cats that I can't keep track of them."

I hung up and resisted the urge to try a few tango steps on the carpet. I wasn't exactly out the door yet, but the officer would be along shortly. Caron and Inez could incorporate him into Act Two as their bodyguard. Everybody would have a fine time, including me. I decided my excursion merited a touch of lipstick, and I was headed for the stairs when the phone rang. Desperately hoping Peter had not returned to the PD before I could make good my escape, I retraced my steps to the den.

"Claire Malloy is not available for comment," I said into the receiver. "Please hang up and call someone who is."

"This is Christopher Santini, Sara Louise's father. I need to speak with her immediately."

He sounded quite as irritable as Madison's father. Reminding myself that I was not a neglectful nanny who'd allowed the girls to cross the street without holding hands, I said, "She's not here right now. Would you care to leave a message?"

"Where is she?"

"I don't know. She borrowed Dolly's car a couple of hours ago and left."

"Dolly Goforth's car."

I sat down on the ottoman. "That's right. Shall I assume you've spoken to Madison's father?"

"Yes, I have. I had my assistant do an Internet search, and he found a very bizarre story from your local newspaper. What the hell is going on down there—and is Sara Louise involved in some way? Her name wasn't mentioned, but Richard said she and Madison are staying at this particular address. He also said you gave him some garbled story about Madison disappearing. Naturally, I'm concerned."

I may not have elaborated on the story, but I certainly had not garbled it. Rather than point this out, I gave him a general idea of what had taken place during the week (omitting personality conflicts and catty exchanges). Apparently I did so with so much precision that he remained silent for a long while.

"Have the police identified the body?" he finally asked.

"A man from Brooklyn named Mordella. He had a record and served some time in prison, but has been a model citizen since then. Is the name familiar? Was he a friend of Bibi's?"

"I do not socialize with petty criminals, Mrs. Malloy, and I have no idea if he was a friend of Bibi's. It seems obvious that Dolly is the one to offer an explanation. Have the police located her?"

"No, but they're working on it." It occurred to me that I'd answered that particular question a mere zillion times in the past few days.

"Have they traced her calls to you?"

"Yes, they have, Mr. Santini. Now let me ask you something. The police have determined that Bibi neither owned a factory nor died in Illinois. Where were he and Dolly living when he had the heart attack?"

"Upstate somewhere. I don't recall the name of the place."

"Upstate what?"

"New York, but he didn't own any factory. He was just an old family friend who enjoyed having kids visit him in the summer. He and his first wife had a son, but the boy died in a car accident and his wife passed away a few years later. We were all surprised when he married this second wife, but it wasn't our place to dictate to him."

"Because he remarried so quickly?" I asked.

Santini hesitated. "She seemed too energetic for him. Had we known about her mental illness, we would have intervened. However, Bibi excused her extravagances and appeared quite enamored of her. I know for a fact that he went into debt to pay for her psychiatric care and medications. Her past may not be as savory as she's led you to believe. Someone told me she'd been married several times previously, and not to upstanding citizens. I was also told that she was involved with an agency that arranged fraudulent marriages with women from Eastern Europe. I can't swear to any of this, of course. My wife and her friends love to gossip; they were convinced Dolly married Bibi for his steady salary and gullible nature."

I remembered Dolly's glowing face when she spoke about Bibi. She'd clearly lied about some things, but I doubted that she was a skillful enough actress to fool me. "I think she was enamored of him," I said mildly. "The police are having a problem tracking down information about her and Bibi. Since he was an old family friend, you must know his proper name."

"He died a year ago, Mrs. Malloy. Whatever is going on down there has nothing to do with him." His voice grew icy. "Tell Sara Louise to call me the minute she comes back."

"She said you were in Hong Kong."

"I am in Hong Kong. She has my cell phone number."

I hung up. Despite both fathers' claims to be concerned about their daughters, they seemed more interested in the status of the investigation. The only information they'd shared concerned Dolly's purportedly shady past. I wasn't ready to buy it without more evidence, in that I would have to acknowledge that I was as gullible as Bibi. Humility and self-reproach are not high on my list of personal virtues.

Caron and Inez had lost the attention of their friends, who were in the pool. I sat down and said, "Did you run out of suspense?"

"The problem," Caron said grimly, "is that we don't have a grand finale. We can go only so far, and then it stops. No one has been arrested. Dolly hasn't confessed or returned in a blaze of glory to accuse the culprit. There's no smoking gun. The police can't even find the body."

"That's why we had to stop writing," added Inez as she fastidiously applied sunblock to her nose. Nobody's going to buy a book that's missing the last three chapters."

Caron sighed. "It was a dumb idea, anyway."

I saw no need to agree with her. "Maybe Peter will think it's okay for you and your friends to go to a movie tonight."

"What friends?"

"The ones in the pool," I said, surprised.

Inez put the sunblock bottle down and said, "They already have plans. The mall's having a talent show next week, so they're going over to Rhonda Maguire's house to work on an act. Rhonda's going to do a Britney Spears thing while they sing backup."

"And everybody else throws up," said Caron.

"The winner gets a two-hundred-dollar gift certificate that's good in all the shops," Inez said, now scratching her nose. "What's worse, we'll get to hear all about it the rest of the summer. They'll probably even show up for the first day of school in their matching short-shorts and spangly tops, and autograph the freshmen's notebooks."

"Emily says Rhonda's going to get her belly button pierced," said Caron. "It's so totally gross."

"That it is," I murmured. "Why don't you and Inez concoct a dramatic scene in which you stumble over a body in the pine needles?"

"While we twirl batons and yodel? Now that would get a lot of votes."

"You have to sing or dance, Ms. Malloy," Inez explained carefully. "Last year some sophomore did an act with her trained poodle. Everybody called her Puffy and tossed dog biscuits at her the rest of the summer, and she had to transfer to a private school."

"Remember Twinkle Toes from about three years ago?" said Caron. "She did a ballet routine and fell off the stage. Afterwards, she dropped out of school and is waiting tables at a café out by the highway."

The four not-so-friendly friends came out of the pool and began to dry themselves. "Thanks for letting us swim," said Carrie.

"Yeah," said Aly, "and call us if you find any more bodies." She glanced at me. "Just joking, Mrs. Malloy. I mean, the police have him in the morgue. It's not like he's going to show up at midnight or anything."

Giggling, they picked up their clothes and went into the house.

Maternal wisdom was called for, but I couldn't come up with even a beginning that wouldn't be dismissed as lame. "A police officer is going to come any minute and padlock the gate. He or she will then stay to keep an eye on things while I go to the grocery store. Is there something you'd like?"

"Whatever, as long as it has cyanide in it," said Caron.

Inez groaned, albeit softly. "Who can eat at a time like this? I wonder how much Twinkle Toes makes in tips every night?"

"Don't be ridiculous, Inez," Caron said. "We've got all summer to apply to boarding schools. We'll get to wear plaid skirts and cardigan sweaters. If we're really lucky, we can play field hockey."

"Aren't you a bit premature?" I said. "You don't have to enter the talent contest, you know. Just sit in the audience and clap unenthusiastically."

Caron looked at me. "So we should give up? Is that what you think? Aren't you supposed to be a role model?"

"Even John Dewey had to defend his decimal system," added Inez. "It was very controversial at the time."

Caron snorted. "Controversial? Did the other librarians light torches and storm his castle? Give me a break."

"Well, then," I said, "I'll just go inside and make a grocery list. I shouldn't be gone long."

Before I could make it to the door, the woman officer who'd been at the house at noon came in through the gate. She stopped to attach a padlock, then came to the patio. "Hello," she said to the girls, "I'm your bodyguard for a while."

I was so grateful that she hadn't said "babysitter" that I wanted to give her a hug. "Did Sergeant Jorgeson tell you what to do?"

"Yes, ma'am," she said. "Protect and serve—that's what I'm here for."

"I hope you weren't pulled away from mall surveillance."

"No such luck. I was back on desk duty, tracking down addresses for scofflaws. It's amazing who ignores piddly little parking tickets. Even some of our city council members have piled up quite a few."

Caron and Inez were lost in some gloomy reverie of plaid skirts and knee guards. I shrugged at the officer, then went inside to get my purse.

At this particular moment, I had no intention of going anywhere except the grocery store. I wasn't even planning to drive by my apartment or the Book Depot. I would buy steaks, potatoes, salad, rolls, and whichever frozen dessert appealed. Bread, olives, and gorgonzola. Thirty minutes, max.

My intentions were honorable. They really were.

Chapter Ten

I drove in the direction of the grocery store, comparing my mental list with the contents of the refrigerator. Pistachios, pears, and pretzels. Steaks and accouterments. A can of fruit cocktail. Maybe a couple of pints of gourmet ice cream, since Caron and Inez would recover from the impending horror of the talent show at the mall and rediscover their appetite for junk food and gangster movies.

Petrolli Mordella had probably been a gangster, I thought with a frown, although not of the stature of Al Capone—who'd ultimately been nailed for tax evasion, as had Mordella. Peter might offer more information, but I could hardly count on it. I had a feeling our next conversation would focus on untaped telephone calls, which would leave both of us annoyed. And require me to find out what I could on my own.

I parked in front of the grocery store and cut off the engine. It was obvious that Mordella had come to Farberville to see Dolly. She'd spoken to him on the phone, and then in person, at which time he'd either given her his cell phone or she'd taken it without his knowledge. She could have shot him, I thought, and left his body behind the gazebo for some obscure reason. As hiding places went, it was a poor choice. Caron and Inez might have decided to explore the yard after returning from the airport. The gardener could have dropped by to fertilize the japonicas or sweep up pinecones. A meter reader might have come in through the gate. The body could have been found while Dolly was still at the airport.

Not that she'd necessarily stayed there for any length of time. She'd been seen when she entered it, but unless she was still crouched in a corner of the lost luggage room, she'd found a way to leave. Considering the nonexistence of public transportation in Farberville, Mordella must have had a car. Had he pulled up to the curb as Caron drove away, helped Dolly load her luggage into his trunk, and then spirited her away? He clearly hadn't driven her to Atlanta, in that dead men are notoriously slow drivers. She could have easily done it herself by the following evening, with plenty of time to eat at ubiquitous chain restaurants and spend the night at a motel along the interstate. If Mordella had a car, that is.

Regrettably, he was not available to answer that question. It occurred to me that I might be able to find out more at the Fritz Motel, where he'd checked in (and possibly checked out). The police had already searched his room and interviewed the manager, but Peter would be disinclined to share the details. In fiction, the classic cop-boyfriend is willing to spill every investigative breakthrough with his doting amateur sleuth, but for the moment, that convenient venue was blocked with concrete barriers, flashing lights, and signs warning the unwary not to enter.

Therefore, in spite of my exemplary intentions, I pulled out of the grocery store parking lot and headed for the highway that kept the more toxic traffic at the perimeter of the city. Tucked among used-car lots, fast-food places, garages, and rusty metal buildings surrounded by sagging chain-link fences was the Fritz Motel, a yellow-bricked paean to the tremulous taste of the 1950s.

I went inside and smiled at the woman behind the desk. Grumbling, she pushed stringy orange hair out of her face, stubbed out a cigarette, and picked up a remote to lower the volume of a television set on a high shelf in one corner. The lobby decor, to use the term loosely, consisted of stained linoleum, folding chairs, and a plastic plant with dusty leaves.

"You wanna room?" she asked, resigning herself to the arduous task of exchanging a key for cash. "Thirty a night, two hundred for the week, payable in advance. No pets, no parties, no paying customers. Ten-dollar deposit for towels."

"I was hoping for some information," I said.

"You a reporter?"

"I'm merely an acquaintance of someone who stayed here several days ago." This did not seem to be an overly egregious lie, since Mordella and I had been in close proximity at one point.

She gave me her full attention. "Your face is familiar. Not on TV or anything like that. . . . Wait a minute—you're the one that found the body in the freezer. You ought to sue the newspaper for running that photograph. You looked like you'd been spit up by a bear."

"It was awful, wasn't it?" I said with a weak laugh. "I realize the police have already been here, but—"

"Oh, lordy, I thought they'd never leave." She leaned forward, resting her chunky breasts on her forearms. "Three, maybe four truckers came scuttling out of their rooms, yanking on their pants. I don't reckon the women with them were their wives, or even their girlfriends. It was pretty damn funny."

"Did anyone visit Mr. Mordella?"

"The cops must have asked me that fifty times. This is my place, and I can't afford to hire any help. I keep the office open until midnight, then lock up and go to bed in the room right back there. Unless I'm cleaning rooms, I can't see who or what goes in and out, which suits me just fine, thank you very much. As long as I get the cash in advance, I don't care, either. This Mordella guy seemed polite, despite having a real funny accent. He paid for three nights, asked about making long-distance calls—I don't allow 'em—and wanted to know where he could get something to eat. I told him about the café next door. I didn't see hide nor hair of him after that."

"He did get a telephone call, didn't he?" I asked.

"Like I told the cops, some woman. I transferred the call to his room."

I'd learned nothing more useful than the libidinous proclivities of

156

truckers, but I wasn't ready to give up. "I suppose the cops searched his room thoroughly?"

She made a face. "They crawled all over it, even brought in a dog to sniff for drugs. I told 'em that when I went in to change towels and make the bed, I didn't see any signs that he enjoyed the companionship of any of the hookers that hang out at the truck stop. I can tell."

Dearly hoping she wouldn't, I said, "Did you happen to notice his car?"

"A rental, according to the cops. They had it towed off after they finished searching the room. They wanted me to sign some piece of paper, but I told 'em what they could do with it. It wasn't any of my business, same as I told that private detective that came by. I don't ask to see a driver's license or a suitcase like they do at fancy hotels. I heard that in places like New York City, you have to pay more than a hundred dollars a night. It goes to show some people have got more money than sense."

"A private detective came by? When was that?"

She scratched her head as she mulled it over. "You know, I kind of forgot about that, what with the cops and all. The day Mordella arrived, I think, but the guy wasn't looking for him. He was after some kid that had jumped bail over in Oklahoma. He asked to look at the registration book, and I said okay, thinking he wouldn't have much luck unless the kid's name was Smith or Jones."

"He didn't find him?"

"Said he didn't expect to, that he was just going by all the area motels. He described the kid, and I told him I was pretty sure I hadn't seen him. I've had private detectives before, but they're usually doing divorce work." She glanced at my left hand. "You ever been divorced, honey?"

I shook my head. "Can you describe this private detective?"

"Nothing to write home about. Average size, dark hair, not real old or young. I didn't pay a whole helluva lot of attention to him, since I was watching one of those shows where everybody is having sex with everybody else, so they all get mad and throw chairs at each other. Sort of like professional wrestling, I guess. No matter how wild it turns, nobody ever seems to get hurt." She looked over her shoulder at a clock on the wall. "In fact, it's about to come on. I can make some coffee if you want to stay and watch."

"I wish I could," I said, backing away, "but I promised to go by the grocery store. Did the private detective leave his card or a number to call?"

"He just said thanks and left. Now I'm wondering if I ought to have told the cops. What do you think?"

"You probably should," I said virtuously.

She reached for the remote. "Yeah, when I get around to it. I don't see how it has anything to do with Mordella. Hey, I bet you could get on one of these shows and talk about how you found his body in the freezer. Course you'll have to say you had sex with it. Now that's a creepy thought, isn't it?"

It was not one I cared to think about. I returned to my car. My brilliant theory about Dolly absconding with Mordella's car dimmed, then flickered out like a sickly firefly. The appearance of a private detective was a remarkable coincidence, considering Mordella had checked into the Fritz Motel that same day. Mordella had not been using an assumed name, in that the proprietor had put through Dolly's call without hesitation. Therefore, his name was in the registration book for anyone to see, including a private eye purportedly chasing down a bail jumper. And whoever had shot Mordella hadn't done so at the motel, unless he—or she—had been willing to risk hauling the body out to the parking lot. Although at the moment there was only a lone white car parked at the far end of the building, I suspected there was quite a bit of activity throughout the night.

I looked at my watch. There was no way I could make it to the grocery store and back to the house in my allotted half hour, even if I ran red lights and bullied my way to the front of the express checkout lane. On the other hand, Caron and Inez were in good hands with Corporal McTeer, who seemed more than capable of fending off obstinate reporters. None of them would mind, or even notice, if I was a wee bit late getting back. As Jorgeson had glumly observed, I wasn't under arrest.

Having rationalized my behavior to my satisfaction, I pulled out of the motel lot and into that of the Cardinal Café. A few dispirited customers were scattered along the counter, drinking coffee. I sat down at a booth and picked up a menu.

A stocky young waitress approached. "Get you something, ma'am?"

"Iced tea, please," I said. "If you have a moment, I'd like to ask you a few questions."

She glanced back at the counter. "Long as one of them doesn't have a heart attack, go ahead."

"Do you happen to remember a man who came in here last Sunday? Short, balding, wire-rimmed glasses, probably with an accent?"

"Real mannersome he was, and a good tipper. He said he was staying at the Fritz. He was startled when I gave him the bill, said I must have made a mistake. I added it up again, but he was real sure it should have been more. I had to get out the menu and show him the prices. We both ended up laughing about it."

"Was he alone?"

"Both times. He came in for supper, and then breakfast the next morning. I figured he was some kind of salesman. I never did get a chance to ask him where he was from or what his business was. Friend of yours?"

I was not making what might be described as significant progress. Petrolli Mordella had been polite. He'd rented a car. He'd probably chosen the Fritz Motel because it was the first one he'd seen coming from the airport. He'd been used to New York prices. I had no idea if he'd had biscuits and gravy for breakfast, but it didn't seem relevant. He had not entertained a hooker in his room. Dolly had called him. She'd ended up with his cell phone but not his car.

I realized the waitress was looking at me. "He wasn't exactly a friend," I admitted with a shrug. "He came to Farberville to visit someone I know, and she's worried about him."

"The blond woman with the red Mercedes? That first evening, I stepped out back to take a break and noticed him talking to her in the motel parking lot. It surprised me, what her looking so classy and him kind of shabby and a lot older. Not that it was any of my concern, mind you. He was getting in her car when I went back inside. I almost said something about it to him the next morning, but we were busy."

I put down a dollar. "I just realized I have to go. Thanks for your time."

"Wish I could have been more help." She tucked the dollar in her pocket, then frowned at me. "If you don't mind me saying so, you look familiar."

I waited to hear how she was going to describe the picture in the newspaper. Opinions of my appearance had thus far been less than flattering. No doubt even Jorgeson had offered a few acerbic remarks to his wife over scrambled eggs.

"Don't you have a daughter at the high school?" she asked. "A sophomore now, or a junior? Red hair like yours, only longer? I can't recollect her name."

"Caron Malloy."

"Yeah, that's right. Maybe I saw you dropping her off at school or something. It's been a couple of years."

"That must have been it," I said, then left with unseemly haste. Once I was in my car, I sternly ordered myself not to so much as entertain a certain image, then sank back and reviewed what she'd told me. Dolly had shown up at the Fritz Motel the night Mordella arrived and taken him for a drive. The following morning he'd been healthy enough to have breakfast at the café. Dolly had left for the airport at noon. It was unlikely that within that small window of opportunity, she'd killed him, transported his body to her yard, showered and freshened up, packed her bags, and been waiting for Caron. It might have been possible—Dolly was a highly organized woman—but it was hard to swallow.

Therefore, I thought as I drove toward the grocery store, he'd given

160

her his cell phone on the first night. Which was curious. If she'd felt the need to have one, she could have afforded to buy a new one. From what I'd found in her files, she hadn't bothered to do that. Why would she want one with a New York area code, making every call long-distance?

I glanced at the rearview mirror and realized I was driving well below the speed limit. Several trucks and cars were trapped behind me, not baying like hunting dogs on the scent of a fox with a limited life expectancy, but likely to run me off the road if given a chance. What's more, my minor field trip had put me at least half an hour behind schedule. I did not want to find Lieutenant Peter Rosen sitting on the porch when I returned. All I could do was hope the level of acrimony at the mayor's office had not yet reached its climax.

I raced through the grocery store, grabbing whatever caught my fancy and tossing it in the cart. I bought five steaks on the assumption Sara Louise might return, then added another in case Madison did, too. I toyed with taking my chances in the express lane, but I wasn't in the mood to be publicly harangued by potentially militant shoppers. I drummed my fingers on the cart handle, fumbled with my wallet when the time came, and refused the advances of a sacker whose primary goal seemed to be helping the elderly, disabled, and distracted with their groceries. After I'd stashed the bags in the backseat, I backed out, narrowly avoiding a car jockeying for dominance in the small but crowded domain, and drove to Dolly's house.

There were no vehicles in the driveway. I parked in front of the door and carried the groceries to the porch. The door was locked, so I shifted the bags until I could free a finger to push the doorbell. Corporal McTeer opened the door and immediately held out her arms to help me. As we went into the hall, I was startled to hear sultry Latino music from the den.

"Having a party?" I said as we headed for the kitchen.

"Nothing like that, ma'am. I put the padlock key on the table in the hall in case you need it later. And I want you to know I've been keeping an eye out for the media. A reporter and photographer from the local paper showed up, but I flashed my badge and warned them they were trespassing. Other than those two, nobody's come by. Sergeant Jorgeson called a few minutes ago to make sure everything was okay, and said to tell you the lieutenant would be here in an hour. A guy from a florist shop called to say he had more flowers to deliver. I told him to call later. Oh, and someone called from a print store to say that the brochures were ready to be picked up. Ms. Goforth must have a busy life."

"And I'm very sorry she's not here to deal with it," I said as I began to unload the groceries on the island. "But why the tango music?"

Corporal McTeer blushed. "I'm afraid it's partly my fault. Caron and Inez got to talking about the talent show at the mall, griping about how they didn't have a chance to win. I told 'em they most likely couldn't unless they came up with something really unique. I usually go watch, and every year it's the same flat-bellied teenaged girls wiggling their asses and trying to sing whatever's high on the pop charts. Most of them sound like starving piglets. I just pointed out that the judges are the same age as their parents. Not to be disrespectful, Ms. Malloy, but how much time do you spend watching MTV?"

"I don't even know what it is."

"That's what I told them. They kicked it around, then Inez saw the videotapes on the shelf. I don't know if they'll chicken out, but at the moment they're swooshing all over the room and having a fine time. If I should have kept my mouth shut, I'm sorry. At least they're not moping anymore."

"Oh, no," I said, "I think it's—well, interesting, and decidedly preferable to moping. And I owe you an apology for being gone so long."

"My shift's not over for another two hours, and this sure beats paperwork. Feel free to ask for me by name tomorrow if you need to run more errands."

"I certainly will." I assured her I could fend off the media for the remainder of the afternoon. She was reluctantly calling the police department for a ride as I went to the doorway to the den to see what progress Caron and Inez had made. The music was erotic, evoking images of alley cats in heat, circling each other in a stylized ritual with an obvious conclusion. I found myself in the murky area between being aghast and impressed. Inez was bent back so far that her hair brushed the rug, with an arm flung toward the ceiling. Caron was poised over her. I averted my eyes and looked at the TV screen, where the same scene was being reenacted by a black-haired woman in a scarlet gown and a man who surely moonlighted as a gigolo when not making instructional videos.

Caron spotted me. She mumbled something to Inez, who awkwardly stood up. Both of them stared as if I'd caught them filching cookies from the proverbial jar (or in this day and age, downloading essays concerning vengeful whales or doomed love). After a moment, Caron found the remote and turned off the VCR.

"Don't let me interrupt," I said. "I just thought I'd let you know I'm back."

Caron flopped down on the ottoman. "We were just fooling around. Dolly told us to help ourselves to the videos."

"We were getting bored with the gangster movies," added Inez.

"That's right," said Caron. "There's nothing worth watching on afternoon television. It was just something to do."

"For the talent show," I suggested mildly.

Caron rolled her eyes. "It's not like either of us is willing to get half naked and pretend to be a pop diva. That sort of thing is so juvenile. I mean, we'd have a better chance doing a taxidermy demonstration onstage."

"Not that we'd actually kill an animal," said Inez, appalled. "Too gross."

"Besides," Caron continued, having adopted verbosity as her best defense, "the tango has historical significance. Its origins were in brothels in the late nineteenth century in Argentina. It was considered vulgar until it became the fad in Paris in the 1920s. It's terribly symbolic of seduction and sexual—"

"I can see that," I said.

163

"We've already done the first video," Inez said. "It's really much easier than you might think, once you've mastered the tango close, the pivot turn, and the left open walk. We've about got down the dip and the flip, but the fan's tougher. Do you want to try any of it? It's all about the hip movement and the basic slow-slow-quick-quick-slow rhythm."

I noted her beaming expression. "You seem to have discovered a hidden talent, Inez."

"Not really," she protested, although without conviction. "I mean, Caron's pretty good at it, too. She's much more dramatic than I am."

Caron flopped onto the sofa. "No kidding. Peanut butter's more dramatic than you are, along with algebra homework, gym class, C-SPAN, and vanilla ice cream."

"Excuse me for being ever so drab," Inez shot back. "Why don't you call Rhonda and see if she wants another backup singer? That way you can wiggle and jiggle your way into stardom. You will let me wash your limo, won't you?"

"Now, girls," I intervened, reminding myself that they might also be in the throes of cabin fever, "as they say, it takes two to tango."

"Or tangle," Inez said sulkily.

Caron clutched a pillow. "But it only takes one to throw a temper tantrum. I was merely pointing out that I have a certain flair for interpretive dance."

"If falling on your butt when trying to master the left flick qualifies."

"At least my lips don't move the entire time."

I felt a pang of envy for those still wheeling carts past the produce counters, weighing potatoes and gravely examining apples for evidence of abuse. "I'm going to finish putting away the groceries, and then go out to the patio. I don't want to find smears of blood on the upholstery—okay?"

By the time I'd found a spot for the gorgonzola in a drawer in the refrigerator, folded the bags and put them in the pantry, and made myself a drink, I could hear tango music from the den.

And the doorbell.

And the telephone.

I did a very fine slow-slow-quick-quick-slow, with a flick and a flip, and what might have been a fan (as if I had any idea what any of that meant). I then banged down my drink, went out into the hall and picked up the receiver, said, "You're on hold, so think Mozart," dropped it on the table, and then opened the front door.

Cal was on the porch, grinning at me over an arrangement of frivolous spring blossoms. "Put them anywhere," I said to him, then went back to the table in the hall and randomly punched buttons on the black box before picking up the receiver and saying, "Claire Malloy, here to protect and serve."

Peter sounded bemused as he said, "You want Chinese?"

"No, I have steaks," I answered, relieved that it wasn't Dolly, a testy father, Don Corleone, Don Juan, Don Ho, the pool guy, or anyone else who would require diplomatic attentiveness. "Potatoes, salad, wine, all that stuff."

"Do I hear music?"

"After dinner, there will be ballroom dancing, so slick back your hair and wear your shiniest shoes."

"Is everything okay?"

"Everything's dandy, Peter. When shall we expect you?"

"Mozart?"

"Mozart had to cancel. Some sort of problem with his visa. Half an hour?"

Peter made a small noise, then said, "About half an hour, unless you want me to rent a tux on my way over."

"I thought all you rich dilettantes owned your own tuxes and diamond cufflinks. I will definitely have to rethink this marriage proposal. I'll see you shortly." I hung up, pushed the only buttons that weren't blinking, then turned around and smiled at Cal, who was hovering nearby, still holding the flower arrangement.

"You're sounding battier than a belfry," he said. "Guess you have a right to feel that way, but what the hell does Mozart have to do with it? Is that who was in the freezer?"

"I couldn't say. Do I need to sign something?"

Cal studied me. "What I think, Mrs. Claire Malloy, is that you need to sit down and have a sip of something soothing. You've got the worst caffeine buzz I've seen in years. I'm finished for the day, just dropping this off on my way home. Why don't we go in the kitchen and have a nice chat about flowers? You can even offer me a beer if you want. I'll bet there's all kinds of imported lagers and ales in one of those cabinets. I myself am more accustomed to whatever's on sale. My dog, though, he's real particular. He turns up his nose at all those so-called light beers. I keep telling him that if he wants the pricy stuff, then he needs to get himself a job as a guard dog."

I gestured at him to follow me into the kitchen. I found my untouched drink and sat down on a stool. "There are all sorts of beers on the bottom shelf of the refrigerator. Help yourself."

"Tough day?" he said as he opened the refrigerator and bent down.

It would have taken me more than half an hour to begin to describe it, so I settled for a sigh and said, "A very busy and confusing day. Did you find something to your liking?"

"Oh, yes." He closed the refrigerator door, then opened a bottle of some exotic beer and sat down across from me. "Well, at least you've got flowers. Flowers are cheerful and you don't even have to talk to them—unless you want to. Some folks do."

"While others prefer to talk to their dogs."

"I can assure you that I don't prefer to talk to the mangy hound, but he's the only one waiting for me when I get home." Cal took a drink of beer, then pointedly waited until I'd taken a swallow of my drink. "Feeling better?"

"I suppose," I said. "Who sent these flowers?"

"I don't know. My job is to deliver them."

I frowned. "The flowers that you brought this morning didn't have a card. Could it have fallen off in the van?"

"Maybe you have an anonymous admirer. Ever think of that?"

I scooted over the arrangement he'd brought and pawed through the petals, so to speak. "There's no card with these, either."

"Then you've got a real determined anonymous admirer. A few

166

years back, I delivered a dozen roses every blessed day for a month to a woman working in an insurance office. She pretended to be annoyed, but ol' Cal didn't buy that. She's probably married by now—and hoping she'll get a new vacuum cleaner on Valentine's Day."

"How very touching," I said, "but I'd like to know who's sending these. Who takes the orders at the florist shop?"

"The boss's wife, but it's after five. You can call her tomorrow. I tried to come by earlier, but you weren't here. I was just taking a chance on my way home." He took another drink. "I happened to drive by your bookstore this morning. There were police all over the place. Had some trouble, did you?"

I shrugged. "A vandal."

"Do you think it had anything to do with that body in the freezer?"

"It must have," I admitted for the first time. "Somebody's looking for something, but I don't know what it is. It must have to do with the mysterious Dolly Goforth. No one's tried to break in here, but I don't see how he could with all the activity during the day and the alarm at night."

Cal tugged on his nose. "It seems to me, and I'm no brilliant detective, that she's the one who needs to come forward and start explaining. Have you heard anything at all from her?"

"She called earlier, but I don't know where she is. I'm also beginning to acknowledge that I don't know *who* she is, either. She led me to believe that she was a rich widow, but she doesn't own this house or the furnishings. She signed a six-month lease. She has no history. Well, she does have a history, but I don't know how much of it is true." I put down my glass. "The man in the freezer was some sort of hoodlum from Brooklyn, for pity's sake. They obviously knew each other. I don't know any hoodlums from Brooklyn or anyplace else. Do you? I mean, what sort of person knows hoodlums from Brooklyn?"

"Calm down," said Cal. "You might be amazed at who all you know. You don't demand résumés and detailed autobiographies from your customers at the bookstore, do you? Maybe this hoodlum was a distant cousin, or even someone she sat next to on an airplane. We bump into all kinds of people while we're ambling along. My nephew's son is doing time for second-degree homicide. Not my fault. I got an old army buddy who lives in a shack in Wyoming and has more guns than your basic battalion. Not my fault. Some guy comes in your store, buys a book, and then you find out he's a serial killer. You supposed to take responsibility for that?"

"Not if he bought a book on how to build a better bluebird house. But if he wanted a book on body decomposition or how deep to dig a grave, maybe I would."

"If you don't mind a personal remark, Mrs. Malloy, you're sounding real weird. That boyfriend of yours is coming over, right? The two of you are going to tango?"

I realized my hands had been flitting like deranged moths and put them in my lap. "I appreciate your tactfulness, Cal. I'm agitated, but I'll get over it. It seems as though all day long the world's been beating a path to my door—and I don't know why. Dolly Goforth was a customer, not a confidante. I don't know where she is or why she left the way she did. If I hadn't had a rat in my apartment, I'd be sitting on my own sofa, drinking tea and reading a novel. My daughter and her friend would be having a pizza with their friends." I paused for a moment. "Well, that's not true. They'd be at the computer lab at the campus trying to hire a hitman on the Internet."

Beer spewed out of his mouth, just like in a movie. "A what?"

"Metaphorically speaking," I said as I handed him a paper napkin and tried not to giggle as he mopped his chin. A giggle would be dangerous, in that it might evolve into hysterical laughter and a total loss of what little control I still had. Hercule Poirot never giggled, I told myself sternly, and Miss Marple would never allow herself to stoop to unseemly behavior. "They've moved on to mastering the intricacies of the tango. Tomorrow one of them may launch a campaign for Congress."

He glanced in the direction of the den. "But a hitman . . . ?"

"They're annoyed, but undaunted." I looked at my watch. "Thanks for bringing the flowers, Cal. My boyfriend, as you call him, is on his way. I would like to call the shop tomorrow and find out who's sending the flowers. I couldn't make out the name on your van."

"Aunt Bessie's Bloomers," he said, sounding abashed. "Do whatever you want, but I think you ought to just enjoy the flowers and stop worrying about who's sending them. It never hurts to have a little mystery in your life."

If only that was all I had, I thought as I let him out the front door and watched him drive away. If only I hadn't found a body in the freezer.

If only I hadn't seen the damn rat.

Chapter Eleven

I was sitting on the patio when Peter showed up. For the record, he was wearing neither shiny shoes nor a tuxedo and diamond cuff-links, but I forgave him and participated in an agreeable, if not passionate, kiss.

"Pour yourself a glass of something," I suggested.

"Are you aware that Caron and Inez are stalking across the den, each with an arm outstretched, clutching hands, and glaring defiantly at the wall?"

"Is that to be construed as an accusation of motherly malfeasance?"

He shook his head, went back in the house, and reappeared shortly with a glass of something that looked very much like scotch. He sat down next to me. "So you were serious about the ballroom dancing? Shall I call Jorgeson? He and his wife did a mean rhumba at the Christmas office party."

"I'm too tired to explain," I said. "How was your afternoon?"

"On a scale of one to ten? When I was obliged to take algebra, I never quite accepted the concept of negative numbers. I applied all the formulas, solved the equations, and slithered by with a passing grade. Now I know better."

I let my head fall back. "If you want sympathy, I can give you the home telephone number of a really nice guy who works for a florist shop. Have you been sending me flowers?"

Peter caught my hand. "Should I have been?"

"Probably, but someone's already beat you to it. I'm keeping all of them on the dining room table so I won't be tempted to talk to them."

"I assumed they were silk, and Dolly's doing. My mother has arrangements like that all over her house. The maids dust them twice a month."

"Then you'd better watch out, Don Juan," I said, "because I've got an anonymous admirer. When's the last time you gave me anything more romantic than an egg roll?"

"I let you have the extra packet of soy sauce. Would you have preferred a diamond-encrusted wedding ring?"

The conversation was moving into an uncomfortable area. I slipped my hand out of his and reached for my drink. "Any news from Brooklyn?"

"Quite a lot, actually. Petrolli Mordella, known as Petti to his friends, lived in a brownstone in Flatbush. According to his neighbors, he was an Italian gentleman of impeccable manners and old-world charm who helped elderly women with their packages, played bingo at the parish hall, and bought gelatos for the children on Sunday afternoons. According to the precinct detectives, he was a low-ranking member of the Velocchio family."

"The what?" I gurgled, nearly dropping my glass.

"The Velocchio family, as in the Mafia. Drug trafficking, prostitution, sanitation, union busting, bribery—the usual things. Is there something you'd like to share?"

I was grateful that I was sitting down, thereby saving myself from months of rehabilitation and physical therapy. "Remember Madison— the girl who was staying here until she left yesterday? Her father works for an antiques gallery called Velocchio and Associates. It's in Manhattan."

"And the reason you know this is . . . ?"

I wondered if I could sink any farther into the chair, or slither out of it and crawl under a shrub. "I called him this afternoon. I had no idea he . . . well, he . . ."

"Might be affiliated with the Mafia?"

"That truly never crossed my mind. He was rude, but I didn't—"

"Why did you call him?"

"I called him because I thought he should know about Madison. Maybe I was hoping he'd say that she'd turned up at home or called to tell him she was on her way to Europe. I shouldn't have, but I felt like something had to be done." I took a deep breath, as no doubt errant Catholics did before entering the confessional. "And I thought he might tell me about Bibi and Dolly."

Peter gazed coldly at me. "Were you planning to mention this to me?"

"I tried to call you earlier, but you were at the mayor's office," I said truthfully. "I knew you were coming by later."

"This was a trivial bit of information that could wait until after dinner?"

I opted to go on the defensive, at least for the moment. "If I had known that Petti was a member of some Mafia family, I would have realized the significance and sent the Mounties thundering to city hall. I just thought I was talking to a brusque businessman. Was I supposed to think his business included drugs and prostitution, along with Louis the Fourteenth armoires? I may be perceptive, but I am not clairvoyant."

"No, you're Claire Malloy. Your name came up at the meeting several times. The chief wants me to haul you in as a material witness. The prosecutor's combing his files in case you have an unpaid parking ticket or a library fine. The mayor is sending inspectors to the bookstore to make sure it's not a fire hazard."

"What a bunch of grumpy old men," I muttered. "However, since you're neither grumpy nor old, I suppose I can tell you the gist of the conversation with Madison's father, as well of that with Sara Louise's father. He called from Hong Kong, by the way. The reception was remarkably good. If there were water buffalo rumbling in nearby rice paddies, I couldn't hear them."

"Have you totally lost your mind?"

I took my time while I pondered his question. At the moment, the polls would not be in my favor. I would not have received a vote of confidence in the House of Commons. I most certainly would not have been nominated for the Supreme Court, or even allowed to sit in the visitors' gallery. "I may be crumpling under the stress," I said at last, hoping I wasn't speaking gibberish. "I do believe my reaction is justified, however. I can either burrow under the gazebo or relate the conversations as best I can. Your choice."

Peter might have preferred to call for men in white coats, but he pulled himself together and said, "Did you happen to tape any of these conversations?"

"I did not," I said with what I felt was admirable aplomb. "I have yet to be seduced by technology." Before he could respond, I proceeded to tell him every last detail that I remembered of my conversations with both fathers, and then embellished them with my impressions.

He was not impressed, alas. "How did you get Hayes's number?"

"The same way that you should have. I looked through her purse and found his business card in her wallet. Her home address is in Sands Point. Is that anywhere near Flatbush?"

"Geographically, yes. Socially and economically, they're not even on the same planet. The per capita income of any resident of Sands Point is apt to be larger than the gross national product of a Caribbean nation."

"What about Bedford, Connecticut?" I asked.

"What about it?"

"I'm pretty sure that's where Sara Louise is from. Is it comparable to Sands Point?"

"In that league, yes. Why do you think that's where Sara Louise is from? Did her father mention it when he called?"

"It's the address of the pharmacy where she got the pain pills. Madison told me that after they left the emergency room, they drove all over Farberville looking for a place to get the prescription filled. If they really went to the emergency room, that is. They may have realized they were in danger of being evicted, and used the assault as a means to exaggerate Sara Louise's symptoms and play on my sympathy."

"I'll look into it," said Peter. "Hospitals are reluctant to give out any information about patients, so we may have to get a court order. Their story about her car is true, though. It did have to be towed in because the key was snapped off in the ignition. The garage owner's having a hard time locating another switch because of all the anti-theft devices. There aren't a lot of Maserati dealerships between the coasts."

"Which they knew perfectly well. I can't see either of them crawling under the car to disable it, or tossing random parts in a ditch. Breaking off the key was tidy and painless, and could be attributed to carelessness. Maybe they weren't confident that Dolly would be delighted to see them, so they created a situation in which she might feel as though she ought to take them in. A variation of the emaciated kitten on the porch. It worked with me, and I'm not nearly as kind-hearted as Dolly."

Peter stood up and took my glass. "I need to make a few calls, then I'll freshen these and we can continue. Who knows what other tidbits you've conveniently failed to pass along?"

"Such as my shopping list?"

I followed him inside and went to the doorway of the den. Although Caron and Inez were hardly ready to take on the competitors in the Catskills, they appeared to be making progress. I was surprised to hear Inez hissing orders, and even more surprised that Caron was responding to them. It was the antithesis of their typical modus operandi. But if one were to judge proficiency by the degree of confidence, Inez had found an entirely new niche to display her heretofore unseen talent. Where it might lead her was problematic, of course, since competitive ballroom dancing might not prove to be a lucrative career.

Inez caught Caron before she toppled over backwards, then said to me, "Do you think it's okay if we look around for peacock feathers and rhinestone tiaras?"

Caron's face was flushed, from either embarrassment or exertion. "There are some dress boxes on a shelf in the closet. We really don't have time to make costumes. The next time Dolly calls, you can ask her if she minds if we borrow some things."

"If it doesn't slip my mind," I said. "Have you selected the music?"

"Not yet," said Inez, neatly cutting off Caron. "We can't use any-thing on the how-to videos because of the instructor's voice. We found a tape made at some hotel, but the dancers are all old and the music's kind of tame."

"Whoever was in charge probably didn't want anybody to have a stroke," Caron said. "Some of them looked like they'd been smuggled out of nursing homes. We need something with shock value, as well as class."

"I can't help you," I said. "Go ahead and see what you can find to use for costumes, but understand that you'll have to get Dolly's per-mission. They may be of sentimental value."

Caron gave me an offended look. "It's not like we're going to steal them. I can't see myself at the prom with peacock feathers stick-ing out of my hair. If I even go to the prom, which isn't likely to hap-pen unless I hire someone from the next state. We're going to make total fools of ourselves at the talent show. Nobody will even talk to us at school. We might as well take baloney sandwiches and eat lunch under the bleachers in the old gym. Rhonda Maguire will be elected senior class president and assign us to the concession stand at the prom. I'll get terrible grades and end up at a vocational school, learn-ing how to be a welder. Some fat slob named Bubba will be my only hope of getting married, even though it means living with his tooth-less parents and his three frumpy sisters. You won't recognize me af-ter I gain fifty pounds and bleach my hair."

"Oh dear," I murmured, "that does sound bleak."

Inez stuck out what little chin she had. "I think it sounds dumb. We'll win the talent show, and when school starts, everybody will still be talking about how creative we were. We'll give lessons during gym class. Rhonda can be on the cleanup committee after the prom."

"At which time you'll be swept up by a dashing gaucho on a black stallion, and the two of you will ride off across the pampas at sunset," said Caron. "I can hardly wait to see that."

"Adios, girls," I said. "I'll turn on the grill and start dinner in about an hour. In the meantime, Peter and I will be on the patio."

"What about Sara Louise?" asked Caron. "Are we supposed to

wait to eat until she waltzes back in? I think you should report the car as stolen."

I returned to the patio and sat down near Peter, who was stretched out on a lounge chair. "Caron thinks Sara Louise should be nailed for grand theft auto."

"You told her she could use the car and gave her the keys, and she's only been gone for a few hours. I think she went off to meet Madison for some screwy reason. Unfortunately, we don't have a clue where she's been holed up all this time."

"Did you trace Madison's calls?"

"Yes, but with a curious lack of success. She used a cell phone, but there's a security block on it. We can't access the number, the account, or the location. It's as if she's calling from an alternate universe. Two of my men are trying to get information from the feds, but they haven't had any luck. They keep getting transferred to different departments, put on hold, and then disconnected. They are not happy."

"That is curious," I said. "Wouldn't the FBI cooperate with you if they were behind it?"

"The FBI doesn't have to brake for local and state law enforcement agencies. The only time we hear from them is when they want something from us. They do not reciprocate. When I left the office, my men were on their way out to buy a Ouija board in hopes of channeling J. Edgar Hoover. But this doesn't mean the FBI blocked the cell phone account. There are plenty of other intelligence agencies with the capability, including ones we've never heard of."

I raised my eyebrows. "It's hard to imagine Madison working for some top-secret British counterintelligence office."

"All I can say is that it's piqued our interest and we're working on it," said Peter. "We had better luck with the call from Dolly. Mordella's cell phone again, this time from Miami. She's obviously using false identity documents. We did get the passenger lists of all the flights out of the Farberville airport that afternoon, and we have the names of the women who were flying alone. There were no matches from Dallas or

Memphis to Atlanta, or out of Atlanta to Miami. What's more, she changed her appearance at the Farberville airport, so we don't have a description. Airport security personnel can't pull aside every woman traveling by herself. We don't have a strong enough case to issue a warrant for her arrest."

"She didn't kill Petti," I said, then bit my lip.

Peter scowled at me. "You have proof?"

"According to the waitress at the Cardinal Café, he was—"

"The Cardinal Café?"

This was not going well. I took a breath and said, "The owner of the Fritz Motel told me that—"

"You went to the Fritz Motel?"

"If you insist on interrupting me like this, we won't have dinner until the mosquitoes have gone to bed. When you feel able to control yourself, I'll tell you what you should already know from reading your detectives' reports. It's possible they didn't hear about the private investigator—"

"The what?"

"I give up. Why don't you try to relax while I make a salad and put the potatoes in the oven? I strongly suggest you do not go in the den, where an uncivil war is revving up. Perhaps a few languid laps in the pool might help. Did you bring a suit?"

"Just tell me what you learned this afternoon while you were supposedly at the grocery store."

"I was at the grocery store. Do you think the salad and potatoes came from a vegetable garden next to the garage?"

His teeth were so tightly clenched that I could see a nerve twitching along his jaw. "I'm waiting," he managed to say.

"As long as you don't interrupt," I said, then repeated the conversations with the motel owner and the waitress. "Therefore," I went on blithely, "Dolly couldn't have shot Petti. There simply wasn't time. Someone else must have lured him out of the motel room and killed him after breakfast, and then left the body behind the gazebo. I suppose it was meant to frighten Dolly."

Peter walked across the patio and turned on the grill. It occurred to me that he might continue around the corner of the garage, get in his car, and leave, so I was pleased when he came back to the lounge chair. "If Petti didn't tell his killer that she was leaving town."

"If Petti knew. She may have lied and told him she'd call him the following day. We don't know if they were friends. He could have come here to blackmail her. She gave him some money the first night, and promised to pay him the rest of it after the banks opened in the morning."

"And why was he blackmailing her?"

I gazed at a bird silhouetted on a power line. "I do believe that's a scissor-tailed flycatcher. Inez says they're rare in residential areas." When he failed to express appreciation for one of nature's more whimsical designs, I crossed my arms and said, "Sara Louise's father said Dolly had been married to several other men of dubious morals. Maybe Petti was one of them. He could have threatened to expose her."

"Expose her to whom? Dolly wasn't in a heated political race or nominated for a Nobel Prize. She wasn't even a local celebrity. If she had been married to him, it was a very long time ago—and he wasn't exactly a kingpin of organized crime. Very few of Farberville's elites could withstand intense scrutiny of their indiscretions, past or present. They have walk-in closets to store the skeletons."

"How about this? In her youth, Dolly had a psychotic episode and went on a cross-country killing spree, slaughtering CEOs from Bangor to Burbank. She was captured and locked away in a high-security mental facility. When she was released, she was given a new identity to protect her from media scrutiny. Petti tracked her down and told her he would go to the tabloids if she didn't pay him off."

Peter's smile was almost evil. "Was it only this morning that you were categorizing her as a candidate for beatification and eventual sainthood? Kind, generous to a fault, dedicated, and so forth? Did you politely overlook her history as a demented serial killer? You can't serve both devil's food and angel food cake at teatime, Miss Marple."

"I guess not," I conceded crossly, "and that doesn't explain the

178

peculiar connections with Velocchio and Associates. Dolly was married to Bibi, who's been described as an old family friend. I assumed 'family' meant aunts and uncles and jolly cousins, but I may have been wrong."

"The Velocchios may not compare to the Partridges or the Brady Bunch, but there is a family reunion of sorts planned for next week. A federal judge is convening a secret grand jury to examine their finances. Of course, after subpoenas were issued two weeks ago, it wasn't much of a secret. The patriarch has taken to shuffling around his neighborhood in a bathrobe and slippers."

"A bathrobe and slippers?" I asked. "Shouldn't he be shopping for a new suit?"

"It's in preparation for a plea of diminished mental capacity. 'Ladies and gentlemen of the jury, how could this addled old man who reeks of urine and cat food possibly be aware of the hundreds of millions of dollars being laundered overseas? He can't find his way home from the newsstand on the corner.' It's considered a tradition in this situation. If it doesn't sway the jury, then he'll stage a heart attack in the witness box to delay the process."

"Did Dolly receive a subpoena?"

"I was told there were no women on the list. It's not an equal-opportunity profession."

I nodded. "It wouldn't be, would it? Most women prefer to explore options and seek compromises instead of gunning each other down in the street. Besides, it's difficult to imagine a wife asking hubby to take the kids to school because she has to pick up the dry cleaning, stop by the bank, have lunch with a friend, beat somebody senseless with a baseball bat, hijack a truck, and be home in time to start dinner."

Peter did not seem to have a ready response. After a moment, he said, "You have to admit that the timing is curious. Petti, Madison, and Sara Louise all came to Farberville within a few days after the subpoenas were issued. It would be helpful to know why." He picked up his glass and shook it gently to make the ice cubes bobble and clink. "It would also be helpful to know Dolly's real name, as well as

Bibi's. Unsurprisingly, no one with the last name of Goforth died in New York State in the last five years. I may end up having to fly to New York to persuade the prosecutor's office to cooperate with us. My mother will insist on meeting me at the Savoy so we can attend whatever opera's being staged at the Met. She'll invite my ex-wife to meet us for cocktails, who'll drone for an hour about the challenge of squeaking by on half a million dollars a year. All because you overreacted to one dinky rat in your kitchen." He pulled me to my feet and put his arms around me. After a few minutes of adult interaction of a somewhat intimate nature, he said, "Let's forget about all this. Would you care to tango in the moonlight?"

"Your invitation would be irresistible were there not mushrooms waiting to be sliced and hearts of endive begging to be tossed in balsamic vinegar and extra-virgin olive oil. You're welcome to find out if Caron and Inez would like a constructive critique of their progress."

"You haven't explained why they've taken up the tango. The last time I was here, they were obsessed with Bibi's extensive collection of old mobster movies."

"Considering his family ties, he probably thought of them as documentaries," I said, leading him toward the sliding glass doors. "If you care to come in the kitchen, I will explain why Caron and Inez are flipping and fanning in the living room. The origins lie in whatever section of the U.S. Constitution deals with the electoral process and the evolution of the two-party system."

We ate dinner on the patio. Peter entertained the girls by encouraging them to talk about Latin American dances and music, and suggested they might be able to find costumes at a consignment store. I smiled and nodded on cue, but I had a hard time preventing myself from speculating about all the relationships that kept leading back to the Velocchio spiderweb. Was Dolly a black widow, a brown recluse, or merely a hapless fly that had been trapped? Had Petti been a benevolent old friend, or a ruthless blackmailer?

The phone rang as we were carrying dishes into the kitchen. I was about to pick up the receiver when Peter nudged me aside, pushed what I presumed were the appropriate buttons on the black box, then gestured for me to go ahead. By now I was prepared for it to be anyone except the pope, but I mustered what enthusiasm I could and said, "Hello?"

"This is Jorgeson, Ms. Malloy. Is the lieutenant there?"

I handed the receiver to Peter. "Don't say anything you might not want to be recorded for posterity," I said, then continued into the kitchen. Caron and Inez had the situation under control, although their display of altruism might be motivated not by selflessness but by the need to borrow money in order to purchase discarded promwear for their performance. I hoped Inez's mother would return in time to sew on sequins and satin rosebuds. I have yet to master the art of threading a needle.

Peter came to the door. "I need to leave," he said, his face grim. "Make sure you lock all the doors and windows, and set the alarm as soon as I'm gone."

I backed him into the hall. "What's happened?"

"We just had a report of a body at the country club." He held up his hand. "The witness was too distraught to add any more to that, so we don't even know the gender. Under normal circumstances, I'd wait until the patrol officers followed it up, but I think I'd better get up there as soon as possible."

I sank down on the bottom step. "Who do you think it is?"

"I don't have a clue. It could be a retiree who became disoriented after leaving the clubhouse, or a thief planning to break into the pro shop. It doesn't necessarily have anything to do with the Velocchio mess."

"Will you call me later?"

He started for the front door. "I'll call you when I can. That may not be until the morning, so don't sit there all night. Lock up, set the alarm, and watch a movie with Caron and Inez."

After he was gone, I numbly locked all the doors and made sure the windows were secured, then went into the kitchen to confirm that the door that led to the garage was still locked. Caron and Inez trailed after me as I returned to the hall and turned on the alarm.

"Why'd Peter leave?" asked Caron.

Aware that my voice was unsteady, I told them what he'd told me, which wasn't much. "Please don't ask me if it's Madison, Sara Louise, or Petti Mordella."

Inez blinked at me. "Who's Petti Mordella?"

I realized no one had given them any information all day. I'd been too frazzled to talk to them after they were delivered home from the police department. By the time I'd calmed down, a parade of people had appeared on the porch. Now I wasn't sure how they'd react to the inclusion of mobsters.

"May I remind you that we are no longer children?" said Caron, her lower lip quivering. "If you won't tell us, I'll find somebody who will—even if we have to climb out of an upstairs window."

"I don't think we should go upstairs," said Inez. "What if there's somebody hiding up there?"

"Just because the downstairs windows are locked doesn't mean we're safe," Caron added. She swiped at her eyes, which were rapidly turning red. "Anyone could grab a brick and break the glass. Sure, the alarm would go off, but there aren't any police officers parked in the driveway, in case you didn't notice. We'll have bullet holes in our foreheads by the time they arrive."

"Okay," I said, "let's not get carried away. If you want the whole story, I'll make tea and we'll sit down in the den. I'll do my best to tell you everything I can. You have to agree not to interrupt me, though."

They managed to stay quiet during most of my recitation. When I finally sat back, Caron said, "Sheesh, no wonder that you've looked so frazzled all day. Maybe you should be drinking brandy. Do you want me to get you a glass?"

I smiled as best I could. "No, thank you, dear."

"I'm confused," said Inez, her face puckered like that of a lapdog. "This Velocchio family is in New York. Petti worked for them. Did Bibi, too?"

"It seems likely. He was described as an old family friend, and I don't think they associate with outsiders. Well, I suppose they have to, to some extent, but they couldn't relax with someone who might be shocked at an inadvertent remark and go running to the authorities."

"Yeah," Caron said. "Al Capone didn't exactly grill hamburgers for the neighbors."

Inez was gnawing on her lip. "If Bibi was their accountant and married Dolly, she must have figured out what was going on. But he died a year ago and she came down here. When Uncle Hoover died, Aunt Sophie sold the house, the furniture, both cars, and the dogs, then moved to Florida. Nobody's heard from her since then."

"Is that supposed to mean something?" said Caron. "Should we try to persuade the police to put out an APB for a screwy old lady living in a coconut tree?"

"My mother thinks she moved to one of those retirement homes for sexually active singles," Inez said coldly.

"That's disgusting," Caron countered. She glanced at me, then turned back to Inez. "Old people don't have sex. They sit around the pool and compare varicose veins and liver spots."

I put down my cup with enough vigor to get their attention. "I'm going upstairs. I will carefully look under my bed before I climb into it and read. The two of you may sleep down here if you'll feel safer." I left the cup on the table and stood up, considering the wisdom of Caron's recommendation of brandy. "If the doorbell rings, don't answer it."

"What if it's Sara Louise or Madison?" said Caron.

"Then she can wait on the porch until I come downstairs to let her in."

Inez looked up at me. "But they're part of this Velocchio family, aren't they? I don't think we should trust them, Ms. Malloy. What if one of them shot Petti?"

At least she'd posed a question I could answer. "The police checked out their story. They were in a tow truck when you found his body by the gazebo."

"Well, somebody shot him," said Caron. "Who was it, then?"

"That seems to be the crux of the problem, doesn't it? If you want to play music, keep the volume low so that you'll hear the sound of glass breaking."

"That is so Not Funny."

"I have to agree with you," I said. "I'm going to take the receiver upstairs with me in case Peter calls. Goodnight."

Once upstairs, I resisted the urge to take a tiny peek under the bed or inside the closet. I changed into nightwear and followed the customary rituals in the bathroom. As I climbed into bed, I could hear tango music, but it wasn't loud enough to disturb me. The vicar, however, failed to engage me. I finally put the book on the bedside table and went over to the window to look down at the patio. Not a creature was stirring within the light cast from inside the house. The shadows beyond the pale were black. The conic roof of the gazebo gave it the look of a private mausoleum in an old cemetery. Did the Velocchios have a family vault, a sanctuary in which to bury the bodies alongside their secrets? Whoever had killed Petti was in no hurry to give him a proper send-off, obviously.

I realized that I could not fall asleep until I shook off my macabre thoughts. My best hope might lie in a drop of brandy and one of Dolly's travel books from the bookcase in the living room. Surely looking at photographs of Amazon wildlife would distract me. I might find recipes for piranha potpies and deep-fried tapir tails. Rather than lie awake all night wondering if I'd incurred the wrath of notorious New York mobsters, I could worry about where to find the necessary ingredients. I'd never noticed packages of fresh piranha at my grocery store, but I'd never really looked. I could change my name, move to California, and open a restaurant. Caron and Inez would be my dancing waitresses. We would all wear brightly colored skirts made of handwoven cotton and pretend to speak Portuguese.

I went downstairs and into the living room, where I found a book I'd sold Dolly a few weeks earlier. Caron and Inez had found more tango music and were squawking at each other about who'd stepped on whose toes first. I went to the kitchen for brandy, and was on my way upstairs to mentally decorate my café with wood carvings and other native paraphernalia when the doorbell rang.

The brandy glass slipped out of my hand, rolled down the carpet steps, and shattered on the tile floor of the hall. The tango music stopped.

"Who is it?" called Caron.

"Don't answer it," added Inez.

Déjà vu all over again, or for those slightly more fluent in French than Portuguese, déjà vieux.

"It's probably Peter," I called back, frowning at the shards of glass that glinted like piscine teeth. I hadn't bothered to put on bedroom slippers. Even if I were inclined to answer the door, I had a bit of a predicament.

Caron came out of the den. "What if it's not Peter?"

"Yeah," said Inez, hovering behind Caron. "What if it's somebody else?"

The doorbell rang again.

185

Chapter Twelve

Just a minute!" I shouted in the direction of the front door, then told Caron and Inez to find a broom and a dustpan in the pantry. Neither of them looked enthusiastic, but they did as told and cleared a path for me to come downstairs. One stood behind me with the broom raised, the other with the dustpan, as I opened the door a scant inch.

"Oh, Claire!" said Lucy Hood. "Thank goodness you're okay! Daniel and I have been so worried about you. I don't want to tell you what went through my mind while we waited out here. Daniel thought he should call 911."

"She thought I should, anyway," said Daniel. "I said you were likely to be in the bathroom. Do you mind if we come inside?"

I gestured to my bodyguards to back off, then opened the door. "Why have you been so worried about me? I've been right here all evening."

Lucy glanced at Caron and Inez. "Then you don't know what happened? Is there somewhere we can talk privately?"

"Let's go in the living room." I knew perfectly well that the girls would be able to hear everything from the den, saving me the bother of having to repeat it. "May I offer you something?"

Daniel held Lucy's arm as he steered her toward the living room. "Would you mind if we had some brandy? Lucy's so shaky that I was afraid she was going to pass out on me while we were waiting outside. She's always been emotional."

She shot him an annoyed look, then laughed and said, "Daniel's always been one to exaggerate. When he had a minor sinus infection last year, he insisted that I take him to Walter Reed so they could rule out a brain tumor. To this day, he still believes it was encephalitis."

"Do allow me to fetch the brandy, Mother," said Caron, stopping short of a curtsy. "Inez, will you be so kind as to assist me in the kitchen?"

Lucy studied them as they left the room. "What nicely behaved girls. Most of the teenagers these days are incredibly boorish. I simply cannot shop at any of the malls anymore."

I waited until they settled on the sofa, then said, "So why were you so worried? As I said, I've been here all evening."

"Because of the body, of course," she said.

"The body?" I echoed.

"Up at the country club," said Daniel. "Don't you know about it?"

"I know that a body was found there earlier, but that's all I know." An unappealing image of Petti lying spread-eagled on the eighteenth green, his spectacles glinting in the moonlight, flashed through my mind.

Lucy poked Daniel. "See? I told you we needed to come over here." She gave me a solicitous look. "I'm appalled that the police haven't seen fit to inform you, considering your involvement. There should be a patrol car parked outside. Daniel, we really must complain to the police commissioner about this."

Caron appeared with a tray holding a decanter and three snifters. Inez carried a plate with an artistic splay of wafers. Silently, they placed their offerings on the coffee table in front of the sofa, gave us a little wave, and vanished into the den. It was an interesting presentation of indecipherable motivation, I concluded as Daniel splashed brandy into the snifters and distributed them.

"You haven't really explained anything," I pointed out.

"I suppose we haven't," said Lucy as she fortified herself with a sip. "I need to start at the beginning. We had a barbecue this evening, as you know. Very informal, just a dozen or so of the people in the nearby condos. After they left, Daniel and I decided to take a stroll. We were in the vicinity of the clubhouse when we saw blue lights of several police vehicles and an ambulance."

"On the service road behind the building where they keep the golf carts," added Daniel. "We wandered over to get a better look. There were police officers with flashlights crawling all over the area, looking for evidence. When we got closer, we saw a body being removed from a red Mercedes."

Lucy smiled. "Your lieutenant was there, giving orders. He's quite handsome, isn't he? That photograph in the newspaper did him an injustice."

"Whose body?" I asked, refusing to be distracted.

"The girl with the long dark hair," said Daniel. "We didn't dare get too close, but from what was being said, it sounded as though she'd been shot in the head. Instead of putting her on a gurney and rushing her away in the ambulance, they zipped her up in a body bag. Guess that says it all."

I put down the snifter. "Could it have been suicide?"

He shrugged. "I don't know, but I had the impression the officers were looking for the weapon."

"And the car key, I heard one of them say," said Lucy. "Why would she park on the service road, throw away the key, and then shoot herself? How far could she throw the gun after she'd shot herself in the head? I think it's obvious someone killed her."

I was too stunned to debate postmortem possibilities. Sara Louise Santini claimed to have come to Farberville on a lark, but it hadn't been much fun. She'd been assaulted, then murdered. Petti Mordella had not fared well, either. It seems probable that Madison Hayes might meet the same fate, if she hadn't already. Dolly had been wise to leave town. I wondered if Caron, Inez, and I should do the same, if only up the road a few miles to Waverly, where we could stay in a cheap motel and watch Silkie simper on the local news.

"Let me get you some more brandy," said Daniel, rising.

188

"No, I'm fine," I said, although I wasn't. I'd spoken to her father only a few hours earlier and casually implied she'd wandered off on an errand. He, and presumably her mother, were expecting her to call. I'd left the same message for Caron at Inez's house too many times to count. Caron hadn't always called back, but Sara Louise never would. I went over and stared blindly at the neat rows of books on a shelf by the doorway. Without turning around, I said, "Sara Louise was young and terribly arrogant, but she was brought up with too much money. She had prestigious degrees and was ready to take on the financial world from her corner office in her father's company. Her newly decorated corner office, that is. Still, there might have been a twinge of humanity under her designer clothes or in the glove compartment of her Maserati. Someday she might have used some of her wealth to build a hospital in a Third World country."

Lucy's eyes welled with tears. "I know this is a terrible shock for you, Claire, but you have a responsibility to take care of yourself and your girls. You should demand twenty-four-hour protection by the police."

"And that's a damn shame," said Daniel. "All you did was volunteer to house-sit. Dolly Goforth needs to come forward and explain all this before someone else gets killed. As far as I'm concerned, she's just as culpable for these murders as the person who pulled the trigger—or more so. She must have had some idea of what was going to happen, or she wouldn't have taken off like she did. Does Lieutenant Rosen have any clue where she's hiding?"

"Miami, as of this afternoon," I said.

Lucy came over to clutch my hand. "Miami? Didn't you say she was in Dallas?" She squeezed my hand more tightly. "You have to think, Claire. You've known her for six months. Did she ever mention anyone in Miami, like an acquaintance or a relative in a retirement community? If you can come up with a name, I'll call Information and try to get a telephone number for you. Daniel and I have some friends who moved there several years ago. They might be able to help."

My fingers were throbbing. Before they could split like hot dogs in boiling water, I removed her hand and stood up. "She never mentioned anything about Miami. I'm sure Lieutenant Rosen is using all of his resources to find her, and eventually he will."

Daniel pulled Lucy to her feet. "Come along, dear. There's nothing more we can do."

"But I'm still worried about you," Lucy said to me, looking as if she might fling her body over mine to save me from shrapnel, should a hand grenade be lobbed through a window. "There could be somebody hiding in the backyard and watching everything that goes on inside. Would you like Daniel and me to stay here with you? We wouldn't be much use if someone attempted to break into the house, but at least it would make it seem like there are a lot of people here. The presence of a male always helps, too. That's not to say Daniel could go one-on-one with an assailant, but someone might think twice before charging inside."

I shook my head resolutely. "It's kind of you to offer, but I have no reason to think anyone will bother us. The gate is padlocked and there are patrol cars in the area. Now that Lieutenant Rosen has identified the victim, it's likely he will assign a couple of officers to watch the house." I moved toward the door, hoping they'd take the unsubtle hint. "I can assure you that the girls and I are perfectly safe. Thank you for coming by."

"I just don't like it," said Lucy, doing her best to dig her heels in the Oriental rug. "I could have Gary come over and stay with you. I'm sure he won't mind sleeping on a lounge chair on the patio."

"We'll be fine." I opened the door and waited until Daniel had propelled her to the hall. My hand twitched, but I restrained myself from applying it forcefully to her back. "Thank you for coming by," I repeated, although less cordially.

"Come on," Daniel said, holding Lucy's elbow. "When we get back to the condo, you can bake more brownies."

She made a grab for my hand, but I put it behind my back. "Well, I suppose so, but I feel uncomfortable about leaving you and the girls by yourself. Will you promise to call us if you hear anything suspicious?

We can be here in fifteen minutes. Let me find something to write the number on. Daniel, do you have a pen?"

Daniel pulled her out to the porch. "Goodnight, Claire."

"Goodnight," I said, then closed the door and locked it. I switched the alarm back on, then went into the living room to peek out a window until they left. If Lucy had her way, it was possible I might discover her, Daniel, and Gary camped out on the patio the following morning, along with a small detachment of retirees armed with golf clubs and fondue forks.

"What a pair of loons," Caron said as she and Inez came into the room. "When did they appoint themselves your guardian angels?"

I sighed. "Yesterday morning. They're only trying to be helpful. Did you hear what they said about Sara Louise being found in the Mercedes?"

Caron's face began to crumple. "This is scary, Mother. First that man—Petti whatever—and now her. She was pretty nasty, but still . . ."

"What does it mean, Ms. Malloy?" asked Inez, her glasses so fogged up that her eyes were indistinct. "Are you sure no one is going to break into the house? Maybe we should go to a motel, after all." She looked over her shoulder at the den. "There are so many windows here. Somebody could be watching us right now."

"I understand how you feel," I said. "Do both of you want to go somewhere else?"

Caron wrapped her arms around her shoulders. "I don't know. I mean, we could get shot while going to the car—or we could be followed. Then we'd be in a crummy motel with a cheap lock on the door, and in even more danger."

"I don't know, either," I admitted. I wasn't nearly as confident as I had sounded when I'd assured Lucy that we were safe. However, there'd been no indication that anyone had illicit access to the house. Petti's appearances had been limited to the backyard and the garage. Sara Louise and Madison had been attacked in the front yard. The alarm system appeared to be functioning. I had a feeling that a 911 call from me would provoke a swift response. I realized Caron and

Inez were waiting, and said, "All right, how about this? We leave on all the lights down here, and go upstairs to your room to watch TV. I expect Peter to call fairly soon. If he says we ought to leave, then he can send a patrol car to escort us. Otherwise, we'll stay here but with officers outside the house the rest of the night."

Caron and Inez conferred in low voices. Finally, Caron said, "That's okay with us. If we move to a motel, we can't work on our talent show act, which means Rhonda Maguire will have a lock on the spring election."

"Then let's go upstairs," I said before she lapsed into the litany. "Shall we take some ice cream with us?"

"By all means," Caron said, resigning herself to a fate only marginally less ghastly than being seen with me at the mall. "We'll put on our jammies, paint our toenails silver, and watch Nickelodeon. Maybe we'll get lucky and there'll be a *Gilligan's Island* retrospective. Ooh, and we can make prank calls to Rhonda Maguire."

"Or 911," suggested Inez, smiling just a bit. "We can get a stopwatch and bet on how long it takes them to show up this time."

I told myself that I could handle this response more easily than I could tears and terror. I sent them ahead of me, then loaded a tray with pints of ice cream, spoons, a package of cookies, sodas, and the brandy I'd ignored when the Hoods had invaded.

Peter called an hour later. He was not amused that I already knew the identity of the victim, the location, and the probable cause of death, and even less amused when I told him why. He's never been fond of tourists at crime scenes. Once he quit mumbling, he agreed to send two officers to remain on the property until daylight. Due to teenaged ears straining to hear every last syllable, I politely thanked him for calling, hung up, and asked the girls to lead me into the murky depths of MTV. It proved to be an error.

A rattling noise awakened me the following morning. I stumbled to the window, prepared to see tanks rolling out from the pine trees, but instead saw a lone man shaking the gate. The officers must have left, I thought as I tried to decide what to do. It did not seem likely that mobsters from New York would attempt to break into the yard in a blatantly indelicate manner, but I was inexperienced in such matters. I hurriedly dressed and went downstairs. I was headed for the sliding glass doors for a better look when the doorbell rang. Reluctantly, I turned around and went to the door.

"Who is it?" I called.

"Yard service. I usually come in through the back, but the gate's locked."

I turned off the alarm and opened the door. The man on the porch was short, balding, and apologetic.

"Sorry if I disturbed you," he said as he handed me the newspaper. "You want me to mow and tend to the plants?"

"Yes, please," I said. "I'm afraid there's some damage out by the sidewalk."

"No kidding. I'll do what I can, and in a couple of weeks, it won't look so bad. Is Mrs. Goforth here?"

I'd finally encountered someone who neither read the newspaper nor watched KFAR. "She's out of town. You'll have to settle up with her when she gets back."

"No problem. She paid for the summer in advance."

I almost expected him to invite himself inside for coffee and an interrogation of Dolly's whereabouts, the last time she'd called, the details of Petti's death, and the identity of the girl found in the red Mercedes.

"It'll take me a couple of hours," he said, then went to a pickup truck with a trailer and began to remove the accouterments of his trade.

I closed and locked the door, then went into the kitchen and started a pot of coffee. Leaving it to gurgle and gasp, I went upstairs to better prepare myself for the day. The bruise on my cheek was still visible, but not threatening to evolve into a black eye. The scrapes on my knees and elbows showed no signs of infection. The lump on the back of my head was receding, or so I told myself. At the moment, I didn't have a headache, although I was sure I would before the day was done.

I took a precautionary aspirin, showered, did the necessities, and dressed more carefully. When I arrived in the kitchen, the coffee was delightfully fragrant. I sat down at the island and unfolded the newspaper. No nightmarish photos greeted me. I flipped through the first few pages. The international community was in chaos, and several Third World modes of transport had flipped, crashed, or sunk the previous day. An African dictator had fled his palace when insurgents overran the capital. The murder at the country club, however, had happened too late to make the newspaper. This did not mean that the reporters, reinvigorated by the scent of fresh blood, were not on their way to Dogwood Lane. I considered calling the police department to request Corporal McTeer's vigilance for the day, but decided to wait and see what happened when the vans and reporters dared to infringe on the lawn while the yardman was present. They had cameras and microphones; he had leaf blowers, hedge trimmers, weed whackers, and other lethal weapons. It would not be a fair fight.

As I ate a bagel and glanced through the paper, I almost expected Cal to show up with yet another flower arrangement. Peter had said he was not my anonymous suitor, and I could think of no one else who might be shelling out big bucks to get my attention. Gary might be culpable, but he struck me as the sort who would claim responsibility at his first opportunity (in the manner of a gorilla thumping his chest, or at least his credit card). Why he'd latched onto me was puzzling. I was more than modestly attractive, I must admit, and certainly more stimulating and engaging than the standard fare of women he encountered at cocktail parties. On the other hand, I'd been cool, if not chilly, in response to his advances. And, well, I was older. Maturity has its charm, but I could hardly imagine him going to such expensive means to win me over when he was merely renting the condo for a week or two.

I decided to do a little investigating. After a moment, I remembered the name of the florist shop and found a telephone directory on the table in the hall. Aunt Bessie's Bloomers was located at the mall, which explained why I was unfamiliar with it. Although it was early for many businesses to be open, I dialed the number.

"Aunt Bessie's," chirped a female voice, "home of bountiful blossoms and bouquets for every occasion. Today's special is a nosegay of spring flowers delivered with a small box of gourmet chocolate and a helium balloon with a message for someone you love."

"Is the boss's wife in?"

"Oh, I'm so sorry, but neither of them works on Saturdays. Can I help you?"

I told her my name and temporary address, then asked if she could track down the orders for the flowers I'd received the previous day.

"It's supposed to be confidential," she said. "Sometimes, like, maybe a man calls and orders flowers, but he doesn't have them sent to his wife. She sees the charge on the credit card, and then all hell breaks loose. Last year the boss had to testify in a divorce case. He wasn't very happy about it, so we're not supposed to give out any information."

"There's no such thing as florist-customer confidentiality," I countered. "However, if that's the policy, you'll have to explain it to Lieutenant Rosen of the Farberville Criminal Investigation Division when he arrives in an hour. You'll also have to close the shop when he takes you in for interrogation. I doubt that will make the boss very happy, either."

"What do you want to know?" she said.

"Just find the order receipts for the two arrangements Cal delivered to me yesterday."

"Cal who?"

"The deliveryman. He came in a white van with a rose painted on the side."

"Leila makes all of our deliveries, and she drives a blue station wagon. You've got the wrong place."

"Okay," I said before she could hang up, telling myself it was not inconceivable that Leila and Cal had some sort of agreement that Aunt Bessie might have disapproved of. I described the two arrangements. "Did anyone order these?"

195

"Not yesterday," the girl said firmly. "We did a big wedding last night, so we spent all day doing the pieces for that and getting them to the church and reception hall. Leila dropped off a few bouquets, but she was mostly busy with this wedding. You wouldn't believe how much money people spend on flowers these days. I've always said I'd rather have a handful of daffodils and a honeymoon in the Bahamas."

I assured her that I agreed and wished her well. I flipped through the ads for other florist shops in Farberville, but none of them had names that I might have confused with Aunt Bessie and her bloomers. I didn't know if Cal talked to his dog, but he was not a deliveryman. So who was he? I wandered into the dining room and gazed at the flower arrangements. Could he be some sort of psychotic who saw my photo in the newspaper and wanted to entangle himself in the case? Had he been planning to confess as soon as he had the details? Big-city police departments were plagued with those starved for attention, no matter how inappropriate it was. Cal had sounded sane and sensible, perhaps a bit too concerned for a stranger—but I wouldn't have allowed a stranger into the house. Posing as a deliveryman was an innocuous cover that had won him a cup of coffee and, later, an imported beer at the infamous scene of the crime. He'd given me his home phone number and urged me to call. I tried to think if I'd kept the slip of paper in my pocket or left it in the kitchen, where Squeaky Clean would have promptly disposed of it. And if I could find it, I had no idea what to say to him (or his dog, if that's who answered).

I needed to consult Peter, but I knew he was too busy with the investigation of Sara Louise's murder, as well as Petti's current whereabouts. I returned to the kitchen and started calling the other florist shops. The first two had not yet opened, and the third disavowed any knowledge of the arrangements. The fourth was also closed, but I had success with the fifth, which was perilously close to the end of the listings.

"Yeah, we did those," said a harried man. "Pricy."

"Who ordered them?"

"I don't have a name. We got a call Thursday afternoon. Some guy came by later and paid cash." Anticipating my question, he added, "Old black guy. I was surprised he could afford it, but his money was as green as anybody else's."

I thanked him and switched off the receiver. I'd found Petti's body on Thursday evening, well after Cal had picked up the flowers. He hadn't been reacting to the story in Friday's paper. I could have called all the places in Farberville that did custom auto painting to inquire about the rose on Cal's van, but there were apt to be more of those than Sunday morning hangovers on fraternity row.

It took me more than half an hour to find the scrap of paper, which was under Dolly's address book on the table in the hall. I glanced at the latest accumulation of mail, none of it interesting, and returned to the kitchen to have a second cup of coffee. I had no idea what to say to him. Beginning the conversation with "Just who the hell are you and why do you keep bringing me flowers?" might be taken as overly aggressive. Then again, I wasn't about to invite him by for brunch.

I stared at the number, and even went so far as to pick up the receiver several times before I found enough courage to push the appropriate numbers.

"Fritz Motel," said a familiar voice, already weary although it was not yet ten o'clock.

I gabbled something about a wrong number and cut off the call. The Fritz Motel? Hardly a hotbed of floral arrangements. For a brief moment, I could almost hear the snapdragons snapping as they inched across the hall toward the kitchen, and the birds-of-paradise flapping their wings as they fell into formation. Had Miss Marple ever confronted demonic daisies in her garden?

I went over to the sink and splashed cold water on my face. It was not yet ten o'clock, I reminded myself sternly. Peter had warned me that I might have to make a preliminary identification of Sara Louise's body in the morgue (presuming they could contain it there). As soon as Peter called her father, or Madison's father to try to get the telephone number in Hong Kong, I could expect calls from the Velocchio family. Or a visit, I thought with a shudder. Some families struggle for years to resolve problems; others deal with them expeditiously. I did not want to be dealt with expeditiously.

The doorbell rang. I grabbed a dish towel and dried my face, then forced myself to go out into the hall. I did not, however, race to the door to fling it open. No matter how powerful the Velocchios were, they could not have mastered instantaneous time travel. Lucy, on the other hand, could have stayed up late to bake more brownies. Cal could have plucked a few wildflowers behind the motel. The yardman could have mowed down poor Petti.

I tentatively opened the door, then relaxed and let Peter inside. He gave me a quick kiss and headed for the kitchen. "Any hope of something to eat?" he asked over his shoulder.

"You look terrible," I said as I followed him. "Bacon, eggs, and coffee?"

"No more coffee," he groaned. "Not even Colombia's finest, carried out in a burlap bag on the back of a shaggy burro, freshly ground and brewed to perfection in a three-hundred-dollar machine." He sat down on a stool and glanced at the front page of the newspaper. "The vultures were circling all night, but the paper had already gone to press. Dolly's car was the tip-off. They have no idea who the girl was or how she's involved in this mess."

"Do you?" I asked, my head in the refrigerator.

"Nothing more than I knew yesterday. No one at the country club saw or heard anything. The dining room and bar are on the far side of the building, and the trees and shrubs around the parking lot block the view of the pro shop and sheds. The maintenance staff leaves shortly after the course closes for the day. The witness who found the body was a very drunk young woman who'd had a fight with her boyfriend in the parking lot and stumbled away to find a place to throw up. Which she did, once she stuck her head inside the Mercedes. She swears there was no one else around. The medical examiner said Sara Louise had been killed at least two hours earlier."

"Was she shot in the forehead, too?"

198

"No, the side of her head, and with what's likely to be a .22 caliber. We can't compare the bullet with the one that killed Petti Mordella until he's been autopsied." Despite his avowed aversion to coffee, he got up and poured himself a cup. "Jorgeson and I went ahead and made the identification, so you don't have to worry about that. I tracked down her home telephone number in Bedford, Connecticut—yes, you were right—but a housekeeper answered and confirmed that Mr. and Mrs. Santini left for Hong Kong a week ago. She doesn't have a cell phone number or the name of their hotel, although she did grudgingly produce his office number. It's some kind of international investment firm, and most decidedly closed for the weekend so that the brokers and clients can bond together at the country club or spend a few days deep-sea fishing in Bimini or Cabo. It's amazing how flexible your weekends can be with a private jet and your own villa."

"Is the firm connected to the Velocchio family?"

"That's not the sort of thing you can look up in the Yellow Pages, and it'll take weeks to peel back all the layers of obscure corporate ownership to find out. I called Richard Hayes's house on Long Island and again talked to a housekeeper. She said he's still in Atlantic City and not expected back until tomorrow evening, and she doesn't know his cell phone number or the name of his hotel."

I carried various ingredients to the counter and started looking in cabinets for bowls and pans. "There's no Mrs. Hayes?"

Peter rumbled in frustration. "There is no *current* Mrs. Hayes. The housekeeper thinks Mr. Hayes might be accompanied by a potential Mrs. Hayes. The police in Atlantic City agreed to contact all the hotels, but the most valued clients bypass the desk and stay in private suites and penthouses. Their identities are not known to the staff."

I cracked some eggs into a bowl, having decided to produce something worthy of Dolly Goforth's kitchen. Which wasn't her kitchen at all. "Pretend the prosciutto is bacon," I said as I tossed some in a small skillet. "Any luck finding Dolly?"

"Since we don't know what name she's using, it's a bit tricky. She hasn't called again, has she?"

"I would have mentioned it," I said mildly, resisting the urge to pelt him with a mushroom or two. "Do you want onions and sun-dried tomatoes in the omelet, or just cheese, mushrooms, and a few herbs?" I began to open more cabinets. "If I can find the herbs, that is. How do you feel about anchovies?"

Peter glanced up at me. "Scrambled eggs, toast, and prosciutto masquerading as bacon will be fine. Did you get any sleep?"

"More than you did, obviously. Did you stand guard outside the morgue all night?"

"Lieutenants don't have to do that sort of thing. We stayed at the scene most of the night, looking for the weapon, the car keys, and her purse. I went back to the department, did the paperwork, made all the calls I mentioned, and came here. I feel as though I waded in that damn pond with a rake, but lieutenants don't do that, either. Do I smell dreadful?"

I quit pretending I was Julia Child and went over to wrap my arms around his neck. "Yes, you do. Why don't you sneak upstairs and take a quick shower? I can't offer any clean clothes, though." I hesitated for a moment. "And if Caron should come out into the hall and catch you, you're on your own."

"We wouldn't have this problem if we were married."

"The prosciutto's sizzling," I said. "You'd better hurry."

After Peter had gone upstairs, I pondered his comment for a minute, then took my coffee cup and went into the dining room. The snapdragons were not snapping, nor the birds-of-paradise flapping. I needed to tell him about Cal, but it could wait until he ate breakfast. His initial response would be predictable, but for once I could state in all innocence that there'd been nothing to connect the flowers with the murders until I'd called the florist shop—and the phone number Cal had given me. And why had he given me that particular number? If he'd been aware of Petti's comings and goings, he must have known that sooner or later the Fritz Motel was bound to come into the picture.

Had Dolly not made the telltale call, the police would have shown their grisly photos and made inquiries at all the local motels. They might have started at the higher end of the spectrum (there were very few), but eventually would have worked their way down to less glamorous establishments, where shakers of flea powder were kept in the bathroom for the convenience of the guests.

When Peter came back into the kitchen, rumpled but less redolent, I allowed him to finish eating before I said, "I have an idea."

"But you didn't leave me a note and drive away to look into it by yourself? You must have a concussion, after all."

I politely overlooked his remark. "You have photos of Petti, both mug shots and those taken at the morgue. What's occurred to me is that you can also have a photo of Bibi and Dolly lifted from the videotape of the tango competition. It's more than ten years old, so Bibi might have had a few more liver spots and a little less hair when he died. It shouldn't be a problem, though."

Peter lifted his eyebrows. "Well, it's good to know I can make a scrapbook after this is resolved. Maybe I'll use the one of you that was in the newspaper, along with the crime scene shots."

"What you can do with the photo of Bibi and Dolly," I said, "is send it to the police department in Brooklyn. If they were friends of Petti, then someone in his neighborhood might recognize them. Santini or Hayes—I don't remember which one—said they had an old house. It could have been next door to Petti's, or in the same block. At least you'd have their real names."

"Where's the tape?"

"I'll get it," I said, struggling not to sound too smug as I imagined three grumpy old men (aka the mayor, the prosecuting attorney, and the police chief) finding themselves in the most uncomfortable position of having to thank me for breaking the case. I went into the den and knelt down to look for the videotape on the bottom shelf. It was not tucked behind the how-to-tango cassettes, which were, in fact, on the coffee table amid some exercise cassettes. I finally found it on top of the VCR and took it back to the kitchen. "You've got the photo of

Dolly from the social page. No one was exchanging partners, so you shouldn't have any trouble recognizing the two of them. He's the one in the tux."

Peter failed to express his gratitude. "We need to have a serious discussion about your safety. You keep insisting that this has nothing to do with you, but clearly someone thinks otherwise. Petti Mordella may not have been killed here, but there's obviously some connection. Madison and Sara Louise showed up shortly afterwards. Now one of them is missing and the other's been killed. We know the three of them are associated with the Velocchio family, and they came looking for Dolly Goforth. I think we can rightly assume they did so because of the impending grand jury investigation. For all we know, the two girls came with the intention of killing her."

"But she's long gone, and I've made it clear numerous times that I have no idea how to get in touch with her," I said. "I suppose they may have thought that she'd call and give me an address, which I would mindlessly share with everyone who asked. And pretty much everyone has asked, with the exception of the yardman and the tyrannical cleaning service. I feel as if I should paint a banner proclaiming my ignorance and nail it across the front of the house. Well, maybe not ignorance. Lack of specific knowledge."

"I don't think the three of you should stay here," he said flatly.

"Do you think Sergeant Jorgeson or Corporal McTeer will fool Dolly when she calls? She does keep calling me, as you must have noticed. I don't know why, but it's not just to express sympathy. If Richard Hayes and Christopher Santini wanted to talk to you, they would have. You can track them down eventually, but neither of them is likely to enlighten you. Even if you can get past their housekeepers, receptionists, secretaries, personal assistants, and so forth, all you'll hear is how Madison and Sara Louise came down to surprise Dolly. Santini will probably make arrangements for Sara Louise from his own corner office with its view of the East River. As long as they continue to underestimate me, they may say something indiscreet."

"Your safety is my first priority."

202

I told him what Caron and Inez had said, and we discussed it over another round of coffee. He finally agreed to station someone outside the house for at least the next twenty-four hours. After he'd taken the videotape and left, I put the dishes in the sink and rinsed out the coffeepot.

It was hard not to notice how badly my hands were shaking.

Chapter Thirteen

I was flipping through the channels on the TV set in the den, looking for something more stimulating than cartoons but less stupefying than pundits discoursing on free-trade policies, when the telephone rang. I pushed what I hoped was the button to record the call, then picked up the receiver and murmured my name.

"Oh, thank goodness," said Dolly. "I was so afraid you and the girls might have moved to a hotel. I wouldn't have blamed you one bit. First that man in the freezer, and now Sara Louise. I am so appalled with myself for putting you in this horrible situation! Is it an absolute media circus in front of the house?"

"Just a patrol car for now, but elephants may come tromping up the hill any minute. How do you know about Sara Louise?"

"Well," she said, "I called Jan Burfield to remind her to pick up the brochures for the children's art show reception next week, and she was beside herself. She'd heard that my car was found last night at the country club and that a young woman's body had been discovered in it, apparently murdered. She called her nephew, who's a resident at the hospital, and he told her they identified—"

"Sara Louise Santini," I said coldly. "One of Bibi's beloved nieces, except from what I've been told, not related. He was an old family friend, the family being the Velocchios of New York City."

"Velocchios?"

"Let's not play any more games, Dolly. Where are you? What's going on? Should Caron, Inez, and I be hunkered down in the Fritz Motel, expecting machine-gun fire to erupt in the parking lot?"

"Anything else?"

I took the receiver into the kitchen and sat down on a stool. "Why don't you stop asking questions and offer a few answers? Let's start with why Petti Mordella came to Farberville. Did he come here to tell you about the grand jury subpoenas? Is that why you left so abruptly?"

"You seem to know quite a bit about all this."

"Then why don't you fill me in on the rest of it? Dolly Goforth is not your real name, and Bibi didn't die in Illinois last year. You and he lived in New York, right? Did he work for the Velocchio family?"

"I'd like to tell you everything," she said with a sigh, "but the line's surely tapped. You're correct in saying that Dolly Goforth is not my real name and that Bibi and I lived in New York. After he died, I wanted to start a new life, to go forth, if you will, and Farberville sounded ideal. Rather than making a commitment, I leased the house to make sure I liked the town and the people. When I found out that certain, ah, acquaintances from the past had located me, it seemed wise to leave town for a short while. I assumed the aforementioned acquaintances would return to New York."

I tried to hide my irritation. "If you'd wanted to make it known you were gone, all you had to do was close the house and let the news-papers accumulate in the driveway. Instead, you invited us to stay here, and offered your car to Caron."

"I thought it might be prudent to allow myself an extra day or two before they realized I was gone. You have to believe me when I say that I truly thought that would be the end of it. I realized you might be asked a few questions about my whereabouts, but that was all."

"Unless your acquaintances decide to chop off my fingers one by one until I blurt out the pertinent information," I said. "Or harm Caron, or burn down my bookstore. Did that occur to you?"

"That's a bit melodramatic, Claire. Have you been watching those old gangster movies?"

"I've been too busy watching my back, as well as finding bodies in the freezer and wondering who might be hiding in the backyard. We have twenty-four-hour police protection now, but it's about five days late. Did Petti Mordella come to Farberville to warn you about these acquaintances? Did he tell you that Sara Louise and Madison were on their way here?"

After a moment of silence, she said, "He didn't know anything about the two girls, and neither did I. There are some other people involved. I suppose you already know that—and I can assure you that they're not the sort to chop off fingers or leave a horse's head on your pillow. Most of them, anyway."

"Most of them?" I said. "Is that what you said?"

"It was a joke. In any case, this will all be over with soon. My lease is good for another month, and you're welcome to stay in the house. Perhaps you can persuade your landlord to do more remodeling. If he's agreed to put in tile countertops, he might consider doing the floor as well."

If she'd been within reach, I would have grabbed her shoulders and shaken the truth out of her. She wasn't, however, and I needed to get as much as I could from her before she terminated the call. "Let's talk about the Velocchio family," I suggested brightly, as if I hadn't been gnawing my knuckles since my conversation with Peter. "Why are they so determined to find you? You aren't subpoenaed to testify next week. Bibi would have been, I guess, but that's irrelevant now. Are they afraid you have damning information about their illegal operations?"

"They know I don't. What Bibi did was incredibly complicated. He used to describe it as juggling handfuls of sand on a beach, and keeping track of each grain. Only people with extensive training and a special aptitude for numbers could begin to understand what he did all day. He was a different person away from his office. He loved to cook elaborate meals and have dinner parties. Sometimes we'd take off for a weekend and find a country inn, where we could browse in antique shops or have a picnic. You've already heard how much we loved ballroom dancing, especially the tango. Bibi used to say it made his Latin blood simmer as if he were a teenager."

"It must have been very romantic," I said, "but I need to know about the Velocchio family. Exactly who are these other acquaintances in town and why are they so anxious to find you? Two people have been murdered, Dolly. We can talk about country inns and the tango another time. This line is not tapped; a specialist from the police department made sure of it only yesterday."

Dolly made a small noise under her breath. "The technology these days may be too sophisticated for a local police investigator. And it's not just the Velocchios who are involved. . . ."

"What are you talking about?" I demanded.

"I can't say any more. There is someone there who can explain better than I, but if I give you his name, I'll be putting him in danger."

"So you're putting Caron, Inez, and me in danger instead?"

"You're not in danger as long as you don't know anything, so let's change the subject. Has anything come in the mail for me?"

"More invitations, flyers, a few bills," I said. "I gather you're not planning to return to Farberville. Shall I cancel your dentist appointment?"

"Oh, Claire, I know you must feel very bitter toward me. I've admitted that I used you and the girls as a distraction, and for that I'm terribly sorry. I never dreamed it would get so far out of hand. I'd come home and try to intervene, but it really would make things much worse than you could imagine. I'll call again when I have a chance."

She hung up. I put down the receiver and sorted through what she'd admitted—and what she hadn't denied. She'd managed to avoid telling me Bibi's last name, but Peter would eventually find out from the Brooklyn detectives, Richard Hayes, or Christopher Santini. He'd been an accountant for the Velocchio family, so the FBI ought to have a file on him. And it seemed to me, a mere civilian unversed in the intricacies of the judicial system, that the FBI would have to become involved if Petti had been among those subpoenaed. Intimidating a federal witness was a felony of some class or another, and putting a bullet in his head was among the more extreme forms of intimidation.

Dolly had said there was someone who could explain better than she what was going on, but then refused to identify him. Assuming she had used the pronoun in a gender-specific sense, rather than the awkward *he/she,* she'd referred to a male who was currently in Farberville. Who might be dying to explain, but not willing to die in order to explain.

I realized the black box was still whirring, and went to the hall and punched buttons until the green light went off. Feeling virtuous, I called the PD and asked to speak to Peter. He was out of the office, I was told, so I asked for Jorgeson. He was minimally impressed that I'd figured out how to record the conversation with Dolly, but said he'd send someone to fetch the tape.

"Let me ask you something," I said before he could hang up. "Dolly assumed the line is tapped. The detective who hooked up the box said it isn't. Could he be wrong?"

Jorgeson thought about it for a moment. "I don't want to alarm you, Ms. Malloy, but yes, he could be wrong. His detection devices are fairly new; I think the department purchased them last fall. Thing is, once they hit the market, they're obsolete. The intelligence agencies have teams of scientists dedicated solely to coming up with new ways to thwart the current technology, with the focus these days on computers. The other side counters with its experts in the field. Someone in a house across the street from you can track your every step with heat and motion sensors, and listen to every word uttered in your house. That's not to say you should get all paranoid. The toys I've been talking about are expensive, and usually reserved for big-time espionage cases. If we need to maintain surveillance on a residence we suspect of, say, significant drug deals, we use binoculars and a telescope, and try to get into the house under an innocent pretext to plant some bugs."

"Have you interviewed the people in the nearby houses?" I asked in what might have been a somewhat shrill voice.

"Yes, Ms. Malloy, and they're all respectable, longtime neighborhood residents. Not a mobster among them."

"Would the Velocchio family have these expensive toys?"

"I wouldn't think so. Mobsters are more sophisticated than they used to be back when money was stuffed in suitcases and buried under rosebushes. Nowadays, the money's laundered through a maze of legitimate operations and ultimately tucked away in foreign countries with lax banking regulations and a disregard for extradition agreements. But at the same time, they still rely on the old-fashioned way of silencing those who break the code of honor or imperil their source of income. They've got their CPAs—and they've got their hitmen."

I was not comforted by his last remark. "So Petti Mordella and Sara Louise were victims of a professional hitman?"

"That's what we'd like to know," Jorgeson said. "I'll send someone to get the tape shortly. The lieutenant went home to grab a couple of hours of sleep. He'll probably want to talk to you later today. You and the girls okay about staying there?"

"Why, Jorgeson, I didn't know you cared. I'm touched."

"If it weren't for you, Ms. Malloy, I'd retire and take up catfish farming. Somehow or another, whenever you're involved, the case is never cut-and-dried. It's like a pile of spaghetti that has to be unraveled one strand at a time."

"I am flattered to hear that, and honored that I alone stand between your career in the department and the specter of you planting catfish in tidy rows."

"Goodbye, Ms. Malloy."

"Have a nice day, Sergeant Jorgeson."

Caron and Inez came into the kitchen. Both looked tired, which was not surprising since they'd started watching a movie when I'd toddled off to bed. For all I knew, they'd lasted through a sequel or two. Sequels were not a factor with the old gangster movies, since all the bad guys were dead when the final credits rolled.

"Do they know who killed Sara Louise?" asked Caron as she took a carton of orange juice from the refrigerator.

"I'm glad to see you're not overwhelmed by the proximity of death."

"I'd be overwhelmed by the proximity of a cement mixer bearing down on me," she said. "As for death, well, I *have* had a tumultuous adolescence thus far." She sat down across from me and gazed out the window. "But an interesting one. I can hardly wait to fill out the section on the college applications where they ask about extracurricular activities."

Inez brought over toast and jam. "Were there any other witnesses last night?"

"Only the young woman who discovered the body," I said, "and that happened a couple of hours later. I'm sure there are detectives at the country club now, interviewing everyone who works there or was in the clubhouse."

"Or rents a condo, like those weird people," Caron said, more interested in selecting the perfect jam than psychological profiling.

I was not in the mood to be judgmental. "They're just busybodies. He wants to look at retirement properties, and she wants to meddle. She seems to think her life's work will be done if I fall madly in love with the man who's in the condo next to theirs."

"Why?" mumbled Inez through a mouthful of toast.

"I have no idea. He's the one who dropped by yesterday afternoon for a few minutes."

"And rescued you from that smelly old hippie at the bookstore?" said Caron, smirking. "He's not bad looking—the guy, not the hippie—but isn't he a little young for you?"

I smiled sweetly at her. "I thought you'd be delighted with a stepfather who can escort you to the prom."

"Do You Mind?" Caron chomped down on a piece of toast, scattering crumbs on the tile surface. "So what are we supposed to do while all these mobsters run around killing each other? Should we tape bedspreads across the window and have police officers slide pizzas under the front door? Are we allowed to communicate with the outside world?"

"You can communicate with anyone you wish," I said, then hesitated. "Except for the media, in any form or fashion. They'll know about Sara Louise by now, and the fact she was in Dolly's car. The police out front will keep them from encroaching onto the property. You can go out to the patio, but be prepared to hear reporters shouting questions from the gate. You can tango till your toes tingle."

"Tingle?" Inez said. "Mine are so bruised that I can't feel them. Unless one of us pays more attention to the choreography, we'll both be crippled by the time of the talent show. We can't tango on crutches."

Caron's eyes narrowed. "And my toes aren't bruised? My big toe looks like a plum."

"Because your foot was in the wrong place," countered Inez.

"Then so was yours, since it was on top of mine."

I stood up. "Clean up when you're done, then go outside, upstairs, or to the attic, if you can find it. Why don't you go in different directions for a few hours? This enforced togetherness is driving all of us crazy. I'm sorry I got you in this mess, but we're going to have to tough it out for the time being."

"And what are you going to do?" asked Caron. "Go to the grocery store for two hours, like you did yesterday?"

If only I could. "No, I'm going to find a place where I can neither see nor hear you. We three can reconvene at lunchtime and whip up a delicately seasoned potage of eye of newt, toe of frog, and wool of bat."

Caron and Inez glanced at each other. Caron finally cleared her throat and said, "Why don't you try the Jacuzzi, Mother? It's very soothing."

" 'Adder's fork and blind-worm's sting, lizard's leg and owlet's wing,' " I called over my shoulder as I went upstairs. There are some perks to being an English major, although hardly of a financial nature.

The Jacuzzi was indeed soothing. The telephone rang on occasion. Caron or Inez must have answered it, but neither came to the bathroom door to convey a message or demand an immediate response from me. The mystery novel failed to hold my interest, so I set it aside and idly concocted a list of those men who might qualify as Dolly's mysterious informant. Peter and Jorgeson were not likely, nor was my science fiction hippie, who would be stymied if I asked him what day of the week it was. I ruled out all of my usual bookstore customers, as well as the students who came in with grubby reading lists. Someone I'd met since I'd taken possession of Dolly's house, obviously.

Nick and Sebastian from Manny's PerfectPools. Cal. Gary Billings. Daniel Hood. The yardman, although we hadn't bonded. If Dolly had used the pronoun *he* in the broader sense, Lucy Hood, the woman at the Fritz Motel, the Squeaky Clean trio, or even Corporal McTeer. I ruled out the vapid reporter and the waitress at the Cardinal Café. After further pruning, my list was down to the pool guys, Cal, Gary, Daniel, and Lucy. Unless, as painful as it was to consider, the informant might be someone with whom I'd not spoken at all, someone watching from a distance. He, or she, was undoubtedly communicating with Dolly, since I hadn't believed her story about calling a local friend to make sure brochures were collected from a print shop. Then again, I've never been accused of fussing over details.

The doorbell rang as I was getting dressed. I heard voices, but no one sounded agitated, so I took my time. When I arrived downstairs, I saw Caron, Inez, and Peter on the patio, eating pizza. I poured myself a glass of iced tea and went out to join them.

"You're looking mellow," Peter said as he moved a chair to the table for me.

I picked up a piece of pizza. "And you're looking less like a stowaway on a cargo ship. Did Jorgeson tell you about Dolly's call?"

He nodded. "She's still in Miami."

"Does she know who killed Sara Louise?" asked Caron.

"If she suspects someone, she didn't tell me," I said. "She didn't really tell me much of anything, for that matter. She admitted that Goforth is not her real name and that she and Bibi lived in New York, but we already knew that." I stared at Peter. "Could she be in the witness protection program? Is that why she has a Social Security number as Dolly Goforth?"

"Probably," he said. He finished a piece of pizza and reached for another. "I gather you all are happy with pepperoni and mushrooms. I thought about anchovies and black olives, but the combo seemed too exotic for lunch."

"The witness protection program?" Caron squeaked. She turned to Inez, who was gaping like a guppy. "Is this cool or what? We actually met someone in the witness protection program."

I hoped I wasn't gaping as well. "So the FBI sent her here? Have they contacted you?"

"Not yet," he said, "and I'm not going to sit all day in my office and wait for them to show up—if they're even in town. Once they place someone in the program, they're done with him unless he's going to testify. Dolly's not on the subpoena list."

"Maybe she wasn't subpoenaed because she volunteered to testify," I said. "Then the Velocchios found out and came looking for her to make sure she doesn't testify in the grand jury investigation."

Peter finished his soda and sat back. "If that were true, the feds would have shown up and bullied us off the case. Their lack of concern suggests they're not especially interested in her. Or Petti Mordella, for that matter. The witness protection program doesn't imply they're protecting a witness. After Bibi's death, she may have cooperated with them, although I don't know why she'd risk incurring the Velocchio family's ire. Whichever FBI agent was on the case told her that it would be prudent to adopt a new identity and move elsewhere. The federal marshals assisted with the background papers, gave her enough money to get by for six months or a year, and then erased her from their radar screen. I doubt they cared what happened to her after that."

Inez blinked at him. "In the movies, they—"

"In the movies," he said, shrugging. "No one makes a movie about a family that's whisked away to some town in Kansas, never to be heard from again. It happens more often than you think. There could be half a dozen people in the program who're living in this county. The kids are lectured never to discuss their past except in the

213

most general terms. The parents keep a low profile. Apparently, a lot of them can't stand the pressure and leave the program. Others revert to criminal activity to make a living. The marshals don't bother to tip off the local authorities about these people's true identities."

"So Rhonda Maguire's family could be in the witness protection program?" asked Caron, her eyes flickering. "They didn't move here until Rhonda was in the eighth grade, you know. Isn't that suspicious?"

"Highly suspicious," Peter replied gravely.

"Her father sort of looks like a ferret," said Inez. "Maybe he shot Sara Louise and Petti."

She and Caron wandered away to the gazebo to further discuss the ramifications of this startling hypothesis.

"You're a big help, Sherlock," I said as I picked up another piece of pizza.

"It turns out that you are, too. We culled a couple of stills from the videotape and faxed them to the Brooklyn detectives, who passed them on to the beat officers, who showed them around Petti's neighborhood. One of the shopkeepers recognized Bibi immediately. Bibi Barlucci, that is, and his wife, Doris, known to close friends as Dolly. Friends of Petti's. Regular patrons at the local cafés and trattorias. He died a year ago of a heart attack, according to his death certificate. The FBI took photos of everyone at the funeral, which ought to give you an idea of who attended."

"So Bibi was a mobster?"

Peter shook his head. "No, but his clients were. He had a few indiscretions when he was young, then straightened up, went to night school, and eventually earned a degree in accounting and passed the CPA exams. He knew of the Velocchios' illegal ventures, but all he did was shift money to various foreign accounts and cook a set of books that the IRS auditors could never crack. A nine-to-five job, very dry and tedious."

"He would have been a useful witness at the grand jury hearing. Are you sure he died of a heart attack?"

"That's what's on the death certificate under 'cause of death.' According to the paperwork, Dolly found him unconscious in his office on the third floor of their house. She called for an ambulance, and he was transported to the nearest hospital, where he was pronounced dead on arrival. He had all the classic symptoms of a heart attack. The funeral was held at the parish church. Afterwards, his body was cremated and the remains were buried in the village where he and Dolly owned a lake house. There was no hint of foul play. He was seventy-seven years old, smoked cigars, drank, and ate rich Italian food."

"Okay," I conceded. "I suppose we already have enough bodies. No sign of Petti, I suppose?"

"His body could be in the trunk of a car, in a freezer, weighted down in the bottom of a lake, covered with leaves out in the woods, or buried in a basement. No one on the night shift at the hospital Thursday night admitted seeing someone in the vicinity of the morgue. No one saw a vehicle in the delivery parking lot after six o'clock." He paused for moment. "If we got married, we could send Caron to boarding school and buy a boat. I've always wanted to sail around the world."

"Do all guys have this Magellan complex?" I said. "If you sail around the world, then you conquer it? Or are you looking for a heretofore undiscovered tropical island to claim as your own? I hate to break it to you, but all the natives have satellite dishes and earn their living day-trading in coconut futures."

"We could live on a remote farm in Australia."

"So you can shear sheep and I can knit sweaters?"

He looked at me. "You're avoiding the issue."

I sat back and looked at him over the rim of my glass. "Yes, I am, but I'm distracted. I guess it has to do with the influx of mobsters. Perhaps I shouldn't have fallen asleep during *The Godfather,* but I did. I don't even know the terminology. What I do know is that they've descended on Farberville, murdered two of their own, kidnapped another, assaulted me and vandalized the bookstore, and sent Dolly into hiding. I'm really not in the mood to talk about sheep, dear creatures that they are."

"If you put it that way . . ."

"I just did." I stopped while Caron and Inez walked past us and went in the house. I had no idea what they might have been plotting, so I was relieved when after a brief moment I heard tango music from the den. "I need to tell you about the guy who's been delivering flowers."

"A victim of unrequited love?"

I told him what I'd uncovered concerning Cal, then said, "Why would he have given me the telephone number of the Fritz Motel if he wasn't involved? I think he wanted me to know that he is, although I have no idea why."

"But he doesn't work for Aunt Bessie's whatever, and he bought the flower arrangements himself?"

"If I look in the Yellow Pages, I can tell you the name of the place where he bought them, and for a lot more than pocket change. He did ask about Dolly's whereabouts, but so did a significant percentage of the population. Can't you put out an APB on the van?"

Peter wrinkled his nose. "Because he bought you expensive flowers?"

"No," I said testily. "Because he wrote down the number of the Fritz Motel. Because he lied about working for Aunt Bessie's Bloomers. Because he accepted an imported beer under false pretenses. Because he told me his dog might answer the telephone. What more do you need?"

"Evidence of a criminal act or the intent to commit one."

"Don't be such a stickler, Peter," I said as I gathered up the napkins, glasses, and pizza box. "You should have gone to law school."

"I did," he said.

I spun around, almost losing my grip on the makeshift tray. "You did?"

"All Rosen boys go to Harvard Law School. Most of them join prestigious firms and dedicate their lives to corporate tax breaks and hostile takeovers. A few of them actually argue in court, but they loathe every second of it. They work sixty-hour weeks, sleep with their secretaries, and spend August with their families on Nantucket or the Vineyard."

"You've never mentioned brothers."

"And I've never mentioned Aunt Belinda, who lives in the carriage house on my mother's estate and raises pygmy hedgehogs. What do I know about your family?"

"Everything you need to know," I said, then went inside and headed for the kitchen. Peter trailed after me, but I pointedly ignored him as I covered the solitary piece of pizza in plastic wrap and put the glasses in the dishwasher. The pulsating music from the den was not helping the situation. Slow-slow-quick-quick-slow. I wasn't sure where we were, whose turn it was to make the next move, whose toes might be trampled. And, to my mortification, I was having difficulty catching my breath. I finally managed to say, "Shouldn't you be off investigating Sara Louise's murder or looking for Petti's body?"

He seemed to have no better idea than I about how to proceed. "I'll call you later," he said at last. "I'll make sure one of the officers checks the backyard every half hour."

"That's a good idea. Caron and Inez may want to swim."

"All right, then," he said. "Call me if anything happens that makes you uneasy."

"I will."

"So I'll talk to you later." He left, although his presence lingered like the faintest whiff of pepperoni—or something much more potent.

Despite a decent night's sleep and the session in the Jacuzzi, I felt exhausted. I sat on a stool for a long while, reflecting on our relationship and the secrets we were unable to share. If they *were* secrets. However, brooding has its limitations, so I stashed away the issue for future consideration and went into the den, where Caron and Inez were diligently stalking, fanning, flinging, and flipping. I waited until they arrived at the climax, in which they turned their backs on each other, then reeled around and dropped into a pose that looked painful to those of us with less than supple spines.

"Very impressive," I said, clapping. "Original, dramatic, and entertaining."

Caron glared at me. "It's supposed to be a parody."

"And amusing," I added quickly.

Inez wiped her glasses on her shirt, resettled them, and gave me a baleful look. "Do you think everybody's going to accuse us of being lesbians?"

"Everybody being Rhonda Maguire?"

Caron flung herself onto the sofa. "Everybody, as in everybody at the high school."

Maternal wisdom failed me. "I don't know. I would think that emphasizing that it's a parody ought to preclude that. Maybe if you look less serious, throw a few winks at the audience and ham it up, they'll realize it's a joke. After all the teen diva look-alikes, you'll be like a cool breeze sweeping through the food court. The judges will love it, even if you make a few wrong moves and stomp on each other's feet. Pretend that you rehearsed it that way."

"Yeah, right," Caron said morosely. She clutched a pillow and buried her face in it. Inez blinked a few times, then sat down on the ottoman and stared at the rug. I wasn't sure what to say; I'd either failed to offer the proper encouragement or insulted them by suggesting that they ought to act like buffoons. Dr. Spock had never dedicated a chapter to a quandary such as this.

"You can always change your mind," I said. "If you don't want to participate in the talent contest, then don't do it."

When I received no response, I retreated to the patio and stared at the placid surface of the pool. The girls were too old for me to make their decisions. Peter and I would have to make some of our own, but I refused to think about it until the case was resolved and I no longer had to worry about New York mobsters and .22 caliber bullets. Dolly Barlucci was history. When her lease expired, the agent would have the personal items stored and start showing the house to newly tenured professors and franchise moguls. Caron and I would return to our apartment, and eventually stop imagining the worst with every minuscule sound from another room.

I was annoyed that Peter had failed to take even minimal interest in Cal. He was involved, I told myself. Of course, I had no idea why, but if Peter wouldn't find out, then I had no choice but to look into it myself. It could hardly be construed as meddling, since I'd freely shared the information. The Farberville CID was obligated to move slowly and relentlessly, but I'd always held the tortoise in contempt, even as a child.

I went inside, picked up my purse, and continued to the den. Caron and Inez were scrunched on opposite ends of the sofa, presumably enthralled by men in black shirts and fedoras hauling bodies out onto a pier. Neither responded when I told them I was going out for a while. The police car was parked in the driveway, the driver reading what appeared to be a comic book and his partner snoring. I knocked on the window until they roused themselves, then told them I was going to the grocery store. This seemed to cause no consternation.

The parking lot of the Fritz Motel was empty, and the sign in the window promised vacancies. I went inside, where I found the orange-haired woman watching a cartoon show on the TV set. She was so engrossed that I had to tap on the counter to get her attention.

"Hi," I said, almost chirping. "Remember me?"

"Yeah, sure, you were here yesterday, right? You were asking about the guy in number eleven, Mr. Mordella. You ever find him?"

"In a manner of speaking," I said. "Now I'm looking for a man named Cal. Is he staying here?"

"Nobody's staying here right now. The truckers and the salesmen try to get home on weekends. This being Saturday, I'll probably get some college boys who've paid for the services of the ladies over at the truck stop. You're not undercover vice, are you?"

"No, most definitely not. Has anyone named Cal stayed here in the last week or so? He's black, in his eighties, with gray hair."

She took a cigarette out of a crumpled pack and lit it. "I don't rent to coloreds. You got a problem with that?"

I was not inclined to engage in an argument about civil rights and illegal discrimination. "He gave me this number, so I assumed—"

"You assumed wrong."

I returned to my car to think. Cal was a dead end, at least for the time being. I could hardly spend the rest of the afternoon driving

219

around Farberville in hopes of spotting a white van with a rose painted on it. If the rose hadn't been scrubbed off along with the mud. There was no point in going to the student union. A few students might be shooting pool and hanging out in the lounge, but the offices would be closed.

However, it was a lovely day, the sort that sends children and their parents to the park and bicyclists out to pedal to their hearts' content. And golfers to the links to hit balls into the ponds and sandboxes.

I headed for the country club.

Chapter Fourteen

Cookie-cutter condos lined three sides of the golf course; the fourth was delineated by a creek and a bluff. I drove through the parking areas, looking for a car with Virginia plates. Other states were sporadically represented, but not the one I'd hope to spot. Gary had never mentioned his home state.

I pulled into the parking lot in front of the clubhouse and drove up and down the rows until I'd ascertained that Daniel and Lucy's car was not there. A gravel path, wide enough for golf carts, led toward the pro shop. Access roads to the maintenance buildings and the golf course had a separate, unseen entrance. I could think of no reason to walk down to wherever Dolly's Mercedes had been found, since it would have been towed away before the course opened for the day. It was highly unlikely that Sara Louise's purse, the car key, and the gun would be glinting in the grass.

I parked between a black BMW and a gold Cadillac. As I walked toward the main entrance, a beep sounded behind me. I glanced back, then leapt out of the way as a golf cart carrying two very convivial male golfers tore past me in the direction of the condos. "Pardon our dust!" called the passenger as they careened around a corner. Clearly, the bar was open and business was brisk.

I wasn't sure of the etiquette required to stroll into the clubhouse. There was no sign with a reminder that only members were allowed inside and that interlopers would be beaten senseless with golf clubs and tennis rackets. I interloped into a wide hallway, expecting to find a tactfully dressed security guard with a list of bona fide members and invited guests. If such a guard existed, he was not on duty. A foursome of tanned women came past me, jabbering among themselves. A sullen man dressed in a lime green shirt and plaid Bermuda shorts brushed my shoulder as he headed for the door. In the main room, which was large enough for formal balls and Republican Party fund-raisers, a scattering of people were seated on leather sofas and chairs. The plants were exuding oxygen, and the artwork on the walls was original. Syrupy music played in the background. A dark-skinned waiter in a white jacket collected glasses from the coffee tables and replaced ashtrays. Two teenaged girls murmured into cell phones as they strolled through the room; I wondered if they were talking to each other. I drew no more attention than a shopper at a post-Christmas sale.

On the far side of the room was a long, screened-in porch that presented a view of undulating vegetation and the eighteenth green. Several tables were occupied by grim-faced bridge players, mostly women. Others were occupied by less-competitive members eating lunch. Another waiter was taking orders from those reading newspapers or gazing at the golf course. It was all very genteel. Had the green been replaced with a croquet court, the setting would have been perfect for a weekend party at a country house down the lane from St. Mary Mead.

As I went onto the porch, I could hear thwacks from a tennis court and whoops and splashes from a swimming pool. An outburst of profanity came from one of the golfers on the green; none of the bridge players looked up from his or her cards. Lucy was not among them, nor was Daniel puttering around the putting green.

I was about to give up when Gary Billings came through a door at the opposite end of the porch. He was dressed in white shorts and a shirt, and carried a tennis racket, leading me to astutely deduce that he'd been responsible for some of the thwacks. He spotted me and waved, then said something to a voluptuous young blonde in a skimpy

222

tennis dress. She nodded in response, shot me a venomous look, and ambled into the clubhouse proper.

Gary joined me and pulled out a chair. "Lucy told me about last night," he began with great earnestness. "How horrible for you." He beckoned to the waiter. "What would you like to drink?"

"Club soda and lime," I said.

Once he'd ordered two of them, he leaned forward and said, "You can imagine how distressed everyone here is. There was talk this morning of a membership meeting to discuss increasing security at night. One couple renting a condo packed up and left after the police questioned them. Nothing this exciting has happened since a caddy was bitten by a water moccasin and had the audacity to drop the bag he was carrying in order to go to the emergency room."

"Everyone seems to be holding up pretty well."

"Well, yes, but there's a lot of anxiety. Do the police have any leads? Did they find the gun?"

"I don't have a badge, so I'm not privy to the reports. Did you happen to see or hear anything last night?"

He batted his eyelashes like an abashed choirboy. It was a well-rehearsed gesture that had no doubt set many an heiress's heart aflutter. "I went for a walk with a divorcée from Chicago. She was dizzy and needed some fresh air. I heard a noise that could have been from a gun, although it never crossed my mind at the time. I told the police I thought it was about eight o'clock, give or take a few minutes. When the damsel in distress felt better, we returned to the Hoods' condo in time for dinner. You really should have come, Claire. The level of banality was enough to ruin my appetite."

"Did you later go to the pro shop with Lucy and Daniel?"

"No, I wanted to watch the ten o'clock news. These people are more interested in gossip than international affairs."

"What did you expect when you rented the condo—evening lectures on the GNP and Greenspan's latest assessment? Seminars on bioethics? Slide shows on poverty in India and environmental destruction in Appalachia? Why did you rent the condo, Gary? You don't even play golf."

"Just on a whim. I've never been to this part of the country."

"And I've never been to Mongolia." I crossed my arms and stared at him. "You came because of Dolly, didn't you? A hitman for the Velocchio family? Are you on retainer, or do you prefer to work as a freelancer?" Raising my voice, I began to sing, "Here a hit, there a hit, everywhere a hit-hit . . . Don Velocchio had a mob—"

Gary grabbed my wrist. "Why don't we continue this conversation elsewhere?"

I resisted his attempt to pull me up. "I'm not inclined to take a hike with you in the woods, if that's what you're suggesting. No one's paying any attention to us. You know, you're not at all what I envision a hitman to look like, but my experience is limited to fiction. Maybe that's what accounts for your success. What do you think?"

"I am not a hitman," he growled.

"You're hardly going to admit it," I said lightly. "You really ought to make an effort not to frown like that. One of these days the wrinkles will persist and you'll have to take the Botox route." I allowed him to smolder for a moment, then added, "If you're not a hitman, then you must be an FBI agent. Did you come to Farberville to keep an eye on Dolly Goforth, aka Doris Barlucci? I suppose that means you knew the Velocchio family had sent some representatives of its own to find her."

"I thought you were an innocent bookseller rather than a conspiracy nutcase."

I stiffened. "I thought you were a shallow womanizer rather than a quasi-successful undercover operative. Life's full of surprises, isn't it?"

"All right," he said, still sounding a bit grouchy, "I don't suppose it can hurt to tell you that I am with the FBI. After Bibi Barlucci's death, we advised Dolly to enter the witness protection program as a precaution. She persuaded the marshals to let her relocate here. When we got word last week that the Velocchio family might be on her trail, I was sent down to assess the situation."

"Let me see your badge."

He took his wallet out of his pocket and slid it across the table. "Try to be discreet."

"I am always discreet." I flipped open his wallet. His FBI badge looked authentic, but I had nothing with which to compare it. "If I copy the number and call the headquarters in DC, will they confirm your identity?"

"What do you think?"

"Will they confirm it for Lieutenant Rosen?"

Gary nodded. "I'm planning to drop by his office later today and have a word with him. It's imperative that I find out where Dolly is. So far, I've just been sitting back and waiting, but it's time for the Bureau to intervene."

I had a feeling Peter would not go quietly into the night. "Why is it imperative that you find Dolly? She's not going to testify in front of the grand jury. When she called this morning, she acknowledged that Bibi worked for the mob, but was adamant that she herself knew nothing about what he did. Why are the Velocchios so worried about her?"

"She called this morning? From where?"

"Miami. You didn't answer my questions."

"No," he said, "and I'm not going to. The less you know, the better." He signaled to a hovering waiter. "I'm ready for something more potent. How about you?"

I agreed to a vodka and tonic. Once the waiter was gone, I said, "Then we won't talk about Dolly. It's obvious that Petti Mordella came to Farberville to warn her about somebody, and then was killed. She swore that neither of them was aware that Sara Louise and Madison were headed this way. Were you?"

"You're relentless. If I were an antelope and you were a lioness, I'd just flop down in the grass and expose my throat."

"I'll take that as a compliment. Madison's father works for the Velocchios, and I assume Sara Louise's father does as well. That makes the girls third-generation, born and bred in the USA, homogenized and sanitized, sent to college instead of Italian cooking school. Is feminism impinging on tradition?"

"From what I've heard, they weren't sent here on official business. I don't know about Madison's motives, but in Sara Louise's case, she's determined to make a place for herself in the hierarchy.

She needs approval from the old man and his most trusted advisers."

"So she came here to kill Dolly?"

He winced, then looked over his shoulder at the bridge players. "No, that's not why she came. Why don't we discuss bestsellers or movies, or even birds? For lack of anything else to do, I've been studying the field guide. Did you know that nuthatches are among the few species than can creep down tree trunks?"

"I'd rather speculate." I waited while the waiter put down fresh drinks and whisked away our empty glasses. "If Petti wasn't aware of the impending arrival of Sara Louise and Madison, he must have had someone else in mind. Will you swear that you're not an FBI agent who moonlights as a hitman?"

"I swear." He appeared to be getting frustrated, although I couldn't imagine why, since my question was infinitely reasonable. "And before you ask, I have no idea who killed Sara Louise. I was at the party, took a walk with a slightly inebriated woman, and returned in time for ribs and baked beans. I told the police the woman's name, and she confirmed the story. You've disliked me from the first day I came into the bookstore. Now that I've admitted I work for a big, bad government agency, you probably loathe me. There's nothing I can say or do to make you trust me."

"You could stop groveling," I said. "That won't make me trust you, but I might feel less antagonistic. I don't like to be used. Did you think my heart would go pitter-patter because you feigned attraction?"

"Your boyfriend cop's name didn't appear in the brief. Otherwise, I wouldn't have come on so strong."

"The brief?"

"I had you checked out the day you moved into Dolly's house. It's standard procedure. I only know the bare facts about your childhood, but I have your college transcript, a copy of your marriage license, the police report of your husband's fatal accident, your voting record, your credit report, your bank balance—which is less than robust— the names of your friends, and copies of the newspaper stories concerning your frequent intrusions into official investigations."

"You found all this out the day I moved into Dolly's house?" I asked incredulously. "Were you spying on the house?"

Gary shrugged. "Let's say it was under surveillance."

I was too stunned to be properly outraged. "Were you perched on a roof with a pair of binoculars?"

"These days we're a little more sophisticated than that."

"Is the house bugged? Are there hidden cameras in the bathrooms? Did you entertain yourself watching me in the Jacuzzi this morning—or do you prefer watching teenaged girls take showers?" I pushed aside my glass. "I think I'd better go. Thanks for the drink."

Rather than protest, he stood up and said, "We must do this again sometime."

I wanted to slap the smirk off his face, but instead stalked out of the clubhouse and floundered around the parking lot until I found my car (which was, of course, precisely where I'd left it). A good deal of proper outrage ensued. I didn't really believe there were cameras in the bathrooms, but I felt violated. All he'd done was snap his fingers and my curriculum vitae was laid open like the morning newspaper. Did the government know that I'd smoked pot in college? That I'd sweet-talked myself out of a speeding ticket three years ago? That I'd written a letter to my senator protesting one of her votes? That I'd fudged my business expenses?

Gary must have been disappointed with my "brief," which didn't sound as though it had been all that brief. After all, I'd never been arrested, joined the Communist Party, been suspected of trafficking in cocaine, smuggled illegal immigrants into the country, or conspired to assassinate a world leader. I was much too boring for that. But still, the government had documented my every cough and sneeze since the day I was born. And it could all be called up at a moment's notice.

I sat for a long while, lost in highly irrational plots to expose the FBI on *60 Minutes* or in *Newsweek*. To start a grassroots letter-writing campaign to Congress. To punch Gary Billings in the nose, dig up J. Edgar Hoover and do the same, and then move to a country that lacked the financial and technological resources to keep dossiers on its private citizens. I finally calmed down and considered the conversation. Gary Billings was an FBI agent, sent to Farberville to keep an eye on Dolly. She'd apparently gone about her typical business until Petti arrived at the Fritz Motel on Sunday. That afternoon, she'd invited me to house-sit, and on Monday was on her way to Dallas or Atlanta while Petti was being murdered, but not by Sara Louise and Madison.

Sara Louise had come in an attempt to ingratiate herself with the family, dragging Madison along as part of her cover story. She could have learned where Petti was going, and presumably why, but she'd chosen to drive instead of fly in order to give herself an excuse to stay at Dolly's house. But Gary had told me that she hadn't come to kill Dolly. The detectives had searched the house and found nothing as damning as a second set of ledgers on the premises. Did the vandal at the Book Depot think she'd hidden them there? Was she alternating calls to me with calls to the home office in Manhattan, so to speak, demanding money in exchange for the ledgers that she'd squirreled away in Atlanta or Miami?

It was as good a theory as I could come up with, although it was hard to believe Dolly would be so reckless. Surely she knew there was no island too small or country too big to ever feel safe again. Some of the Velocchios might end up in prison, but not all of them. They might consider blackmail as treacherous as cooperating with the federal prosecutors.

In that I'd never taken it upon myself to delve into mobster philosophy, I drove to the bookstore, merely for comfort. Jorgeson had not only locked me out but also barricaded the doors with yellow tape, which might be good for business if and when I was allowed to reopen the store. I'd have some tidying up and dusting to do, but perhaps my science fiction hippie could be coerced into helping—if he'd recovered from finding the store quite so spooky. I sat in the parking lot and debated my options. Gary had told me all that he was willing to share. Daniel and Lucy could be anywhere, looking at properties, shopping, or attending a matinee. There was no way to find Cal unless

228

he drove by in his van. That left Nick and Sebastian, headquartered at Manny's PerfectPools.

I left my car where it was and walked half a block to Sally Fromberger's health food restaurant. She came out of the kitchen with plates for the two diners in the corner, then spotted me and froze. "Oh my gawd, Claire," she gasped, then banged down the plates on their table and hurried over to hug me. "I'm so glad you're okay! You must be going out of your mind! Let me fix you a cup of camomile and rosehip tea. Sit down right here. I've been so worried about you!"

"I'm sorry I don't have time for a cup of tea," I said. "I came in to use your telephone directory."

Her eyes widened. "Are you in danger?"

"I'm not going to look up the number of the police department. I just need an address."

"Now?"

"Well, yes," I said, trying to hide my irritation. "That would explain why I came in and asked for your directory."

If her eyes widened any further, surgery might be required. "Are you sure you're not in danger? I can throw the customers out, close the blinds, and lock the door. No one will know you're here."

"No one cares that I'm here, Sally. The directory?"

"I think you need a cup of tea," she said firmly. "You've behaving very oddly. That's not to say any of us wouldn't after finding a body in the freezer, and then having a houseguest steal a car and get herself killed at the country club. The woman who owns the house should be ashamed of herself! Here you are doing her a favor, and she can't bother to come back and sort all this out. If she dares set foot in here, I'll refuse to serve her."

"Is the directory behind the counter? Shall I get it myself?"

The two customers in the corner were ignoring their alfalfa sprouts and tofu burgers in order to gawk at me. Sally glared at them until they turned away, then brought me the directory. She seemed determined to stand over me, but I raised my eyebrows and waited until she reluctantly started for the kitchen.

Once I'd found the address for Manny's PerfectPools, I closed the directory and left before Sally could bear down on me with tea and sympathy, as well as thinly disguised curiosity. Okay, brazen curiosity. Sally's much easier to tolerate when she's organizing local events and browbeating the innocent into serving on committees. Her weapon of choice is a clipboard.

I drove across town to an industrial area and parked in front of a metal building. Weeds, gravel, and chain-link fences dominated the landscaping. A van at the far end of the lot gave me a flicker of optimism that Nick and Sebastian might be there. I had no idea what I was going to ask them, then reminded myself that my undeniable quick-wittedness would see me through. I pushed open the door and went inside what was basically a warehouse. The smell was pungent and the air thick with dust. A counter with a cash register indicated that Manny made some retail sales, but I presumed most of his business came from service contracts.

"Hello?" I called.

The only response was the scurrying sound of startled rodents, a sound I knew too well. I forced myself to go around the counter and into an office, where I found an elderly lady grumbling under her breath as she sorted through stacks of papers. "Hello?" I said more loudly. "Are you Miss Groggin?"

She spun around. "Who are you?"

"I'm looking for Nick and Sebastian."

"Why?"

I hadn't been so intimidated since third grade, when I'd been berated for dirty fingernails in front of the whole class. I couldn't recall the sadistic teacher's name, but she'd had the same white hair in a bun, thin lips, and beady eyes. "I need to ask them something. Are they here?"

"You think lazy bums like them work on a Saturday afternoon? Go look for them at a bar or pool hall. If Manny only knew how sloppy and rude they are, he'd have never let them so much as set foot inside this shop. Manny's a real professional."

"He was called away for a family emergency, right?"

"So they told me. I've worked for him for seventeen years, and not once has he ever taken a vacation without giving me warning so I could make plans of my own. Last summer I went to the Galápagos Islands. No one told me I had to clamber in and out of a rubber dinghy and hike up mountains just to look at giant tortoises. A giant tortoise is no different from the ones I find in my backyard, only bigger. And some of the young Europeans on the boat behaved scandalously, as if none of the rest of us could guess what they were doing under a blanket in a deck chair. This summer I'm going on a bus tour of antebellum houses in Louisiana and Mississippi. We'll be staying in four-star country inns with such basic amenities as bathtubs and down comforters."

"Manny didn't tell you that he was leaving?"

Miss Groggin shook her head hard enough to dislodge a hairpin. "I came in Monday morning and there Nick was, sitting in this very chair, making a mess of the invoices and work orders. He told me he was in charge until Manny came back. He was so snooty that I almost turned around and left, but I know how much the business means to Manny. And to me, too, since I'll have a nice pension when I retire. I told Nick to move his butt, then explained the procedure and gave him the service schedule for the week. He was polite enough after that, although he didn't fool me. If he'd paid any attention to what I told him, I wouldn't be working on a Saturday afternoon, trying to sort through the bills and the checks. I don't understand why he finds it so difficult to keep the paperwork in the folder I gave him. He seems to enjoy wadding it up and stuffing it in his pocket instead."

I put my hands behind my back in case my fingernails had a trace of dirt. "And Sebastian?"

"I have no idea about him. As far as I can tell, Nick hired him from a homeless shelter or the unemployment office. I had a nephew like that many years ago. He blew himself up making pipe bombs in his bedroom."

"Sebastian didn't work for Manny?" I asked, puzzled. "I was told that he did."

"And you were told that the Easter Bunny laid chocolate eggs." Miss Groggin's eyes narrowed. "Friends of yours, are they?"

"Not at all," I said hastily. "I'm house-sitting for Dolly Goforth. They came by last week to clean the pool, and I wanted to ask them a few questions."

"Ah, yes, I saw your photograph in the newspaper. You looked as though fire ants had crawled into your panties. All I can say is that it's a good thing you found the body in the freezer instead of the pool. Dead flesh is a carrier of all kinds of vile insect larvae and fecal contaminants. Manny would have to drain the pool and scrub it down with muriatic acid. Even then, you couldn't be sure you might not be swimming with maggots. Some microscopic worms burrow under your skin to lay their eggs."

I was beginning to feel queasy, but I took a breath and said, "Then you don't have addresses for Nick and Sebastian?"

"If I did, I wouldn't tell you," she said, now gloating as if she could sense my physical discomfort. "Ask them yourself on Monday, if they show up."

I did not flee to my car, but I certainly wasted no time wandering around the front room to admire the nets and brushes. Manny must be a prince, I thought as I sucked in quantities of fresh air. That, or he locked her in the office in the morning when she arrived, and released her at five o'clock. I would have thrown away the key.

I had no one else left to question, so I drove back to the house. The police car hadn't moved, and the officer who'd been snoring earlier was still at it.

I was obliged to ring the doorbell, since Sara Louise had taken the house key with her the previous afternoon. I made a note to look through the drawer in the table in the hall for a spare one.

Caron finally opened the door. "Nice of you to come back so quickly. Did it occur to you that Inez and I are trapped here? We might have liked to get away for a while, but the only car in the driveway was the police car. I doubt they would have given us a lift to the mall. Besides, what could be more entertaining than to wait around for a sniper to get us in the den—unless Dolly had the windows re-done with bulletproof glass? Do mobsters do that?"

I edged around her. "Did anyone call?"

"Two television stations, four newspapers, and some pervert who asked to be alerted if we found another body. Would you like to know what he wants to do with it? It's too gross."

"Then let's not discuss it. What are you and Inez up to? Is the tango in or out?"

"We're thinking about it," Caron said as she followed me into the kitchen. "We don't have to sign up until Monday." She took a pint of ice cream out of the freezer in the top of the refrigerator, found a spoon, and perched on a stool. "What do you think? Are we going to be cool or moronic? I don't want to spend the next two years of my life being called 'Thumper.' That would be too humiliating."

I put on the teakettle, then sat down across from her. "That won't happen if you quit."

"So you're saying I should quit?"

"No, but you have to weigh the risk. Based on what I've heard, if you make fools of yourselves, you'll have to slink around the back halls until graduation. If you win, Rhonda will be the one slinking. The third option is not to take this so seriously. Win or lose, the world will continue to rotate on its axis. Some children in Africa will starve, and others will be rescued by international relief agencies. Congress will continue to find ways to waste money and whine about the deficit. Some species will become extinct, but scientists will dis-cover new ones. Threats of nuclear warfare will arise. California will have earthquakes. A mousy microbiologist will discover a cure for a fatal disease. What goes on in the halls of Farberville High School for the next two years will be of no significance."

"So you're saying I shouldn't quit?"

So much for eloquence, I thought as I straightened a ribbon on the flower arrangement. The flower arrangement that hadn't been there when I left the house. There was no card. "Where'd this come from?" I demanded.

Caron stopped sucking on her lip and eyed me curiously. "I'd guess a florist shop."

"They were delivered?"

"Inez and I didn't climb over the wall out back and go down to Thurber Street to buy them, if that's what you're thinking. One of the cops brought them to the door."

"I'll be back in a minute." I went down the hall and out to the driveway. The officer in charge of the perimeter scrambled out of the car.

"Something wrong, ma'am? Did you see somebody?" He pulled out his gun and waved it unsteadily. "Do I need to call for backup? Erwin, wake up, dammit! We've got us an intruder."

I was weaving to stay out of his line of fire. "Calm down. There's no intruder. I just need to ask you a question. Who brought the flowers to the house earlier this afternoon?"

Visibly disappointed, the officer lowered his gun. "An old black guy. Said they were for you, ma'am. I hope I didn't do anything wrong by bringing them to the door."

"Did you see what he was driving?"

"He parked on the street, so I didn't get a good look at his vehicle. I got a glimpse of a white van when he drove away."

"Go back to your comic book," I said. "I'll scream if I need you." I returned to the kitchen, muttering under my breath. Caron was no longer there. She'd put the ice cream away, but the spoon remained on the island in a puddle of gourmet goo. I rinsed it off and wiped up the minor mess. Cal was having a fine time, I told myself angrily. He must have known that sooner or later I'd call Aunt Bessie's Bloomers and, if I'd saved the scrap of paper, the Fritz Motel. Was he teasing me, or threatening me? And if the latter was the case, why? Could the charade with Petti's body and this influx of flowers be intended to drive us out of the house so that someone, Velocchio or fed, could search the house for a set of ledgers?

I called the PD and asked for Peter, who was, as usual, unavailable. I then asked for Jorgeson, who had a much better track record.

"The lieutenant's in a meeting with the chief, the mayor, the prosecutor, and the director of the country club board," Jorgeson said gloomily. "This may be a long one. Stealing a body from the morgue's one thing, but upsetting the membership at the country club is grounds for life imprisonment without parole. It seems the ladies are refusing to play the tenth hole because it goes behind the cart shed."

"Did Gary Billings come by to see Peter?"

"Who's he, if you don't mind me asking?"

"He's an FBI agent who was sent down to keep an eye on Dolly. He's staying in one of the condos at the golf course."

Jorgeson took a moment. "And he told you he was an FBI agent? Why would he do that?"

I was not inclined to tell Jorgeson how close I'd come to shrieking, "Hitman!" on the screened-in porch at the country club. "It's a long story. He did say he was going to go to the PD to announce that he's taking charge of the case."

"The lieutenant's gonna love this. I'm thinking I may go home and weed the vegetable garden."

"I wish I could, too, except I don't have a vegetable garden. I suppose I could go to the paint store and look at chips. Mr. Kalker's crew should be ready to start on the walls in the next few days. How do you feel about sage green?"

"At the moment, my face is sage green and I doubt it's all that attractive. You'd better stay where you are, Ms. Malloy. The lieutenant will want to talk to you when he gets out of this meeting. If you're not there . . ."

"Weed till you weep, Sergeant Jorgeson," I said, then hung up.

I went to find Caron and Inez. They were on the patio, conversing intently. I wondered for a brief second if Caron had actually heard what I said in the kitchen, but I doubted it. Until she reached a certain level of maturity, she was the center of the universe. She read only the comics in the newspaper and retreated to her bedroom whenever I watched the news. If I told her a meteorite was plunging toward Earth, she'd dash into the bathroom to wash her hair. And I would try to finish the last chapter in whatever mystery novel I was reading. "I knew all along it was the housekeeper" would be my last words.

I opened the sliding door. "I need you to help me."

"Yeah, in a few minutes," Caron said.

"Now. We are going to search every inch—no, every centimeter of this house, from the pantry to the mustiest closet. We need to do it in the next hour. Your conversation will have to wait."

"Search for what?" asked Inez.

Caron rolled her eyes. "Have you forgotten that the police already searched the house a couple of days ago? Do you think someone managed to smuggle the dead guy back into the house and fold him up with the extra blankets and pillowcases?"

"We are going to search for ledgers. The police may have passed right over them, assuming they were of no consequence. And we need to do this before Peter gets out of a meeting and starts pounding on the door. If you refuse to cooperate, I'll tell the officers outside that it's too dangerous for you to stay here any longer and they need to take you to a cheap motel without cable."

"You are Too Peculiar, Mother," Caron said. She stood up and waited for Inez. "Okay, we'll search the house. What exactly is a ledger? Would one expect to find it on a ledge? In a hedge? As a wedge?"

"Enough of the Dr. Seuss," I said.

I explained the basic concept of a ledger. We split up and opened every drawer, suitcase, box, cabinet, closet, and hatbox. I pulled out all the files and folders in the desk and looked through them. Caron pranced through the den with a purple boa wrapped around her neck and went back upstairs. Inez, to her horror, encountered a dead mouse in a cabinet in the pantry and nearly fainted. I forced myself to go into the garage and make sure the storage room contained only empty boxes, a half case of wine, and a multitude of spiders.

At last I called it quits and we went into the kitchen for beverages.

While Caron gleefully described a box of costume jewelry she'd found, I poured myself an inch of scotch and dropped in an ice cube.

So much for that brilliant theory.

Peter showed up an hour later, bearing hot dogs, buns, and chips. His greeting was less than exuberant. I took the groceries into the kitchen, then brought him a beer while he turned on the grill. After he'd flopped down in a lounge chair, I said, "Jorgeson told me you had another meeting today."

"Oh, yes."

"Did you tell them about the Velocchio connection?"

"It went over really well. They demanded that I call in the FBI, the CIA, the FTA, the DEA, and everybody else short of their mothers-in-law, which I suppose would be the MIL." He rolled his head to look at me. "It seems I don't have to call in the FBI, since you've already done that."

"I did nothing of the sort," I said indignantly. "It just sort of happened."

"Why don't you explain how it just sort of happened? I'm sure it will be fascinating."

"If you'd listened carefully to the tape of Dolly's call earlier, you would have come to the same conclusion."

Peter did not appreciate my tacit reproof. "I was distracted by the murder at the country club last night. The media are hounding the PD for a press conference, or at least a statement as to our progress. First a body in a freezer, then a beautiful girl in a red Mercedes. As soon as word gets out about the Velocchio family, you'll have news helicopters over the house tomorrow. You and the girls may want to stay inside."

"Caron and Inez are more likely to be out here doing the tango in their bathing suits, or in Sara Louise's and Madison's bikinis." I took a deep breath, then related in great detail the conversation with Gary. "I suppose I pushed him into a corner," I admitted, "but he's a professional. He could have told me I was crazy and walked away. I didn't have any proof that he was even involved."

"He was going to have to step in sooner or later. Neither Petti nor Dolly was on the subpoena list, but they were clearly players. Federal charges, federal grand jury, federal indictments." He took a long drink of beer. "This Billings guy was questioned this morning, along with all the other residents in the condos. His story was verified by the hosts of the party and the woman he escorted outside for a short while. He had no reason to flash his badge."

"What about Daniel and Lucy, who hosted the party?"

"Neither of them left their condo until the event broke up at ten, nor did anyone else. Do you think they're on one side or the other?"

"I don't know what to think," I said. "Dolly did say that there was someone here who might confide in me. They showed up in the store earlier on the day I found Petti in the freezer, and later they asked about Dolly's whereabouts. Oh, and guess what? Cal dropped off another flower arrangement this afternoon. You need to find him."

Peter sighed. "We need to find Madison Hayes. After what happened to Sara Louise, it's getting harder to believe she's holed up with some college boy in an apartment. Then again, it's possible they've found more stimulating things to do than look at a newspaper or turn on the TV. Anything else?"

I told him about my encounter with Miss Groggin, which he found highly entertaining. After he quit chuckling, I went into the kitchen and returned with the wieners. We charred them to perfection, then called Caron and Inez to eat on the patio. We all lacked the energy to engage in even superficially clever conversation; most of the remarks involved ketchup and mustard. Before Peter left, he told me that officers would remain at the house all night and periodically patrol the backyard. I promised to lock up and switch on the alarm. His kiss was perfunctory, as was mine.

I left Caron and Inez making monstrous sundaes and went upstairs to my bedroom. I read for a long while, although by the penultimate chapter, I was unable to stop yawning. I put the book on the bedside table, scrunched up a pillow under my head, and went to sleep.

I awoke to a faint sound from downstairs. I rolled over and found the alarm clock, which read 3:17 A.M. Blinking, I sat up and strained to grasp what I was hearing. Music, I finally realized, nearly inaudible, but the same music Caron and Inez had been playing earlier. Perhaps one or the other of them had gone down to the den to reflect on the wisdom of doing the tango at the talent contest.

I went along the hallway and opened their bedroom door. Both of their dear little heads were on pillows, and lumps under the blankets suggested the rest of them was also there. Curiouser and curiouser, I thought as I eased the door closed and went to the top of the stairs.

The police officers who were parked in the driveway had no access to the house. The alarm had not shrieked. Had a devious FBI agent, namely Gary Billings, found a way inside, he would hardly idle away the night listening to music, nor would an even more devious hitman. Hardly professional.

I could have gone into the bedroom vacated by Sara Louise, opened a window, and pitched a lamp in the direction of the police car. I could have returned to the girls' room, locked the door, and called Peter. I could have armed myself with a can of pepper spray, but I'd never owned such a thing.

Having dismissed my other options, I took a breath and went downstairs.

Chapter Fifteen

A small lamp in a corner was adequate for me to identify the back of Dolly's head as she sat on the sofa. She was swaying with the music, as if imagining herself in Bibi's arms in the center of a glitzy ballroom.

I suppose I should have been shocked, stunned, and flabbergasted, but I was no more than bemused. If Petti had appeared from the living room, accompanied by Scarface, Bugsy, and Bibi, I would have introduced myself and offered them wine. The past week's events had transcended any semblance of rationality; I was beyond being overwhelmed. "Hello," I said as I came around the end of the sofa and sat down on the ottoman. "I thought you were in Miami."

"Good evening, Claire. I'm so sorry if I disturbed you. Now that you're up, would you like a cup of tea? I know I would."

"I thought you were in Miami," I repeated.

"And indeed I was," she said. "Then I flew to Dallas, took one of those alarmingly bumpy commuter flights here, and rented a car. I thought it best to park it at the bottom of the hill. The police officers out in the driveway failed to notice me when I stayed in the shadows along the fence. I let myself in through the side door of the garage and reset the alarm. I must admit it's been a long day. I do believe I'll make some tea. Are you sure you won't join me?" Without waiting for an answer, she headed for the kitchen.

I followed her. "Okay, now I know how you got here. Shall we move on to why you decided to come back?"

She filled the teakettle and set it on the stove. "Have the detectives made any progress finding out who killed Sara Louise?"

"Did you come back to help them, Dolly? Is that why you're here? Wouldn't a phone call have sufficed?"

"I wish I could tell you, dear, but it would put you and the girls in even more danger. It's imperative that no one, including that handsome lieutenant of yours, knows I'm here. Rest assured I won't be staying long."

"You've already put us in danger," I said, grinding out each word. "I deserve to know what the hell's going on!"

Dolly waggled a finger at me. "Let's not wake the girls, Claire. Is Madison here, too? It would be most inconvenient if she learns that I've returned."

"She disappeared a couple of days ago. I suppose it would be inconvenient, since she and Sara Louise came down here to . . ." I grappled for a euphemism, then gave up and shrugged.

"Kill me? They most certainly did not come here for that purpose, but it's possible they might have eventually. Well, they probably would have. Sara Louise has always been impetuous. When they used to come to the lake house, she was the one who bartered drugs for beer with the local boys. Bibi and I could not control her. I always thought her parents sent her to us simply to get her off their hands for a few weeks. Once she went away to college, she settled down and focused on getting her degrees."

"And preparing herself for a position in the Velocchio family? A degree in international banking would have been useful when it came to moving money all over the world. Was Bibi her inspiration?"

Dolly took out teacups and a box of tea bags. "Sugar? Milk?"

"I'd prefer answers."

"She was always fascinated with what Bibi did, although he was reluctant to discuss it with her. In this day and age, however, with all the electronic transfers, encryptions, and heightened scrutiny by dreary federal agencies, complex computer savvy is so very necessary. Bibi accepted that, and had decided to retire when he had the heart attack. We had such glorious plans for the future."

"We've already had that conversation," I said without sympathy. "Why don't we talk about your old friend Petti? Did he come here specifically to tell you about the subpoenas? Couldn't he have called or sent a postcard?"

Dolly put a teacup in front of me, then sat down. "There was a certain urgency, but neither of us could trust the telephone. He called someone else with the message that he was coming. I was subsequently informed where he would be staying. I should have known it was too risky to call that motel."

"You weren't worried that someone might follow you when you went to meet him Sunday evening?"

She smiled. "I took great care not to be followed, and at that point, I didn't really understand how serious the situation was. In retrospect, I should have arranged a drop-off, but I was so eager to see Petti. He was a dear friend for many, many years. He and Bibi grew up in the same neighborhood, went to the same schools, played stickball, ate dinner at each other's house. They were closer than most brothers. He and I were going to take Bibi's ashes to the lake house and bury them on the hillside near the terrace where the three of us spent so many pleasant evenings."

"Not in a Catholic cemetery?"

"I knew what Bibi would have wanted. Instead, I didn't even have a chance to say goodbye to Petti after the funeral."

"Because the FBI whisked you away and put you in the witness protection program?"

"You have been busy, haven't you? Five minutes after the funeral was over, I was taken to the airport and given a new identity and a ticket. Five hours later, I landed at the Phoenix airport."

"So you weren't at home to receive visitors after the funeral. That must have aroused suspicion," I said.

Dolly shook her head. "Not really. I'd told everyone I was going to stay with a cousin in Arizona. The Velocchios were supportive after

Bibi's death, even offering financial help, and I think they believed me when I said I needed to get away. A few weeks later, I sent a letter to Bibi's sister, telling her I couldn't bear to go back to the brownstone and was planning to buy a home in a retirement village near Phoenix. It was postmarked in Arizona, so I doubt any one of them even gave it a thought. The FBI is amazingly adept at that sort of thing." She gazed at me, her eyebrows raised. "Which leads me to wonder how you found out."

It was tempting to give her a dose of her own maddening medicine, but I said, "I had a drink this afternoon with an agent named Gary Billings. With a bit of provocation on my part, he showed me his badge."

"Gary Billings?" Her spoon rattled in the teacup. "Here, in Farberville? That's a silly question, isn't it? You hardly could have flown to DC and back again. What did he have to say?"

"Then you know him?"

"He was one of the agents who took me to the airport, so I don't know why I'm so surprised he's here. Where did you tell him I was?"

"Miami," I said. "He said he was aware that the Velocchios had come to find you, and that he'd come, in his words, 'to assess the situation.' Was he planning to relocate you?"

"That may have been his plan," she said vaguely. "I'm exhausted, Claire. I'll sleep in whichever room Sara Louise was using, and stay out of sight in the morning. Is there any chance Caron and Inez will go out tomorrow?"

I'd had enough of her evasions and lies. It was nearly 4:00 A.M., my head was throbbing, and I'd learned virtually nothing I wouldn't have figured out on my own (although possibly later rather than sooner). "If you so much as put one toe on the floor, I'm going to call Lieutenant Rosen and tell him what's going on. He will have you picked up immediately and offer you a thin, lumpy mattress for the remainder of the night. In a few hours, you'll be served watery coffee, powdered eggs, and cold toast. Marmalade will not be an option. You'll then spend the day in an interrogation room, as well as the day after unless Gary Billings takes you into federal custody. Two people

243

have been killed. No one is taking it lightly. I am not going to do anything to help you unless you tell me the truth."

"I thought you were my friend, Claire."

"And I thought you were mine, until I realized that all you've done is lie to me."

She stared at her teacup for a long while. "Perhaps we can compromise. I'll tell you part of it now, and after I've had some sleep and time to think, I may be able to give you enough information so that you'll understand better. Do I have your permission to make another cup of tea?"

Now I felt like a churlish child whose hand had been slapped. "Go ahead, but start talking."

She went to the stove and switched on the burner. "Petti realized that when the subpoenas were issued, the Velocchio family might suspect that I had pertinent information concerning certain testimony. He heard rumors that they had located me, so he sent the message that he was coming and I picked him up at the motel so we could drive around and talk. He gave me his cell phone and several sets of false identification. After I dropped him off at the motel, I never saw or heard from him again. Someone must have followed him here and killed him."

"Why his cell phone?"

"Because I didn't have one and we wanted to stay in touch. He figured he could call me on it safely. He never did, obviously."

"You could have bought one," I pointed out.

"I didn't think I had time. I had to pack and be ready for Caron to take me to the airport. Petti said he'd buy another one when he got home."

"And you have no idea who killed him?"

"Or Sara Louise, either, if that's your next question. Petti's body was left in my yard to frighten me. I assumed that whoever the Velocchios had sent here would learn fairly quickly that I was gone, and that would be the end of it. I don't know why Sara Louise and Madison stayed on like they did."

I grimaced. "Their cunning plan involved disabling the car so that you'd feel obligated to take them in for a few days. You did call, however, and they must have thought I would be able to tell them where you were. They weren't the only ones. You'd be flattered by the number of people who've been concerned over your whereabouts and indignant that you didn't return immediately to clear things up. Everybody who saw the story in the paper has demanded updates, including customers at the store, the owner of the health food restaurant, the pool guys, and even the florist."

Dolly glanced at the flowers at the end of the island. "The florist? It sounds as though you've been pestered incessantly. I'm truly sorry, Claire. As soon as I can, I'll leave. It may be a few days, though. Is there any way you can explain my presence to the girls?"

"They know what's going on, and they're not happy campers," I said. I thought about it for a moment, then added, "This is a long shot, but it might work for a day or two. They're determined to learn the tango. If you can convince them that you're not guilty of anything—which may take some work—and then offer to give them lessons, they may go along with it."

"Teenagers want to learn the tango? How very quaint. I would have thought they'd be more interested in this insipid contemporary music. Then again, I did notice that the videotapes were piled on the table and there was a CD in the player. I'll talk to them in the morning, if it's all right with you." She put her cup in the sink. "I really need a few hours of sleep. You have every reason to distrust me, but I do hope we can reestablish our friendship."

"You still haven't told me why you came back."

"I wish I could, but I can't. Which room was Sara Louise's?"

I left my untouched teacup where it was and gestured for her to follow me. She waited at the bottom of the stairs while I went into the den to turn off the lamp and the music, and said nothing as we went upstairs. I indicated the room, and returned to mine. Whatever, I thought as I crawled into bed. Whatever.

———

The following morning when I awoke, I lay in bed for a long time, wondering if my encounter with Dolly had been nothing more than a diabolic dream. Each word and nuance were still clear, and I eventually concluded that I would find one teacup on the island and another in the sink. Which, regrettably, led to the question of whether I should have called Peter immediately—or should as soon as I got out of bed. I pulled a blanket over my face to block the sunlight and stayed where I was. The scenario I'd described to Dolly during our bizarre conversation would most certainly take place, most likely within minutes of my call. Gary Billings would swoop down like a buzzard. Ranting and raving would ensue as the FBI battled the Farberville CID. Judges might be hauled off golf courses to settle the custody dispute. The chief of police might be interrupted during brunch, which would make him all the more determined to have me pilloried on the courthouse steps. The prosecuting attorney, dragged away from his bloody marys and the Sunday newspaper, would charge me with harboring a fugitive—even if Dolly wasn't technically one. He might opt for conspiracy instead, or high treason, as long as both carried the possibility of the death penalty.

And then there was Peter.

I had even less desire to get out of bed than I'd had the morning after giving birth to Caron, who, being a night owl even in utero, had refused to cooperate until nearly dawn. Thinking of her was enough to propel me to my feet and into the shower. I needed to be downstairs when she and Inez came to the kitchen for breakfast so that I could at least warn them of the considerable surprise awaiting them. I had no idea how they'd react, but I rarely did.

Dolly was asleep in the bed most recently used by Sara Louise, and the girls had flopped around since I'd last peeked in on them but were snuffling and snoring. I went downstairs to the kitchen, started a pot of coffee, and then switched off the alarm before opening the front door. Officers Blinken and Nod had been relieved by two new officers of a similar appearance. I waved to them as I picked up the morning newspaper and went back inside.

A blurry photograph of Dolly's Mercedes dominated the front

page, but the factual information in the story was sparse. The identity of the victim could not be released, pending notification of the next of kin. The officers at the scene, and specifically Lieutenant Peter Rosen, had deferred questions about the cause of death to the medical examiner, who'd had no comment. In that the car provided a link to my discovery of the body in the freezer, that story was rehashed. Petti's name had been discovered, perhaps from a garrulous orderly, but all the story could relate was that Petrolli Mordella was a retired building consultant from Brooklyn. That was adequate, in the eyes of the reporter, to make him seem sinister, although justification for the implicit accusation was noticeably absent.

I tried to immerse myself in the rest of the newspaper, but I felt as though the sword of Damocles, currently incarnated as a blond woman with a good heart and a penchant for lies, was dangling above my head in both a figurative and literal fashion. The phone was only a few steps away. Peter was undoubtedly in his office, making futile calls and abusing a computer keyboard for further information. If I ratted out Dolly, she would be held as a material witness (despite not having witnessed anything), and possibly torn to tatters in the ensuing custody war. Six hours ago, I'd been perversely pleased that she'd returned; now I found myself wishing she'd taken the next flight from Miami to Anchorage.

I was skimming the business section when Dolly appeared, dressed in a plush terry-cloth robe I'd seen in the closet of the bedroom in which I'd been sleeping. I'd encountered such robes in hotel closets, but had been too intimidated to wear them for fear I'd be charged as an imposter. Her hair was impeccable, as was her makeup. I ran my fingers through my damp, limp curls and said, "There's fresh coffee."

"How thoughtful," she murmured. "Why don't I see what I can find in the refrigerator and whip up a soufflé? I do so love Sunday mornings. Bibi used to make the most divine blueberry muffins and cinnamon rolls, and we'd spend hours reading the *New York Times* and slaving over the crossword puzzle. Shall we have mimosas on the patio with breakfast?"

"A lovely idea. I'll invite the two police officers parked out front to join us. They must be starving."

"I think not, dear." She took eggs, mushrooms, peppers, and various other items from the refrigerator and set them on the counter next to the sink. "Has anyone called?"

"If you're worried that I called Peter, the answer is no. I'm still considering it, though. I'm in an even worse position than I was yesterday. Are you sure that no one knows you're here? What if this Velocchio person followed you from the airport?"

Dolly smiled. "I used a false driver's license and wore a gray wig. My limp was so pronounced that the clerk at the car rental agency expedited the paperwork and walked me to the car. No one could have recognized me, including Bibi."

"What if the police find the rental car?" I persisted.

"I left it in the Ferncliffs' driveway. Lucille mentioned a few weeks earlier that they were going on an extended tour of Asia. It won't be noticed." She found a bowl and a whisk, and began to crack eggs. "Will Caron and Inez be joining us?"

I stared at her fuzzy white back. "Eventually."

"I'm looking forward to finding out why they've become interested in the tango. So few teenagers appreciate ballroom dancing these days. They'd rather gyrate at each other from several feet away rather than luxuriate in physical contact. When they condescend to slow dancing, all they seem to do is drape themselves over each other and shuffle their feet. There's no passion in that, no exuberance, no drama, no joie de vivre."

While I was searching for a response, and admittedly having no success whatsoever, Inez came into the kitchen. She spotted Dolly, who was chopping mushrooms, then blinked at me as if I were entertaining a mutant life form or a Hollywood celebrity.

"Is that . . . ?" she gurgled.

"Good morning, Inez," Dolly said cheerfully. "I suppose you're too young for coffee. Would you like a glass of orange juice? Will Caron be along soon? I'm almost ready to put the soufflé in the oven. Once it's done, it waits for no one."

Inez positioned herself behind me in case the mad woman with the whisk threatened to attack. "Caron's in the shower."

"Then we're in good shape," Dolly continued. "I'll just beat the egg whites, pop the soufflé in the oven, and see what I can find upstairs to wear. I noticed that you and Caron are staying in my bedroom. Do you think she'll mind if I tiptoe in and look through the dresser?"

I felt Inez's fingernails digging into my shoulder. I removed her hand before she drew blood, then said, "Of course not, Dolly. It is your room, after all. Inez, you go with her and let Caron know what's going on. The soufflé can wait until the three of you have a nice, long conversation about past and current events. I'll wait here."

"That's an excellent idea," Dolly said, putting down the whisk. "Come along, Inez. We have issues to discuss, but I'm confident we can negotiate an agreement."

Too dumbfounded to protest, Inez followed her out of the kitchen. I suppose I should have accompanied them, but I hadn't yet decided whether or not to call Peter. I opted to pour myself another cup of coffee rather than give serious consideration to the moral dilemma that had plopped into my lap. I could throw Dolly to the hyenas, or trust her despite her noticeably poor record thus far.

I was still musing when the telephone rang. I went into the hall, punched the obligatory button, and picked up the receiver. "Hello?"

"Ms. Malloy, this is Nick, Nick Lambert, from Manny's Perfect-Pools. Remember me?"

"If you're calling about the pool, it's still perfect."

"No, it's not about the pool, although I would like to say I take pride in my work. I heard you went by the office yesterday, and I think we should talk about it. Would it cause you undue inconvenience if I was to come over?"

"Did Miss Groggin tell you I was there?" I asked.

"Miss Groggin is a suspicious woman. After you left, she began to wonder if you had taken what little cash there was in the drawer or availed yourself of cleaning supplies on your departure. She felt that you were behaving in an odd manner and took it upon herself to call me. Normally, I would have paid no attention to her, but then I learned that you had engaged in an enlightening conversation with Gary Billings. That is what I desire to discuss with you. If you do not object, I can be there in ten minutes."

I sat down on the bottom step. "I do object, Nick. What's this about?"

"It would be better if we had this discussion in person, Ms. Malloy."

I had no idea how long it would take Dolly to convince the girls that they should accept her proposition. Caron had received a poor grade in her sophomore debate class, primarily because of her tenacity despite whatever contrary evidence was presented. I certainly didn't want to add Nick to the convoluted equation. On the other hand, I was more than a little intrigued by his reference to Gary.

"You can't come here," I said, "and I'm not going to meet you at the so-called office in that desolate wasteland of warehouses."

"I understand, Ms. Malloy. There's some sort of organic restaurant very close to your bookstore. I should think we can have a private conversation in a back booth. Is that acceptable?"

"I guess so," I said, not attempting to disguise my lack of enthusiasm. "This afternoon?"

He cleared his throat. "I am thinking of more like fifteen minutes. I'm worried about you, Ms. Malloy. I do not think you realize how much danger you're in right now. Gary Billings is not who he says he is."

"Who is he?"

"Fifteen minutes, then. Please don't let anyone know about this, including Lieutenant Rosen. If I so much as sense that he or any of his detectives are present, then you and I will discuss chlorine, pump maintenance, and the wisdom of draining pools in the winter. Am I clear?"

He hung up without waiting for a reply. I replaced the receiver, then sat back down and tried to think. At this point, I'd dug such a deep hole for myself that I could barely see a patch of blue above me.

And it was a cloudy patch, at best. I'd left my watch upstairs, but I could hear the minutes ticking away.

I concluded that I would be in no danger at Sally's restaurant on a sunny Sunday morning. I wrote a note stating I would be back shortly, and left it on the island. The two police officers looked up as I walked past their car. I said something to the effect that I was going out to get a copy of the *New York Times,* then drove to the Book Depot and parked behind the building. As I entered the restaurant, I saw Nick in the back booth. Ignoring Sally, which is harder than one would think, I sat down across from Nick and said, "Please explain."

"Would you care for coffee and a muffin?"

In that Sally was bearing down on us, I nodded and kept my eyes averted as he ordered. Once she had moved out of earshot, I said, "What do you know about Gary Billings? Are you going to claim he's not an FBI agent?"

"He was suspended last month. I do not know the details, but I do know he's not on active duty."

"How do you know this?" I demanded.

Nick paused as Sally put down coffee mugs and muffins. She seemed inclined to linger, but we remained silent until she reluctantly went to another booth to take an order. "My supervisor told me," he said in a low voice. "Billings made a serious mistake that weakened the government's case against the Velocchio family. His excuses were not satisfactory."

I dumped a spoonful of brownish-gray granules in my coffee. "Are you telling me that you're an FBI agent? And Sebastian, too? I find that hard to believe. Why don't you show me your badge, Nick?"

"I am undercover, Ms. Malloy, and I do not carry my badge unless I anticipate the need to produce it. Sebastian is just a guy who works for Manny."

"No, he's not," I said. "Miss Groggin told me you hired him."

Nick sucked on his lower lip for a moment. "Sebastian is not a regular employee. On account of some trouble he incurred in the past, he prefers to be paid in cash. Miss Groggin would not have gone along with this, so Manny never told her. Since all I know about swimming pools is how to jump into them, I need Sebastian's expertise, limited as it may be. He is not what you would consider a prime candidate for cloning. He just grunted when I told him that Manny asked me to run the business for a few weeks."

"And why did Manny do that?"

Nick gazed at me. "He is a very accommodating fellow."

While I thought, I tried the coffee, which tasted as though it had been made from roots and berries. "For starters, Nick, why should I believe you? Gary has a badge, as well as a somewhat credible explanation for being here."

"He also has ties to the Velocchio family. I do not suppose he mentioned that."

"How do I know you're not the one with ties to the Velocchio family?" I countered coolly, praying he wouldn't hear the faint tremor in my voice. "Does the FBI have a toll-free number I can call to verify your story?"

"Like I said, Ms. Malloy, I'm undercover. Remember that show called *Mission: Impossible*? The man on the recording always said the secretary-general or whatever would disavow any knowledge. We have the same policy."

"So I just take your word? I don't think so."

He took a sip of the coffee and wrinkled his nose. "I have never tasted horse piss, but I imagine it would be similar to this. But to return to the problem, I agree that you have no reason to believe me. That cannot be helped. All I can do is warn you not to believe Gary Billings, either. It is probable that he is responsible for Petrolli Mordella's death, and the girl's, too. It is imperative to him that he find Doris Barlucci, currently known as Dolly Goforth, before we do. Obviously, we cannot let that happen."

"Why does he have to find her? Better yet, why do you have to find her? She's not going to testify at the grand jury investigation next week. During one of our conversations on the telephone, she made it clear that she has no incriminating evidence. She wants to put Bibi's death and his association with the Velocchio family behind her. Why this sudden urgency to find her?"

"It's safer for you and your daughter if you don't know," said Nick.

"I've heard that too many times."

"In this case, the truth really is stranger than fiction, Ms. Malloy. You should heed all these well-intentioned warnings. Look at what happened to Mr. Mordella and Miss Santini. I do not want something like that to happen to you and your daughter."

I stared at him. "Is that a threat?"

He held up his hands. "In no way should you interpret that as a threat. The FBI does not threaten law-abiding citizens. The Velocchios, on the other hand, have a different philosophy. Once they're satisfied that you've told them everything you can, they do not leave witnesses, including members of their own family whom they no longer trust. That is why it's taken us so many years to even attempt to get grand jury indictments. It is most unfortunate that you are now perceived as a key player. If you wish, I can make a few calls and have you and your daughter relocated within hours."

"Temporarily?"

He shrugged. "That will depend on your degree of complicity. Even if the head of the family and his trusted captains are imprisoned, others may feel a moral obligation to make an example of you. The federal marshals will choose a random location, offer limited assistance, and give you fresh identities. This way, no one, including your closest friends and relatives, will be able to inadvertently give away any information. It will be difficult, but at least you'll be safe."

"Will they find me a job as a library aide or a custodian? Pay Caron's college tuition? Send Christmas cards on my behalf?"

"This is not a joke, Ms. Malloy," said Nick. He leaned forward, his hands clutched on the stained tabletop, his voice low and intense. "You will remain in danger until we find Dolly and take her into protective custody. Those sent here by the Velocchio family are convinced that you know where she is. They know, as do we, that she continues to call you every few days, and now they suspect that she is much closer to home than Miami. They will not leave you standing in their way. Think of it as a dog race. The rabbit, a mindless machine, goes around the track, while the dogs pound after it, jostling each other, snarling, determined to catch it and rip it to shreds. This rabbit made of scraps of metal and artificial fur lacks the capacity to be afraid. A real rabbit would dive into the nearest burrow and stay there until the race is over."

"That is a very poor analogy," I said sternly. "I have no reason to believe you, or to accept your story that Gary Billings is a rogue agent who killed two people. Maybe you killed them."

He tried to look offended, but it was unconvincing. "The Bureau has strict policies about such things. Had I gotten to Mordella first, I would have taken him in for interrogation. Although I was aware of the Santini girl's affiliation, I had no reason to think she had intimate knowledge of Dolly's whereabouts. If I had, she too would have been interrogated. The FBI is overseen by the federal government, and we operate under legal strictures. The Velocchio family's primary instincts are based on self-preservation—and revenge."

I took a nibble of the muffin, which was surely made from the same roots and berries as the muddy coffee. I vowed never again to grouse about the coffee at the police department, presuming I lived long enough to grouse about anything at all. "Okay, Nick, if that's your real name, why haven't you done anything about Gary? You told me he'd been suspended."

"He is not aware of my presence. Furthermore, he broke no law when he rented the condo."

"Well, he did if he killed two people," I pointed out as I kept trying to swallow the muffin crumbs lodged in my throat. "Why hasn't he been arrested?"

"That is a matter for the local authorities, who appear to have no evidence of his involvement. The victims were not under federal protection. You're beginning to look ill, Ms. Malloy. Would you like a glass of water?"

Sally Fromberger would have been delighted to fetch water, thump my back, and drag me into the kitchen to demand details. I shook my head. "Gary told me he was going to the police department to identify himself and take over the case. Why don't you do the same, Nick? Tell Lieutenant Rosen to flip a coin and call me with the winner's name. We have around-the-clock protection at the house, so don't bother dropping by later with some feeble claim about testing the bacterial levels in the pool." I refrained from knocking over the mug as I stood up, although it would have been interesting to find out if it could eat through his clothing and do considerable damage to his ability to sire children. "Your story is compelling, but I didn't just hop off a truck packed with illegal immigrants. I hope you enjoy the muffin."

"You're making a big mistake, Ms. Malloy," he said softly.

"Such is the perilous life of a bookseller." I left before Sally could catch me, and walked to the bookstore. I gazed at it as if it were a holy shrine, with all the answers contained on neatly printed pages, along with footnotes. If only, I thought longingly, I could slip inside, sit down between the racks, and flip through pages until I stumbled on answers.

Or a list of the cast of characters.

Chapter Sixteen

Despite the innumerable questions and few answers pinging inside my head, I recalled the purported reason for my outing and went to a newsstand owned by a pair of expatriates from the English department. After a congenial discussion of the latest campus scandals, I talked them out of a copy of the *New York Times* and drove back to the house. The two police officers nodded at me as I went to the front door and rang the bell.

Caron opened the door and dragged me inside. "Is what she says true?" she whispered, clinging to my arm. "I mean, I have No Idea what to think. Does she really have all these false driver's licenses? Isn't that illegal? Did she tell you why she came back? Doesn't she know about these mobsters and how they've murdered people? She closed all the curtains and blinds, and it's like a mausoleum. I keep waiting for Petti to come stumbling in from the freezer with an icicle dangling from his nose!"

"Calm down, dear," I said as I extricated my arm. "I don't have any idea what she told you, but she is certainly aware of what's happened since she left on Monday. I do think we're safe as long as the police are parked in the driveway and the gate's locked."

"She managed to get inside the house."

"She has a house key," I said. "No one else does, including me."

"Yeah, because Sara Louise took it with her when she left two days ago. Who's got it now?"

It was a very good question, one that I hadn't considered. Sara Louise's purse had not been found at the scene. Possession of the key did not guarantee a free run of the house, however. Once the alarm was switched on, anyone using a key had only a minute to punch in a code on the keypad. I wasn't sure what would happen if the sequence was disrupted, but images of Keystone Kops and paratroopers descending from all directions had charm. "What did you and Inez decide to do about Dolly?"

"It's okay with us if she stays here. What are you going to say to Peter when he finds out? Will all of us be arrested? Inez says her parents will absolutely kill her if she gets sent away to some juvenile lockup for the next two years. They've already paid for her to spend August in Honduras or Guatemala with her church group, building an orphanage. She'd do better in a cell. I can just see her sleeping in a tent with spider monkeys, tarantulas, six-inch leeches, and poisonous snakes."

I went into the dining room and put down the newspaper. The den was unoccupied. "Where is everybody?"

"Dolly's cleaning up the kitchen, and Inez went upstairs to read. I've been trying to watch TV, but all that's on are either church services or politicians spouting platitudes. The only way to tell the shows apart is by what they're wearing. The politicians avoid polyester and pastels."

"No tango lessons yet?"

"This afternoon, unless we're locked in those nasty little rooms at the PD with one-way mirrors and all the modern conveniences of a Moscow apartment."

I put my arm around her shoulder and tried to sound wise. "We'll be okay, dear."

"Wasn't that the motto of the *Titanic*?" Caron went into the den and flopped down on the sofa.

I went into the kitchen. Dolly was in the pantry, putting cardboard containers and plastic wrappers in the trash can. "I'm so sorry you didn't get to share the soufflé," she said as she wiped her hands on a dish towel and joined me. "It was spectacular when I took it out of the oven. Did you find a copy of the *Times*?"

I sat down on a stool. "Yes, but I also found out some other things of perhaps greater interest. Are you familiar with someone named Nick Lambert?"

She dropped the towel by the sink and turned around to look at me. Her lips barely moved as she said, "I've heard the name. Why?"

"He and I had an interesting exchange this morning. He claims that he's an FBI agent and that Gary Billings was suspended for bungling evidence concerning the upcoming grand jury investigation. Nick also said that Gary most likely killed Petti and Sara Louise."

"Did you believe him?"

"I don't know who's telling the truth," I admitted frankly. "Gary has an alibi for the time Sara Louise was killed. That's more than Nick has. The police aren't sure when Petti was killed, partly because of the tissue damage caused by the freezer." I did not volunteer the primary reason why the autopsy had not yet been completed.

Dolly's eyes filled with tears. "Poor, sweet Petti. If only he'd stayed in Brooklyn instead of rushing to my rescue. The only family he had was a cousin who lives in Australia or New Zealand. Has anyone made arrangements for his burial?"

"Not that the authorities are aware of," I said. "But what about Nick Lambert? Is he the FBI agent—or is Gary? Why are they so interested in locating you? And why did you come back here?"

"I can't tell you, Claire. I really must go lie down for a while. Please tell the girls we'll start our lesson in an hour or so." She gave me a wan smile and left the kitchen.

I might as well have been questioning a scissor-headed flyswatter, I thought glumly as I gathered up the *Times* from the dining room table and went into the living room. I would have preferred the patio, but it seemed too exposed. Dolly had experienced no problems getting inside the house despite the vigilance of Farberville's finest. The backyard was a veritable playground of hiding places, from the gazebo to the upper branches of the pine trees. I wished

I felt quite as confident about our security as I had when glibly telling Caron that we were perfectly safe. Which we probably were. My gravest danger was likely to be that of indigestion from the coffee and muffin.

The first section of the paper was, as always, a compilation of international disasters, from attempted (and successful) assassinations to ferries that had flipped, insurgencies that had flopped, and pious pronouncements from duly-elected political leaders and insecure dictators. Medical breakthroughs held great promise for those of us who would be long gone before the drugs went on the market. Pomp and circumstance. Breakthroughs and breakdowns.

I moved on to the metro section. Sanitation workers planned to strike, as did teachers. Vacant lots in war zones had been graced with benches and proclaimed to be community parks. A ceiling had collapsed in an elementary school, luckily during the night. A neighborhood coalition had vowed to eradicate drug dealers from abandoned buildings. A church and a synagogue had been vandalized, reinforcing the American illusion of religious equality. The police were baffled by a series of electronics store robberies over the past several months, but had promising leads. They had no leads in the arson investigation of a funeral home in Flatbush, in which the body of the owner had been discovered after the fire had been extinguished in the early hours of the morning. At least his family had not been burdened with the cost of cremation.

I pulled back the drapes long enough to assure myself that the police officers were present, then found a pencil and tackled the dreaded Sunday crossword puzzle. The blank squares remained as blank as my mind. I could usually dash off a good deal of the puzzle by relying on my innate acuity and flexibility, but even the most elementary vocabulary challenges eluded me. Asian rivers, Polynesian capitals, chemical compounds, and lethal South American toads rarely slowed me down. Wondering if I was in need of a nap along with everybody else in the household, I pulled off my shoes, stretched out on the sofa, and tucked a pillow under my head. Snippets of dreams tumbled by like scenes from a poorly staged farce.

My eyes flew open when I felt a hand press down on my mouth. Inez stared at me, her expression as solemn as that of a juror preparing to read a verdict that did not forebode well for the defense. "Ms. Malloy," she whispered, "don't make any noise." She withdrew her hand, but stayed nearby in case I could not restrain myself. "There's something you need to see. Follow me."

She led me to the hall and then through the dining room to the doorway of the den. I could see Caron's feet dangling off the end of the sofa and hear her faint snores. It was hardly worthy of a magazine cover. I elbowed Inez and whispered, "This?"

Inez held up one hand as we advanced into the room. As we edged past the desk, I saw Dolly on her hands and knees, groping under the sofa. She finally sat back, sighed, and glanced in our direction. Her face, which had been pink, turned pale.

"Oh, my goodness, you startled me," she said with a deprecatory laugh. "This must look quite peculiar." She stood up and brushed at invisible carpet fibers on her knees. "I can't imagine what you're thinking."

"Neither can I," I said.

She licked her lips. "I lost an earring last night, and thought it might have rolled under the sofa. It could also be under one of the cushions, but I didn't want to disturb Caron."

Caron had been disturbed. She sat up and blinked at Dolly, then at Inez and me. "What's going on?"

Dolly sank down beside her and patted her knee. "Nothing, dear. You had such a pretty smile on your face while you were sleeping. Were you dreaming about a special boy?"

"I was dreaming about pigsties," Caron retorted grumpily. She pushed her curls out of her face and glared at me. "Is there some reason all of you are standing there staring at me like I'm covered in pig poop?"

I gave Inez a nudge in the back. "Why don't you help Dolly search for her earring—or whatever it is? I'm going to make coffee."

"What a lovely idea," Dolly chirped. "I'll make some little sandwiches. I seem to recall that there's a box of raspberry tarts in the freezer. It's unfortunate that we can't go out to the patio and enjoy the sunshine."

"I'll handle it," I said to her, unable to put up with any more of her pig poop, so to speak. "Why don't you put on some music and give the girls a few pointers?"

Dolly maintained her bright smile. "Well, girls, why don't you show me what you've mastered thus far? I know how much it will mean to you to win the talent contest, and I think I can help you. Caron, do stop yawning and find the remote. Inez, please push the ottoman out of the way so we'll have adequate space. It's impossible to concentrate on the moves if you're worried about crashing into furniture."

I'd just reached the kitchen when the doorbell rang. I hurried back to the den and said, "Dolly, you need to go upstairs. Girls, grab the newspaper from the living room and settle down in here." The doorbell rang again. "Now," I added urgently.

Dolly scampered past me and went up the stairs. I waited until Caron and Inez were back on the sofa, feigning fascination with the financial pages, then took a deep breath and opened the front door. One of the police officers stood on the porch, his face twitching with anxiety.

I was about to offer him immediate use of the guest bathroom when he said, "Ma'am, there's sort of a situation. I was gonna call the lieutenant, but they said not to. I will, though, if you want me to."

I peered around him and saw Lucy. Beside her was Daniel, his arm supporting Madison. When she saw me, her knees crumpled and only Lucy's quick grab kept her from collapsing.

"Bring her inside," I said, stunned. I told the policeman to wait in his car, then stepped aside and allowed Daniel and Lucy to guide Madison to the sofa in the living room. She collapsed with a groan. I noted a bruise on her chin, dusty streaks under her eyes, and blood-caked scratches on her bare arms and legs. There were no other visible signs of damage, but I was not a trauma specialist.

"What happened to her?" I asked Daniel.

Lucy came around him. "We don't know. We found her under our deck, whimpering. I wanted to take her to a hospital, but she insisted we bring her here."

"Silly girl got damned hysterical about it," Daniel said huffily.

"I don't think she's been . . . well, sexually abused," Lucy said in a low voice, glancing at Madison. "I've seen enough television shows to know the symptoms. Her underclothes are intact and she doesn't have any bruising that might indicate . . ."

"Could I have some water?" asked Madison in a weak voice, then rolled over and buried her face between the throw pillows.

Daniel snorted as Lucy dashed toward the kitchen. "She ought to be examined by a professional, be tested and all that."

"She was under your deck?" I said. "How long had she been there?"

"Not long. Late yesterday afternoon when we got back from viewing property, we sat on the deck and had a few cocktails with Gary. All we heard was cursing from the golfers and birds in the woods. We went to the clubhouse for brunch this morning, so it's possible she crawled under the deck during the night. Shouldn't you at least call a doctor?"

"Doctors don't make house calls," Lucy said as she returned with a glass of water. She looked down at Madison, who was snuffling into the pillows. "My nonprofessional diagnosis is that she's suffering from shock and exhaustion. All she needs is rest and plenty of liquids. Why don't we get her upstairs and in bed?"

I shook my head. "I should call Lieutenant Rosen. I'm certain he'll want to question her."

Lucy crossed her arms. "She's in no condition to be questioned until she's had some rest. She was nearly incoherent when we found her, and her condition hasn't improved. If he storms in and badgers her, she may fall apart completely. She's already asleep. I suggest we leave her for at least a little while before she's subjected to a brutal interrogation."

"I could use a drink," said Daniel. "After we've all calmed down, we can decide what's best for her."

"One drink," I said, "and then I'm calling Lieutenant Rosen. He will not show up with a rubber hose and a cattle prod, but if Madison was in the vicinity of the golf course when her cousin was killed, he'll have some questions. So will I."

I figured Caron and Inez, who were in the doorway that led to the den, would be able to restrain Madison if she had a miraculous recovery and attempted to bolt. And even if she eluded them, she'd encounter more problems with the two officers in the front yard. I gestured for Lucy and Daniel to go to the kitchen, then opened the front door and called, "Everything's under control. I'm going to call the lieutenant, so you don't need to bother."

Daniel had located the bourbon and was mixing drinks when I joined them. He offered to fix me one, but I shook my head and sat down on a stool.

"I have a question," I began coolly. "When you learned that Sara Louise had been killed behind the cart shed, you came here to tell me. Why did you think I had any knowledge or interest in her? She wasn't here when you dropped by to invite me to your party. Neither was Madison, for that matter."

"There must have been a mention of them in the story in the newspaper," said Lucy.

"No," I said flatly.

"Then perhaps Gary said something," she countered blithely. "Yes, he must have said something. He's not the type to ignore attractive young women."

"They weren't here when he came by, either. And where is he, by the way? If Madison was so desperate that she took refuge under your deck, she must have knocked on your neighbor's door first." I paused to think. "Unless she was escaping from him. Instead of crashing into the woods, she chose the nearest place to hide."

"Gary would never do such a thing," Daniel said as he set down a drink in front of Lucy. "I'm an excellent judge of character."

"As well as his supervisor at the Bureau?"

Daniel looked at Lucy. "How could I be? He works for some regulatory agency, something to do with tariffs and quotas. I believe his supervisor is an undersecretary at the Department of Commerce."

"That is correct," said Lucy, nodding her head so adamantly that I expected it to topple off her neck and roll across the floor, coming to rest in the butler's pantry. "He was home when we returned yesterday. He came over with a pitcher of martinis, and we played gin until it grew chilly. He declined my invitation to stay for dinner, saying he had a date. I don't know which bureau you referred to, but I can assure you that we'd never met him before arriving in Farberville. His family is well known in Virginia; his grandfather served four terms as a congressman. His father owns an investment firm, and his mother is renowned for her charity work. Gary attended a good college, and then spent two years as a Peace Corps volunteer in some African village. The very idea of him keeping a young woman prisoner is preposterous."

"I don't think it matters if his great-grandfather was the last king of Prussia," I said mildly. "He told me he works for the FBI."

"The FBI?" echoed Lucy.

"That's what he said." I gave them a few minutes to shoot guarded looks at each other, then continued. "And I'm certain that you do, too. Would you like me to wait outside while you concoct another passel of lies? You'd better keep your voices low, though. I can't swear every inch of the house isn't bugged."

Daniel downed his drink and refilled his glass. "You would have found out in the next day or so, anyway. We're here because of Doris Barlucci. She has significant information in her possession. We have to find her before Velocchio's thugs get to her. They will not treat her kindly."

"Has she done something criminal?" I asked.

Lucy reached across the island for the bottle of bourbon, then poured the last of it in her glass. "It's convoluted, but the answer is no. She has not been charged with anything, and mostly likely will not be in the future. We're trying to save her life. And yours, too."

I didn't bother to ask what significant knowledge Dolly possessed, since I knew perfectly well they wouldn't tell me. They'd probably have to get clearance from headquarters to tell me my hair

264

was on fire. "So you two and Gary came down here to locate Dolly before Sara Louise and Madison did. Who killed Petti?"

"Hard to say." Lucy took the empty bottle into the pantry and dropped it in the trash can. She came back into the kitchen and began to hunt through the liquor cabinet. "I've never seen so many liqueurs in a private home. Is there another bottle of bourbon?"

I poured myself a glass of water while she and Daniel rattled bottles and mumbled at each other. Daniel finally arose with his trophy. "Actually," he said as he opened the bottle, "we thought you might have killed him."

"Me?" I squawked. "Why would I do that? I never even met him."

Lucy leaned against the counter and regarded me with a complacent smile. "Well, you were Dolly's only confidante, so you might have known that Petti Mordella was in town. Maybe the Velocchio family got to you and offered a tidy sum to dispose of him. You certainly could use the money. Your bookstore is picturesque and charming, but hasn't shown much of a profit since you opened it. What with college tuition looming . . ."

If I hadn't been so outraged, I would have been flattered. "I am not some sort of amateur hitman. I don't even put out mousetraps. How can you accuse me of putting a bullet in a stranger's head? Do you think I killed Sara Louise, too? Did I kidnap Madison and stash her under your deck?" I took a gulp of water and wiped off my chin with the back of my hand. "And how do you know if the Book Depot makes a profit? What business is it of yours?"

"We have connections," said Daniel. "You'll be relieved to know that after a lengthy analysis, we concluded that you were nothing more than a somewhat inept small-town bookseller. When we met you, we realized that was why Dolly had selected you to assist her in her scheme to avoid both the FBI and the Velocchio family."

I would have sputtered had I not known how unbecoming it was. "I am astounded at your perspicacity. It often takes me half an hour to tie my shoes in the morning. Why, just the other day I turned on the microwave and sat down to watch the news. I was relieved to learn that nothing had happened all day. My worst problem now is how to extricate the pizza from the VCR."

"He didn't mean it like that," said Lucy.

I stared back at her. "Then who killed Petti and Sara Louise? Gary Billings?"

Daniel shrugged. "We don't know who killed them, but I can tell you unequivocally that Gary did not. He's been working on this case for more than five years. Grand jury indictments will ensure him a major promotion. Why would you think he did?"

"There's a rumor he's been suspended." I left them in the kitchen and went to the doorway of the living room. Madison did not appear to have moved. Caron left Inez to stand guard at the foot of the sofa and came over to me.

"Did you call Peter?" she asked. "This is getting Way Too Weird."

"I promise I'll call him in a few minutes."

"What about Dolly? She must be going crazy, since she doesn't even know who's here. Crazier, I mean. While she was fixing breakfast, I went in to ask if I could help and found her digging through the trash. The best she could come up with was some inane excuse about looking for an expiration date on the egg carton. I pointed out the carton was on the counter, and she just kind of laughed."

"Run upstairs and tell her about Madison. The two in the kitchen seriously underestimate me, and I want to find out what else they have to say. Negotiations are delicate, dear, so don't even think about listening at the door."

Caron rolled her eyes. "The only thing I'm going to think about is moving to Argentina to become a famous dancer. I wish I hadn't slept through Spanish class last year."

I waited until she had gone upstairs, then returned to the kitchen. "I don't recall that you mentioned where Gary is right now. I would have thought you might have wanted his help with Madison. She's not exactly a featherweight."

"We don't know where he is," said Daniel, "but you're the one who needs to answer some questions. Who told you Gary was suspended?"

"Not that he is," Lucy added. "We were all three assigned to come here and take Dolly into custody. Normally, only one agent would be sent, but the involvement of the Velocchio family made things more complicated. Now who told you this about Gary?"

"Why, I do declare it's gone right out of my mind," I said, simpering like any inept small-town bookseller. "I went to Sally's for a quick bite to eat, but I can't imagine her saying any such thing. I bought the *Times* at a newsstand up the hill from my store. Billy and Anastasia are better informed about faculty wife-swapping than FBI plots. Maybe I heard something on the car radio."

Lucy's brownie-baking role was long gone. "You are impeding a federal investigation. We can transport you to Quantico if that might improve your memory."

"Will they let me play with an Uzi?" When they failed to answer, I said, "If you're working so closely with Gary, why don't you know where he is?"

"We don't hold hands on assignment," said Daniel, whose face was turning mottled from either bourbon or frustration. "Lucy, call Lieutenant Rosen and tell him to get over here. I don't believe Ms. Malloy understands how much trouble she'll find herself in if she refuses to answer our questions."

And he doesn't know the half of it, I thought as I sat down. I was beginning to think I did, although no more than that. I had a pretty good idea why Petti had come to Farberville, why Dolly had fled with his cell phone, and why she'd come back despite the infestation of federal agents and mobsters.

The kitchen door swung open. "Let's not make any calls just yet," Madison said in a remarkably level voice for someone who'd been quivering like aspic only a few minutes earlier. In that she was pointing a gun in our general direction, no one seemed inclined to argue.

Chapter Seventeen

She stepped back and shoved Inez into the room. "Everybody have a seat. Where's Caron?"

"Upstairs, uh, in the bathroom," I said. "She has a nervous stomach. Why are you doing this, Madison? Do you know who these two people are?"

Daniel cleared his throat. "How could she? We're just a couple hoping to retire here. Lucy's always wanted to live in the mountains."

Madison pointed the gun at his head. "All of you feds have the same rancid stench. Where's Gary? Shouldn't he be here with you?"

"Why don't you put down the gun, Madison?" said Lucy. She began to approach her cautiously. "It's liable to go off if you keep waving it around like that. You haven't committed any crime that we're aware of, so we can all just forget about this unfortunate moment. Daniel and I don't know where Gary is, and neither does Claire. We haven't seen him since eight o'clock last night when he left our condo." If she'd had a plate of brownies, she would have whipped them out like a gunslinger. "Would you like a glass of wine and something to eat? I can make you a sandwich—"

"Shut up," she said shrilly. "I thought I told all of you to sit down. The last one standing will be the first one bleeding out on the floor."

It was not the version of Musical Chairs most often played at children's parties. Daniel, Lucy, and Inez all scuttled to the stools nearest them. I realized we'd have a problem if Caron came into the kitchen, with or without Dolly, since there were only four stools. No one seemed to have much to contribute, so I said, "Why are you so determined to find Gary, Madison?"

"Because he's a son of a bitch! No one treats me like that. He knows who my father works for. My mother's maiden name was Velocchio, dammit! All I have to do is make one phone call, and Gary Billings won't be buffing his badge on some whore's bare ass ever again." She pointed the gun at me. "Recognize this, Ms. Malloy? The little ol' .22 caliber Beretta? It was thoughtful of Dolly to leave it in plain sight, wasn't it? Inez, would you be a sweetie and fetch me a glass of wine?"

"You didn't have the gun when you left the house on Thursday," I pointed out. "The pool guys would have noticed any, ah, unsightly bulges."

Madison accepted a glass of wine from Inez, then waved her back. "Oh, I didn't take it. That would be stealing, and the nuns drilled that into my head. Okay, so maybe I shoplifted when I was younger, but that was for a lark. Even Daddy understood when he had to pay off the store owners. Everybody goes through a phase like that. Isn't that true, Inez? Don't you have some cheap pieces of jewelry and cosmetics in the bottom of one of your dresser drawers?"

Inez looked horrified, but had the sense to nod. "Yeah."

"Then your record is clean," proclaimed Daniel. "Put down the gun, girl, and we'll drink a toast to the statute of limitations. As for Gary, not one of us can help you. We haven't—"

"Shut up!" she said with even more vehemence. Her hair was dangling in her eyes, giving her the look of a feral feline. Sweat (which I'm sure she would have referred to as perspiration) was beading on her upper lip. "I don't know *where* he is, but I damn well know who he's with and what they're doing! He tried to pretend he wasn't getting rid of me last night. His big plan was for me to hang out in the country club parking lot until a couple of drunks came out, then wheedle them into giving me a ride back here in case Dolly called again. Like I was supposed to buy that crap. We had a fight"—she touched her chin—"and he actually hit me. Me, of all people! Then he told me to get out before he got back with his hot little date. I was going to follow him to the clubhouse, but then I changed my mind and went back to wait for them. Which is when I realized I'd locked myself out, if you can believe it. I felt incredibly stupid. I haven't done something like that since I was thirteen and so drunk I lost the key while I was throwing up in the bushes. Anyway, I decided to hide under your deck until they came back, but they never did. He didn't come back this morning, either. I guess I finally fell asleep."

"You've been with Gary since you left here on Thursday?" I asked, shaking my head. "Do you know he's an FBI agent?"

Madison giggled. "That's what made it so exciting. I had no idea at first, when he came on to me at a fabulous club in the Hamptons last summer. He said he was a lawyer from DC, and, to be honest, he was so hot that I wouldn't have cared if he was a bricklayer from the Bronx. We had an absolutely wild summer, then I didn't hear from him until a couple of months ago, when he took a suite at the Plaza. We were in his room, and while he was taking a shower, I went through all his stuff and found his badge and ID card. It was too funny! I mean, Daddy would have had a stroke. Sara Louise was the only person who knew, and she swore not to say a word."

"Does he know who you are?"

"Well, of course," she said, giving me a pitying smile, "everybody knows who I am. My friends at school thought it was a riot. They couldn't believe Daddy had me on this silly little allowance. He keeps saying that if I don't get married, I'm going to have to get a job. Can you see me super-sizing fries?"

Apparently none of us could.

I waited in case Lucy or Daniel wanted to jump right in, then said, "Surely you weren't planning to marry an FBI agent?"

Scowling, she turned the gun back on me. "He told me that he'll resign and that he'll have enough money for us to live in a villa on the Riviera. He can occupy his time playing polo and baccarat, and I can have elegant dinner parties for the right people. During the summer, we'll cruise the Mediterranean or visit friends in Paris. Daddy will get over it when he realizes he doesn't have to support me anymore. Maybe I'll send him a genuine mummy for his next wedding present." Tears began to dribble down her cheeks. "At least that's what Gary said. But now he's gone off with some slut who's spent more time with plastic surgeons than she has with personal trainers and therapists. When she looks in a mirror, she probably doesn't recognize herself. This is so not fair! Now I'm the one who's in all kinds of trouble, not Gary."

"Why are you in trouble?" asked Lucy, adopting the role of a deeply concerned high school counselor. I wondered if one of her training courses had included kung fu or something equally useful. Daniel appeared to be too absorbed in his glass of bourbon to fling himself off the stool. Fall, perhaps, but not fling.

I will admit to a small sigh of relief as Madison turned the gun on her. "A few weeks ago Gary told me he had to go on a business trip, but he wouldn't tell me where. I thought it'd be fun to surprise him, so when he went out to buy a couple of shirts, I got on his computer and found the e-ticket he'd printed, along with the confirmation for the condo. Sara Louise agreed to drive down with me."

"You didn't know he was coming here to find Dolly?" I said, hoping the Velocchio empire never fell under her control. She'd be more likely to order the elimination of cheeky car valets than members of rival families. Bombs would be special-ordered from Gucci. Automatic weapons would be issued in tasteful hues of seashell blush and champagne mist. Even the lowliest goons would be required to have manicures on a weekly basis and take elocution classes.

Madison's forehead wrinkled, as if the wine was slightly sour. "No, but the funny thing is that Sara Louise did. She said that if we could get to Dolly first, she'd earn a lot of points with her father, and that mine would be so grateful that he might let me run off with Gary. It was her idea that we turn up like a couple of ragamuffins. Sara Louise was really pissed when you answered the door, but she

271

thought it was possible that Dolly was in Dallas and might come back—especially when Petti started popping up and then disappearing. It's not like I know where Dallas is, but Sara Louise said it wasn't very far. I feel real bad about Petti. He was always nice to me. He used to take me to the races every Saturday when I was kid, and let me use his binoculars. He took me to see *Cats,* even though he had allergies."

I could see that Madison was beginning to sag, and the last thing I wanted was for her finger to slip on the trigger. "Madison, why don't you sit down on Inez's stool and let her go upstairs to check on Caron?"

"And give her a chance to call the cops? I don't think so."

Inez arose to the occasion, as well as to her feet. "I'll bring the phone receiver in here so nobody can call from upstairs. I'm getting kind of worried about Caron. Last year she had a—what's it called?—bleeding ulcer and passed out on the bathroom floor."

Madison studied her for a moment. "And you won't hang out the window and alert the cops outside?"

"Not while you're in here with a gun," Inez vowed solemnly.

"All right, then," Madison said, wafting her free hand. "Get the receiver, then bring the stool over here and go upstairs. I'd better not hear anyone creeping down the steps, though."

"I never creep." Inez did as ordered, then banged the door as she left and stomped up the stairs.

Lucy stood up. "Well, if we're finished, then perhaps—"

"Sit down," said Madison. "You still haven't told me where Gary is. Call him on your cell phone."

"I'll try. Daniel, pour Madison another glass of wine. Claire, would you like something? You're looking a bit flushed." She took a cell phone out of her purse and flipped it open, punched some buttons, listened for a moment, and then shook her head. "He's not answering. Maybe he's back at his condo, taking a nap. We could all drive out there and find out."

"Excellent idea," mumbled Daniel. "He's treated Madison abominably. She deserves an explanation."

I most definitely did not want to go on a Sunday drive, particularly with a driver who was pie-eyed, despite having managed to spit out the word *abominably,* which I can rarely do in more lucid situations. "Have you been with Gary since you left on Thursday?"

Madison smirked. "I couldn't bear the idea of playing nursemaid to Sara Louise, so I called him and told him to meet me in the alley. I was just going to tease him a minute about how I was a better spy than he was, and maybe arrange to meet him later, but we kind of got carried away. He begged me to go to his condo for an hour. We ended up in bed all afternoon, and before I realized how late it was, it was already dark. It seemed easier just to stay instead of trying to come up with some kind of explanation. Besides, it was a helluva lot more entertaining." She giggled like a bride at a lingerie shower. "Gary said it might put more pressure on you if you thought something terrible had happened to me. That's why he kept having me call you and sound all breathless and terrified. Pretty convincing, wasn't I?"

I was in no mood to assess her theatrical talents. "Especially your call on Friday about going to the bookstore. Did he attack me?"

"I'm sorry about that, Ms. Malloy. He thought maybe Dolly had left a message on the answering machine, or arranged to have a letter sent there. When he couldn't find anything, he called me and told me to call you. He was plenty angry. If that goofy guy hadn't shown up, he was going to keep you in the back room until you talked."

Lucy sat up. "Gary would never do anything like that. It's against regulations."

"That's right," added Daniel as he refilled his glass. "Got to go by the book. It's how we operate. Ask anyone."

"Call him again," Madison ordered Lucy. "And keep calling. If he doesn't answer, I may have to shoot one of you."

Before any of us could come up with a rebuttal, the doorbell rang. Madison stood up and pointed the gun at me. "Who's that?"

"I have no idea," I said.

"Then let's go answer it," she said. "You first, and me right behind you with this little ol' Beretta against your back."

273

I glanced at Lucy and Daniel, who offered no suggestions to the contrary. I led the way to the door, trying not to wince as the muzzle bit into me, and opened the door. Both police officers were there, panicked and barely able to speak.

"So sorry, Ms. Malloy," said the slightly more articulate one, "but these guys are here and they say it's an emergency. A water main ruptured up on the hill. The city's already working on it, but these guys say if they don't cut off the line to the pool, it'll crack, and then the lines will back up and flood the bottom story of the house."

"These guys," I murmured.

Nick and Sebastian propelled the officers in the direction of the sliding glass doors, and told them to start searching for the valve. "We'll be there as soon as I explain," Nick called to them as they stumbled out to the patio. He locked the door and turned around. "My apologies for barging in like this, Ms. Malloy."

He stepped around me and yanked the gun from Madison's hand, then kept a grip on her wrist. "You are in some kind of trouble, young lady," he said to her. "Sebastian, please ask those in the kitchen to remain there until we have left. Also, remind them that it would not be wise to attempt to use their cell phones."

Sebastian lumbered by me and went into the kitchen.

"Let go of me!" squeaked Madison, trying to jerk her wrist free. "Remember that conversation we had in the kitchen after you showed up, pretending to be a pool guy? Sara Louise warned you that she knew all about that truckload of DVD players you claimed never arrived. You swore you wouldn't interfere with us. Daddy may be pissed at me for coming here, but he's going to be livid when I tell him you were ripping off the family!"

"Which I'm sure you will do shortly. At this moment, your father's private jet is landing on an airstrip in the next county. From what he has said to me, he is not pleased. When I told him that I knew where to find you, he told me to bring you to him at once. I suspect you and he will have much to talk about on your flight back to New York."

"Daddy's here?" she said slowly.

Nick ignored her. "I told you not to trust Gary Billings, Ms. Malloy."

"You also told me you were an FBI agent."

"I did not think the truth would sit well with you. Now, if you will excuse a further intrusion, I will allow Sebastian to restrain Miss Hayes while I invite Mrs. Barlucci to join Mr. Hayes and his daughter on their trip." He dragged Madison to the kitchen door and shoved her inside. Her colorful language suggested that they would never become friends.

"I told you Dolly called from Miami," I said.

"And I'm sure she did. Private jets are a luxury that most of us cannot afford, but commercial jets are an affordable option. I am aware that your daughter and her friend are upstairs as well. I will not harm them unless they attempt to interfere."

"I'm going with you."

"You are a feisty lady, if you will permit me to say so. Please feel free to accompany me, but keep in mind that I have a gun and am experienced in using it. Ladies first."

As we went upstairs, I wanted to shriek a warning, but I was afraid it would only make matters worse for all of us. Thus far, Nick had been soft-spoken and polite. This did not preclude his loyalty to his employee and what I suspected was his job description. "Did you kill Sara Louise?" I asked as we reached the top step.

"Good heavens no, Ms. Malloy," he said, sounding shocked. "She was the daughter of Christopher Santini, as well as the boss's favorite goddaughter. I would never treat her or Miss Hayes with anything but the utmost respect." He paused. "It was unfortunate that Petti's body ended up in the freezer, which would have caused them some awkwardness if the police did background checks and discovered the family connection. But it could not be helped. Sebastian and I were carrying the body to the van when the Mercedes pulled up. I was afraid the two girls were your daughter and her friend, so I told Sebastian to stash the body while I . . . well, diverted their attention. He couldn't take the body to the backyard, since you might still be looking out the window. There was only one place in the garage to conceal it. We were leery of returning later that night because of the police cars patrolling the neighborhood. Regrettably, you found the body before we could retrieve it."

"But you had no problem retrieving it from the morgue at the hospital."

Nick gave me a puzzled look. "Why would we do that, Ms. Malloy?"

"Well, you killed him, for starters. Maybe you're some sort of perverted collector."

"What I like about you is your wit, Ms. Malloy. Petti violated the family trust. It was known that he stayed in touch with Mrs. Barlucci this past year, but they were old friends and no one thought much about it. Then events occurred that cast him in a bad light. After that, he was closely followed, first to Miami and then here. If you would please move along, we can get this over without any fuss."

I took a couple of steps and peered down the hallway. "You didn't answer my question about Petti."

"Technically speaking, you did not ask one. Surely you've heard that gag line that goes, 'If I tell you, then I'll have to . . .' I can see that you have. Now, please call quietly to those who seem to be hiding that they need to come out in the hall. If I have to search through closets and under beds for them, my good nature may become less apparent. Mr. Hayes does not like to be kept waiting." He touched the gun to the side of my head. "Please do as I ask, Ms. Malloy."

"Caron? Inez?" I said obediently. "This is really not a good time to play games."

"Don't forget your friend Mrs. Barlucci," Nick whispered in my ear, his mouth so close that I could feel moisture.

I batted away the gun and frowned at him. "Just why are you so sure she's here?"

"Because we have been monitoring conversations from the van for the last few days. Had it not broken down last night before we could park within range, we would have been at your doorstep early this morning to deal with the water main and all that bullshit, if you'll

276

excuse my language. As it was, we had to wait until an auto parts store opened at noon so Sebastian could make the necessary repairs before we could take our position down the hill. Sometimes the best-laid plans are at the mercy of a pimply-faced boy who does not know a fan belt from a pair of suspenders."

"A pity," I said drily.

"And also a pity that we will have to search the rooms one by one. Like Mr. Hayes, I can be impatient. On the other hand"—he raised his voice—"if no one appears in the next five seconds, I will punch you so hard that you will slam against the wall. Your diaphragm will contract and you will be gasping for breath. I will wait another five seconds, then kick you hard enough to cause serious damage to your gallbladder. Luckily, it is not a vital organ, although I'm told it's somewhat utilitarian."

"Okay," said Caron as she came out of the bedroom at the end of the hall, "let's not get overly dramatic about this. Inez is with me."

"And Mrs. Barlucci?" said Nick, holding on to my arm.

"She's gone. You can pummel Mother until both of you are blue in the face, but it won't do any good."

"Gone?" I said.

"As in no longer here. She said to thank you for taking care of the house, and that we're welcome to stay until the rental agent runs us out. I don't know about that, though. This place is getting weirder by the minute."

"Gone where?" demanded Nick.

"Like you think she'd tell me? She just waited until everybody was in the kitchen, then went out the sliding glass doors. She called somebody before she left, although I don't think it was for a taxi. After she found the wrapper in the wastebasket from the music store in Buenos Aires, she said we could keep the tango CDs. I thought that was nice of her."

"How'd she get out through the backyard?" I asked. "The gate's locked."

Inez eased into the hall. "I noticed the key to the padlock was missing when I went to get the phone receiver."

277

Nick was having trouble finding the wherewithal to speak. "When—I mean, how long ago did she leave?"

"I'd estimate about twenty minutes ago," said Inez, consulting her watch. "It could have been thirty, or even a little more than that. Madison kept babbling on so long that I thought I'd expire from boredom. If anyone was ever in need of therapy. . . ."

"Or a brain transplant," added Caron. "One that requires a flock of surgeons and forty-eight hours in the operating room. Even then, they'd probably miss a few screwed-up connections and her mouth would keep firing at random."

"You let her leave just like that?" said Nick.

"Madison?" said Caron. "Oh, you mean Dolly. We're sixteen years old, for pity's sake, and she's older than my mother. Were we supposed to ground her for breaking curfew last night? Give me a break."

"You'd better get Madison out of here while you can," I said to Nick. "You don't want to keep Mr. Hayes waiting in his private jet."

"Cool," said Inez. "I saw some private jets at the airport when my parents took me to New York City. Limousines were driving right up to them. I'll bet the passengers get more than pretzels and little cups of soda."

Caron snorted. "They have filet mignon and entire bottles of champagne. Can you imagine someone ordering Donald Trump to buckle his seat belt and put his tray in an upright position? On *Air Force One,* there's even a bedroom and a bath with a shower. You are so naive, Inez." They continued their argument as they went back into the bedroom and closed the door.

"Should I believe them about Dolly?" asked Nick. "Maybe she's hiding in there."

"Satisfy yourself, or better yet, follow me." I led him into the room that Madison had occupied and pointed out the window. "There's the gate, and there's the padlock on the ground. Once Dolly found out Madison was here, she wouldn't have lingered. She might even have recognized Lucy's and Daniel's voices. Search all the nooks and crannies if you wish, but you won't find her."

"Mr. Hayes is going to be unhappy," Nick said as we started toward the stairs. "Not that he was happy to begin with, having to disrupt his weekend and all. Madison and Sara Louise should have had more sense than to blunder into what might have been a simple snatch."

"If Petti hadn't tipped off Dolly," I pointed out.

"That was a very bad thing he did. He should have stayed in Flatbush and made boat models out of balsa wood or something like that. The family made sure he had enough to live on after he retired. My aunt Flora had her eye on him. Maybe they could have learned the tango like Bibi and Dolly. I always thought that was kinda sweet, two senior citizens like them living out their romantic fantasies. Everybody else sniggered about it, but Sebastian and me, we understood."

I kept my lips clamped shut as we went downstairs. Peter, Sergeant Jorgeson, and an untold number of other officers were waiting for us. Nick prudently dropped his gun and allowed himself to be handcuffed. Lucy and Daniel were seated on the sofa in the living room, silent for the moment. I glanced out the open front door and saw Sebastian in the backseat of a police car, his head lowered.

"Nice of you to show up," I said to Peter.

"We've been outside for a while, trying to decide how to intervene without anyone getting hurt. Once the officers in back saw you and this guy go upstairs, we went into the kitchen from the garage and hallway. No one except Miss Hayes had much of anything to say. She was a bit agitated."

"And where is Miss Hayes?"

"In the kitchen, drinking wine. I wanted to talk to you before we start transporting these people to the department for formal questioning. You and Dolly Goforth, that is. Is she upstairs with Caron and Inez?"

I told him what Caron had said, then glanced at the kitchen door. "Before you start trying to sort this out, I'd like to speak to Madison. You can trail along if you'd like."

"How gracious of you," Peter said. He held open the door and gestured for me to proceed. "Your witness awaits."

Madison was sitting on a stool, her elbows propped on the island, while two young officers hovered nearby. Rather than concerned, she looked deeply annoyed, as if her hairdresser had died. She gave me a bleary glare. "I hope you're satisfied, Ms. Malloy. If you'd had the sense to tell us where Dolly was, none of this would have happened." She redirected her glare toward Peter. "Look, the only thing you can charge me with is waving a gun around. Nobody got hurt. My lawyer will claim that I was under stress from spending the night under the deck, not knowing if a spider or snake would slither under my clothes. In fact, just tell me what the bail will be and I'll write you a check."

I sat down across from her. "I think it may be more complicated than that, Madison. Surely Daniel and Lucy told you about Sara Louise's murder."

"Yeah, I feel really awful about that. We practically grew up together. Daddy was always telling me I should be more like her—study harder, stop going to clubs all the time, act more mature." She refilled her glass and took a gulp. "Not that she was perfect, of course. She was just smart enough not to get caught."

"But for once you were smarter than she was, right? Did you call her on Gary's cell phone and tell her to meet you behind the pro shop?"

Madison grimaced. "No, the bitch called me after Gary had gone next door for the barbecue. She knew where I was, since I'd told her about the condo before we left New York. She said the whole situation was getting out of hand and we needed to leave the next morning. Her big idea was that we'd fly to New York and let Nick drive her car back when it was fixed. She ordered me to meet her behind the pro shop. Ordered me, if you can imagine!"

"So you cut across the golf course," I said encouragingly. "Did she have the gun in her purse?"

"She said she was worried that Gary might show up and persuade me not to leave. She couldn't stand him, but I think it was because she was jealous. Sure, she went to fancy schools and all that crap, but Gary would barely speak to her when we were all together."

"You and Sara Louise argued, I assume."

"I wasn't about to leave until I had it out with Gary. When I told her, she got furious and tried to drag me into the car. She took out the gun, and it sort of went off. It was an accident." She paused, her nose wrinkled. "Or maybe more like self-defense. I thought she was going to shoot me, and I panicked. I barely remember what happened."

"But you remained cool enough to take her purse, the car key, and the gun with you when you went back to Gary's condo and discovered you were locked out. Is the purse still under the Hoods' deck?"

"It was self-defense," Madison said sullenly. "Is there any more wine?"

What ensued after that was lengthy, tiresome, and therefore unworthy of further description.

It was well after dark when Peter returned. Caron, Inez, Corporal McTeer, and I were in the den playing cards, having all agreed that neither gangster movies nor tango tapes had any appeal.

"You may leave now, Corporal," he said.

"Just a sec." She played her last card and sighed. "It's a good thing I didn't decide to become a professional gambler. You girls still planning to show up that friend of yours in the talent show?"

Caron shrugged. "I guess so."

"I'll be out in the audience cheering for you." She got to her feet and gave Peter a nervous salute. "Sorry, sir. Am I still on duty outside?"

"The officers who were here earlier were unlucky enough to draw the second shift. Sergeant Jorgeson's waiting to take you back to the station."

After she scurried away, Peter went into the kitchen and returned with a beer. "Quite a scene here this afternoon," he commented. "Feds, hitmen, cops, and of course, the usual collection of innocent bystanders. That's not to say that I consider any of you innocent. It's just a phrase used on TV cop shows, and typically refers to witnesses who happened to be on the sidewalk when a drive-by shooting or knifing takes place. They never have much to contribute, but they try."

"Should I hire a defense lawyer?" I asked, gathering up the cards. "If you're planning to read us our rights, you're way too late. Nothing we said can be used against us in a court of law."

"Very good, Mother," Caron said. "As long as you don't admit we buried Petti under the gazebo, we're safe. I just wish we were home free, as well. This place is beginning to feel spooky."

Her last word caught my attention. "That's what my science fiction hippie said when he came in the store while Daniel and Lucy were there, and then repeated it while Gary was pretending to rescue me. He must have some sort of radar for FBI agents, a seventies flashback."

"Just where is Gary?" asked Inez, blinking at Peter. "Madison admitted that he attacked Ms. Malloy. What if he's in the backyard, waiting for another chance?"

Caron, who'd hours earlier cheerfully told Nick to pummel me until we were both blue in the face, blithely dismissed the threat to her mother's well-being. "He doesn't have any reason to hang around Farberville, now that Dolly's gone once and for all, and those icky FBI agents are after him."

"If he knows," Inez said, pulling off her glasses to clean them. "It's not like any of this was on the local news."

Peter put down his beer and leaned forward. "Let's make a deal," he said to them, his expression intent. "I realize that you've both been disappointed that you've been kept away from the media—for your own safety. Tomorrow at two o'clock, there's going to be a press conference in front of City Hall. I will personally introduce you and allow you to tell your story. The story's already been leaked to the AP, so it's likely that the national newspapers and cable news stations will send reporters because of the Velocchio connection."

"The FBI won't try to hush this up?" I asked.

"They've been playing on my turf," he said, his voice icy. "If they'd bothered to give us one clue about what they were doing, we'd have picked up Dolly and held her in protective custody until they got here. I guess they didn't think our dinky backwoods department could handle such a delicate matter."

Caron's eyes were glazed. "So we can tell the media everything?"

Peter gave her a sharp look. "Unless it's something you haven't told me. Have you picked up some bad habits from your mother?"

"We told you everything," Inez said hastily. "I mean, we told you everything we know for a fact. Everything that's happened from the first time we found Petti's body out by the gazebo until Dolly left."

"She didn't say anything that might give you an idea where she went?" he persisted.

"Not a word," Caron said. "She made a call, then gave me the cell phone and asked me to wait fifteen minutes before I called you. I swear I have no idea who she called or where she went after she left through the gate. I just stayed in the bedroom, watching the clock. Then, when Inez showed up, we sat for another five minutes and then called you. She wasn't a criminal or anything, and it wasn't her fault all these horrible people were looking for her. She was very nice."

"That's right," Inez added. "She told us to help ourselves to anything we found that could be used as costumes." She looked down for a moment. "She even told me I could have a bottle of really expensive perfume, but there's no way I'd dare use it. My father would throw a fit and my mother would make me stay in the shower until it was rinsed off."

Caron looked inquiringly at me, but I shook my head. "Don't even think about it. Okay, Peter, you mentioned a deal. What do the girls have to do if they want to be on CNN tomorrow night?"

He politely overlooked the muted squeals. "They have to go upstairs, wash their hair, polish their story for maximum impact, and then go to bed. They will not leave the room until tomorrow morning. Sound fair?"

"Oh, yes," breathed Inez. "We're going to be more famous than Rhonda, even if she does win the stupid little talent show. We can skip it and forget we ever tried to learn that ridiculous dance. We'll be invited to speak to classes about our experience, and not just at the high school." She took off her glasses and wiped them on her shirttail. "Can you imagine us on national TV?"

"Did you bring mascara?" Caron asked as they left the den. "I have some, but it's kinda old. Not as old as Mother, though."

I looked at Peter. "Time for the same trite discussion, I suppose. Shall we have some brandy on the patio while I explain why I didn't call you in the middle of the night, or why I didn't tell you about meeting Nick this morning? How it all got out of control? Why I didn't want to toss Dolly into the lions' den until I figured out which ones were the lions?"

He caught my shoulders. "Brandy on the patio, yes. While you get snifters and the bottle, I'll send the officer on patrol to the front yard to commiserate with his pals. I thought we might go for a swim."

"Did you remember to bring a suit?" When he shook his head, I grinned. "Neither did I."

Later, as we lay on lounge chairs, pleasantly exhausted from the swim and the ensuing amorous exertions on a towel spread on the pine needles, I said, "I realized something earlier today, when Madison and then Nick were pointing their guns at me."

"That it might hurt to get shot?" murmured Peter, sipping brandy.

"I suppose that came to mind, but what really bothered me was that I might end up dead without ever having . . ."

He sat up and caught my dangling hand. "Without ever having what?"

"Well, I didn't want you to remember me as meddlesome Miss Marple. That would make it too easy for you. Before too long, you'd be entertaining a new batch of rookies with stories of my indisputable prowess. I'd be nothing more than a legend around the department."

"How would you have preferred that I remembered you?" he asked quietly.

"As your meddlesome wife. I didn't want to end up dead without ever having made a commitment to you. Maybe it would have been a mistake, or maybe it would have been every bit as wonderful as I imagined it. But I'd never have known."

"Then we'd better correct the situation before Farberville hosts another crime worthy of your attention." He tugged at my hand until I joined him on the lounge chair, which wobbled alarmingly. "It could happen as soon as next week, you know."

"I was thinking more along the lines of the end of the summer. That will give Caron some time to adjust to the idea, as well as your mother."

"As you may have already discovered, I don't have a ring with me. Tomorrow night, a candlelit dinner, wine, a slightly more formal proposal?"

"If no one gets murdered in the morning," I said, then gave my attention to returning his increasingly insistent advances.

Chapter Eighteen

A week later, I was back in the Book Depot, glumly watching pedestrians wander by without so much as a thought to the wealth of wisdom and solace to be found within the covers of my stock, along with lurid sex on the bestseller rack, travel guides to places one would never dream of going, leather-clad maiden warriors on the science fiction rack, and a disquieting silence surrounding the cash register. Caron and I had moved back to the apartment, where the kitchen appliances were antiques and the only pool was a puddle on the bathroom floor. The tile on the counter was pleasing, and I'd opted for a reliable beige on the walls, as opposed to seashell blush.

Daniel Hood and Lucy Loomis, as I learned was her real name, had won the jurisdiction squabble and departed with Madison, Nick, and Sebastian. Gary had vanished, but I wasn't especially worried since I had a vague idea what might have happened to him. I had a pretty good theory about where Dolly was, for that matter. There was no reason to tell Peter, since there was nothing he could—or would—do about it.

A bouquet of flowers sailed past the window, and I wasn't surprised when the doorbell jangled and Cal came inside. "Got something for you," he said.

"These bugged, too?" I asked.

"Figured that out, huh?" He put the flowers on the counter. "I was thinking we might have a little talk. You have any coffee in your office?"

"I do indeed." Once we'd settled in the back room, I regarded him coolly. "Do you even have a dog?"

"I sure do. He's next to worthless, but I'm fond of him. Except when he farts, of course. I have to open every window in the house."

"Then you didn't lie about everything," I said. "Shall I call you Manny or Cal?"

Cal took a sip of coffee, made a face, and put down the cup. "Whatever you prefer. Fellows back in New York took to calling me Cal, on account of the way I could divide up the dinner bill right down to the taxes and the tip, just like a calculator. When I retired and moved down here, I didn't have much need of that."

"Retired from the mob, I presume?"

He held up his dark, arthritic hands. "I wasn't no hitman like Nick or Sebastian. I was nothing but a runner, a gofer, a chauffeur when some wife wanted to shop on Fifth Avenue all day. All I did was hang around saying, 'Yes, sir,' and 'I'll wait right here, ma'am,' and 'Aren't you looking particularly fine today?' It wasn't a bad job, and I had a lot of time to read."

"You and Bibi were friends, weren't you?"

"We used to play chess together, things like that. When he got married to Dolly, he wanted me to be his best man, but that was impossible. I drove them to Niagara Falls for their honeymoon. I kept offering to close the screen in the limo so they could have some privacy, 'cause they sure were acting like a couple of horny teenagers. We stayed friends, though. Some weekends I'd drive them and Petti up to their lake house, and we'd sit around playing cards and drinking half the night. That place up in the Catskills where they won a trophy for their dancing, I was the one with the camcorder. I could have done better if Petti hadn't kept poking me in the back and making wisecracks."

"You must have been devastated when Bibi died," I said, watching him closely. "Did you attend the funeral?"

"It was so crowded that I had to stand in the back of the room. I

287

was hoping to have a word with Dolly afterwards, but she left through a side door."

I tried to keep a properly somber expression on my face. "Did you drive Petti to the church by the lake house to bury Bibi's remains?"

"I sure did. Once it was done, we opened a bottle of scotch and toasted him until it got dark. I can hardly remember the drive back to Brooklyn. Guess we made it, though."

I took a box of tissue out of the bottom drawer and tossed it at him. "Help yourself. It took me a long time to realize that you were the reason Dolly persuaded the marshals to let her come here. Farberville's a charmingly quirky little place, but it lacks exotic appeal except to those who aspire to tenure at a second-rate college. How'd you end up here?"

"My family had a farm at the far edge of Stump County. Instead of attending one of those summer camps where the offspring of the wealthy learn to sail and perfect their tennis techniques, I was sent here to help out. I rode mules instead of pedigreed polo ponies and fished for crappies instead of rainbow trout, but I always had a fine time. When it came time to settle down, I couldn't think of a better place. I convinced Dolly to move down here so I could keep an eye on her. It might have worked out better if she hadn't confided in Petti, but there wasn't any reason to think the Velocchios would come looking for her like they did."

"Because of the subpoenas," I said. "That's when they got all hot and bothered."

Cal gave me a broad smile. "Reckon so."

I rocked back in the chair, hoping I wouldn't get so carried away with my theory that I ended up in the wastebasket behind me. "When the subpoenas were issued, they realized the FBI had a stronger case than they'd anticipated. A witness, for instance, who could testify about laundered money and overseas accounts. Someone like Bibi."

"Dead men don't testify," he drawled. "Digging up evidence is one thing. Digging up witnesses is a sight harder."

"I'm not thinking about the urn in upstate New York. The feds must have pressured Bibi until he agreed to cooperate, so they had to keep him alive while they pulled together the case. They staged the heart attack, the death certificate, and the funeral. Dolly dressed in black, sniffled into a hankie, and let it be known that she was moving to Arizona. Did Bibi prefer Florida?"

"She had to stay away from him in case some member of the family got curious. The feds wouldn't even tell her where he was. Petti was sort of the middleman, getting the word about Bibi from one of his racetrack buddies and about Dolly from me. The feds had promised Bibi that once he testified, he and Dolly could leave the country for good."

"And buy them a yacht?"

Cal's eyes shifted away. "Bibi was dealing with more money than you and I can imagine, shifting it from the Caymans to Switzerland to Singapore, then using it to buy floundering corporations and strip their assets. That's what he did every day for the last thirty years, just played one long game of international Monopoly with real money."

"While diverting some of it to his personal accounts."

"Could be he was skimming a little bit here and there, to the tune of something along the lines of twenty million dollars. The FBI said they'd overlook it, but Bibi didn't trust them not to hand him over to the IRS after the trial. He was staying quiet down in Florida, acting like he was ready to testify when they needed him, but all the while he was figuring out how he and Dolly would make a final exit. Then all of a sudden the subpoenas were issued, and he didn't know how to get in touch with her. According to what she told me, he was going to finalize plans and then contact her through Petti."

"Why not call her?" I asked, having always admired simplicity over duplicity.

"He didn't know who might be tapping the line or getting to her mail. He could have called me, but he was afraid the Velocchios might make the connection. He told me before his so-called death that he wasn't going to trust anybody except Petti."

"So Petti gave Dolly his cell phone in case Bibi called. When she didn't hear from him, she started thinking he must have mailed something to the house, something that looked innocent. Something like a package of CDs from a store in Buenos Aires, so she'd know how to find him. Too bad the package came after she left town. And too bad I didn't realize its significance. I should have, you know. I looked through all her credit card bills and didn't see a charge. Somebody paid for the CDs, but obviously it wasn't Dolly. Is that where she is now—in Argentina?"

"We won't know for sure until one of us gets a postcard." He started to stand up, but I waved him back down.

"A few more questions before you leave, Cal. How did the Velocchios find out Dolly was living here? You didn't tell them, did you?"

"Hell, no! According to what Nick and Sebastian told me, after the subpoenas went out, the capos got to thinking maybe Bibi wasn't dead after all. They sent some fellows over to the funeral home to have a look through the files."

"And when they found out the truth, they killed the owner and burned the place down," I continued for him. "I saw something about that in the *Times*. I suppose at that point they took a hard look at Petti."

Cal whistled under his breath. "You're good, Ms. Malloy. They tapped his phone line, bought him plenty of drinks, talked to his neighbors, and kidded him about going to Florida. Then Nick and Sebastian simply followed him. Once they found out which motel he was staying at, they hung around until Dolly showed up. When Petti clammed up, Nick decided to kill him and try to scare Dolly into panicking and calling Bibi. He's the one who insisted I keep delivering flowers so he could hear what was being said in the house; the fact that you left them in the dining room was driving him crazy—and he wasn't all that stable to begin with. It's hard to believe, but Sebastian's the one who thought it was funny to keep moving Petti's body. I even heard him plotting to steal it from the morgue."

"So you decided you'd had enough of this disrespect and took it yourself."

"Buried him next to my sister. One of these days I'll put up a stone marker or maybe a brass plaque. I'm real sentimental. Kinda odd, considering my past."

"You buried Petti. What did he bury in place of the urn?"

"Two sets of ledgers, one cooked. I imagine Bibi will mention it to the FBI one of these days. He never did approve of the family's shadier businesses, but he couldn't have upped and quit. It doesn't work like that."

I shrugged. "He didn't seem to mind putting some of this filthy lucre aside for his retirement."

"Don't suppose he did." Cal stood up and smiled down at me. "Now, if you'll excuse me, I got to go to the office and find out what Miss Groggin's lined up for next week."

I walked out to the front room with him. "One last question. Should I be worried about Gary Billings?"

"No, ma'am, you should not. Before Sara Louise was killed, she called Madison's father and told him what was going on, along with the fact that Gary was using his FBI credentials in hopes of blackmailing Dolly and Bibi. Mr. Hayes didn't like any of that, especially the way his daughter was being exploited sexually just so Gary could keep track of what the family knew. Nick and Sebastian were very proud of the way they handled that. As long as Miss Groggin doesn't find a reason to go out back and open a metal drum full of muriatic acid, nobody's ever going to lay eyes on Agent Billings."

"Is that why Madison killed Sara Louise?"

Cal nodded. "Madison sure wasn't happy that her father knew about Gary, and as much as I hate to say it, there were some rumors that Sara Louise went to Atlantic City a time or two with Mr. Hayes. Gary realized what had happened, but he couldn't exactly tell anyone, could he? He must have thought his only chance was to disassociate himself from the whole mess. He should have known better than to piss off a Mafia princess." He gave me a wry look. "Or underestimate a bookseller. If you don't object, I might come by one of these days and pick us some books. Shall I bring my dog?"

I opened the door for him. "As long as he behaves himself."

"Oh, he'll promise, but it's hard to know who to believe these days. Goodbye, Ms. Malloy."